HANA YIN

A Leaf in a Small Town

First published by Hana Yin 2023

Copyright © 2023 by Hana Yin

This novel is entirely a work of fiction. The names, characters and incidents portrayed in it are the work of the author's imagination. Any resemblance to actual persons, living or dead, events or localities is entirely coincidental.

Hana Yin asserts the moral right to be identified as the author of this work.

First edition

ISBN: 9798853329072

This book was professionally typeset on Reedsy. Find out more at reedsy.com

To Brian

Contents

1

Fallen Fu

Tall, whitewashed walls. A dense bush of dusty green bamboo, leaves stretching, whistles in the wind. A giant, moulting willow, casting a deep shadow over the crumbling temple, sighs. She pounds on the faded wooden doors, but no one answers. On either side an aged white marble lion statue stands in silence, eyes bulging, mouth open. The jasmine scent stirs the air; the sound of babies crying echoes faintly from deep inside. She turns around; the small boat disappears, leaving a ripple of silver fish scales...

The wind had eased, the crackling fire had softened and was swaying an amber lullaby, and the night had ripened like a frost-licked persimmon. Jade-Lotus stared at the page in front of her, but the words were like cranes flying in formation, one minute condensing into a line and the next evaporating into clouds.

'Sorry, Miss Brontë, it's not you.' She sighed, closed the book, and placed it on the plump white pillow. The digital alarm clock glowed an eerie green: 2.30 a.m. *Must find a way*

1

to dream valley, otherwise there will be panda eyes in the morning. She nestled under the soft down duvet and shut her eyes. *One carp, two carp, three carp, four carp... All would be logical in the morning. One carp, two carp...* But her eyes sprang open, and she turned as if pulled by a magical string. By the fireplace, the floor lamp tentatively arched over an old chestnut leather armchair, illuminating its sunken seat, as if to highlight the hollowness that William had left behind. In the downy halo of the light, two Spring Festival cards, which had arrived earlier that day, stood conspicuously on the marble mantelpiece like stone tablets on an altar. Tablets were considered to have the solemn power to summon one's respect towards one's ancestors. The cards grew invisible hands, beckoning her; the letter, attached to the inside of the red card, stirred up a desire that she had tried hard to bury.

Don't look, just don't look! She turned over. The muted bamboo pattern on the curtains somehow came alive, fluttering gently; the teddy bear in the corner looked sullen and lonely; the rocking horse in the far corner sulked at being used as a clothes hanger. It was as if the objects in the room wanted to politely ask why they had been chosen to be there. *Oh, go away!* She bent like a cooked prawn, covered her eyes and resisted touching the mole above her lip. The prawn spread out into a starfish, and then curled back again. She turned one more time, her eyes drawn to the cards. *Stop it, just stop it!* She peeled off the duvet, knelt on the bed and folded into the child pose, her favourite way to relax. Breathing in and out slowly for a time, instead of finding the realm of serenity she finally gave up and snorted, 'So ironic!'

Jade-Lotus got up; it was futile to try to sleep. *Just go and get a coffee and wake up from this madness!* But instead of heading for the door, her feet took her to the mantelpiece. She reached for the red card, hesitated for a moment, and then picked up the other one, a postcard of Johannesburg, on which big characters took up all the available space:

Short break with hubby.
* HAPPY GOLDEN PIG YEAR!*
* Snow-Flower xxx*
* PS: When are you coming home to see us all?*

Jade-Lotus could almost hear her childhood best friend, in a massive floppy hat and dark sunglasses, shouting in a bell-like voice. Every year Snow-Flower asked that same question, but she never answered. She stared back at the red card for a while before picking it up. Fingering the embossed golden pig on the front and the bulging letter beneath it, she felt her heart yo-yo between her chest and throat. She opened the card, unfolded the letter and read it again:

Dear Jade-Lotus,

*   Happy Spring Festival! We wholeheartedly wish the Year of the Golden Pig brings you and William good health, prosperity and happiness!*

*   If you don't get this letter before the festival, please forgive me. I've been very busy with the school, and your cousin Little-Blossom has been poorly – she's in fact pregnant again (I'm whispering). We have to be secretive and cunning: Little-Blossom will go for an illegal scan with a doctor friend in Shanghai next week, and we're hoping for a miracle. If not, you know, we can't bend the one-child policy any more, although Little-Blossom would be despondent about what she would have to do.*

My parents are out travelling, enjoying their retirement; our two little girls are well and send their sweetest love.

Yours sincerely,

River-Cloud, from your old hometown

January 2007

'Pregnant? For the third time? Was she a rabbit in a former life?' *Oh, did I just say that?* She bit her tongue, her face burning. That wasn't a kind thing to say about a dearest cousin!

What miracle were River-Cloud and Little-Blossom hoping for? She tightened her lips into a sarcastic smile. Nine-Pound Old Lady's words rumbled like thunder, 'A baby boy is, has always been, and will always be, the seed of the family, carrying the family name generation after generation. What use is a girl? A leaf only falls away from the tree and becomes the property of someone else!' And when each of their daughters – Summer-Lily and Spring-Cherry – was born, a dim leaf lantern would have been dangled dispiritedly by their front gate; a handful of leaves would have been thrown into the river next to their house to float far away; and there would have been no family flag, no fireworks, no banquet, nor visitors wishing loudly for the family's prosperous future. If townspeople happened to pass their leaf lantern, they would reverse back to avoid bad luck; and when people bumped into Little-Blossom in the town centre, some would sympathetically pat her on her arm and others would simply look away...

How could Little-Blossom and River-Cloud fall for this pathetic tradition? Jade-Lotus sighed, her chest heaving. That small town, Blushing Lotus – her old hometown – was really a fermenting urn, in which even great souls would rot and become covered by its thousand-year-old smelly mould; running away from it had been the right decision. But all things tend to have a silver lining; through the crack in a ruin comes light. What if Little-Blossom was with a girl again? River-Cloud had implied that they would have no choice but abort her, right? Jade-Lotus frowned, thoughts turning in her mind. Could they be each other's saviour? So Little-Blossom needn't have an abortion, and she could fill her unfillable hole. Her shoulders tensed up, her fingers clenched hard on the letter, and her heart knocked so wildly that she had to put a hand on her chest.

In the fireplace, sparks danced up from the dying ashes.

But William had never wanted to adopt. Not even after their final painful attempt at IVF. She took a yoga breath and slowly sat down in the sunken chair, William's favourite, as if wanting to feel what he felt and see what he saw. Another spark flared up, and with a crackle a tiny flame burst into life, giving out orange warmth, much like it had on that autumn night eighteen months ago, as she held the edge of the mantelpiece with her eyes tightly shut.

A chill vibrated in the air as William approached with a long needle in his hand. 'OK, little lamb, just a gentle kiss on the bum.'

She squeezed her eyes shut harder. 'You'd better not be a big bad wolf. Quick!'

There was a slight rustling behind her; she gritted her teeth.

'Ow!' She shot her elbow backwards.

'Ouch!'

She turned to look. The syringe was hanging from her

buttock; William was on the floor, covering his right eye. She hopped around, yelping, 'Get it out, get it out!'

When the needle came out, it was bloody and bent.

She collapsed to the floor with her sore buttock tilted up.

'I'm sorry,' William said.

She reached a hand out to him. 'Sorry about your eye.'

They nestled together in silence for a long time.

William shifted slowly. 'I think we should give up this IVF business, don't you? I just hate to see you get hurt.'

She didn't answer and gripped his hand harder. In a mosquito's voice she eventually said, 'Um, we could still try to adopt?'

He was quiet for a moment and leaned his face against her head. 'Darling, I'm sorry, I really am. But as I've said before, I want a child with you, not a child from a stranger.' He caressed her shoulder. 'Even if we can't have a child, we still have each other.' He kissed her head.

The flame in the fireplace died out.

Much like the wilted orange flame in front of Jade-lotus was doing now. The eerie green digits changed shape to 3.20 a.m. Yes, that was what William had seen and how he had felt. It would be unfair to ask him to hoist the sails on that abandoned ship; it would be unkind to make him do things against his will.

Tap tap, the February rain gently rapped on the windows; an owl hooted faintly in the distance. The night stretched on, its silky solitude spinning a giant cocoon. The emptiness in the room slowly unrolled like a strip of black and white film; although the dark negative was set off by the bright positive of William coming home in the morning after his monthly business trip to the US.

Another spark shot up in the fireplace, like a shooting star. He didn't want a stranger's baby, right. But this baby was her cousin's, blood related. She leapt up from the chair and paced, her heart leaping too. 'Oh my gosh!' Would this change the equation? *Breathe, breathe, and breathe!* But it had been eighteen months since that autumn night and their life had taken on a different shape; new plans had been made. *Time to get that coffee.*

She put on a dressing gown and furry slippers, and rushed out of the bedroom door. As she skipped past the giant mirror leaning on the landing wall, she stopped and stepped back. A slim woman with waist-long dark hair stared back; the small black mole above her upper lip stood out on her pale face, like a drop of ink on a minimalist Chinese painting. She shook her head and descended the stairs.

As she opened the kitchen door, she touched the Fu, a shimmering golden Chinese character printed on a piece of glossy red handkerchief-sized paper, which she had firmly stuck to the door as a festive decoration for good fortune and happiness. *Hope it brings just that!*

She filled up the coffee machine; it hissed moodily as it dripped.

Without thinking, she opened the cupboard and got out a mixing bowl and some flour.

'Dig a well in the snow, slide salt and water in the hole; weave all in with your hands, a sticky dough will soon land!' she sang the mnemonic Grandma had taught her as she worked. 'The most enjoyable bit is kneading, there's nothing we can't knead out,' she said out loud, just like Grandma had, all those years ago in her tiny kitchen when they made dumplings together for the first time.

'Come, my little treasure, I'll teach you how to knead,' Grandma said, patting the dough she had just made. She then lowered the flour-board onto the top of a nearby wooden crate and knelt to demonstrate. 'Look, you push and then knead. Push away your problems, and knead them out. So, why the donkey face when you've just successfully finished your first school term? What happened?'

'Nothing,' Jade-Lotus muttered.

'Come, you try this, push away your problems and knead them out. Was it a classmate?'

Jade-Lotus poked the dough; it was nice and soft. She began to push and knead. After a few rounds, she said, 'It was the teacher. She announced the dancers for the coming Spring-Festival Red Gala, but she didn't announce me, even though she knows I'm much better than the others.'

'Hmm. Confucius said, "Lack of forbearance in small matters will destroy great plans." We can't control others, but we can choose how we deal with them, my little treasure. Push your teacher's prejudice against us away and knead her stupidity out.'

'Yeah, push away teacher's prejudice and knead her stupidity out!' The dough soon became silky smooth.

'We now make the filling by chopping the snow cabbage and dried prawns, but that's too dangerous for you. Tell me your worries and nightmares, and I'll chop them up for you. Chop chop, chop worries, chop chop, chop nightmares…' Grandma hammered her choppers on a thick wooden block, one in each hand, up and down, up and down, like a chicken pecking for grain. In no time all the unhappiness from primary school was chopped into a hundred pieces...

Now, under the bright kitchen lights, what was it that needed to be kneaded out? Jade-Lotus drove the dough in an anti-clockwise direction, gathering flour and thoughts. Was it the right time to have a baby now? In a couple of months, the big four-oh would be knocking; a new project at work, one of the perks of a new promotion, would begin in a week's time after many months of bidding; and William would probably take a job in the USA. Yes, so many things had changed since that needle-crushing night. But, but... would any time be right to have a baby? At the age of ten, she had once announced, 'I want to have a proper family when I grow up.' Could having children be wired into one's brain from a young age? It might have gone into hibernation, like a honey bear, but at the first sign of the sun it would wake up.

She kneaded in the opposite direction. Now say Little-Blossom was carrying a girl and couldn't keep the baby, and was happy to give it up for adoption – so many assumptions – how to get the baby? She took a deep breath and let it out through clenched teeth; it sounded like an old bicycle tyre leaking. The only way to get the baby was to go back there. Really? Go back to the place with mould-stained walls, shallow smelly canals, claustrophobic streets and tiny bridges? A place with stubborn traditions and bitter memories? Running away had been the only choice; in sixteen years she had never missed it.

She slowed down her kneading. What to do? What to do? Grandma's words rang aloud, 'Ah, my little treasure, Mencius once said, "I want fish; I also want the delicacy of bear-paws. If I can't have both, I have to give up fish for bear-paws."

You can give up anything, your principles, pride, fear, even your love if you want the other thing enough.' Her words of wisdom always came at the right time. Was there anything more important than a baby to complete a family? Jade-Lotus resumed the kneading. Little-Blossom's baby could be an iron tree blossoming, the best possible gift that needed to be grasped by both hands. Yes, GRASP! As in 'Grasp, grasp, tightly grasp; pull, pull, pull the rope!' the chant that had enabled her Duck team to beat the Chicken team in the tug-of-war at William's company's Family Day, just before Christmas. And right there on the fridge door was the photo of her in a mother-duck's hat, nestled among the children in yellow duckling costumes. That Christmas holiday had been full of giggles about the win, and William quacked each time she giggled. *Now I just need William to sing the same tune as me again.* She patted the dough; it was smooth and ready.

Time for the filling. Luckily, there was no need to hammer with choppers like Grandma; she got the food processer out. She pulsed the Chinese leaves, raw king prawns and fried eggs; what would mince up William's resistance? Deep down he had wanted children too. She added seasoning and tasted; what would be palatable to him? She added a little more five-spice and sesame oil; what would be compelling for William? The mixture became a fine filling; a plot began to take shape. Time to make the dumplings. She rolled out the dough thinly and cut it into tiny circle wraps; 'one hand can't clap', William would need to be on board. With a spoonful of filling on each wrap, she carefully formed them into dainty fat-bellied dumplings; with delicate handling, William would come around. Soon rows of dumplings stood on the countertop like terracotta soldiers; the plot was ready, and would hopefully run as smoothly as the First Emperor's mercury river... *Wow, I really ran away with myself there!*

A flop ambushed the busy quietness in the kitchen. Jade-Lotus looked around and squealed, 'Oh no!' The glossy red paper that had been prominently and perkily welcoming good fortune had fallen, folded and lay paralyzed on the floor, the shimmering golden Fu totally hidden. She froze, her jaw having dropped with a mind of its own. 'Absurd! Superstition! There's nothing in a fallen Fu!' she shouted, but unconsciously touched the mole above her lip with a floured finger. She stared at the picture next to the door, a Chinese watercolour painting, a wedding gift from River-Cloud long before he had married Little-Blossom. In it an ancient stone bridge spanned a small river, and under the arch a narrow dark cloth-covered boat rocked. The recurring dream of the crumbling temple behind tall whitewashed walls that had woken her up in a sweat yesterday morning came back. Some years ago a monk from her hometown had said, 'Dream may be the moon in the sky, or just its reflection in the water; dream may be a palm tree in the desert, or simply a mirage.'

2

Spring Festival

'Darling, I'm home!' William shouted from the hall. His suitcase thudded on the wooden floor and the taxi ground its way back up the long gravel drive.

Jade-Lotus ran downstairs.

He hugged her tightly, almost lifting her off the floor. 'Oh, I missed you so much!' He kissed her.

'I missed you too!' she said as she came back down to earth.

'Now, I've got great news!' A tuft of his blond hair bounced; he took off his coat.

She passed him his slippers. 'What news?'

'The board created a new job for me. We're going to move to California at last! Isn't that great?' He kicked off his black brogues and walked into his slippers.

'Wow, that's good! No, I mean it's great! Really great!'

'We have a month to sort out stuff here. Hope it's enough notice for your company too. Can't wait! So it's a double celebration this weekend!'

'Indeed, darling, indeed. Let me make you a coffee, the

machine is on.'

'You're going to keep me awake?' William winked.

'Well, you're excited, you won't be able to sleep, will you?' Jade-Lotus smiled.

'You're right. Actually, I slept quite well on the plane. I'll have a quick wash and change.' William kissed her again and took his suitcase upstairs.

'Good smell! Oh, you've made dumplings? I thought we were going to make them together?' William said as he came back into the kitchen.

'I'm here,' Jade-Lotus waved from the sofa. William sat down next to her, and she passed him a china mug with the characters for China on it. 'Well, I couldn't sleep, so I got up early and made dumplings.'

'Oh? Couldn't sleep and made dumplings – do I need to worry?' He stared at her.

She smiled sweetly. He had many reasons to worry. The first time it had happened they had relocated back to England, and moved their wedding away from China. The next time, eight years later, they had moved out of London to the current house, a Georgian wreck at the time, to shoot two eagles with one arrow – make a new home and a baby. The house had been all done up, but there was still no baby. 'No need to worry, really.' She looked down at the foamy swirl in her mug. 'I know what I want for my birthday now.'

'Oh! That's great! What do you want?'

'Darling...' She raised her eyes. 'You said I could have anything in the whole world, right?'

'Of course. It's your big four-oh! Just say what you want, providing I can afford it.' He patted her thigh with a grin.

13

She gave him an even sweeter smile and picked up the red card from the coffee table. 'Look, this is from River-Cloud and Little-Blossom.' She passed it to him.

'Nice! Don't tell me, it's the Pig Year isn't it?' He touched the golden pig on the cover. 'It's good of them to send us a card every year. What does the letter say?'

She translated the letter and stared at him affectionately.

'What? Oh, please send my festive wishes when you call them,' William said.

'Darling, Little-Blossom will have to have an abortion if the baby is a girl.'

'Yes, it's not nice. But they have no choice, do they?'

Jade-Lotus picked up his hand and gently caressed his palm. 'But we have a choice, don't we? We could help her out by adopting the baby. It would be the best birthday gift ever.' She kissed his hand.

William turned slowly to her. 'What? Adopt the baby? Are you serious?' The stubble on his chin seemed instantly darker. 'You know how I feel about adoption.'

'Yes, but I've done a lot of thinking.' She glanced at the rows and rows of 'terracotta soldiers'. 'This is my cousin's baby, a blood relative, not a stranger's. The last thing in the world Little-Blossom wants to do is have an abortion. We would be helping her and ourselves.' She patted his hand.

William looked at the dumplings, then slowly turned back. 'But we've talked about this and moved on. Now we have the chance to live in the place we dreamed of.'

'But adopting this baby won't stop us moving to California! We can bring her up there just as well.'

'Hmm, I'm not sure, I'm not sure. The baby could well turn out to be a boy; fifty-fifty isn't it? So, don't you think you're being premature?'

'You're right. If it's a boy, congrats to my cousin; and we'll live our dream life in America. But if it's a girl, I think we should try to adopt her.'

He put down his coffee mug and shuffled his feet. 'OK. Say hypothetically it's a girl, how are we going to adopt her? I'm curious now.'

'Well, I'll quit my job, go there to sort everything out and wait for her to be born.'

'You'll *what*? You just got promoted! And you would actually spend time in the place you hate the most?'

She sighed. 'A job is just a job. But Grandma is no longer young.' Nudging her knees towards his, she leaned forward and took out her pendant. 'I also want to use the time to find out what happened to Mama.'

'Oh!' He threw an arm on the top of the back cushion behind her and scratched at the seam, sat up and then took his arm back. 'Are you sure? Have you talked to Grandma about it?'

'Yes I'm sure, but Grandma's in the Northeast at the moment.'

'Oh yeah, her annual royal tribal tour.' His tone was bordering on sarcastic.

'It's not a tour. How many times! It's better to spend the festival with your relatives than on your own, isn't it? She gets treated really well as their last living royal. I wanted to talk to you first, and if you're happy I'll tell her.'

'Darling…' He cleared his throat. 'I know you want to know what happened to your mum, but won't you be causing trouble for Grandma even now?'

'I can't go all the way there and not try. It's about time we found out the truth.' She stared at the disappearing foam in

15

her mug.

William cupped his hands around his mug; his fingers tapped it rhythmically. 'What about me?' he said eventually.

'You? You can go to the US first, maybe find a nice place to live, so we can join you once the baby is born?' She found herself speaking fast, her heart thumping.

He caressed the characters for China on his mug. 'But we always do things together. We should be bringing a child into our life together, don't you think?'

'So you agree to adopt?' she shrieked.

He turned and tapped his finger gently on the tip of her nose. 'At least you won't suffer this way. It's our last chance for a child.'

'Oh my gosh, oh my gosh!' She kissed him.

He kissed her back and hugged her tightly. 'Now, what's *our* plan? I'm going to come with you.'

'Really? You really want to come? But can you? I mean… your work schedule?' She brushed the air with her hand, as if to throw caution to the wind. 'OK, if we're quick we can get there for the Lantern Festival, two weeks today.'

'It would be fantastic to see the lanterns for real. I could clear my diary. Shall we call Little-Blossom now?'

Jade-Lotus looked at the time. 'They'll be busy having their big meal; so later, when their New Year arrives. My cousin and River-Cloud will no doubt let us adopt if it's a girl.'

'I hope so. "Everything is set, the only thing we need now is the east wind."'

'You're quoting Chinese.'

They laughed, and in their laughter the pair of red paper lanterns hanging on the ceiling above them revolved.

'I've got my new red socks on, have you?' Jade-Lotus said.

'Of course. Look!'

'Let's trample down our little enemies together, before the new year arrives.'

'Absolutely. We don't want bad luck for the whole year.'

They chased upstairs to their bedroom. 'OK, ready? "Trample trample, little enemies crumble!"' Jade-Lotus skipped around the room, followed by a stamping William.

They repeated their actions in each room of the house, shouting and laughing, before rushing over to the chain of small golden bells near the front entrance, and ringing them together. 'Ring the bells, all year will be well!' they shouted.

Later, when they sat down for the Spring Festival Eve's meal, the most celebrated meal, Jade-Lotus just stared at her chopsticks, unable to pick anything up from the six dishes that she had spent hours making; a tight sensation bubbled in her stomach. Would the baby be a girl? Would Little-Blossom and River-Cloud be happy to give it away? Would it be like fetching water with a bamboo basket again?

'Darling,' William said gently, stretching his rice bowl over to her.

'Sorry.' She shook her head, spooned a couple of tiger prawns into it, and added some of the steamed seabass. 'Prawns bring good luck and fish makes you rich.'

'OK, I can live with that. But you need to eat too.'

'I'll have tofu with mushroom, so my new year will be peaceful and prosperous.' As she played with a small piece of tofu in her bowl, her other hand unconsciously held her pendant.

'Ganbei! And may all your wishes come true!' William raised his glass.

'Ganbei!' She took a sip of champagne, its warmth calming her feverish body and mind. Comfortably numbed everything would be fine. But her heart still skipped a beat at the thought of having a baby.

Dong! The antique grandfather clock in the hall struck, its echo lingering.

She looked at him, and pressed her hand onto her chest, which seemed to be resonating with the chime.

He looked back at her, his eyes intense. 'It's 3.45, almost midnight in China.'

'I'd better make the call.' As she got up, she felt her hands shake. In a short time, it would be clear what kind of new year it was going to be.

'Good luck!' He got up and gave her a firm hug.

Jade-Lotus dialled, but no one answered. She redialled and redialled until she got through. Her hand held the phone so tightly it hurt.

'Festival greetings from England!' she said in a high-pitched voice.

'HU-LLO, it's you! The flown-away sparrow! What do you wan... want?'

'Oh hello River-Cloud,' she frowned, 'William and I want to wish you all excellent health, great luck and huge success in the Pig Year!'

'Oh! Happy Spring Festival to you too! But... but when the temple bell rings at midnight, there must be something ur... urgent – so what do you w-want?'

'Oh dear, are you drunk? Umm, well, thank you for your lovely card and letter. Can I ask... do you know the scan result? I mean is the baby a boy... or a girl?'

'Girl! Of course a girl! What do you expect?' River-Cloud snapped. 'Unlike you, living in your glorious cocoon, we're always the unfortunate ones! Happy now?' Then he chanted, 'Heaven knows, earth knows, but little people like us, don't know our own fate…' He burped.

'Hello Cousin! Ah ah, so sorry – he's been rude to you, hasn't he? He's very drunk! We just came back in from our family shrine. Go, please go River-Cloud, please take the girls out and light the fireworks, but don't let them go too near! Sorry, Cousin. Happy Spring Festival to you and William.'

'Happy Spring Festival, Little-Blossom! I can hear the fireworks, wish I was there.'

'It's very pretty outside. It seems families are competing for the best display. Ah Buddha, it's so loud. Let me shut the door.'

'Um, River-Cloud said you have another baby girl; are you going to…?'

'Ah ah, yes… abort it.' Little-Blossom heaved a long sigh. 'I just don't have boy-fate, you know? I shouldn't complain at this festive time.'

'I'm really sorry. But do you really want to abort it? Sorry, it's not the right time to talk about this.'

'Don't worry, Cousin, everyone is outside with the fireworks. New Year is any minute now. Aihh, I don't want to, you know I don't, but I have no choice. When the Lantern Festival is over I'll get it done.'

'Little-Blossom, can… can we adopt your baby girl?'

'What? You and William want our baby? It's a *girl*, you know?' *Bang!* A firework exploded.

'Yes, yes, we'd love a girl. Perhaps you need to discuss it with River-Cloud. I'll call you tomorrow if that's OK?'

'Ah ah.'

'I'll let you join the fireworks. Happy Chinese New Year!'

As Jade-Lotus put down the phone, the grandfather clock in the hall struck. She could almost hear the town clock in her hometown strike too. Dong, Dong, Dong... Twelve loud dongs and their echoes, mingled with loud bangs and little cracks to announce the Year of Golden Pig – a year of hope, plenty and family happiness – colourful fireworks blossoming in the air, bright light raining from above, shining on every happy face.

3

Journey to the East

Zhuangzi once dreamt he was a butterfly, dancing vividly in the air, feeling jubilant. On awakening, he was shocked that he was still himself. Had he dreamt of being a butterfly, or had a butterfly dreamt of being him?

Jade-Lotus had a similar feeling now that she was on the plane heading to China; reality was like newly brushed ink, struggling to seep through the cooked rice paper. The cabin light dimmed; William was watching a film. She looked out of the window at the gilded dusky clouds. What would Blushing Lotus be like today? Little-Blossom and River-Cloud had seemed a bit reluctant when she had called.

'Ah ah, it's really nice that you want her,' Little-Blossom said on the phone. 'But being your dearest cousin, I'd ask you again: are you really sure?'

'Quite, quite,' River-Cloud said. 'I'm sure you haven't forgotten what it's like here – I mean our dear townspeople and officials. You'll have to face them for the adoption, you know?'

'Yes, I'll be all right, with your help obviously,' Jade-Lotus said.

Their speakerphone went silent for a second.

'Oh, I hope this won't be trouble for you,' Jade-Lotus added quickly.

'Ah ah, no trouble, no trouble,' Little-blossom said.

'Quite, quite, we'll work it out, we'll work it out,' River-Cloud said.

'I can't wait to see you guys,' Jade-Lotus said.

'We can't wait either, really looking forward to seeing you.' Little-Blossom's voice was calm and warm again.

In cold and bleak teenage years, Little-Blossom had always been a bonfire, full of warmth. But many years had passed, perhaps it would be difficult to be as close as a worm in each other's tummy. Hopefully by spending time together, the small holes in the magic carpet that had kept their friendship flying before would be patched.

But what Grandma had said on the phone was a complete surprise.

'Grandma, you're back early! How was your holiday? Happy Spring Festival at last!' Jade-Lotus cried.

'Yes yes, my dear little treasure, and to you and William. Ah, I had a lovely time, a really lovely time. A lot of snow this year, we even saw a bear out in the wild; but the snow disrupted transport, I flew back as soon as I could.'

'I've big news for you, Grandma!'

'I know,' Grandma said flatly. 'I've news for you too.'

'OK, you go first.'

'Guess who was on my doorstep just after I got back home today?'

'I can't think of anyone.'

'Nine-Pound Old Lady!' Grandma sounded like she had eaten a huge pot of gunpowder.

'OH! Why? Everyone has to go to kowtow to her, the "Empress Dowager", at festivals!'

'Indeed! "One doesn't visit the temple without a cause." So, I said, "Well, whatever it is you forbid me to do, I'm going to do it! Happy Spring Festival, please leave!" Oh my little treasure, she waved her stick at me and said, as cold as ice, "It won't happen, you and my family, if I still have a breath!" before she was pulled away by Little-Blossom,' Grandma grumbled. 'I had no idea what she was talking about until Little-Blossom filled me in.'

'What did Little-Blossom say?'

Silence drifted in like a mist, followed by a breezy sigh. 'My dear dear Buddha, is it true? Are you sure about this adoption?'

'Oh Grandma.' Jade-Lotus felt her stomach churn. It was as if the idea of the adoption had been swallowed like a whole sweet date; now its stone was rubbing inside her. 'I thought you two ladies had long laid down the flag and stilled the drums. I thought you would be happy.'

'Happy?'

'You often suggested we adopt a Chinese baby, and this one *is* blood related.'

'I'm happy for you, of course.'

'But you sound angry.'

'Ah, my dear little treasure, you know I can never be angry with you. It's just, you know, our two families have never

23

mixed so intimately, and now everyone is talking about it by the river.'

'Oh, the laundry day,' Jade-Lotus said. The women back home would gather by the river for the first time after the festival, wooden clubs in hand, and beat their dirty clothes against a slab, soap bubbling away into the water. The belief was if they launder before the sixth day in the new year, their family's fortune would be washed away. But what they really enjoyed was catching up and gossiping: 'The east family are tall, the west family are short; three frogs have only five eyes, six parrots contest with two wives...'

'But Grandma, it's not their business, is it?'

'Aihh, you seem to have forgotten that everyone's business is business for everyone. I guess we'll sail through it somehow, as we always have.' Grandma uttered an almost undetectable sigh. 'When are you coming back, my dear?'

Like a bursting water fall Jade-Lotus told Grandma her plan.

'Are you OK?' William stretched his head over. 'You looked worried.'

'Worried? Oh no, I'm excited!' Jade-Lotus gave him a weak smile.

'I'll get some sleep now; maybe you should too.'

'Good idea. Night night, darling.'

Outside the clouds darkened, smeared with a sliver of blush. Jade-Lotus lay down, but couldn't settle. The name Nine-Pound Old Lady popped up, like an unwanted advertisement on a computer screen. Being the heaviest baby ever at birth in Blushing Lotus, by tradition she was entitled to be a dictator and a stick-in-the-mud. The old bitterness between them seemed to have snaked back; the memory of their first encounter unrolled in front of her.

'Go to stay in the shade,' Grandma said, eyeing a big umbrella-like tree not far from them.

Jade-Lotus looked up at the bright sun and the long queue for rations. 'OK, Grandma.'

As she walked to the tree, she heard people talking behind the huge trunk. So, she sneaked round and saw some old ladies perching on stools cooling themselves. 'Oh no, it's them!' She cupped her hand over her face; in the past some of them had pinched her face like it was a newly picked persimmon. She tried to tip-toe away.

'Hello pretty little girl, come here.' One of them waved to her.

'Ahya, don't be shy! Give us a smile!' another said.

'Good morning, grandmothers.' She had no choice but to greet them and bow.

The third lady pulled Jade-Lotus's hand and sat her on her knobbly knee, pinched her face and said to the fourth lady, 'See, I told you, her eyes are so big, and her skin is so pale and smooth, so flawless, like porcelain! Just like her mother.'

The fourth lady stared at her, from head to toe.

Jade-Lotus didn't know what to do, but couldn't help staring at her small pointy feet, bound in the traditional manner. She said quietly, 'I've never seen you before.'

'Ah, Nine-Pound Old Lady's been hibernating.' The first lady laughed.

'Are you a snake?' Jade-Lotus said curiously.

Three ladies laughed, dabbing their eyes. 'Oh, you think Nine-Pound Old Lady is a snake? Ohhaha ohhaha…'

25

Nine-Pound Old Lady didn't laugh, continued to stare at her and then shook her head. 'Tut tut tut, what a pity! You have bad fate. Just look at that mole above your lip, that's a sure sign of a bad fate! No wonder you lost your mama so young!'

Jade-Lotus didn't like her mocking tone, and bent herself down into a downward-facing dog. Looking at Nine-Pound Old Lady through her crotch, she said, 'You have smelly feet.'

The other three ladies' mouths dropped open; their hands shot up to cover them.

Nine-Pound Old Lady's eyes narrowed, her lips tightened and her skin coloured.

'And now you look like a giant purple turnip!' Jade-Lotus shouted, still upside down.

Nine-Pound Old Lady breathed loudly and said slowly, 'You poor little devil! Trust me that mole will give you bad fate, you are going to be the next Lin Daiyu! Tut tut tut.'

At that moment Grandma appeared with a small wire basket of eggs, a tiny muslin bag of rice and a bunch of spinach in her hands. 'What poor little devil? What bad fate? Total nonsense! That's a beauty mole, can't you see? My little treasure is going to grow into a very beautiful woman one day, just like Lin Daiyu, but her fate will be so much better, in fact so good you'd never imagine it! Get up, my little treasure, let's go!'

After that introduction, their relationship had never thawed. At Spring Festival people were supposed to be nice to each other and exchanging negative words was totally forbidden by tradition, but that hadn't stopped Nine-Pound Old Lady.

Jade-Lotus blew hot breath onto the thinly spread glue on the back of the Fu, and quickly pressed it onto their front gate. 'Please, please stay up! We've no flour left to make more glue.'

The Fu fell off, for the third time. A gust of wind swirled it around; she gritted her teeth and hopped after it. When the Fu finally stopped, she tried to pick it up, but couldn't. It was held by the tip of a wooden walking stick. Next to the stick was a pair of pointy bound feet encased in new handmade canvas ankle shoes. A ring of fiery red peeped from between the top of the navy shoes and the cuffed hem of the padded trousers. A foul smell wafted in the freezing air.

Jade-Lotus took a deep breath and at once regretted it. Looking up, she squealed at the sight of Nine-Pound Old Lady, cloaked in a long dark hooded cape. Under the hood, her round face, framed by neatly combed hair, looked paler than usual, its few fine lines seemingly frozen; her small pointy nose breathed out cold sneers; her purple lips were pursed tightly and the auger-like gaze from her narrowed eyes felt colder than the weather.

'Hel… hello, Grandaunt Shan, your stick is on my Fu,' she meowed.

'Humph, Bad Fate, you are ruining the luck,' Nine-Pound Old Lady said, and beating her stick on the ground to emphasise each word, 'for you, your family, and all of us! You wait and see!'

Later that year, although only nine years old, Jade-Lotus had a list of 'crimes' against her name: Grandma's ankle, twisted on the Red Star Farm – a communist labour camp – while slaving to harvest snow cabbages; the collapse of a well in the town centre; and the diarrhoea that afflicted the townspeople after their late spring rations of mouldy pickles. As well as the unfortunate things that happened more widely, like the death of Mao, a meteor shower in a north-eastern province and the Great Tangshan Earthquake.

'Ma'am, would you like a cup of chamomile tea to help you sleep?' an air stewardess leaned in and said.

'Yes please. Thank you.'

Jade-Lotus sat up, stretching to see William, who was fast asleep. It was good that he could sleep; perhaps the less he thought about the destination, the better. He appeared enthusiastic about going back to Blushing Lotus, but had he forgotten his only trip there and his encounter with Nine-Pound Old Lady? She sighed and blew her tea, wanting to blow away that memory for William's sake, but it lingered.

'They must go to walk on the Three Bridges,' a friend of Grandma's had said, looking at Grandma; the crowd that filled Grandma's home all nodded.

The three single-arched stone bridges, named Golden Koi, Evergreen Pine and Swooping Bat, that loosely chained the riverside paths of three different rivers into a ring, had long been considered sacred. At each momentous event in one's life, one had to walk on them to ensure prosperity and happiness.

Jade-Lotus stared at Grandma, her palms sweaty.

Grandma didn't answer, kept on blowing her tea and occasionally glanced at William. Maybe she didn't approve because William was an Englishman, a foreigner, a word that had often made her pale and always stirred up uneasiness with the townspeople. She then sipped her tea slowly, pausing to think between each small sip, as if she was a tea master. Time tick-tocked like a leaking tap; everyone in the room held their breath. With the tenth sip, she gently nodded, which elicited a round of applause from her friends.

Jade-Lotus let out a heavy breath; it was a sure sign of Grandma's acceptance of William.

They arrived at the bridges. Jade-Lotus held William's hand, with Grandma and her friends looking on, and they started to walk, smiling at each other.

Their path was suddenly blocked by a hooded figure with a walking stick.

Jade-Lotus squealed, squeezing William's hand hard. 'Oh hello, Grandaunt Shan. This... this is William, he loves... loves our traditions.' *Why did I say that?*

'No foreigners are allowed to walk on these sacred bridges,' Nine-Pound Old Lady said loudly. Her gang of friends gathered behind her, like a fan.

'Why? You want everyone to follow traditions,' Jade-Lotus said.

'Nine-Pound, please don't make trouble,' Grandma said.

Nine-Pound Old Lady took her dark hood off and stared at William. There was a moment of silence; perhaps she would be won over by William's handsome and benevolent face. 'I'll tell you why, Jade-Lotus. Because throughout our long history, no foreigner has ever been good to us. They always made us kneel for them. If you want to kneel for him, or crawl after him, fine. But we won't.'

Jade-Lotus stared at Nine-Pound Old Lady, speechless.

Grandma froze.

William whispered to her, 'We'd better leave.'

Jade-Lotus stood there, eyes burning. Seeing Grandma's ashen face she backed down.

For the rest of their stay, it felt like she and William were unwanted street rats. The seafood restaurant said there was no table for them, even though half the room was empty. The pretty temple on the hill closed its doors in their faces. No rickshaws would take them, even though they had been lining up on the street waiting for customers for ages...

Jade-Lotus finished her tea and put the cup down. She yawned and lay down again, to try to get some sleep. The plane bounced gently. Whatever lay ahead, the only way was to face it. When waves ebb away, there might be gold left behind; after years of sieving out bad memories, there might be peace to be found. It would be wonderful to see her hometown from a distance, or under the moonlight, its painful flaws and blemishes invisible. All that remained would be the whitewashed walls, the grey tiled roofs, the fragrant tea houses, the canals, the small wooden boats, the narrow cobbled streets, the clack clack of wooden clogs echoing on a quiet rainy afternoon, the women's shy smiles, the children's innocent faces, the old friends, the old school... But, would it accept a runaway soul? Accept that its return was not like the dragonfly hopping over the water, but an altogether longer and deeper affair – to adopt an unborn baby girl and take her abroad, the like of which had never happened before?

She finally fell asleep, and dreamt that she was back in the classroom at her old school, reciting a classic poem with all the children, again and again:

'... The road ahead winds like a rope,
Up and down I go, to pursue my hope...'

4

Meeting Old Rain

Hazy sunrays and a warm willow breeze brushed her face as Jade-Lotus stepped off the plane. She shut her eyes, greedily breathing in the moist air, gently scented by the honey plum blossom. Ah, Shanghai, back again. Inside they had to carefully follow the signs, weaving left and right through the shiny terminal where the chilly air had a whiff of fresh paint and sealant, and cranes nodded outside the tinted glass walls.

'Are we at the right airport?' she said as they marched towards immigration.

William laughed. 'It's modern, isn't it? So different from the old one. This passage must be the longest in the world.'

Jade-Lotus nodded, her heels click-clacking on the granite floor. 'Hope we won't be worn out before we get to Snow-Flower.' Thinking of her old friend, she felt her heart skip a beat. For the past sixteen years, their lives had been run separately like parallel railway tracks, each with its own rhythm, occasionally meeting at a junction to say hi before rolling off again. This time, Snow-Flower had insisted on coming to pick them up and having them stay for the night in her new apartment.

'Are you OK?' William eyed her boots.

'They're killing me,' Jade-Lotus muttered. 'And no!' She gave him a mean glance.

'OK. I won't say I told you so.'

Of course he was right, she sighed. Would a new pair of teetering Prada boots really be a winning edge when meeting Snow-Flower with the four Ps – Pretty face, Professional job, Perfect husband and Powerful connections? Aihh! The competition had always been on, even at their first meeting.

Waiting at the train station, Jade-Lotus shifted her weight from one foot to the other. Her sweaty hand smoothed the skirt of her new dress - a white broderie dress that Grandma had stayed up late making, so she wouldn't look like a country bumpkin in front of a fashionable person from Shanghai. In her other hand she held two Magnolia champak flowers tied together with a pink ribbon, and a tiny bamboo cage, containing a green long-horn cricket, dangled from her wrist. She looked from the corner of her eye; River-Cloud stood bolt upright and his mother, Auntie White-Azalea, stretched her neck looking in the direction the train would be coming from.

Jade-Lotus nudged River-Cloud and whispered, 'How do I look?'

'You're just fine,' River-Cloud whispered back, and pushed up his spectacles.

The air was still and sultry; Auntie White-Azalea paced along the platform, as if trying to make the train come quicker.

'Is she really your sister?' Jade-Lotus said. 'I thought I was your sister.'

'Well, strictly speaking, you're like a sister; she and I share the same parents.' River-Cloud shrugged.

'What's she like, do you remember?'

'No. I was only two when she was born and given away to an auntie in Shanghai.'

'Will you love her more than me now she's back?'

'Don't be silly. I might not even like her; who knows.'

Jade-Lotus smiled and stroked the pink ribbon.

A distant whistle and a puff of white cloud heralded the impatient green dragon; Auntie White-Azalea hurried back and they huddled together to face the roaring creature. It became tame and spat out its passengers, who were quickly claimed, but there was no sign of Snow-Flower. Auntie White-Azalea ran a few steps, and looked left and right along the train. Then Jade-Lotus saw a girl still standing in the corridor of the next carriage, wiping her eyes, so she shouted. The girl leaned out and climbed down the four steps. She was wearing an unbuttoned duffel coat, despite the June heat; underneath was a white shirt with a pink Peter-Pan collar and a matching pink skirt; her canvas plimsolls were blindingly white. She walked up, dropped her small suitcase, swung her army-green satchel behind her, and held out a hand to Auntie. 'Hello, you must be White-Azalea Shan, my new mother? I'm Snow-Flower. Nice to meet you.'

Auntie nodded keenly, shook the small hand and bursting into tears said, 'Yes, yes, I am, I'm your birth mother.'

Snow-Flower was about the same height as Jade-Lotus but, carrying herself like a ballerina, looked taller; her dimples made her look like she was smiling even though she wasn't;

her eyes were a little red, but sparkled; her teeth were the neatest and whitest Jade-Lotus had ever seen.

'You're home, you're home!' Auntie held on to the hand, crying and laughing.

Snow-Flower smiled generously, and used her other hand to gently pat Auntie's arm, as if to calm her new mother down.

'Is she really just ten years old?' Jade-Lotus whispered.

'Yep, the same as you,' River-Cloud said.

After she was finally released, Snow-Flower walked up to Jade-Lotus and River-Cloud. 'Nice to meet you too.' Her dimples deepened alluringly.

Jade-Lotus just stood there and stared at her. Only when she felt a nudge on her elbow from River-Cloud did she remember. 'Um, welcome home. I'm Jade-Lotus and these are the best things I have, I want you to have them.' She presented her the flowers and the little cage.

Snow-Flower stared at the cricket, but didn't take it. Instead she pulled something out of her coat pocket and said proudly, 'This is my best toy.' In her hand was a frog made of metal and painted with green stripes. She then wound the little key in the frog's tummy and put it down on the concrete floor. The frog started to jump and croak at the same time. 'Isn't it better than your cricket?'

Jade-Lotus was captivated by the frog; it was like nothing she had ever seen before. But she said quickly, 'These magnolia champak flowers have the best scent in the world and you can hang them on your shirt button. See the little loop here?'

Snow-Flower pulled out a book from her satchel and said, 'My picture storybook is better than your flowers.'

River-Cloud snapped, 'Why are you so competitive? Jade-

Lotus just wants to give you nice gifts, she's spent days choosing them.'

Jade-Lotus glanced appreciatively at River-Cloud.

Snow-Flower stared at them and smiled again, dazzling them with her perfect teeth, which made Jade-Lotus quickly close her mouth to hide her slightly crooked ones. 'I'm not, REAL big brother! Thank you, Jade-Lotus, for your kind gifts, but I have better things.'

'Come on, children, let's go home.' Auntie had finally sorted herself out and led the way.

Snow-Flower didn't come to the airport, and instead sent a limousine with a uniformed driver.

'So Snow-Flower!' Jade-Lotus muttered.

'She could just be busy,' William said.

'Yeah, she could be…'

The driver negotiated the traffic, edging into the city, where cars packed together like steamed buns in a wok, and snailed along the dear old Bund. The European-style buildings, once imposing and proud, seemed assaulted from all directions by shiny skyscrapers. Across the Huangpu River the needle-shaped TV tower, once the tallest landmark, was crowded by many new neighbours, all wearing glistening jackets as if they were visiting their in-laws at a festival. The cherry trees that lined the road were blossoming gloriously, but they no longer stole the scene, now just laces softening the roads of metal. Accompanied by a chorus of hooting, their car shuffled out of the traffic, swung into a neat planetree-lined street and stopped in front of a white 1920's art deco building. *Does she live in the French Concession?* As if the driver had heard her thoughts, he said, 'The top floor penthouse is where you're staying.' He hurried to press the buzzer next to a glossy dark door. 'The concierge will show you the private lift and Mother Li is waiting for you. I'll bring your luggage up later.'

'Who's Mother Li?' William whispered.

'No idea,' Jade-Lotus whispered back.

'Wow, this is very different from their old flat.' William looked up at the building.

'A shotgun replaced by cannon!'

Once out of the mirrored lift they were met by a smiling lady who looked to be in her late fifties; a scar crawled on her cheek like a baby scorpion. She quickly bowed and made a lotus-bud gesture with her hands. 'Welcome,' she said very quietly.

'You must be Mother Li,' Jade-Lotus said warmly and stretched out her hand.

Mother Li nodded, but stepped back and bowed even lower.

So Jade-Lotus bowed too, as did William.

When they rose up, Mother Li gestured towards an open door without saying anything, her eyes fixed on her embroidered slippers as she let them pass.

The hall was a world of dazzle: white walls, a white marble floor, bright light streaming through rooftop windows bouncing between giant mirrors, and a huge polished lampshade hanging down from the ceiling, like an upside-down wok.

'Slippers are underneath,' Mother Li said, a little louder than before, pointing at a pair of horseshoe chairs not far from the door.

William obediently sat down and changed out of his shoes, while Jade-Lotus gave her boots a lingering glance before peeling them off.

'I'll show you to your room,' Mother Li said and turned to

lead the way. Her grey hair was neatly tied in a chignon, and the cloisonné hairpin bobbed with each step she took. She was slim, and the clothes she was wearing – a navy mandarin jacket and a pair of matching-colour crop trousers, both embroidered with a spray of small white flowers – appeared to float around her. For a second, it was as if Jade-Lotus had already arrived in her old hometown. 'Once fresh up, please make yourself comfortable in the drawing room.' Mother Li pointed at a pair of moon-shaped doors as they passed. 'I'll go and make some tea; Snow-Flower will be back any moment.'

'Hello Mother Li, I'm back!' Snow-Flower's voice rang from the hall; the click-clack of high heels on the marble floor gathered pace towards the drawing room, accompanied by soft singing: 'Weeping willows sprouting again, sitting by the window I miss you in vain, where is, where is, my dear dear old rain…'

Jade-Lotus and William stood up as Snow-Flower rushed in. Wrapped in a slim-fitted cream suit and balanced on a pair of red stilettos, her hair in a smooth high bun, her face luminous and her lips stamped post-box red, she looked like a politician and superstar rolled into one.

Jade-Lotus stared at her like she was ten again.

As Snow-Flower marched forward it was as if a high-wattage bulb had been switched on and they were being showered by its generous radiance. She fell into the arms of Jade-Lotus and hugged her tightly, a powerful cloud of Chanel No. 5 shrouding them.

'My dear, dear old rain!' Snow-Flower squeezed Jade-Lotus, then pulled back and surveyed her from head to toe. 'Or rather young rain?' She then went across to kiss and hug William and in perfect English said, 'Hello, stranger, long time no see. How are you?' But before William could answer, she pulled Jade-Lotus to her side and continued, 'Who looks younger? Ha ha, you can lie, William... Now, how have you been keeping, handsome?'

Jade-Lotus smiled; this old friend hadn't changed. When the sun shone, everything else was in its shadow.

'Hey, young rain,' Snow-Flower turned to Jade-Lotus, 'you haven't changed a bit.'

'Really! I have more lines now than the news scripts you read! But you seem to grow younger, prettier and richer!' Jade-Lotus eyed the tennis-court-sized drawing room. 'You've definitely won!'

'Hahahaha! Our old game!' Snow-Flower laughed like a peal of bells. 'But thank you my dear.' She pointed at herself. 'This is the "get noticed and get what I want" work me. All made up! Oh, by the way, I'm so sorry that I couldn't come to the airport, a last minute meeting popped up.' She pouted dramatically. 'As for the apartment, it was all Wave's money, not mine! Oh, I must get changed. Mother Li said dinner is ready. She's cooked our favourite dishes. And I have something important to tell you.'

'You're not going to tell me you're the mayor of Shanghai as well?'

'Hahahaha, you remembered that too! But no, not yet, not yet.' She gave Jade-Lotus a wink before echoing away on her stilettos.

What could it be? Jade-Lotus frowned at William. Paralleled railway tracks seemed an understatement; they were in two different worlds. After all these years of sharing not much more than festive cards, would it be possible to pick up from where they had left off?

Sitting at the round table, facing giant drunken prawns, sweet and sour seabass and some other familiar dishes, and smelling their fragrance, Jade-Lotus felt a soft lump in her throat.

'Mother Li has cooked our old hometown's specialities!' Jade-Lotus said.

'Oh yeah, Mother Li can cook anything. I just need to describe a dish to her, and she cooks it like a pro!' Snow-Flower got up and flip-flopped to the wine cooler that was the size of an upright fridge freezer, her navy jacquard silk dress floating around her. 'I have this vintage white wine from South Africa; you've got to try it.' With a bottle in hand, she came back.

'How did you find Mother Li?' Jade-Lotus said.

Snow-Flower poured wine into each glass. 'She is a relative of a relative who needed a job when Wave bought this place. But I have to say she's great, I can't do without her. Now, let's toast: to our reunion.'

'To our reunion!' Jade-Lotus and William raised their glasses.

'And to your cannon!' Jade-Lotus added.

'Hahahaha, and yes, to my cannon!' Snow-Flower took a swig and twirled her wine. 'But, as I said it's all Wave's money. I'm sure Mother Li would have given you the grand tour and told you how Wave bought it for me as a token of his love. She likes to tell everyone about it.' She waved for them to tuck in.

'This prawn is great,' William said, sucking his finger. 'I thought Wave was just a government official?'

'Oh William, you English are so direct.' Snow-Flower tutted. 'Wave is clean, I'm sure. He was in the first group of government officials sent to Africa to invest and he chose a gold mine; the rest is history. You could say Wave is a gold digger nowadays.' She laughed, her laughter bounced like pearls on the marble.

'Still congrats for making it into the French Concession!' Jade-Lotus said.

Snow-Flower brightened up. 'You remembered that dream of mine too! Oh, I've missed you, my dear old friend!' Pressing her hand affectionately onto Jade-Lotus's: 'It's been six years. I've really missed you.'

Jade-Lotus smiled. Surprisingly she had remembered the number of years since their last meeting; maybe the old friendship would spark again, like a dormant flint struck by steel. 'Now I'm back, and will be here for a long time! You'll be bored to death by the end of it.'

'Hahahaha. I'll tell you when you get annoying.' Snow-Flower drank some more wine. 'Now, I have important news. A warning, in fact.' Her face turned a page.

'A warning?' Jade-Lotus dropped the fried oyster she had just picked, her stomach tightened.

'Do you remember High-Fly Lee?' Snow-Flower said. 'The boy who used to chase her by writing political-slogan-like poems,' she whispered to William. 'Oh, remember the one you told me about: "Climb high, dive low; besides giving my red heart to Chairman Mao, I want to give a bit to you!" I'll never forget that!' She burst into laughter again.

'What about him?' Jade-Lotus frowned.

'Well, he's taking a special interest in you again,' Snow-Flower said, winking at William. 'The mayor's office and our TV station run an annual competition called the Golden Communist Road amongst the small towns around Shanghai.

We follow officials in each town for a period of six months, and whoever has the most innovative and unique idea to show leadership and loyalty to the Party will win a six-figure prize for the town. We decide the contestants. Guess what? This year our hometown entered – again,' she rolled her eyes, 'and High-Fly's Blocking Foreign Adoption got my attention. Little-Blossom had told me about you coming back to adopt. So, I called him.'

Jade-Lotus froze.

'I hate that monkey-like squeaky voice of his! He's tried to endear himself to me many times in the past. When I asked him whose adoption he was trying to ruin he just laughed; but when I told him I wouldn't let them enter without more details he admitted it was yours.'

Jade-Lotus dropped her chopsticks and they fell onto the floor.

'Can he do that?' William said.

'I think he can,' Snow-Flower said, and picked up the chopsticks. 'They would spin it from the one-child policy; it would make them look very loyal, and they might actually win... and that monkey told me he was dreaming about collecting the prize, watched by thousands of officials, and imagining endless future opportunities... Grrr, there's nothing that monkey and his father wouldn't do for fame, power, money and...'

Jade-Lotus felt the blood drain from her face and tuned away from Snow-Flower's ringing voice.

'And you let him enter?' William said.

'I said to him, "You do know that the person you're trying to expose for flouting the one-child policy is my sister-in-law, and the person adopting the baby is my best friend, don't you?"

And guess what? He just laughed and said, "You're a journalist, you must see how newsworthy and gripping my proposal is? I bet your manager will agree with me…" I couldn't believe that monkey was threatening me, and wondered why I was wasting my time. A toad is always a toad. Obviously, he didn't know I'm the editor in chief, so, I said, "We'll see", hung up, and crossed our hometown off the list.'

'He's definitely off?' Jade-Lotus said weakly.

Snow-Flower nodded. 'But I don't know what he'll do back in Blushing Lotus, so you need to be prepared.'

Jade-Lotus nodded too. Everything would be twisted back home; old armour needed to be dusted off. 'Thank you.' She grasped Snow-Flower's hand; the back of her eyes moistened.

Snow-Flower gave Jade-Lotus a hug.

In the embrace, Jade-Lotus blinked hard.

Snow-Flower let go, reached for the wine and filled their glasses again. After taking a slug she said in a subdued tone, 'You don't need to thank me really. I also stopped High-Fly for myself. I didn't want to take a risk again.'

William raised his eyebrows.

Snow-Flower took another swig of wine and said, 'Well, back in January, I had to drop one of my best documentary programmes just before it was due to be aired. Guess what? My wrist got slapped twice, once by the top, the communist party leaders, and once by the mayor. I'm still angry, angry at their interference, but mostly angry at myself for having given in.' She paused, twirling the wine in her glass and looking at the ripples, and sighed. 'Your story, no matter how we spin it, touches the very same nerve as my axed programme called *Unwanted*, which was about people abandoning baby girls. My team spent three years filming it, but in the end, the top said it was too damaging to our country's image since we are hosting the Olympics next year.' She shook her head. 'Well, enough of my work problems; let's finish our dinner and have coffee in the library.'

The library was a more intimate space. One wall was entirely covered by honey-coloured bookshelves, neatly filled with books and small objects. On the wall opposite, many different-sized black picture frames were hung harmoniously together, each with a black and white photo of a girl in it.

'Who are these girls?' Jade-Lotus asked.

'Ah, they're the pride of my life!' Snow-Flower said, beaming. 'They're the girls that my charity has helped over the last ten years. All cast out by their families, just because they're girls.' She sighed. 'Ten years ago I was a fearless journalist. I did what a journalist should do and I did what society wanted me to do – report on the real issues in life. Now I'm at the top but a coward, no bones at all. Ah, I'd better not go there again as it's getting late. Tomorrow we have to get up early to travel!'

Outside, the sky had turned dark velvet, covered by clouds. There wasn't a single star on the horizon. Across the river one or two beacons of light flashed on top of the skyscrapers, lonely and incessant, their faint rays suffocating in the darkness. Dawn was still far away.

5

Dead Ashes Burn Again

As the train rhythmically rocked, and the hazy, chaotic, steel and concrete world of Shanghai was being left behind, William and Snow-Flower fell asleep. Jade-Lotus took her pashmina from her neck, unrolled it and gently covered her safari-suited friend. After all these years, Snow-Flower still watched out for her. The old friendship might have been stretched thin by distance, even buried under the thick dust of modern life, but given time and effort it would shine again.

She looked out at the grey monotonous suburbs, her heart heavy. Among the faces that had been stuffed into a 'suitcase', its key deliberately thrown away, and left deeply buried in Blushing Lotus, was High-Fly's. Because they had never seen eye to eye, right from the first day of primary school. In fact, High-Fly had crab-like eyes, only god knew what he was looking at most of the time and what sick ideas he was having as he swivelled his eyeballs.

'Everyone, this way please,' shouted Teacher Tan, a smiling

ponytailed new graduate from Shanghai.

Jade-Lotus skipped, her little green satchel swinging behind her; at last she had been accepted by the school!

All the children sat down in the classroom; a woman and a man marched in.

'Let's give a warm round of applause to welcome our school's secretary of the Communist Party,' Teacher Tan said, turning to the stick-like woman with a horse face and slit eyes, 'and our town leader.' She gestured to the short stout man with shiny swept back black hair, dressed smartly in an army jacket.

Slit Eyes waved her hand at the children in a forceful manner and ground her thumb and fingers together, as if grabbing a fly and crushing it.

At once, everyone quietened down. Teacher Tan stood still in the corner, her hands tightly clasped in front of her.

'Long live Chairman Mao!' Slit Eyes shouted, her raised fist hitting the air, her spittle flying. 'And thanks to him, we're the masters of the New China! But we must stay alert and sweep away any class enemies! Now, let's start with the blow-on-the-head: listen carefully, announce your family class before you say your name and "I am a red communist sprout."'

A small pale boy sprang up and shouted, 'Glorious Worker's Class! High-Fly Lee, a totally red communist sprout, taking after my dad.' He pointed at the stout man.

'An exceptional red seed!' Slit-Eyes beamed at the same man.

When it was her turn, Jade-Lotus hesitated and omitted her family class.

The Secretary chided her, 'How can you be a red sprout? Your parents are anti-revolutionist, rightist, capitalist-roaders and more! Black puppy is more like it.'

The stout man clapped slowly.

Teacher Tan followed suit and waved for all the children to join in. Her ponytail bobbled to the rhythm of the clapping.

'Black puppy! Black puppy! Down black puppy!' High-Fly shouted, like a dog barking because its master had told it to.

Jade-Lotus swallowed and blinked back the tears that were forming. Enough crying had been done already; Grandma had fought to the bitter end to overcome their family background and get her into this primary school.

Slit Eyes nodded satisfiedly, and marched out with the stout man.

Teacher Tan quickly closed the door, and stood holding the door handle for a moment before turning around. 'Welcome to your new school,' she said, squeezing out a smile, 'now please all come to the front, you need to be re-seated, the taller ones sit at the back.'

When High-Fly, probably the shortest of the fifty children and thin as a matchstick, was called, instead of sitting in the front row, he chose the back row, where Jade-Lotus sat.

'High-Fly Lee!' Teacher Tan raised her voice.

'What?' Seeing the teacher's steely face, he stood up, which didn't seem to make much difference to his height from when he was sitting down, and shouted, 'You know who my dad is, don't you? Say you know who he is! Say it!'

Teacher Tan coughed, as if to clear some annoying phlegm. 'He's the reddest in the region – the leader of the worker rebels, the leader of the town's communist party, the leader of the Maoism study classes, in fact the leader just about of anything and everything.' She sounded like a tape recorder.

'Good!' High-Fly sat down. 'Daddy says to keep comrades

close, but enemies closer.' He leaned forward and eyed Jade-Lotus; the two children between them leaned back.

Jade-Lotus glanced at him, but was unsure who he was looking at.

Teacher Tan shook her head and carried on getting the rest of the children seated. Once the room was in order, she said, 'Now, who'll tell me what you'd like to learn in your first class? Please raise your hand.' She sounded like an actress in a movie.

'I will!' High-Fly shouted.

'Do I see a hand?' Teacher Tan insisted.

High-Fly waved his hand impatiently.

'Good! So, what's it you'd like to learn?'

'I want to know how to write Black Puppy, so we can all write her name correctly.' High-Fly laughed shrilly, beating the desk like a drum with both hands. Everyone in the room laughed, including the teacher. 'Now, everyone, repeat after me, Black Puppy! Black Puppy!'

The room was like a troop of apes chanting and drumming. Something was crystallising in her eyes again, and her throat closed, but Jade-Lotus swallowed hard, and bit her lip with such force that it hurt. Grandma's 'Teary silkworms don't stop people poking them' came to her rescue. When silkworms spit silk, the local people say they're shedding tears. Instead of storming out of the room in tears, she opened the little book in a red cover that was placed on her desk and saw the first line, 'Imperialism is a paper tiger!' She didn't know the characters for Imperialism, so she just shouted, 'Paper Tiger!'

Teacher Tan's mouth dropped open; the classroom quietened down. The power of a line from Mao's little Red Book worked the other way too.

'Come on Children, please open your textbooks,' Teacher Tan said, her face completely serious.

Outside became greener; in the distance, pylons marched like soldiers. Jade-Lotus looked at her watch; about half way already. The ratty old train no longer felt slow, it was reaching the old hometown too quickly. She sighed. The rocky road with High-Fly had continued, the bully turned into a spotty annoying teenager.

'You really want to walk on your own on your birthday?' Snow-Flower said.

Jade-Lotus nodded; her emotions were running high, again.

'Come on, we should give her space,' River-Cloud said.

Jade-Lotus squeezed a smile to him; he was always so understanding.

'OK, don't be long,' Snow-Flower said. 'Remember we'll come over later? I can't wait to have your grandma's hand-made noodles!'

Jade-Lotus waved, turned and headed towards the river; it was quiet there in the mid-afternoon. She wanted to resume the ritual she had started on her last birthday: to thank and remember Mama.

Suddenly her path was blocked; it was High-Fly, whistling, hands in pockets, eyeballs skidding around. 'Happy Birthday!' He took something out of his pocket and thrust it into her hand, his spotty face the colour of the flag on the badge he was wearing on his chest.

'What do you want now, Communist Youth League secretary?' Jade-Lotus frowned, looking at what was in her hand – a folded silk handkerchief with her name embroidered in one corner. 'No thanks.' She handed it back.

'I begged my sister to make it; it cost me one yuan.' He forcefully pushed it back into her hand. 'It's my gift.' Then he pulled out a pile of papers from his schoolbag and shoved it into her bag, like a pick-pocket in reverse. 'They're for you too, all my work.' He turned and walked slowly away.

She took the papers out. There were about ten pages, and each page had a short poem. She read the first one quickly: 'One thousand songs, two thousands songs; each song was for the reddest sun! You sing them, I sing them; we hold hands together to sing Maoism!' She snorted. 'Hey, you come back!' she shouted after him.

High-Fly almost jogged back, his estranged, soy-bean-sized eyes burning bright.

'Let's go to the water.' She glanced at the river that was right ahead of them.

He whistled with delight, skipping down the short path.

Jade-Lotus knelt down and spread all the pages of poetry on the ground. As he stared, she threw them, one page at a time, into the river, and finished by throwing the handkerchief in after them. 'Your love is floating away; perhaps some other lucky girl downstream will enjoy it more.'

Bright sunlight slanted across Jade-Lotus's face and she closed her eyes, shutting out the winding past. She raised a hand to shade her face and looked out.

As if a painter had been hard at work, the landscape had changed completely. Lush green fields stretched as far as the eye could see, interwoven by gleaming waterways; straw-thatched cottages dotted here and there, light smoke rising from their humble chimneys. It was the beginning of March, but spring was like a peacock in full display. Under the bright sun, pink cherry blossom, pale peach blossom and snow-like pear blossom competed like in a beauty pageant. The mulberry trees alongside the railway line had all woken up, a fresh green coat on their bony branches. Farmers led buffalos to plough; women planted, their bamboo hats floating in the air.

The train took a bend and reduced speed; Jade-Lotus sat up rigidly. She shook William and Snow-Flower, as the old town revealed itself like an unrolling scroll painting – the whitewashed walls, the grey tiled roofs, the stone bridges and the canals. Abundant pairs of red lanterns hung guarding each front door, like eyes dotted on sleepy dragons.

'Ah, home!' Snow-Flower said.

'The Lantern Festival!' William said.

'River-Cloud is coming to pick us up,' Snow-Flower said as they got off the train,

'That's nice. I hope I can still recognise him,' Jade-Lotus said.

'Well, I won't say anything then,' Snow-Flower said.

But there was no sign of River-Cloud on the platform or outside the small station.

'Where is he?' Snow-Flower said as passengers dispersed. She dialled her mobile phone. 'Voicemail!' She shook her head and walked away to leave a message.

Jade-Lotus raised her face to the sun and closed her eyes; every cell in her body surrendered like morning glories. The air, scented with new shoots, vibrated to the fluting melody of yellow orioles. *Ah, this feels good...* But her thoughts were cut short by a nudge from William, and she opened her eyes.

A suited, official-looking man stood a few paces in front her, hands in pockets, smiling at her. On each side of him was a waistcoated youngster holding a professional-looking camera. Jade-Lotus stared at the man, who was short both in height and width, lacking the prosperous girth normally found in a Chinese official. His face was bony and dull, but his small, estranged eyes were astonishingly animated and lively. She frowned, and cried out, 'High-Fly Lee!'

'Ohhaha, just knew you'd remember me!' High-Fly said, walking up and stretching his hand towards her.

Reluctantly, Jade-Lotus extended her hand.

'Welcome, welcome! Dear dear old classmate! You haven't changed a bit!' He held her hand, turned to a camera and smiled.

The two youngsters bobbed around taking shots.

Jade-Lotus was speechless, unconsciously turning away from the cameras.

High-Fly turned to William and said in English, 'Welcome, welcome, my dear classmate's husband!' He held on to William's hand even longer, turning again to the camera with a wide toothy smile.

Snow-Flower returned, 'What's this? Good Heavens! What are you doing here, High-Fly?'

'Ohhaha!' High-Fly's face changed from dull yellow to red. 'What a surprise, our famous TV star is back too. Wonderful! Wonderful!' His high-pitched voice quivered as he beamed at Snow-Flower.

'STOP them taking pictures!' Snow-Flower shouted.

'Of course.' High-Fly's smile stiffened as he waved away the youngsters. 'Who can disobey your order, TV Star? But I'm here for the best of reasons, our town leader sent me to

51

welcome our foreign guests; our local newspaper wants to capture that.'

'Oh really?' Snow-Flower sneered. 'Just go away, chop chop.'

High-Fly shrugged and walked off.

'River-Cloud!' Jade-Lotus shrilled, much relieved to see her old friend appear ahead of them.

Sporting a navy silk mandarin jacket, its high-collar tightly buttoned, matching silk trousers, and a pair of black round wire-framed spectacles, River-Cloud looked like a scholar from a period drama. 'Sorry, sorry I'm late,' he said and ran the last few steps to Snow-Flower, before turning to Jade-Lotus and William. He joined his hands together in front of his chest in a hand-over-fist salute. 'Greetings, greetings! Long time no see.'

Jade-Lotus opened her arms, wanting to give him a big hug and a tight squeeze, to wring out the years of being apart; but all she did was a gentle curtsey, as if dragged back to old Imperial China.

William, who loved to watch kung-fu films, returned a perfect hand-over-fist salute.

'Sister here is also curtseying, Real Big Brother,' Snow-Flower tightened her voice as if in an opera.

River-Cloud smiled kindly and said, 'The motor rickshaws I've arranged are waiting. Shall we go?'

He led the way to a quiet back street. But there were no motor rickshaws; instead two shiny black Mercedes limousines were parked neatly at the roadside, each with a uniformed driver holding open a rear door.

'Gosh, you call Mercedes rickshaws nowadays?' Jade-Lotus said.

Before River-Cloud could answer, High-Fly stepped out of one of the cars, with a Machiavellian smile, and said, rather pompously, 'Our foreign guests deserve better! I sent away the ratty old rickshaws.' He waved to Jade-Lotus and William, 'Come, come, we'll give you a smooth ride to the moorings.'

'Thank you, Mr Lee, but we won't trouble you and your nice cars,' River-Cloud said with a gentle and placid tone. 'Jade-Lotus and William aren't your official guests. Thanks for your kindness, we'll find some other rickshaws.'

'Ohhaha! You may find that all the rickshaws are busy somewhere else by now,' High-Fly said with a wink.

'Are you making trouble?' Snow-Flower cut in.

High-Fly rolled his eyes and said, 'Am I?'

River-Cloud raised his arms, palms downward, like an orchestra conductor calling for smoothness. He turned to Jade-Lotus and shrugged. 'Maybe it's better we take the cars?'

Jade-Lotus exchanged a glance with William and nodded.

While helping Jade-Lotus with her luggage, River-Cloud said, 'Well, you can now see the modern side of your old hometown!'

Jade-Lotus smiled at him, watching as he helped the driver load the car, his willowy frame under the silk suit working hard to lift her luggage, his spectacles repeatedly slipping down his nose.

Once they left the railway station, High-Fly came alive. 'We've made huge strides in modernising our town since you left,' he said, twisting his body from the front seat and glancing at Jade-Lotus, before pointing out, 'this is our modern cinema, that's the state-of-the-art Worker's Cultural Palace; and look, look, William, we've even got high-rise blocks in the distance, I'm sure as modern as what you have in England.' He grinned

53

smugly.

'Very modern indeed,' William said. 'What's that tall building over there?'

'Oh, that's our Red Watchtower, a new tourist attraction. And look at the one next to it...' High-Fly talked incessantly to William.

Jade-Lotus turned to look outside. A sense of annoyance at being trapped with High-Fly and having to follow his script sank in. She had mentally prepared herself for him after Snow-Flower's warning, but hadn't expected to see him so soon, and was now rather confused by his warm welcome. What tricks did he have hidden in his calabash?

The scene outside was unfamiliar; the old hometown was almost unrecognisable. But had this deeply conservative town really changed? Had High-Fly really changed? And even if he had, what was it that the changed High-Fly wanted?

'I need your help now, Jade-Lotus,' High-Fly said in Chinese, 'I've used all the English words I know trying to talk to your husband! Did I hear right that he won't be staying long?'

'Yes, he has to go to USA next Thursday,' Jade-Lotus said.

'OK, OK, you must insist he has lunch with our town leader. Mark Lee really wants to meet William. Oh, and of course you too! Please, please come next Tuesday, I'll send a car.'

'You should know William can speak pretty good Chinese.'

'Thanks for the invitation, we're pleased to accept,' William said in Mandarin.

6

Pirate

Thank God, the old hometown was the size of a sparrow, and the journey with High-Fly to the mooring only lasted six minutes. Jade-Lotus climbed out of the car as fast as she could, but William enthusiastically shook High-Fly's hand, and thanked him for the ride. How interesting to see William do that, like it was a business meeting. High-Fly, on the other hand, looked overwhelmed as if William was some kind of superstar, holding on to his hand and patting his arm, his face a blossomed chrysanthemum. He even rolled down his window and waved as his car glided away.

'You don't need to be nice to him,' Jade-Lotus whispered.

'But we can't make enemies of the officials,' William whispered back.

Jade-Lotus sighed; he was right.

'You survived High-Fly?' Snow-Flower had arrived too.

'Just about,' Jade-Lotus said.

River-Cloud smiled at her. 'Let's get on board then.'

In front of them was a shiny wooden boat, its windows all

intricately carved, and its honey hew so fresh that it looked brand-new.

'Nice boat,' William said.

'His new luxury toy,' Snow-Flower said.

'Haha, not that grand. I use it for the school.' River-Cloud gestured for everyone to board. As William passed, he added, 'Please sit in the front.'

'Now we can talk like we used to.' Snow-Flower wrapped her arm around Jade-Lotus's. 'Tell me who you miss the most.'

Jade-Lotus looked at her with wide eyes.

'I know, I know, apart from me.' Snow-Flower giggled.

Before Jade-Lotus answered, Snow-Flower's phone rang. 'Sorry, I have to get this.' She wrinkled her nose and pressed Jade-Lotus's hand before getting up and stepping out of the cabin door.

The river breeze combed Jade-Lotus's hair and thoughts. Of course, Snow-Flower knew; who else could it be? Who had single-handedly brought her up? She vividly remembered seeing Grandma for the first time.

The heavy sun-bleached wooden door squeaked open; a lady slowly leaned out half of her face. But then the door was thrown open with a big clunk, and the lady stood there, staring. She was in a long black dress, tall and slim; her hand holding a walking stick, her dark-brown hair reaching down to her waist, and on her marble-white face, one of her eyes was covered by a black patch.

Little Jade-Lotus ran to a nearby shrub and hid behind it.

The lady threw away her stick, rushed out and knelt down. With hands stretching out towards Jade-Lotus, she said, 'Aiya, don't be scared. I'm your grandma.' A tear ran from her uncovered blackened eye.

Jade-Lotus wasn't entirely convinced.

Grandma patted her eye patch and said softly, 'We're going to play a game. I'm your pirate and you're my most precious little treasure. I'm here to protect you. Come, come,' she beckoned, 'see that boat with a red flag? We can use it to treasure hunt.'

Jade-Lotus followed Grandma's pointing finger to a shabby wooden boat, its paint faded and peeling. She had never seen a boat or a pirate before, although Mama had told vivid stories about them in the south, and she liked them. So she slowly walked over to her grandma and gingerly fell into the arms of Pirate. Her lamb-horn hair-buns were caressed by Pirate's hands, her shoulders wet with hot tears. The swirling yellow leaves became calm…

'You still don't want to talk?' Pirate asked the next morning.

Jade-Lotus shook her head.

'OK. Let's go treasure hunting, shall we?'

She shook her head again.

'Hmm, how about Mama-hunting?'

She nodded slowly.

'OK. We need to pack some food.' Grandma stared at the empty basket, and then at the half cornbread and boiled egg on her plate. 'I can't possibly eat all of this.' She went to the kitchen and came back with a chopper, and carefully sliced the bread and egg.

Jade-Lotus pushed her plate of one egg and a smaller piece of bread to Grandma.

'You need to eat them; we have nothing else.' Grandma pushed it back.

She pushed it back again.

'Pirate gives orders. So how about you have the egg, I'll take the bread.'

She eventually nodded.

'Let's make little parcels; they're our treasure. Will you look after them?'

She nodded again.

'Now, cover your legs with this blanket,' Grandma said on the boat. 'Hold on to our treasure no matter what.'

The river was muddy; the sky was gloomy. Her little hands were cold, but she held their parcels firmly against her chest as she shivered. Pirate rowed and rowed, her dark brown hair flying in the wind.

They docked at the first house. Grandma knocked hard on the door. After a long while a woman came out; her eyes widened, staring at Jade-Lotus.

'We've got you a little food parcel,' Grandma said, gesturing to Jade-Lotus.

The woman immediately leaned forward and took the parcel.

'Did you see where my daughter went?' Grandma said.

The woman at once shook her head. 'No. I know nothing. Don't ask me.' Her hand shook a little, but her fingers gripped the parcel tightly.

'It's OK,' Grandma said. 'You can keep it. Thank you,'

They moved to the next house. Although there was the muffled sound of someone approaching the door and the peephole being checked, the door remained firmly closed.

When their parcels had all gone and all the doors had been knocked upon, they returned to the boat. Pirate looked pale; her eyepatch starkly black. In the icy wind, with her hair flying, she sang as she rowed:

58

'The reeds and rushes are green,
  White dew turned to frosty sheen.
  The one I love so much
  Is somewhere near the stream.
  I go upstream searching for her,
  The journey long and dire.
  I go downstream searching for her,
  She stays in the midst of water...'

Jade-Lotus quietly hummed the same old song, accompanied by River-Cloud's boat's engine. As a little lost shell that had landed on Pirate's shore she was cherished. In the distance, the tea-bush smothered hills looked moody; above them, dark clouds and light clouds entwined and exchanged conspiratorial glances. On the bank, the dense, whitewashed, centuries-old houses nudged each other; along the river, small granite bridges passed whispers. The river breeze brushed her face; the fishy smell was like a long lost friend. As the boat surged forward, closer and closer to the old hometown, the sense of being caged – by the grey tiled roofs that dangled with red lanterns, by the dark feathery vegetation on the banks – crawled back over her. Like a tiny pea in a tight-fitting pod.

Snow-Flower came back. 'Are you alright? You look miles away.'

Jade-Lotus nodded. 'I was thinking about Grandma. I've left her on her own all these years.'

'Ah. But was there any other way? She wanted you to have a better life, didn't she?'

'Yes, I know. But still, "Children should never be far away when parents are alive".'

59

'Oh God, that rubbish Confucian guilt! I can't believe you even remember that.' Snow-Flower stared at her. 'Cheer up, my dear! Your grandma's an iron lady and I think she's quite happy.'

Jade-Lotus stretched a smile. 'Your grandaunt keeps trying to change that.'

'Although she can be a pain in the arse, Nine-Pound Old Lady is just a paper tiger really.'

Jade-Lotus smiled again and looked away. In the front of the boat, William and River-Cloud were talking like old friends. The nudging townhouses began to space out, their intimacy cooling.

'What?' Snow-Flower said.

'Nothing,' Jade-Lotus answered.

Snow-flower took her hand and looked softly into her eyes. 'What's really on your mind?'

Jade-Lotus twisted her bottom on the leather seat, which squeaked.

'Come on, you can tell me,' Snow-Flower insisted.

'I want to find out what happened to Mama.'

Snow-Flower dropped Jade-Lotus's hand, her eyes widening. 'Does Grandma know?'

Jade-Lotus shook her head.

Snow-Flower sucked in air sharply.

Silence shrouded them like river mist.

'You'll talk to Grandma about it, won't you?' Snow-Flower eventually said.

'Yes.'

'Shall I come?'

'No. But thanks. I should be OK.'

'Here we are,' River-Cloud announced loudly.

After the last in a row of whitewashed houses, their boat turned into a quiet side canal. Jade-Lotus's heart jumped as Grandma's stone-mooring came into sight.

At the top of the steps stood a lady in a long dark dress, one hand holding the front of a dark shawl peppered with red dots, and her other hand waving frantically at them. As their boat reversed into the mooring, a gust of wind tightened her dress, sketching out her slender body and lifting a few strands of her grey hair. Tears welled in Jade-Lotus's eyes and she bit her lip hard.

Ah, home. Ah, Grandma.

As she stepped over the stone threshold, Jade-Lotus felt her legs soften. She held the wooden door, on which the scent of tung oil was still detectable, and gently slid her fingers up and down its edge before closing it. Was this really the old courtyard? The threshold seemed not as deep and less tall.

'We go up here.' Grandma led them to the side stairs. 'You're going to stay in Mama's room.'

'Really?' Jade-Lotus said.

Growing up, Mama's room had always been locked. Although at first she had often sat on Mama's bed looking out for Mama's boat on the river, waiting for her to come back. But then Grandma padlocked it; only on Mama's birthdays would Grandma open it up so they could go in and light a candle for her.

The corridor that overlooked the central courtyard felt shorter; then Mama's room was right there, its double doors open like welcoming arms. Grandma and William strode in, but Jade-Lotus entered gingerly, tiptoeing quietly on the wooden floor as if trying not to wake someone up. The lattice windows were all open too, but the air still had a musty hint. Mama's room hadn't been inhabited for well over forty years. It had been a sacred place for immortals.

'Very nice,' William said.

Grandma smiled.

'Where are Mama's things?' Jade-Lotus said.

Grandma stared at her, as if surprised, before raising her chin towards the connecting door to Mama's old reading room. 'They're all in there. Oh, I'm doing an early lunch; I bet you're hungry. See you down in the dining room as soon as you're ready.'

'Thank you, Grandma,' William said. 'I'll go and get the rest of the suitcases.'

Jade-Lotus stood in the middle of Mama's room; how interesting that Grandma had put them here. Had she given up holding it as a sacred place for her dear daughter? That look she had just given, was it a rebuke? Jade-Lotus shook her head. Surely Grandma knew her granddaughter was about to be forty, not fourteen any more.

The yellowing newspaper with many articles circled by a pen had all disappeared from the walls, as well as the two big faded posters of Mao. The only adornments on the now cleanly whitewashed walls were three wooden frames, each with a picture in it. The desk, once the dominating feature of the room, on which teenage Mama had written poems for the local newspapers, seemed to have shrunk, and was pushed against the wall sandwiched between two windows. Mama's old single bed had been replaced by a big four-poster one, draped with a white muslin mosquito net, matching the muslin curtains. To call it Mama's room wasn't accurate now, as nothing of Mama remained.

Jade-Lotus slowly sat down on the bed as if feeling out the mattress, raising her eyes to look out of the window and down at the river. There wasn't a boat, only haze; but her memory of the train trip with Mama in the autumn of 1969 was crystal clear.

Little Jade-Lotus puffed as she climbed onto the window seat on the train and leant on Mama, who was also puffing, her heart thumping hard. Before they had their breath back, a big girl on the seat opposite, in army-green overalls and wearing a cap pinned with a red star, shouted at them, 'Foul baggage!'

What baggage? Jade-Lotus was startled and looked at Mama. They had been in such a hurry that all they had with them were the clothes they were wearing: Mama's faded navy overalls clinched with a brown belt and her own sun-bleached army green overalls – Baba had said earlier that she looked like a little communist soldier. Mama didn't say anything and sat Jade-Lotus on her lap; she held her small doll tightly.

The big girl lurched forward, grabbed the doll, threw it hard onto the floor and stamped on it with an ugly plimsoled foot.

Jade-Lotus's mouth dropped open. The doll's arms had broken off, its face smashed; one eye had popped out and was staring harshly through messy brown hair.

The big girl opened the window, scooped up the doll's little carcass, threw it out and shut the window. She curled her lips into a satisfied mean smile, thrust her fist into the air and shouted, 'Down with the bourgeoisie! Long live the Cultural Revolution! Long live Chairman Mao!'

Jade-Lotus broke away from Mama's arms, wanting to bite the ugly girl; but all she did was turn her back on her and stand looking out of the window.

Mama's arms wrapped around her and she whispered: *'One butterfly, don't cry, two magpies, don't cry; three orioles sing a song, four white cranes soar to the sky!'*

Outside it was completely dark; the reflection of the vainglorious ugly girl stared back at her. She blew hot air onto the cold window, and the girl's insane obnoxiousness dissolved.

Mama nudged her; when she turned, the nasty girl had indeed disappeared.

They sat back down silently; Mama sighed and put her arm around her little shoulders.

The back of the carriage went mad with youths singing 'The East is red...'

Mama looked around cautiously before opening the top button of her overalls and taking a small package from inside her bra. She unwrapped it to reveal a gold necklace, quickly put it around Jade-Lotus's neck and buried it inside her clothes. 'You've been a good girl.'

Jade-Lotus touched the teardrop-shaped jade pendant; it was still warm.

'It's a magic pendant,' Mama said, cradling her face in her hands. 'When we arrive, you must behave with Grandma. And remember Mama loves you very much.' Mama's big dark-brown eyes glinted and she hugged her tightly. 'When you miss Mama, talk to the pendant, Mama will be back.' She felt a tear, then another, and another drop onto the back of her little neck, so warm and so wet...

Jade-Lotus caressed the pendant that had dangled from the same necklace ever since that fateful day. She had talked to the pendant a thousand times, but Mama never came back.

'One butterfly, don't cry, two magpies, don't cry; three orioles sing a song, four white cranes soar to the sky!'

Sunrays slanted a square on the polished wooden floor, which in turn reflected onto the three picture frames on the wall. She rolled off the bed, and tiptoed across the room to get a closer look at the black and white photos. The one on the left was of a young girl nestling against a lady that looked like Grandma; both of them were smiling slightly, and the handwriting in the corner said, 'Age 9 Shanghai 1955'. The middle one looked familiar; yes, it was Mama's graduation photo, marked: 'Beijing University 1965'. The photo on the right had the words 'Happy family Beijing 1969'. They were all Mama's photos; it was as if Grandma was narrating Mama's life. She looked again at the family portrait: Mama wore a long stiff dark dress, looked incredibly young, and cradled a baby in her arms; next to her stood a tall young man in a Mao suit, presumably Baba. She narrowed her eyes, but couldn't really remember him. He had tidy, wavy hair and a chiselled face with rather handsome well-defined features. Both Mama and Baba had a tiny curl in their lips, but their smiles didn't extend to their eyes. In front of Baba's leg stood a little girl with a gloomy sad face, presumably hers. The baby must be Didi, Great-Aspiration. She couldn't remember anything about the photo being taken, but since it had 1969 on it, it was probably the last family photo. Although Grandma hadn't said, in her heart Jade-Lotus knew that Mama died right after the train trip in 1969. What had happened to Baba and Great-Aspiration? They hadn't come with them on the train, and it would be impossible to find anything out about them after all these years.

'Is that your family?' William embraced her from behind.

Jade-Lotus nodded.

He leaned forward to get a closer look. 'They look so young! Have you worked out how to talk to Grandma?'

'Not really.' She sighed. 'Do you think she's put us in this room for a reason?'

'I've no idea. But I never read the subtleties of what people say, or most of the time don't say, in your culture. Let's go down for lunch.'

'Dumplings for departing; noodles for home-coming!' Grandma gestured warmly to the bowls of steamy noodles on the table and a ring of dishes next to them. 'Help yourself to the toppings. All local delicacies.' As they sat down, Grandma added a big spoonful of topping to William's bowl. 'You must try this braised smoked duck, the best in the region!' She then pointed, 'Little Treasure, that's your favourite.'

'Oh, your fried eel slices! I dream about them all the time,' Jade-Lotus said and tucked in. *Must get the tone right with Grandma.*

'The duck is delicious,' William said.

Jade-Lotus chewed her eels slowly. *How to bring it up?*

'How are they, dear? Still taste like they used to?' Grandma asked.

'They're out of this world,' Jade-Lotus said. 'Absolutely!'

Grandma stared at her for a moment and smiled. 'Now have some prawns.' She waved at the dish. 'Is there something on your mind, my little treasure?'

William reached for the egg-fried prawns.

Jade-Lotus cleared her throat. 'Grandma, I'm staying here for a few months, you know, for the baby to be born.'

'Yes dear, that's wonderful. I couldn't be happier,' Grandma said, and added some dressed bamboo shoots to her own bowl. 'Although, about the baby, it's a Shan baby...' She busied herself spooning prawns into Jade-Lotus's bowl, and turned to William. 'How are the prawns? They were still alive when I got them home.'

Before William could reply, Jade-Lotus said, a little hotly, 'But it's Cousin Little-Blossom's baby too.' She softened, quickly adding, 'I'm sorry, Grandma. I'm really sorry that this baby has brought up the old sesames between you and Nine-Pound Old Lady.'

Grandma stared at her noodles, tucking away a hair that hadn't actually loosened, and eventually looked up. 'Maybe you're right; it's all old sesames and rotten grains. Aihh, at least this baby isn't just anyone's baby, it has some family blood.' She nodded several times as if trying to convince herself. 'Anyway, I've already declared to Nine-Pound Old Lady that I'll support you.' She laughed a short and dry laugh.

'I love you Grandma!' Jade-Lotus wrapped her arm around Grandma's shoulders and gave her a squeeze.

'I'm so glad you're back,' Grandma said.

'Me too. These prawns are unbelievable, aren't they?' Jade-Lotus glanced at William.

'The best I've ever had,' William said.

'Grandma. There's something else,' Jade-Lotus said slowly.

'Anything, my little treasure, now that there's no hidden grit in our rice.'

Jade-Lotus took a deep breath. 'I'll have a lot of time on my hands; of course, I'd love to spend time with you.' She stretched a sweet smile. 'But I also want... um... to find out what happened to Mama.'

Grandma froze, her serving spoon, just filled with slices of preserved egg, stopped in mid-air before it could reach Jade-Lotus's bowl; her face paled as she shook her head. 'We've long agreed that you won't do that.'

Jade-Lotus organised the toppings in her bowl into a pattern of stripes. 'I'm a grownup now, Grandma, not a teenager any more.'

'Ah, but you'll still need him for the adoption.'

'What do you mean Grandma? Need who?'

Grandma plopped the egg into Jade-Lotus's bowl, put the spoon back on the dish and buried her face in her own bowl, quickly eating her noodles.

Jade-Lotus exchanged a look with William and said, 'What is it, Grandma? You just said there's no hidden grit in our rice.'

Grandma continued eating, drank the last drop of stock, slowly put her bowl down and carefully balanced the chopsticks on top of it. 'Yes, my little treasure, you've grown up safely and been long out of the reach of his claws.' She let out a heavy sigh. 'I hated that I had to choose; I hate even more now you're on his chopping board.'

'Is that a riddle? Whose claws? Choose? And between what?' Jade-Lotus said.

Grandma studied her folded hands for a long time before raising her eyes. 'Years ago, Mark Lee visited me and said, "If I were you, I'd stop digging into what happened to your daughter and watch out for your little one."'

Jade-Lotus widened her eyes.

Grandma gathered her eyebrows together, like a child's pencil drawing of a wave. 'I've heard he wants to stop you adopting the baby.'

'He's invited us for lunch next Tuesday,' William said.

'Ah, he's a renowned chameleon and full of poison,' Grandma said. 'It's hard enough to adopt here without making an enemy of him. Don't you think?'

7

Lantern Festival

The following day fireworks crackled from dawn and incense smoke swelled in the air. On the roof terrace, in the spacious silence after a deafening cacophony from the firecrackers that William had lit, Grandma, with joss-sticks in her hands, bowed to the west sky and uttered, 'Goodbye, ghosts of our ancestors. Hope you all have a safe journey back to heaven and see you next time!' She then softly chanted Buddhist scripts.

Jade-Lotus bowed with Grandma in the heady sandalwood smoke. *Is Mama's ghost around? Had she heard the conversation with Grandma? Would she be happy? Had she been disappointed all these years that her body hadn't come home? I'll find out and bring your body home, Mama! But is there a risk of having to choose the baby over Mama, just like Grandma had?* Paper snowflakes from the fireworks lingered in the air, obscuring her vision.

'Do you two want to stay here a bit longer?' Grandma said.

Jade-Lotus nodded. 'It's a nice morning.'

'Don't be too long. I'll get breakfast ready.'

'Thanks Grandma,' William said.

The breeze was as gentle as willow shoots, and the sun-rays wove a silky blanket. The rolling hills of tea bushes stretched into the distance; a dark diamond lake strode across the boundary between the gardens, its waters lapping the property of Yang and of Shan alike. Pink cherry blossoms skirted around the roof terrace; yellow orioles sang.

'It's so nice here. Your ancestors must've been proud of this place,' William said, taking the lens cover off his camera.

'Yeah,' Jade-Lotus said, managing to swallow her next sentence, 'but it gave us nothing but trouble' before it emerged. She still remembered the fate of her old essay.

The Beautiful History of Our House

Our house is located at the end of the town centre, away from all other houses, apart from one, the Shans' house, where my best friend River-Cloud lives.

Grandma said that people used to call it Ghost House. After we were liberated in 1949, the communist government wanted our house to be shared with proletarians. Many families in succession moved in, but after their first night, they moved out. They believed the house was haunted.

But all the time Grandma and I have lived here, we have never seen any ghosts. I wish I could see one so I could ask it to be more welcoming to our proletarians.

Like many houses in the region, our house has leaks, and many of them. In rainy season, Grandma and I have to move from room to room, trying to find a piece of dry land. Our Town Leader, Mr Mark Lee, says our life has been improved a thousand-fold since the new China, and we are truly grateful, only our house doesn't feel it. Maybe one day. Grandma and I remain hopeful.

Despite all of this, Grandma says it has a beautiful history and we should celebrate it.

Our house dates back to the Qing Dynasty, and was originally built as a residential palace with twenty acres of beautiful gardens for the dear uncle of Emperor Guangxu. It had a lovely name: Jasmine Pavilion and Gardens. Before the uncle died, he gifted it to his favourite nephew, the emperor.

A succession of defeats – two opium wars with the British, a war with the French and a war with the Japanese – had humiliated and weakened the Qing dynasty. The young and more open-minded Emperor Guangxu was determined to grow the economy and improve education, and issued many imperial edicts for reform and the speedy development of capitalism.

So, in one of his campaigns, he decided to select the top performer in each trade and reward them handsomely, to set up as an example for others to follow. It so happened that two of the selected businesses came from the same region. One was ours: Yang's Silk. Our silk had been recognised as the best in the country for decades, supplying the Qing court and trading with Europe. The other was Shan Academy, a private school that had the overall top score for students passing the notoriously difficult imperial examinations.

Although he knew that scholars tended to look down on business people, and business people thought that scholars lived in ivory towers, Emperor Guangxu decided that the two families should become neighbours and start the process of reforming these age-old prejudices. So the Jasmine Pavilion and Gardens was divided in two, each family being gifted half indefinitely. For over three quarters of a century now, the Yang and Shan families have been neighbours.

Like our townspeople are proud of our town's historical name,

Grandma and I are proud of our house as it has a beautiful history.

'Bravo! It's great,' Teacher Tan, her ponytail now a common bob, applauded after Jade-Lotus finished reading in front of the class.

With a shrill whistle High-Fly jumped up and marched to Jade-Lotus, cleared his throat and drawled, 'Interesting.' Staring at the teacher: 'You think this is good writing?'

'Well,' Teacher Tan said, standing unusually tall, 'it's fresh, simple, and fits the requirement of "no slogans, denunciations, or fake passions". I believe it's true to her heart, I learnt something and I was captivated. Yes, it's excellent writing, befitting our exciting new era. In fact, it's so good that I'm going to enter it into the county writing competition.' She stood even taller.

High-Fly sneered, grabbed the essay from Jade-Lotus, tore it into pieces and threw them on the lectern in front of Teacher Tan. 'Gone! No More! How dare you enter a black puppy's work into the competition? The body of our greatest helmsman isn't yet cold and you want to restore the old imperialism?' He took out a folded page from his pocket and threw it at the teacher. 'Enter my essay!'

Teacher Tan was speechless; the school bell rang.

When Jade-Lotus left the classroom, High-Fly shouted, mimicking her, 'Our house has a beautiful history!' Other students followed, 'Our house is a beauty! A beauty!'

'It is a beauty,' Jade-Lotus muttered walking over to William, who was clicking away.

'Yes, so picturesque from every angle,' William said. 'Oh look, Snow-Flower.'

'Looks like she's out for a jog.' Jade-Lotus shouted, 'Good morning!'

Snow-Flower stopped and looked up. 'Morning!' She bent over and breathed hard before straightening up. 'I'm coming right up.'

A minute later Snow-Flower emerged onto the terrace, 'It's a beautiful day, isn't it?'

'Good morning,' William said. 'Indeed!'

Snow-Flower gave him a sunflower smile and skipped over to Jade-Lotus. 'So, have you talked to Grandma about finding out about your mama?'

'Yeah,' Jade-Lotus said.

'Yeah? Is she OK about it?'

'Um, no. I may have to give up.'

'Give up? That's not you! Why?'

Jade-Lotus avoided looking into Snow-Flower's sharp eyes. 'Grandma said that it's hard enough to adopt here as it is, without making an enemy of officials. I think she may be right.'

'Officials? You mean Mark Lee? Oh come on, he's always been your enemy hasn't he? It can't get any worse, can it! What's the problem? You can't hide from me, you know that; we're the worm in each other's tummy!'

Jade-Lotus puffed out her cheeks. 'OK. Years ago, Mark Lee blackmailed Grandma by threatening to harm me so she had to give up digging into what happened to Mama.'

'Ooh, reeeally! I wonder why he did that.' Snow-Flower narrowed her eyes. 'Now he could use the baby to blackmail you too, is that what you're worrying about? But doesn't it make you want to dig even more?'

'I'm not sure. Grandma would have wanted to dig more

too.'

'Well, that was during the Cultural Revolution, and Grandma had nobody who would dare help; but today you have me, and River-Cloud and Little-Blossom.'

'How is Little-Blossom?'

'Ah, I almost forgot. River-Cloud wanted me to tell you that lunch will be at two, as Little-Blossom is delayed.'

'Is she OK?' Jade-Lotus asked.

'Yeah.' Snow-Flower looked away. In a much quieter voice, she added, 'If you ask me, I think she chose the later train on purpose.' She brushed her hand in the air, as if a mosquito was annoying her.

'Really? That's not like her, is it?'

'Well, what can I say? She's definitely been different lately, I can tell you that.' Snow-Flower rolled her eyes and shook her head. 'I'd better get going. See you all at two.'

As Snow-Flower jogged away in the spring sunshine, Jade-Lotus thought of Little-Blossom. How different could she be? Yes, she had sounded somewhat hesitant on the phone about the adoption; but she had always been a rock, right from the moment they had met.

The school summer holiday had started; the air was scented with jasmine.

'We need to go faster,' Jade-Lotus said as she hurried towards the train station.

'Sorry, it's my fault,' Snow-Flower said, her side ponytail bobbing as she hurried beside Jade-Lotus.

'Yes,' River-Cloud huffed. '"Can't decide what to wear"!' He thinned his voice to imitate his sister.

'We should be OK. I think Little-Blossom would say don't

worry,' Jade-Lotus said. Although she and her cousin had never met, she felt she knew her. Ever since Mao had died five years earlier and it had become safe for their families to contact each other again they had been writing. In her letters, Little-Blossom sounded older and wiser, even though she was actually two years younger. When Grandma had made enough money from her new teahouse, she sent some to Little-Blossom, so she could come and stay for the summer.

'Do you have a photo of her?' Snow-Flower said.

'No. They don't do photos in their village,' Jade-Lotus said.

'Is her village in the third world?' Snow-Flower laughed, bells ringing.

'Don't be so unkind,' River-Cloud said. 'You wouldn't like it if other people looked down on you.'

Snow-Flower's ponytail jerked into an exclamation mark.

River-Cloud ignored her and said to Jade-Lotus, 'But how will you find her if you don't know what she looks like?'

'I'll just know,' Jade-Lotus said.

They arrived at the platform as the train was approaching on the other side; then the heavens opened. They dashed to a shelter and watched the train come and go, leaving a chaos of disembarked passengers fighting for cover. Luckily the rain didn't linger, and they ran to the opposite platform, but it was deserted. Only drips rapped the puddles.

'Are you sure she'll definitely come? She could just spend the money, you know?' Snow-Flower said, shrugging.

'You haven't met her yet, and you're already belittling her!' River-Cloud said.

'Oh, come on,' Jade-Lotus said. 'She won't; I trust her. We've promised each other that we won't leave until we meet.'

'How noble!' Snow-Flower said.

'Ah ah, is that Cousin Jade-Lotus?' a girl mewed.

Jade-Lotus turned around and saw a small barefooted girl coming out from behind a young French sycamore, one of the newly planted trees replacing the gigantic ones that had been chopped down by Red Guards. She was wearing a faded red vest, which wrapped limply around her skinny body, the legs of her dark trousers were rolled up to her knees, and a pair of jellybean sandals, tied together by their straps, dangled across her shoulder. She had a gentle round face, nicely tea-coloured, and framed by the hair from her short bob; her eyes were softly round too, looking shy and kind. Her hands were holding a basket, covered by what looked like her pullover.

'Little-Blossom!' Jade-Lotus ran up to her.

'Is it her?' Snow-Flower and River-Cloud followed.

'Yes, yes!' Jade-Lotus introduced them.

'Are you really twelve years old? You're so small,' Snow-Flower said.

Little-Blossom nodded.

'And why are your sandals on your shoulder?' Snow-Flower said.

'They're new; I don't want to get them dirty. I'm used to walking barefoot at home,' Little-Blossom said, gently brushing raindrops from her face, 'although my grandma always tells me off. "A good girl should always smile shyly without showing her teeth and walk elegantly without exposing her toes," she would say.' She smiled, her teeth happily on display, and then lifted the pullover from the basket and said to Jade-Lotus, 'My parents picked these wild bayberries this morning.' She patted a small cage next to the berries. 'And this is for you.'

'For me? Oh, so cute!' Jade-Lotus felt her eyes popping.

'A white baby rabbit!' Snow-Flower screamed. 'I've always wanted one!' She was pulled back by her brother.

'Can I help you with your luggage?' River-Cloud said with a shy smile.

'I don't have any,' Little-Blossom said, sunset-red clouds climbing her cheeks.

'But you're staying the whole summer!' Snow-Flower said.

'Grandma always says travel light,' Jade-Lotus said quickly. 'Thank you for your gifts! Let's go.'

'I'll carry the basket,' River-Cloud said.

Little-Blossom stood inside her front door, behind River-Cloud and half-shaded by the deep doorway, waving. She still wore her hair in a bob, but her face was much paler and rounder, like a full moon. Her body seemed to be living up to the expectation of filling the tent-like long dress she was wearing. The only festive colour was the red embroidered slippers peeping out underneath the dark dress. Summer-Lily and Spring-Cherry – looking very much like in their photos – cautiously stuck their heads out from each side of their mum's skirt, before running towards Grandma and shouting, 'Great Nana!'

River-Cloud, in a crimson silk mandarin jacket printed with a golden pattern of music staves and notes, came over and shook William's hand. 'Welcome to our humble little home.'

Jade-Lotus rushed over to her cousin and hugged her.

Little-Blossom hesitated, but then hugged her back, even tighter, her chin digging into Jade-Lotus's shoulder.

Jade-Lotus was unable to speak. In that embrace, the years of being apart evaporated; the physical distance dissolved. For a fleeting second, the skinny girl with jellybean sandals on her shoulder reappeared. But the soft tummy cushioning their hug heralded a new life; the ribbon of hope for a family that had dangled for so long could finally be tied into a perfect bow. As her linen shirt dampened with falling tears and her body quivered with Little-Blossom's rhythmic sobs, she stroked her cousin's back, and murmured, 'Thank you! You're my rock,'

'Thank you for wanting her,' Little-Blossom whispered. 'Thank you!'

'Ooh!' Snow-Flower appeared, in a red apron, and bear-hugged both of them. 'Just like old times!' She giggled. 'The meal is ready if you cousins would like to join.'

As they sat down at the round table, Snow-Flower brought in the last dish, two head-to-tail carp. 'To bring you riches and good luck!' she announced happily.

Jade-Lotus nodded to Little-Blossom, who smiled, tears still hanging on her eyelashes.

River-Cloud stood up and raised his glass. 'Firstly, to our elders.' He nodded to his grandpa, Autumn-Rain, and then to Grandma, 'secondly to our home-coming guests! Happy Lantern Festival!'

Just as everyone took a sip of the yellow wine, Summer-Lily and Spring-Cherry ran in and shouted, 'Mum, Mum, come and look, there's a huge boat at Great Nana's dock!'

Little-Blossom blushed. 'Sorry.' She turned to her daughters. 'Shh, shh – try to behave like ladies.'

Jade-Lotus looked at Grandma, who frowned and shook her head.

'Excuse me.' Jade-Lotus stepped over to the window. A two-story pavilion boat, lit by chains of red lanterns, and with a communist flag fluttering at the stern, was trying to moor at Grandma's dock.

Snow-Flower and Little-Blossom came over too.

'Whose boat is that?' Jade-Lotus said.

'Oh, that's Mark Lee's emperor yacht,' Snow-Flower said.

'What's he doing here? I'd better go and find out,' Jade-Lotus said.

'Maybe River-Cloud should go?' Little-Blossom said quietly.

'Nah, it's our dock, so I should go.'

'Are you OK there?' William said from the table.

'All fine, darling. Just excuse me for a moment,' Jade-Lotus said.

'I'll come with you,' Snow-Flower said.

'OK.' Jade-Lotus turned to look at Little-Blossom. 'Will you come too?'

'Me? Ah ah.' Little-Blossom blushed again, but her eyes brightened as she nodded.

'What could Mark Lee possibly want?' Jade-Lotus said as they headed to the back door.

'Maybe he's just being festive and polite,' Little-Blossom said.

'Ah, when a weasel pays hens a New-Year call, it won't be with the best intentions!' Snow-Flower said.

As they came out of Shan's back door, they bumped straight into High-Fly.

'Oh ha ha,' High-Fly said, 'Three golden flowers! Happy Lantern Festival!'

'Happy Festival,' Little-Blossom said with a gentle bow.

'Where's your father?' Jade-Lotus said.

'Three times in two days. We seem to be seeing you a lot,'

Snow-Flower said.

'Oh ha ha, TV Star, sharp tongue! Sharp tongue!' High-Fly said, taking a step back. 'Well, there's no town leader today, just me. Am I not enough for you pretty ladies?' He gave an over-the-top affectionate stare and a display of his yellow sweetcorn-like teeth. 'Now, I'm serious and let's talk business. It's the Lantern Festival; my father wants me to send his best wishes to our foreign guests.'

'Oh, thanks,' Jade-Lotus said.

'Message received, you can shoot,' Snow-Flower said.

Little-Blossom gently tugged her sister-in-law's sleeve.

'Umm,' High-Fly slowly rubbed his hands together and turned to Jade-Lotus, 'he also wants you to take his boat to the Lantern Fair.'

'No thanks, we have everything organised,' Snow-Flower cut in.

'Well,' High-Fly took another step back, 'you two families can enjoy the boat together, you know? It's much more comfortable than yours and you'll be guaranteed to moor right at the temple pier.' He flashed a toothy smile again.

'Oh, I see,' Snow-Flower said, 'but we all know that "the old drunk scholar's real interest wasn't the wine".'

'We're grateful for your father's generosity, but no, thanks. Please take the boat home, and happy festival!' Jade-Lotus said.

Little-Blossom nodded.

'Oh no,' High-Fly said, colour draining from his bony face, 'please accept my father's boat. Please?'

Jade-Lotus raised her eyebrows; she'd never heard him say please before.

'There's no better boat in the whole town,' High-Fly said

quickly, 'think of William, eh? What face will we have if our foreign friend sees how chaotic it is at the public mooring? Shabby boats, floating like driftwood; uncivilised people, crowded like in a slum?'

'Really!' Snow-Flower said.

'Jade-Lotus, please take the boat. Please say you will.' High-Fly put two hands together as if to pray. 'Father said I can't go home if you don't accept the boat, and my little boy will be disappointed that I can't take him to the Lantern Fair.'

Jade-Lotus thought for a second – Summer-Lily and Spring-Cherry would be very disappointed if they couldn't go to the Lantern Fair. 'OK, we'll take the boat.'

'You will! Thank heaven and earth you will! Thank you, thank you, and thank you!' High-Fly dropped his shoulders. 'You'll have an easy ride, everyone knows the boat, and when you get there, someone will even moor it for you if you like. Enjoy the Fair!' He had a skip in his step as he left.

'You're too soft,' Snow-Flower said.

'Ah ah…' Little-Blossom said.

The day closed like the petals of a daisy; the night unpeeled its soft robe revealing its silky dark skin and a white-jade moon tattoo. Jade-Lotus, along with both families, boarded the glorious pavilion boat, Mark Lee's toy, and headed to the Golden Buddha Temple for the Lantern Fair. The communist flag fluttering next to her was somewhat comical. Tangling so closely with the Lee family was unimaginable and certainly a compromise. William was right: Mark and High-Fly Lee had the power to stop the adoption. Was this a price that had to be paid to be a mum?

The boat picked up speed; the night air caressed their faces like feathers. The moon, so gigantic and close, was showing off its fine drawing of Chang'e, the moon goddess, and her pet, Jade Rabbit. The glittering river generously copied the moon, stars, red lanterns and white houses. Lonesome fireworks fizzed up here and there, giving a taste of what was to come. Having travelled the world, would the Lantern Fair be as enchanting as some twenty years ago? And would William enjoy it?

'Is it your first time, William?' Snow-Flower said.

'Yes,' William said. 'But I've heard about it a lot.'

'Then I'll be your guide,' Snow-Flower giggled, 'we're coming to the end of our small town and starting to join…'

'It's been years since we went to the Lantern Fair together,' Little-Blossom said.

'It has, hasn't it?' Jade-Lotus said, wrapping her arm around her cousin's. 'We should enjoy it as much as we can, along with the tiny baby.' She felt her inner moon as bright and big as the one in the sky.

'Ah ah, quite, quite,' Little-Blossom said, and then lowered her voice, 'if I'm rude, please just tell me off; but do you really want this baby girl? You're not ridiculing me or pitying me, are you?' She fanned her face.

Jade-Lotus turned to Little-Blossom, and in the moonlight saw tears in her eyes. 'Oh Cousin!' She stroked her hand. 'Of course, we want her. You know how many years we tried for a baby; but now, all thanks to you, we can have one and be a complete family. You can't imagine how happy we are! You really can't!' She hugged her cousin. 'A boy or a girl really doesn't matter to us. OK?'

Little-Blossom nodded and wiped her eyes.

'Hurrah!' Summer-Lily and Spring-Cherry shouted from

the front of the boat, 'We've arrived!'

'Oh yes, the Golden Buddha Temple,' Snow-Flower said. 'William, can you believe it's over two thousand years old?'

Nestled at the foot of a mountain and cocooned in miles of yellow boundary walls that stretched up a slope, with lantern-lit tiers of ascending palaces and at the top a magnificent grand palace that housed the tallest gilded Buddha in the region, the Golden Buddha Temple looked impressive. When it reopened in 1980 after thirty years of closure due to political turmoil it was a wreck; it looked like it had been restored to its former glory.

The river turned into a lake. On approaching the temple pier, their pavilion boat was directed to moor right next to the steps that led to the temple. Once they climbed up, they had the whole platform to themselves, and a panoramic view of the huge brightly lit lanterns floating on the lake: a giant frog perching on a leaf; a colossal lotus flower, its petals opening and closing to the rhythm of music; a drift of gigantic golden pigs...

'It looks like a Chinese Disneyland,' William said.

'I don't remember anything like this before,' Jade-Lotus said.

'Ah, they're light sculptures, a new fashion,' Snow-Flower said.

'Look, Great Grandpa, carp jumping over the Dragon Gate!' Summer-Lily pointed. And indeed, the next lantern was a stupendous serpent, its body curved into peaks and valleys. 'Wish I could turn into a dragon just like that!'

'Haha, you'd only be a little dragoness,' Autumn-Rain said.

'That's Buddha Guanyin, the bringer of sons! How vivid!' Little-Blossom held her tummy. 'Maybe I didn't worship her enough.'

'Well, if you had, I wouldn't be here to adopt,' Jade-Lotus said.

'Ah ah, sorry; you're right,' Little-Blossom said.

'Would you all come here, I'll take a picture of you,' William said.

Continuing up a wide flight of stone steps, they arrived at the gate to the temple. Just as Jade-Lotus was about to step over the foot-tall stone threshold, Little-Blossom grabbed her hand and put it on her own tummy, 'Good luck to us all!'

'To us all!' Snow-Flower piled her hand on top of Jade-Lotus's.

Jade-Lotus smiled as they stepped over the threshold together.

They were now plunged into a 'rainbow lantern tent' – wave after wave of watermelon-shaped lanterns, each wave a different colour, packed so closely that they blocked out the inky sky. Eventually they emerged into the temple square which had been turned into a carnival: on the left, lions in yellow and red costumes were dancing to the rhythm of clanging cymbals and thumping drums; on the right, a troupe in gold costumes was trying to control a green dragon flying above their heads; to the front, on a stage, Madam White Snake in the same-named Yue Opera was hitting the highest note, fighting for love; and cooking smells wafted from the food stalls surrounding the square…

'So amazing!' Jade-Lotus shouted. It was as if flat old memories were being pulled out in ribbons and spun into mythical creatures, bringing back youthful years.

'Better than before,' Snow-Flower shouted back.

'Daddy, can I have a toffee thornapple please?' Spring-Cherry, who was sitting on River-Cloud's shoulders, shouted.

'I'd like one too,' Summer-Lily said.

River-Cloud led his little party aside and said, 'OK. If anyone fancies climbing three hundred steps right to the top, you're welcome, the rest of us are heading to the food stalls.'

'Shall we go up there?' Jade-Lotus said, looking at her friends.

'Absolutely!' Snow-Flower said.

'Love to, I grew up climbing mountains,' Little-Blossom said.

'What about you, William?' Snow-Flower said.

'I'll go with them,' William nodded at River-Cloud.

'He's scared of heights,' Jade-Lotus said.

The three friends set off like a herd of mountain goats up the endless steps, among the many other diehard souls.

'It feels like we're young again,' Jade-Lotus said.

'We're still young!' Snow-Flower said.

'We're grown up really,' Little-Blossom said. 'Less brave, less courageous and more baggage. Ah ah, I mean me, not you two.'

There was moment of silence.

'I'm not that brave, at all,' Jade-Lotus said.

'But you are! You've come all this way to adopt a baby girl,' Little-Blossom said.

'That's more of a selfish instinct,' Jade-Lotus said. 'Any woman might do it.'

'I think I know what you mean,' Snow-Flower said.

Little-Blossom stopped climbing the steps. 'What are you talking about, Cousin?'

Jade-Lotus took a deep breath. 'I was planning to try to find out what happened to my mama while waiting for the baby, but Grandma is against it and I don't think I have the courage.'

'I see,' Little-Blossom said, breathing hard too.

Silence returned.

'But you've always been brave,' Little-Blossom said, 'and you've always wanted to do that; maybe it's about time.' She held her tummy. 'And this might give you drive and focus.'

'Wow, that's the wisest thing you've said in a long while,' Snow-Flower said.

'Thanks. Now I see what you really think of me, Snow-Flower,' Little-Blossom said and turned to Jade-Lotus.

Jade-Lotus stared at her for a moment, her eyes moistening. 'You're right. My daughter needs to know about her grandmother.' A new strength, like nothing before, grew from the soles of her feet as she started to climb the steps again. 'I'm not afraid of Mark Lee.'

'Did you know that Mark Lee used her when she was little to blackmail Grandma, so Grandma had to stop digging into what happened to her daughter,' Snow-Flower said.

'Oh no,' Little-Blossom said. 'I see. And now Cousin, you're worried about the same thing? It's a risk, a great risk.'

'Unless I can do it without him feeling even the tiniest wind,' Jade-Lotus said.

'You do it? Hello, I'm here,' Snow-Flower said.

'OK, you and I can do it,' Jade-Lotus said and then looked at her cousin. 'If you could join us, it'll be even better.'

'Ah ah, if I can be of any use?' Little-Blossom asked.

'Yes of course! We're three, we're one,' Jade-Lotus said.

'We're the Three-Legged Ding!' Snow-Flower shouted and stared at Little-Blossom.

'Yes, we're the Three-Legged Ding!' Little-Blossom shouted too.

They linked arms and together they started to climb again.

'Now we need to think about how to persuade Grandma,' Jade-Lotus said.

'We'll find a way,' Little-Blossom and Snow-Flower said together.

When they reached the top, the fireworks started. Pink pom poms, yellow dandelions, red wheels and blue fountains blossomed in the velvety dark sky, weaving a lush tapestry of bright colours and sparks. Bangs and crackles correlated, reverberating around the mountains. Behind them stood the glorious Grand Palace, where the hundred-foot-tall gilded Buddha sat giving holy blessings, while monks chanted as incense burned, the perfumed smoke winding up and up…. Was it heaven or earth? Could anyone see the boundary? The legend said that the immortal Jade Emperor in heaven wanted to burn people on the earth for killing his pet crane, but his daughter secretly came down to tell everyone to put up red lanterns and light fireworks, around the time of the first full moon of the year, tricking him into believing that Earth was burning already, so they would be spared.

'The mighty Jade Emperor will certainly be fooled tonight,' Snow-Flower shouted.

'We all have a lot to thank his courageous daughter for,' Jade-Lotus shouted back.

'Yes!' Little-Blossom shouted.

8

Blushing Lotus

It was nearly midnight when they returned home from the Lantern Fair.

'I really enjoyed it,' William said as he climbed under the silk duvet.

'Me too.' Jade-Lotus smiled, a little pride for the old hometown sprouting. 'And Snow-Flower and Little-Blossom are going to help me find out what happened to Mama!'

'Oh, that's brilliant! You'll have a much greater chance with their help.'

'We'll have to find a way to persuade Grandma first.'

'I'm sure you will.' William caressed Jade-Lotus's hair. 'There must be something that Mark Lee didn't want your family to know.'

Jade-Lotus nodded and sighed. 'In this town, a frying wok can be sealed with a lid; bottled and corked sesame oil tends to leak everywhere.'

'Let's get some sleep.' William kissed her. 'Love you!'

'Night night, love you too.'

The night changed from opaque hustle and bustle to translucent, desolate silence; William's light snoring harmonised with a distant nightingale's song. Moonlight flooded in; Jade-Lotus stared at the muslin curtains trembling in the breeze. What reason could there be for Mark Lee to stop Grandma digging into Mama's death? Had he been involved? The Cultural Revolution had systematically killed millions of people, but no one had ever been called to account for their crimes. Like dunes after a sandstorm, everything was just covered up and smoothed out; those with blood on their hands changed their mask and moved on. Certainly, Mark Lee would never admit any wrongdoing. 'I just followed orders' would be his master key to unlock any sticky jammed-up situation. But who gave the orders? Was the whole country full of robots that followed the central computer's commands? But if Mark Lee could easily pick the fluff off his sleeves and shake dirty water off his belly, why stop Grandma? And now, would he try to do the same again? Hmm. But the truth of how Mama had died was important; Grandma hadn't been able to bury her own daughter. And now a child was on her way; she would need to know the truth when she grew up. Jade-Lotus nodded and took a long, slow yoga breath; thoughts of the Three-Legged Ding working together ignited warm feelings. She relaxed, and soon she was touching dream valley with her fingertips.

'Aaahhh, aaaahhhh...' A faint groan crawled in from outside like a spider. Jade-Lotus peeled open her heavy eyelids and listened. 'Aaaiiiyaaa, aaaaiiiiyaaaa...' The spider was weaving a web. '... Aiiiiyaaa, you bastard! You bloody killer! Heaven punishes you!' It was in fact a woman's voice, mixed with breathless sobs. Who would be sitting outside in the cold wailing on a festive night, while all around houses were filled with the warmth of gathered families? The townswomen would rarely go out in the dark on their own; their private feelings would never be aired in public. Who was she? Why did she wail? The moonlight dimmed; the wailing faded. Darkness deepened and Jade-Lotus fell asleep.

'Don't we need to wait for Snow-Flower and Little-Blossom?' William said as they were about to head off for breakfast at Grandma's teahouse in the town centre.

'Nope,' Jade-Lotus said. 'Apparently, they're going for a jog together; mad, isn't it? We'll meet them at the well in the square.'

The sky was lead grey, punctured by soft sunbeams, the air still saturated with the smell of gunpowder from the previous night. The narrow lane was framed by tall whitewashed walls freckled with mould; their footsteps echoed hollowly on the stony path. Once out of the lane, they came to a small arched bridge and stopped on it. On the river, a thin mist crept steadily towards them; in the distance, thick patches of fog engulfed the top of the dark mountains. Downstream by the bank, a couple of women were banging their laundry with sticks on slabs, clouds of foam drifting in the water. At nearby moorings, men were readying their boats, the rasping sound of recalcitrant engines vibrating the stale air…

They crossed the river and soon met a rock that was taller than William; on it, the engraved calligraphy – Blushing Lotus – shouted at them.

'That's new! Always loved that name,' William said.

'Beautiful calligraphy! Maybe it is one of the originals that Grandma was always on about,' Jade-Lotus said, remembering the legend behind the name. It had been her favourite bedtime story.

'Long, long ago,' Grandma said, lying beside her and cradling her in the crook of her arm, her voice warm and comforting, like the burning charcoal in the copper pit at the foot of the bed. 'Our town was called Floating Lotus, as it was small and pretty – just like you – sitting on a web of peaceful rivers and canals. When the wars stopped and each king drew up their borders, Floating Lotus, like a small fish escaping from a net, belonged to no country. The townspeople weren't bothered as they just wanted to live a quiet life, fishing, farming and making silk. For a while they managed just that, but then the powerful neighbouring country of Yue came to plunder them, robbing their rice, tea and silk, making life miserable. One day the town leader called everyone together to discuss how to defend themselves, and they came up with an idea. The next day, they sent a messenger to the capital and invited the King of Yue to visit them. When the king arrived, he was presented with the prettiest girl from Floating Lotus to take as his bride in exchange for peace. The king was bewitched by her beauty and noticed that the white lotus flowers nearby seemed to blush in her presence. He happily accepted the proposal, took the town under his wing and gave the town a new name – Blushing Lotus. The townspeople were pleased to accept it and more importantly the peace and protection from Yue, and lived happily ever after...'

Grandma then pulled the sheet up to cover both of them. Shielded from the bright moonlight, she continued in a much lower voice, as if her throat had been stamped on by a heavy boot.

'Aihhh, but in 1966, we were defeated, all thanks to Mao's destruction of the Four Olds. The wretched Lee brothers said that Blushing Lotus was far too decadent and corrosive according to Mao's Little Red Book, so, ignoring its two thousand years of history, they changed the name to Blooming Red. Tut tut tut. They tore down all the stone signs bearing the beautiful calligraphy of Blushing Lotus, and replaced them with the ugly wooden ones that you see today. Tut tut tut. Ugly name, ugly calligraphy! Only Buddha knows when we can have our pretty name back. Remember, my little treasure, always remember you are a child of Blushing Lotus.'

'I wonder when they brought back the signs,' Jade-Lotus said as they continued their walk. They were approaching the square.

'My tour guide Snow-Flower would know,' William said with a laugh.

'Ooh, she must have tailwind ears!' Jade-Lotus waved to Snow-Flower and Little-Blossom, who were jogging diagonally across the square.

'Morning! Good timing!' Snow-Flower shouted, slowing to a shuffle.

'Morning! How was the jog?' Jade-Lotus said.

'Ah ah, it almost killed me!' Little-Blossom stopped, breathing hard.

'… Damn bane! Damn bane! Damn…' someone shouted from near the ancient well, where a group of people huddled together. He was a bald man, looking to be in his late fifties. His voice was resonant and nasal; his features were sunken on his fat face, like buttons on an old Chesterfield sofa. 'Returned again? Drowning herself in alcohol, stumbling in the street wailing, again! What's she playing at this time?'

'Not good, not good,' responded the group.

'It's *not* a good omen!' a low fibrous voice – not the dry, chewed and spat-out sugarcane kind, but the soluble water-celery kind – boomed. Its owner looked to be in his mid-seventies; the gathered wrinkles by his mouth were a sign that he had probably smoked a pipe all his life. 'Remember the first time she did it? What a terrible flood we had, all those stranded mud-loaches!'

'Bad omen! Bad omen!' The wave of muttering was like reeds in the wind.

'Oh Buddha, she's back too,' a woman squealed at Jade-Lotus.

The group fell silent, firing stares at them like arrows.

'Sunning yourselves, are you?' Snow-Flower shouted. 'Just don't burn your tongues!'

'Don't bother about them, let's go,' Little-Blossom said.

'What are they talking about?' Jade-Lotus said after they had passed them.

'Is it a coincidence?' chased the resonant voice.

Jade-Lotus wanted to turn, but was pulled back by Little-Blossom. 'Look, Grandma is waiting.'

'Morning all,' Grandma shouted, waving enthusiastically.

'Morning!' Snow-Flower ran up to Grandma. 'How is my favourite granny today?' She hugged and kissed her.

'Hahahaha…' It was like Grandma was being tickled, her eyes soft crescents. 'It's so nice to see you all together again…'

'Indeed Grandma…' Little-Blossom held Grandma's hand.

Behind Grandma, the old two-story townhouse was no longer anaemic, although memories of it from the 1970s sprung back: a peeling sign, 'State-Owned Sickle Pickle

Factory and Shop' over the door; in the blazing sun or snowy winter, forever-long queues for always short rations – lumps of coal-coloured, fly-kissed turnip or some salted cabbages riddled with fat white maggots. When Grandma bought it in 1980, it wore its mould-ridden walls like an oversized mottled jacket and shook like a leaf at the slightest hint of wind, its patched-up roof pulled low over the warped sun-bleached windows and doors, as if feeling the shame of becoming the first privately owned teahouse in a society that not long ago held 'Material hardship enriches the soul' and 'The poorer, the more glory' as its greatest aspirations. It now had fresh whitewashed walls, deep-chestnut varnished windows and doors, shiny green roof tiles, and ridges teeming with mythical creatures. Above its double doors, a large black lacquered plaque with three carved golden characters proclaimed 'Yi Pin Xiang' – First-Grade Fragrance.

'Wow,' Jade-Lotus said.

'It looks totally different,' William said.

'Come on in!' Grandma said loudly.

As the doors opened, Jade-Lotus was hit by a fragrance like wild orchids after a rain shower, so different to the stale jasmine smell that had accompanied her teenage years. The décor was simple: white walls, flagstone floors and wooden furniture. The amber round tables and horseshoe chairs looked much better than the old flimsy, mismatched classroom furniture made redundant by the Shan Academy; some tables had wobbled so badly that she had chipped many of Grandma's enamel mugs. A few tourists looked to have enjoyed their breakfast and were now taking pictures; several local ladies chatted happily over their morning brew while their husbands read their newspapers.

'I never imagined it would be like this from what you told me,' Jade-Lotus said.

Grandma smiled proudly. 'Now we go upstairs for breakfast.'

'Upstairs?' Jade-Lotus and William said together.

'Oh yeah,' Snow-Flower said with wink.

'I don't remember you saying you did upstairs,' Jade-Lotus said.

'Ah, my little treasure, maybe I forgot, but you were so busy.'

Jade-Lotus said nothing. Yes, there had been a mad period when not many other things in the world had mattered. But now it was time to make up for it with Grandma.

'It'll be a surprise for you then,' Grandma said and led the way, her steps light, her head high, the tiny crystals on her chignon's hairpin sparkling.

Jade-Lotus couldn't imagine what upstairs would look like now. After having scrubbed off the stinky smell from pickle-making, it had been used as the storage for crates and crates of green teas, white teas and black teas; hessian sacks of dried jasmine, lotus, chrysanthemum, honeysuckle, lemon grass, lavender and gingko to add flavour to the tea; and porcelain jars of the stately Longjing green tea. Because of the strong perfumes there were no mice or snakes lurking in corners, it had been a perfect hiding place for her and her friends.

Now it was an open-plan room. One wall was fitted with floor to ceiling shelves that were filled with books; in front of the shelves sat two large sofas and a coffee table.

'It looks like a trendy library,' William said.

'Yes, it is.' Grandma grinned. 'And, I have, oh, what do you call it? Oh yes, internet access, so people can come here to read, get on the spider web thingy and mingle.'

'Haha, spider web! You're so lovely, Grandma!' Snow-Flower said.

'Come Cousin, look what Grandma has done.' Little-Blossom pointed at a roof window.

Jade-Lotus hurried over. 'Oh Grandma, you've restored all the mythical creatures! Do you remember they started our Three-Legged Ding?'

Snow-Flower and Little-Blossom smiled.

The year after they had first met, Little-Blossom again came to spend the two-month summer holiday with Jade-Lotus. They hung out with Snow-Flower and River-Cloud most of the time. In the morning, they helped Grandma in the teahouse, and in return they got lunch and a hiding place upstairs to do homework and anything else they liked.

'I'm really bored,' Snow-Flower grumbled one day after they had finished their studies. She got up, climbed up the steps and leaned out of one of the roof windows. 'Nothing's happening out here either, no boats or birds!' On tiptoes, she leaned out further. 'Oh! There are some clay creatures tucked away here, have you noticed them before?'

'No,' three voices replied together.

'Come here. It looks like there's a lion, a seahorse, a bull and a fish, each about the height of a chopstick. Some have a little green colour. What are they? Why are they here?'

They took turns to look, but didn't know the answers.

'The other roofs don't seem to have any?' Little-Blossom said.

'Maybe we should ask Grandma,' River-Cloud said.

'I think we should find out for ourselves; Grandma's too busy,' Jade-Lotus said.

Snow-Flower, eyes shining and dimples deepening, said, 'I think that's a great idea! Our summer-holiday puzzle!'

'OK,' Little-Blossom said, her bobbed hair sparkling in the sun as she nodded.

They stared at River-Cloud, but he pushed up his big square spectacles and said, 'I need to finish reading these books before starting uni, so I'll pass. But if you're stuck, I'll help.'

'Really!' Snow-Flower rolled her eyes.

Little-Blossom giggled, her button nose blushing.

'I'm sure we can solve it ourselves,' Jade-Lotus said.

'Absolutely!' Snow-Flower said.

Little-Blossom nodded. 'How do we start?'

Jade-Lotus squinted her eyes. 'It'll take too long if we all do the same thing. But if we separate, each doing something she's good at, then at the end of the day, we get together and decide the next step.'

'Sounds good to me,' Snow-Flower said. 'I think we'll need some books about old buildings.'

'But there aren't any such books; all the olds are bad for us,' Little-Blossom said.

'I know the county library has some books that have survived the Cultural Revolution, but it's not easy to get permission to look at them,' Snow-Flower said. 'But, if I use father's name...' She winked.

'I can ask the older people around town; they seem to like me,' Little-Blossom said.

'I'll write everything down. When we've worked out what they are, we can check with Grandma,' Jade-Lotus said.

'Agreed.'

Three weeks later when they had some answers and asked Grandma about the creatures she looked around at the crates of tea and said in a whisper, 'Who wants to know?'

'No one,' Jade-Lotus said.

'It's our holiday puzzle,' Snow-Flower said.

'We'd like to know if our answers are right,' Little-Blossom said.

'Why are you so nervous, Grandma?' Jade-Lotus said.

Grandma sighed. 'We still have to be careful. OK, tell me what you know.'

'They are mythical creatures, normally mounted on the ridge tiles, and auspicious roof charms, protecting the building,' Snow-Flower said.

'They're also a symbol of status, always appearing in odd numbers. The emperor used nine, glazed in yellow, on his palaces. But other royal families used less, depending on their rank,' Little-Blossom said.

'On our roof,' Jade-Lotus said, 'we saw four creatures. One was probably missing – the immortal riding a phoenix. They were all glazed in green, a colour only allowed to be used by royal families. But we couldn't find out why we have them on our shabby teahouse.'

'Well done, you're all right.' Grandma smiled. 'In fact, each roof ridge of our teahouse had five creatures, but they were all chopped off and smashed by the Red Guards. Only these hidden few survived.' She leaned in and whispered again, 'So you really don't know why we have them?'

'No,' the three girls answered together.

'OK, that must remain a mystery,' Grandma said.

'We'd better keep them hidden,' Jade-Lotus said, picturing what would happen if High-Fly and his gang knew about them, even though High-Fly was no longer in the same class, or the same school.

'And keep our findings to ourselves,' River-Cloud said, which won a nod from Grandma.

'How did you find all this out?' Grandma said.

'It was team work. All three of us worked together,' Jade-Lotus said.

'They're a Three-Legged Ding,' River-Cloud said. 'Like in this book I'm reading; an ancient bronze wine vessel that's stood for centuries and won't fall, because of the perfect balance of its three legs.'

'I like that name,' Snow-Flower said.

'The creatures look so regal, don't they? And they rightly belong to this building,' Jade-Lotus said.

'Indeed,' Snow-Flower and Little-Blossom said.

'What do you mean?' Grandma frowned.

'Well, Grandma, I'll tell you our secret; we found out about the *royal seal*,' Jade-Lotus said.

Grandma looked around the room several times, even though there were no other customers. 'Time for our breakfast,' she said and walked towards the two doors at the far end of the room. She opened one, invited everyone in and closed it firmly after them.

'I don't remember there were rooms up here before, right, Grandma?' Jade-Lotus said.

Grandma didn't answer and waved for everyone to sit down at the square eight immortals table that was in the middle of the room, on which sat a large tray with a mesh cover.

'I got dim sum from Sun's restaurant.' Grandma gestured towards the tray, and began to pour hot jasmine tea for everyone. 'Help yourselves.'

'Ooh, the best dim sum in town! You have to order them

days ahead,' Snow-Flower said.

Chopsticks, bowls, plates and teacups played a harmonious symphony.

'This prawn shaomai is unbelievable,' William said.

'Wow, green sticky balls, one of my favourites,' Jade-Lotus said, wondering how long Grandma was going to avoid the topic of the royal seal for.

Grandma squeezed a smile and loaded a couple more balls onto Jade-Lotus's plate. She then picked two dumplings onto her own plate, toyed with one, then looked up and asked, 'Who told you about the royal seal? And how much do you all know?'

Jade-Lotus, Snow-Flower and Little-Blossom exchanged a happy glance.

'Well, Grandma, after we checked our answers with you, we couldn't help our curiosity and went on to find out why this shabby teahouse had mythical creatures on it. It took us a while, but in the end we managed to press Grandad into telling us,' Snow-Flower said.

'But all Autumn-Rain said was the building historically had a royal seal; then he refused to tell us any more and made us promise absolute silence about it,' Little-Blossom said.

'At least we understood why the mythical creatures had been on the roof. But we kept our promise all these years, and haven't told anyone, not even you, Grandma,' Jade-Lotus said.

Grandma nodded slowly. 'I have to say I didn't get the slightest wind that you three had carried on.'

'We can be very discreet if we need to be,' Jade-Lotus said and looked into Grandma's eyes, 'and we can be very discreet again if we look into what happened to Mama now.'

Snow-Flower and Little-Blossom nodded.

Grandma stared at them in turn, and then shook her head firmly. 'I don't think you know how much risk you'll be taking. It could well be the case that you fail to steal the chicken and also lose your handful of precious grain. Don't forget who decides about the adoption.'

'Oh Grandma, I didn't know Mark Lee keeps chickens.' Snow-Flower giggled. 'Now, seriously, are you scared of him, Grandma?'

'No, I'm not scared of him.'

'We are not either,' Jade-Lotus said. 'The three of us working together have a good chance of getting to the truth.'

'I agree,' Little-Blossom said. 'Grandma, only the other day my mum mentioned Jade-Lotus's mother and said she would close her eyes more easily if she knew what had really happened to her dear cousin.'

Grandma stared down at her chopsticks, her face solemn.

Snow-Flower reached out to caress Grandma's arm. 'You do want to know the truth, don't you? Times are different now, and Mark Lee can't harm any of us easily, I promise you that, Grandma. We'll be super careful and discreet, and he won't know a thing.' Seeing Grandma's knitted eyebrows loosening, her dimples deepened. 'For you, Grandma, just for you, we'll steal that chicken, and keep our grain.'

Grandma let out a long sigh. 'Just be careful, all of you.' She spooned some soy sauce onto her dumplings before devouring them. 'Now, do you want to know more about the royal seal?'

'Absolutely,' Jade-Lotus said.

'Well, our teahouse hasn't always been a teahouse,' Grandma said with a gleam in her eyes, like a magician about to show

102

what's inside her sleeve. 'For two hundred years it was our family shop selling our Yang's premium silk. This floor was dedicated to serving the more discerning customers, with a nice seating area – like you saw outside – floor-to-ceiling shelves displaying rolls and rolls of silk cloth, and a couple of private rooms – this room and the one next door – for taking measurements.'

'Our family shop?' Jade-Lotus said.

'When I was a little girl,' Grandma continued, 'my nana often brought me here, and the beautiful women who came here to get their dresses made always gave me such lovely sweets. And it was here we had a little party when your mama was born. Ah, good times…' She closed her eyes, probably wading back to the happy moment of being a new mother. Jade-Lotus watched her, feeling a twitch in her stomach; how little she knew about Grandma's past, and their family's past.

'But how did it become a pickle factory?' Snow-Flower said.

Grandma woke from her dream, and made a throaty, almost angry noise. 'It was confiscated by the communist government in 1950. For thirty years they ran it down and made a stink of it, literally, and I had to buy it back!'

'That's not fair,' William said.

'A lot of things were, and are still not fair.' Little-Blossom sighed. 'Grandma, how did the royal seal come about then?'

Grandma looked at her for a moment as if to calm herself down, and said, 'In our long family history we had three royal ladies. The last was my nana, a cousin once removed of Emperor Guanxu, but because they grew up together and were close he honoured her with the seal. And all our properties were given royal status, with green-coloured roof tiles and mythical creatures.'

Jade-Lotus widened her eyes. Good job that Grandma had always been surreptitious about the family past; just imagine High-Fly's face if he had known this!

'You kept that tight, Grandma,' Snow-Flower said. 'But it's curious, isn't it? I've never heard anyone else in town gossip about it.'

'Ah.' Grandma smiled. '"A tall tree attracts wind; a deep pond gathers fish." In an old town like ours, almost every family's history wasn't clean enough for the communists, so everyone only sweeps the snow on their own path.'

'It's safer that way,' Little-Blossom said.

Grandma nodded. 'You never know which direction the wind will suddenly blow. Now, have more dim sum. I hope they're still warm.' She picked up the tray, revealing the warmer that was built into the table, and loaded more food onto everyone's plate.

'They're really delicious,' William said tucking in again.

Spoons and chopsticks danced.

'Oh, I meant to ask if you all heard a woman wailing last night?' Jade-Lotus said.

'Ah –' Little-Blossom said.

'Oh –' Snow-Flower said. 'Has Grandma never told you the story?'

Grandma stared at her plate. 'Poor Mad Girl.'

'Mad Girl? Who is Mad Girl?' Jade-Lotus said.

'Go on, tell her, Grandma – you were there,' Snow-Flower said.

Grandma raised her eyes. 'Ahya, no one admits they were there, because it isn't something we're proud of.' She sighed. 'It's been eight years, but the guilt still weighs on me.' She rubbed a spot on the table.

'What happened?' Jade-Lotus frowned.

'For once, your old classmate High-Fly didn't listen to his father, and married his true love,' Grandma said. 'A really lovely girl, often came to my teahouse, so I got to know her well. After a few years, she became pregnant, and told me how happy she was. But the next time I saw her she was angry. Apparently, Mark Lee had insisted she should have a scan to see whether the baby was a boy – you know the one-child policy – and High-Fly gave in to him. But the modern technology didn't do any good for them!' Grandma tutted. 'The scan showed it was a girl. Mark Lee told her to have an abortion straight away, but she wouldn't do it.'

'Gosh,' Jade-Lotus said. *High-Fly's wife had an abortion?*

'That Mid-Autumn Moon Festival, I went to the Earth Temple to pray. When I came out, I bumped into High-Fly and his wife, and they told me happily that they were here for a private worship for the safe arrival of their baby girl. I wished them good luck, and sat down on a nearby bench to rest. I saw High-Fly step over the stone-threshold of the east chamber and turn to help his wife, but two burly men seemingly came from nowhere, pushed him inside, closed the door and locked it. Then they tried to take her away, but she wouldn't have it and fought back. A crowd gathered to watch. For a moment she got free and knelt in front of the crowd, begging, "Mark Lee wants to kill my baby girl, please help me!" But no-one moved or said anything. Then Nine-Pound Old Lady's cold voice cackled, "It's a family matter." We all stood by and watched as they grabbed her again and dragged her into a car. I was so shocked and started to shake. Why didn't I go to help?'

Everyone had by now stopped eating.

105

'Later I heard that she was forced to abort the baby girl right away, and the following night, when the moon was at its biggest and brightest, everyone in Blushing Lotus heard her screaming and wailing on the street. It was so desolate and sorrowful that I cried.

'That autumn, we had the worst storm in living memory, the whole town was flooded. When the waters receded, there were dead fish everywhere. So bizarre. Was it some kind of punishment? Before next Spring Festival, High-Fly's wife divorced him. Then she moved back to her parents' town, but came back to haunt us with her wailing at festivals. So everyone calls her Mad Girl. Aihh, sinful, we were all sinful!' Grandma sighed.

'It is shameful that no one helped her,' Snow-Flower said.

Jade-Lotus nodded, shuffling her feet; they were now firmly planted on the soil of her old hometown. She shivered at the thought of High-Fly and Mark Lee deciding on the adoption. The room went silent; all chopsticks had been laid down and untouched dim sum sat cold on the plates. Her ears were filled with the wailing again, high and low, so sad and so mournful. 'What's her real name? Do I know her?'

Snow-Flower and Little-Blossom shook their heads before turning to Grandma.

Grandma raised her eyebrows, pinning hair behind her ear. 'Aihh, we've called her Mad Girl for all these years and I don't remember her real name.' She tutted. 'I don't think you know her, she was from another town, and you had already left when she married High-Fly.'

'Mark Lee seems everywhere, and has done a lot of bad stuff,' William said.

'Oh, tell me about it!' Snow-Flower said.

'Ah ah, and you have to meet him for lunch tomorrow,' Little-Blossom said.

'I'm really curious what he wants from us,' Jade-Lotus said.

'Please be careful,' Little-Blossom said.

'And stay alert!' Snow-Flower said.

Jade-Lotus nodded, and turning to William said, 'Well, we know there are tigers in the mountain, but we have to climb it.'

9

Chameleon

Mark Lee hurried to the window for the third time to peep out of the blinds; but there was still no car. He snorted and let go of the bamboo slats; as they sprung back they scraped his hair. His hand shot up to smooth it and he took out a folded mirror from his pocket. *Thank Buddha, still perfect. The hairdresser's new imported products are certainly worth the extra dime; no one can tell it's been dyed, can they?* He winked at himself. *As to whether it is an Elvis quiff or a world leader's stately mane will be a matter for future historians.* He chuckled.

Feeling calmer he paced back and sat down at the dining table in the private room. Checking his watch, he frowned; still fifteen minutes to go. *Humph! Why can't High-Fly be early for once! Still, it's better to have some peace here than just sitting in my stifling office, staring at the new County Leader's damned Five-Year-Little-Leap-Forward Plan, scratching my head and losing some of my beautiful hair. Aihh, I've lost so much sleep.* He sighed, reached for a cigarette, lit it, and took a drag.

Why am I fretting? Sudden political change is nothing new!

But this damned new leader, according to rumours, has refused several banquet invitations and thrown out many expensive gifts! What's he playing at? Like an unopened watermelon, no one knows whether he's ripe and sweet or crunchy and sour. He hasn't even warmed his golden throne yet, but has already called for reform, replacing the old with new. Reforming what? Replacing whom? Is he trying to squeeze out people like me, nearing retirement age?

He puffed a chain of smoke rings into the air, and as they evaporated into a haze hoped his worries would go the same way. But they lingered, like the smell of his cigarette, permeating every inch of him. *How can Blushing Lotus attract any foreign investment, let alone meet the damned demanding targets? It's obvious to all, isn't it, that Blushing Lotus is too tiny, has no natural resources, and isn't in a prime coastal location? My good friend, the last county leader, understood it and always let me off the hook. He once even said that no matter how MIGHTY I am, it's impossible.*

Haha, mighty. Yeah, of course mighty! But wait, what does everyone in my office call me? 'Eminent'! Oh ho, those arse-lickers! Eminent? Really? But I have to say that it's a better and more precise word, haha. He nodded and his smoke rings seemed to agree. He took out his mirror again. *Indeed eminent, there's not a wrinkle on my forehead; so broad and shiny, full of political wisdom; my skin is so smooth and radiant, like, oh, what did they say? As attractive as a damsel's, haha! OK, my eyes are teeny tiny bit small, but my pupils are so lively, shinning with cleverness! No wonder they say that I look so much younger than sixty-two!*

He took another satisfied drag on his cigarette, and aiming his mirror at his collar straightened his carefully chosen navy silk tie with golden dollars printed on it. *How many Chinese men can tie a perfect tie like this? Bet that husband of Jade-Lotus*

Yang will be impressed! The old saying is so right: 'Men should dress up appropriately; Buddha needs to be gilded luxuriously.' Oh oh, old friends were so jealous when I wore that soldier's uniform when I was a Young Worker Rebel, even though I'd never been in the army! My belt was tight, my sleeves were rolled up and I had Mao's little Red Book at hand all the time. Good old years! Then Deng came to power and the government's wind suddenly blew from the west. But that didn't stump me! With tailored dark suits, a beautifully starched white shirt and a designer silk tie, I demonstrated the sophistication of having money! Smart, handsome and powerful! OK, some nit-pickers pointed out that my height is less than ideal, but great leaders needn't be tall! Look, Napoleon wasn't, nor was Stalin! With my wide shoulders, a prosperous tummy and glowing face, I look just like *them! But I am truly great! How many politicians could have survived like me in politically volatile climates, where an east wind could suddenly become a west one, or even swirl up into a tornado? I've clung to power and stayed in the number-one chair ever since I climbed there nearly forty years ago! The townspeople called me a chameleon and thought it was an insult. They knew nothing about Darwin's evolution; nor anything about what's important in a society where 'All animals are equal, but some animals are more equal than others', as a foreign businessman once told me. Naïve and ignorant townspeople! To survive, you need to adapt! Humph! No one is better than me at adapting. I even changed my name twice!* He stretched the right corner of his mouth up, smirking.

In the war-ridden mid-nineteen-forties, his parents had named him Rich-Peaceful Li, wishing a better life for him. When he turned twenty, they pressed him to follow the tradition of an arranged marriage and produce a grandson. He called them 'frogs at the bottom of a well' and refused to speak to them for weeks. Soon the Cultural Revolution started and the destruction of Four Olds campaign saved the day! He changed his name to Ma-Ke Li and gave his brother – Rich-Knowledgeable Li – the name of En-Ge Li, literally taking the names from Marx and Engels. The two brothers denounced their parents overnight and threw them out of the house, announced themselves as the Proletarian Rebels and Revolutionists and took charge. In no time they formed the Young Worker Rebels and took the eager, adolescent Red Guards under their wing. During the day, they marched to close the silk and guzheng factories, then music and art institutes; at night, they went home to home to purge and destroy all the bourgeois objects and even took the antique bed from the home of Nine-Pound Old Lady, and peeled the tiny embroidered silk shoes from her bound feet. She was so angry she put a curse on them, saying they would never have an heir. They just sneered and went on to cleanse the street names that had any olds in them. Old Buddha Street, Longevity Road and Imperial Canal Lane became People's Street, Anti-Imperialism Road and East-Is-Red Lane. The poor postman was confused for months! The visiting Shanghai officials were absolutely impressed, and called Ma-Ke Li 'a new-born calf, unafraid of a tiger'. They fast tracked him into the Communist Party and asked him to lead the way!

When the central wind had changed direction in the nineteen-eighties, many top officials were simply blown away, but not Ma-Ke Li. He flourished as he was quick to smell the sea – money, money, money, the essence of the Deng era! As the old saying went: 'The fortune that favoured the east bank thirty years ago falls onto the west bank now!' When he saw the leaders' pockets become fat as their coastal cities and towns opened up for foreign investment, he immediately decided that it was time to shed his skin once again. He went to an evening school and learnt some English; then he christened himself Mark and changed the spelling of his surname from Li to Lee, ready for another thirty years! As he was able to mix English words into all official meetings, he became a hot potato again. Many county leaders invited him when they had foreign businessmen around and his tummy became prosperous with all the sumptuous banquets. Wave after wave never sank him; season by season he adapted comfortably!

He nodded and grinned, dabbing some ash off from his cigarette. *Why am I worried about this new county leader? I shouldn't be because I've already got a plan. A SUPERB PLAN! OK, when High-Fly first brought me the news of Jade-Lotus's adoption, I didn't see any opportunity, and told him, 'You know the rules, just deal with it, as always we need to look good.' But then I had a brilliant idea! So good that I actually pinched my arm! With this plan, not only can I achieve my foreign investment target, but also show off High-Fly as a young reforming talent, playing the new tune. Good Buddha, I almost can't believe it myself. When this plan succeeds, I'll no doubt become the new county leader's favourite, and a lot of crumbs will fall into my pocket! Oh my, that'll definitely give me a beautifully comfortable retirement. Oh my!*

He tried to pat his own back, but his arms wouldn't reach. He watched as one last hoop of cigarette smoke dispersed in the air, and smiled. *But will High-Fly pull his weight? It's his future too, surely he'll see that.* He stubbed out his cigarette and forcefully threw its butt into the ashtray. Checking his watch, he frowned. 'Now he's late! Can't he do anything well? Humph, bad seed!' *Oh, did I just say that out loud?* He quickly looked around the room; thank Buddha the waitress wasn't there.

He got up and paced around the room. *Why can't High-Fly be more like me? At nearly forty years of age and with all my tender cultivation, he's still nothing like a leader! Even his physique looks all wrong. After all those expensive, free dinners, how can he still look like a hungry monkey? Annoyingly, this monkey recently suggested that I should think about early retirement. What was he thinking? Did he think he's ready to take over from his great dad? Humph, at this rate, in a million years he won't have evolved into a town leader, let alone an eminent one! Bah! The other day the monkey even questioned my changed attitude towards Jade-Lotus. But hey, if you're called the chameleon, you change quickly. Monkey, 'The ginger is much hotter when it's older!'* 'Humph, bad seed!' *Did I just shout again?* He covered his mouth and looked around. *Good, still no one here. I'd better stop calling him a bad seed. I should stay positive, change the negative into a positive just as I've always done. After all, when Judgement Day comes, I'll be able to kneel in front of my ancestors and say, 'I've completed my family duty.' Can those ancestors in heaven see everything?* He rubbed the scar behind his ear as his right eye twitched. *Oh, what's that noise outside?* He rushed to the window and saw High-Fly's car had just parked in the yard. He took out his mirror again and checked his hair and smile, practising his speech in his mind one more time and reminding himself to joke about his English name.

After getting out of High-Fly's Mercedes, Jade-Lotus saw

Mark Lee gliding down the stairs, his arms open, face radiant and teeth displayed like corn on the cob.

'Hello!' he said in perfect English, nimbly jumping off the last step of the stairs. It was astonishing how smartly he was dressed, like he was attending a wedding, and how agile he was considering the size of his tummy. He strode up with a hand stretched out, seeking one of William's. Once found, he grasped it, gave it a firm tug, and wouldn't let go. 'Welcome, my dear, dear friend! I'm Mark Lee. Surprised, eh – an English name?' He raised his thick broom-like eyebrows a couple of times; his eyeballs darted from left to right. 'Hahahaha, my parents had international vision when naming their golden boy! So, we're close already, aren't we?' He patted William's hand enthusiastically.

William seemed impressed, eyes shining and hair bouncing. As he bent to embrace Mark Lee's handshake he appeared comfortable. Well, he had to deal with many countries' officials in his job. He maintained his smile, smoothly getting his hand back, and shifted his body a little. 'Nice to meet you, Mr Lee. This is my wife Jade-Lotus,' he said.

'Of course, you funny William! Funny!' Mark Lee laughed loudly, his laughter crisp like winter reeds. He prodded William with his elbow, his pupils darting as he turned to Jade-Lotus.

As their eyes met, he was a little hesitant, fear flickering in his eyes, as if he was seeing a ghost. But he quickly recomposed himself and said loudly, 'Hello, our town's golden girl! Welcome home!'

'Nice to see you, Town Leader,' Jade-Lotus said as sincerely as she could. Nausea bubbled inside, as if a piece of pork had been forced into her vegetarian stomach. It was difficult to

114

chisel from memory the image of the short stout man from the first day at school, and the dark clouds he had placed over her head ever since. Maybe it was unfair to blame him for all High-Fly's doings, but apples don't fall far from the tree, and in particular, this apple hadn't, being nurtured by his father.

'Come, come,' Mark Lee said, springing back to William and stretching his arm dramatically towards the stairs, as if he was a balustrade salesman. 'I've chosen the best restaurant and ordered our region's top speciality, so we can have a good talk, my dear friend.' He hung on to William's hand like a child and climbed the stairs side by side with him, leaving the quiet High-Fly to accompany Jade-Lotus. She forbade herself to roll her eyes.

'Ah, Maotai!' William said as they sat down in the ornate upstairs room, pointing at the distinctive white bottle with a shiny red label that stood proudly on the large round table.

'Good Chinese! Good taste!' Mark Lee said, clapping his small fat hands. 'I just knew you'd appreciate it, the liquor for state banquets, eh!' His eyebrows danced and his pupils darted vividly from side to side again. 'But I'd say my great foreign friend is worthy of it!' He elbowed William warmly and waved to a waitress to pour the liquor, 'And Longjing tea for the lady!'

The waitress poured the liquor into the small cups in front of the men, while another waitress brought a pot of the famous tea. Jade-Lotus smiled and said thanks. This was truly the old hometown; gentle women would never drink alcohol in front of men. *Why is Mark Lee so hospitable? Didn't he want to kill off our adoption? What does he want? And what can we possibly give him?*

'Let me make a toast,' Mark Lee said, standing up with his

little cup in hand and beaming at William. 'To our best new friend William! And our best old friend Jade-Lotus! Ganbei!'

Jade-Lotus managed to squeeze out a smile and raised her teacup.

William stood up too and clinked his cup with those of the Lees; they downed their liquor in one.

'So,' Mark Lee said, laid his cup down and beckoned for the waitress to pour some more liquor for William, 'how is your stay? Regrettably I was too busy to come to the station, so today I'd like to make amends.'

'Oh Mark – may I call you Mark?' William said.

On first name terms already? Yes, William had to be friendly, but there was no need to be too close.

'Of course, just like good friends,' Mark Lee said.

'Mark, your kindness and hospitality has been remarkable,' William said, gesturing to High-Fly. 'We'd really like to thank you! So, I propose a toast to you and High-Fly.' William raised his cup.

'Ganbei!' Mark Lee said, beaming. 'I can see we're getting on famously!' He signalled with his hands for everyone to sit down. 'Now, I need to be frank with you, William, before you got here, the news of your adoption caused a big scandal in our town. A BIG SCANDAL!' He drew a large circle in the air. 'And people said to me: "How can anyone be allowed to have a third baby, just so a foreigner can adopt it? You should nip it in the bud!" Oh my, you can't imagine the hassle, tut tut tut…' He reached out and patted William's shoulder.

Jade-Lotus turned to William. *What's he trying to say? Has he called us here just to tell us to our face that we can't adopt? If so, why bother with a banquet?*

William seemed to have understood and said, leaning back,

116

'OK. Do you mean you're going to stop us adopting?'

'Yes,' Mark Lee said, his pupils darting from William to Jade-Lotus and back again.

High-Fly, who had been quiet, looked up, his estranged eyes seemingly further apart.

Jade-Lotus felt her face hot, but her hands that had been warmed up by the hot tea were cold. An urge to dump dirty words like dung on Mark Lee surged up, but in that moment not a single swear word, in either English or Chinese, came. She looked at William, and he looked back. The whirring of the air con suddenly became obvious.

'Ha, got you! Got you! Hahahaha…' Mark Lee laughed ecstatically; his radiant face rippled with mischievous victory.

High-Fly looked confused, but nevertheless laughed too, as if his father's laugh was contagious.

'Very funny, is it?' William said.

'You know,' Mark Lee drawled, his elation disappearing fast, 'this baby is illegal; the Shans already have two, very naughty!' He shook his head, his small eyes squinting.

A long silence followed. The muffled sound of a busy engine on the nearby river came and went.

Mark Lee stared intently at William for a second before carrying on, 'As you know, we have a strict one-child policy, so this baby shouldn't be allowed to be born, end of story.' He jabbed a full stop firmly in the air with his little sausage finger.

The air in the room seemed to have stopped too.

'But,' Mark Lee said suddenly, enjoying every bit of the drama he had just created, 'how can I refuse you, my dear, dear friend? Although my patience is worn thin by people from above and below, I can't deny my kind heart, my strong wish to help you to become a parent. There was no one-child policy in my day and I'm the father of three girls and a son, so I understand how you feel. So, my dear friend, rest assured; even if I have to break through many brambles and thorns, I'll help you achieve your dream! Mark my words, mark my words! Ah, food is coming, good timing, good timing.'

A waitress brought in a large pot of steamed hairy crabs, selected the largest for William and put it on his plate. She then similarly served everyone else. Another waitress placed a small dish of sauce and a toolset – rather like the ones used by dentists – in front of each diner.

'That's kind of you,' William said, glancing at Jade-Lotus with relief, 'but what strings are attached?'

At this question, High-Fly shrunk his body lower in his chair and focused intensely on working on his crab.

'Oh my, you're so clever!' Mark Lee said, raising his crab tool and pointing at William. 'I heard you're a top notch, so true! But can you believe me if I say no strings, no strings at all?' He looked intently at William again, his pupils darting feverishly.

'Actually I can't,' William said.

'Hahahaha!' Mark Lee laughed hysterically, as if William was a lamb falling into his den. He skilfully extracted a large piece of crab meat and popped it into his mouth. 'Wonderful! Wonderful! We have a famous Confucian saying: "Isn't it a pleasure when you have friends coming from afar?" but I want to add a line: "Isn't it beautiful when friends help each other out?"' He carefully placed his crab tool back down on the table and stared at William expectantly.

'What can we do to help?' William said, looking curious.

Jade-Lotus couldn't help but want to add a new saying: Isn't it a bore for an official to play such a silly game?

'Jade-Lotus,' Mark Lee said, turning to her unexpectedly, 'isn't he adorable? I hope you won't be jealous that we love your husband too! Don't we?' For the first time, his intense gaze swept a little wider to include High-Fly, who at once nodded with a mouth full of crab meat.

'In fact, William,' Mark Lee said, 'I've sold you out. Who can blame me when you are so clever? I promised people above and below that you're not just here to take from us, but to help us too. To help us develop our economy, attract investment and create jobs; to make our town more prosperous, and provide a better future for our children!' He finished vehemently, enjoying his own speech as if there were thousands of followers looking up at him and applauding.

So you're asking William to do your job? Jade-Lotus bit her tongue. Must stay focused and avoid taking any risk with Mark Lee.

'What exactly do you want me to do?' William said, undaunted. 'I'll help in any way I can.' His tone was sincere and keen.

'Ha, right to the point. Love you, love you!' Mark Lee pointed his crab tool affectionately at William. 'I heard you're responsible for operations worth multimillions at a global company, surely helping us is a trifle compared to that, eh?' He worked on another crab, and said without lifting his eyes, 'I want you to come up with a plan as to how we can attract foreign investment, and I need quick results.' He expertly extracted a big piece of crab meat, smiled at William and shovelled it into his greedy mouth.

William nodded. It was as if a top student, having prepared for advanced calculus, was being asked to simply find a square root. He put his crab tools down, sat back, and crossed his legs, his shoulders dropped. He looked at Jade-Lotus and then Mark Lee; his eyes sparkled as he ran his fingers through his blond hair. There was an air of renewal about him. 'OK, no problem, I'll make you a business plan. I'm leaving tomorrow, so can I have a copy of your plans and financial reports for the past couple of years, please?'

'High-Fly will give you everything you need, but I need it done in three months' time, at the latest,' Mark Lee said, looking much relieved. Of course, he would! He'd just handed his big problem to William! He put his crab tool down, stroked his tummy, his face glowing.

'Yes, yes,' High-Fly said after swallowing a piece of crab meat, 'I'll get the papers to you this afternoon, but if you need more, Jade-Lotus can always find me.' In contrast to his father's dramatic performance he was almost normal.

'Come, my dear friends,' Mark Lee said, standing up again, 'let's toast to our great understanding, our beautiful friendship and our bright future! Ganbei!'

William raised his little cup and Jade-Lotus raised her teacup. 'Ganbei.'

Jade-Lotus sighed silently. She felt the joy of the adoption going ahead and the disgust of being trapped by Mark Lee in equal measure. The price for having a complete family was to buckle and play Mark Lee's tune. After all, 'He's the knife, and I'm the fish on his chopping board'.

William looked rosy, probably not just from the stately liquor. He was now truly involved and that would make him happy. His fear, that he would be useless once in China, that he would be shut out by the townspeople and wouldn't be able to contribute much to the adoption, had vanished. As the liquor warmed his stomach, it was clear that he had a burning desire to play the part he had been given.

10

Twisted Roots and Gnarled Branches

'So, you sold your souls,' Snow-Flower said as she sat down for brunch in the teahouse the following day. 'I never imagined the Chameleon would ask that, creatively cunning!'

'It could've been worse,' Little-Blossom said, pouring Oo-long tea for everyone. 'At least if William comes up with a feasible plan our children will benefit.'

Jade-Lotus nodded.

Grandma passed around the bean buns and salted eggs. 'What if you get him the investment, but he breaks his promise on the adoption?'

'There's never any guarantee,' Snow-Flower said. 'But I'm sure he'll let you adopt if you give him what he wants; all he cares about is face and money in his own pocket. Many officials I know grabbed as much as they could before retiring.'

'I hope so,' Jade-Lotus said.

'"Know yourself; know your enemy"!' William said.

'Ooh, you're such an old China hand!' Snow-Flower said, her dimples blossoming. 'Now Grandma, are you ready?

Anything you can tell us could be useful.'

'Ah, is it that time already?' Grandma said, taking a few moments to realign her chopsticks alongside her emptied congee bowl.

'Try to relax, Grandma,' Little-Blossom said tenderly, caressing the prayer beads on her wrist.

Jade-Lotus dug her fingernails into her palms. The Three-Legged Ding was about to start the search for the truth about Mama; the long wait had come to an end.

'Right.' Snow-Flower rubbed her hands cheerfully and opened her brown leather-bound notebook. Her face brightened. It was as if the camera was on and she was ready to shoot. 'But I'll let you take the lead,' she said generously.

Jade-Lotus took a deep breath. The desire to know about that autumn day in 1969 had been brewing all these years but, like the unspoken code between residents of leafy suburbs and their binmen about which way round the bins should be placed, she and Grandma had cooperated to avoid the subject. It was wonderful that Snow-Flower and Little-Blossom wanted to help. Snow-Flower being a seasoned journalist would find things that no one else could; Little-Blossom had a knack for getting people to open up and talk. But now for some hard yards. 'Grandma, what really happened on the day Mama brought me back?'

Grandma stared at her, as if trying to see through her. But her eyes dulled; the scar over her eyelid throbbed. It was as if a dusty old locked door into the darkest room had just been pushed open but she was hesitant to go in. She clasped her hands tightly under her chin, studying the teacup; silence drifted in and meandered. 'Aihh, fate!' she eventually began, 'Just before your mama took you on the train, she tried to call me, but I wasn't at home. I was in prison; the savage Red Guards decided I was a spy because my husband had been in the Kuomintang to fight Japanese in the forties.' She paused, her eyes fixed on the white china teapot. It was as if the nightmarish past was cold tea in the pot, and she wasn't sure whether to warm it up. She then turned to Snow-Flower. 'She called your mother.'

Snow-Flower's head jerked. 'My mother?'

'Yes, your mother, White-Azalea, my only friend not arrested at the time,' Grandma said.

'Oh, right,' Snow-Flower rolled her eyes, 'the glorious peasant class again!' Her tone was sour. 'Apparently, my mother's family background saved everyone in the Cultural Revolution! Remember the school forms?' she turned to Jade-Lotus, 'Mother watched me and River-Cloud, to make sure that we filled them with her class, not our father's anti-Revolutionist and rightist class.'

'The wrong family class in those years could get you killed,' Grandma said. 'Anyway, White-Azalea was staying at home looking after you and your brother; your father was in a labour camp. I guess you'd know all of this.'

'We never talk about the past,' Snow-Flower cut in hotly.

Little-Blossom shrugged.

Grandma stared at Snow-Flower, shifting her bottom. 'When you were a baby, White-Azalea hired a wet nurse to feed you, as she couldn't produce enough milk. As a toddler you had weak digestion and the wet nurse continued to come every day. When my daughter called that day, the wet nurse was in your house and the Red Guards were outside. Fearing she would be spotted, White-Azalea arranged for her trusted wet nurse to go to the railway station to meet you,' Grandma looked across the table at Jade-Lotus, her eyes lifeless, 'and bring you both back via a secret path to the Shan Academy's back door. The wet nurse went the following morning, but never came back.' Grandma almost whispered the last sentence, her knuckles all white.

'My Buddha, it sounds like a film. What happened next?' Little-Blossom said.

Grandma glanced at Little-Blossom, before turning back to Jade-Lotus. 'There was still no news by evening; White-Azalea said she was like an ant on a hot wok. Next morning, she put Snow-Flower in a sling on her back, took River-Cloud by the hand and went out to search, knocking on people's doors. At the end of a long day, the mother of a former Shan Academy pupil pulled her aside, and told her she had eavesdropped on her husband and other Young Worker Rebels in their backyard. Apparently, the wet nurse was a true rebel herself; she took you and your mama to the river, and pushed Mama, who was a traitor, spy and anti-Revolutionist into the fast-flowing water. While Mama was being swept away, she kidnapped you and ran away...'

Jade-Lotus felt her eyes widening; the room was deafeningly quiet. Outside the teahouse was the same river; it was easy to see just by standing up. But she didn't move, couldn't move; a picture floated into her mind's eye: swirling water rushing downstream with Mama's body, pure like a white lily. But if there had been a body in the river, why had no one ever found it? For days back in 1969, she and Grandma searched along the river and asked almost everyone in Blushing Lotus, but no one had seen anything. And how could a kind wet nurse do such a thing? Had she gone mad? 'But I wasn't kidnapped, I came to you, Grandma,' Jade-Lotus mumbled. *I was there?*

How could I have no memory of it?

'"Good news stays indoors; bad news travels a thousand miles", Grandma didn't seem to hear her and continued, her voice tight as if she had stifled a sob. 'Soon enough, this story reached every corner of Blushing Lotus, including me in prison. I felt like I had died too.' She looked up, blinking, but a tear rolled down; she fumbled out a handkerchief and dabbed her eyes.

Jade-Lotus swallowed hard. No wonder Grandma had never talked about it. It must be extremely painful for a mother to talk about the moment she learnt her child had died. To fail to have a baby was painful enough, but to have one and have it killed would be a whole new level of pain. She reached out to caress her, but Grandma recomposed herself and said, 'A few days later after that news, a Red Guard came to tell me, "Stop your nonsense hunger-strike, think of your granddaughter." When I asked him what he meant, ahya, he quickly walked away. I thought to myself perhaps the kidnapping and Mama's death wasn't true. Aihh, almost everything at the time was a lie, a conspiracy, and without seeing Mama's body, I refused to accept it. So, I made plans in my head: to look for you both once I was out. That plan kept my spirits high enough to endure the daily beatings.'

Jade-Lotus clenched her fists, Little-Blossom cleared her throat loudly and Snow-Flower uncrossed her legs and dropped her high-heeled foot heavily on the floor. There had been so many stories about torture in the Cultural Revolution, but imagining Grandma, a tender widow who had just lost her only child, going through brutal beatings by some of Mao's favourite thugs, was just unbearable.

'Just like I was put in prison for no good reason,' Grandma

continued, 'two weeks later, I was released without a word. When I got back home, White-Azalea brought you to me. Oh my Buddha, I was so pleased! Apparently, a note had been squeezed under her front door, telling her where to find you. She then told me the story I've just told you, and apologised so many times for having wrongly trusted the wet nurse.'

Snow-Flower and Little-Blossom turned to Jade-Lotus, but she shook her head. *No, I don't remember anything about that either. How could the wet nurse suddenly come to her senses and release me after killing Mama?*

'Was the note from the wet nurse? My wet nurse? Have you still got it?' Snow-Flower asked.

'It looked like a woman's writing, but there was no name on it,' Grandma said, 'and no, I haven't kept it.'

A hush fell over the room, except for Snow-Flower scribbling in her notebook.

'Where was I found?' Jade-Lotus asked eventually. There were no memories between the train trip and Grandma's house.

'Ah, with a good family,' Grandma quickly answered. 'When I saw you, oh my little treasure, you were so pale! For days you didn't cry or want to eat; for weeks you didn't say a word. I was so worried, but little by little you came through.'

Jade-Lotus shook her head. In that man-made maddening time, remarkably, the murderous wet nurse had taken her to a good family. But what would cause a child to refuse to speak or eat?

'Even though you didn't speak, we became a team. You, my little treasure, and me, your Pirate, remember that?' Grandma said.

Jade-Lotus nodded. The swirling yellow leaves, the tall lady in a dark dress with waist-long hair and a black patch on her eye… she remembered all of that.

'We went out in an old boat to search for Mama; I really hoped that she was still alive, just locked up somewhere,' Grandma said, her tone despondent. 'Then Mark Lee came to tell me to stop. Ahya, Buddha punish him!' She pursed her lips, her eyes burning with fire.

'Grrr, Mark Lee!' Snow-Flower grumbled.

'Buddha punish him!' Little-Blossom said.

Jade-Lotus lowered her head. The slowly healing scar of the past seemed to be torn open, the wound sprinkled with salt. Grandma had lost her daughter, and been denied the cause of her death and her body for a proper burial. In deeply traditional Blushing Lotus, that believed in Yin and Yang, without the body, there would be no home in the Yin world of the dead for Mama; her soul would forever drift, unable to unite with her ancestors, and therefore she was unfilial in Confucian terms. And little Jade-Lotus had been used as a weight on the scales – of what? Politics, career ambitions, or pure nastiness? How strong Grandma had needed to be to get through it! She reached for Grandma's hand and caressed her bony fingers. Their roles reversed; she was no longer the tender little girl being cared for.

'You're all I have, Little Treasure. So, I stopped the search. But in thirty-seven years, I've never stopped thinking about Mama.'

Silence fell. The word Mama bounced from one cold teacup to another; a purple, sombre undertone vibrated in the air. Little-Blossom sobbed, counting her prayer beads; Snow-Flower chewed on the end of her pen.

'Did the wet nurse ever come back?' Jade-Lotus asked at

last.

'No, no one ever saw her again,' Grandma said.

'She would be an obvious lead.' Jade-Lotus turned to Snow-Flower and Little-Blossom.

'May I?' Snow-Flower raised her hand, but without waiting continued, 'I'm very sorry about what happened to your mama.' She gave her sad-eyed-sloth look. 'What Grandma has said just leads to more questions. We need to follow the vine to get to the melon! There are three vines here: first, my mother. Yes, my mother! If she hadn't trusted the wrong person, none of this would have happened! She's totally…' She swallowed. It seemed that after all these years, she still hadn't made peace with her mother or herself. 'But, she's out travelling and there's no way we can talk about this on the phone! The second is Mark Lee. Since you need him on your side for the adoption and he was the one who stopped Grandma, we'd better not beat the grass and scare the snake. The third is this wet nurse. Grandma, do you know her? My mother never mentioned her.'

Grandma nodded. 'She was, in fact, a nice person, married to Mark Lee's younger brother. But he also disappeared not long after Mama. No one knows anything about them, and some even said they both died long ago.'

'Mark Lee's brother's wife?' Jade-Lotus raised her eyebrows. 'A *nice* person in the Lee family?'

'Oh my God! She was one of them! And my mother trusted her, and hired her to feed me?' Snow-Flower said, pulling a face like she had just stepped on dog poo.

'She was very different from Mark Lee,' Grandma argued, but her voice wavered; maybe she was still struggling with this conundrum.

'All the crows in that family are black!' Little-Blossom said.

'Does the Lee family have some kind of grudge against you, Grandma?' Snow-Flower said.

'I don't think so. Grandma's only "enemy" is Nine-Pound Old Lady,' Little-Blossom said softly.

'I've thought about it for years,' Grandma said, 'Mark Lee passionately follows communism; I was once a number one class enemy. But I don't think it's that. Mark Lee's mother is Nine-Pound Old Lady's younger sister, but she seemed fine too; we lived cordially, like well water and river water.'

'Mark Lee is related to Nine-Pound Old Lady? You never told me that?' Jade-Lotus said.

'We don't chew our tongues over other people's business,' Grandma said, 'besides, even Nine-Pound Old Lady doesn't want to admit that relationship.'

'Mark Lee is related to us Shans?' Snow-Flower almost screamed, staring at Little-Blossom. 'No one told me that!'

'Oh my Buddha! High-Fly is in fact your distant cousin,' Little-Blossom said covering her mouth.

'Aihh, no family wants to admit their black sheep,' Grandma said. 'Mark Lee kicked out his parents in 1966. Although the communists loved him, he committed the utmost moral crime against Confucius – "Of all virtues filial piety is foremost" – and in the townspeople's minds he was disowned by his clan. Since he has the power to make people's lives hell, no one ever talks about it.'

'You can't choose your relatives!' Snow-Flower shook her head. 'Where are Mark's parents now?'

'They left the town, shamed by their sons, and disappeared. No one has heard from them since,' Grandma said.

'This is so complicated,' William, who had been sitting

silently with his arm around Jade-Lotus, finally said.

Snow-Flower sighed. 'Now we have no leads.' She chewed her lip, staring at her notes. 'One thing I can do though, is check the official records of Mark Lee's family to see if we can find anything about his brother and the wet nurse.'

Jade-Lotus nodded; although a long shot, it was better than nothing. Outside stood an ancient beardy banyan tree, full of twisted roots and intertwined branches; its huge canopy covered sky, but light sipped through between the leaves. 'What about Mad Girl? She was married to High-Fly; do you think she could shed some light? Mark Lee's family seems central to this.'

Snow-Flower slapped her hand onto her forehead. 'Of course, why didn't I think of that! I bet Mad Girl hates Mark Lee, so she could well help!'

'But no one knows where Mad Girl is, she only appears when she wants to,' Little-Blossom said.

'That's true,' Grandma said. 'Ever since she divorced High-Fly, she's never been back to my teahouse.'

'But I can ask around about her,' Little-Blossom said.

'OK. Let's paint with two brushes, and see what we get,' Jade-Lotus said. The window of hope was tiny, but it was still a window, letting in fresh air. How much could they find out? If Mark Lee had sealed everything like kimchi in an air-tight jar to ferment for years, could they really open it without an explosion? And once opened, what flavour would it have?

'And let's see who finds the next breakthrough first?' Snow-Flower winked, closed her notebook and checked her watch. 'Oh, we need to leave now. William, are you ready?'

'Yes, my luggage is downstairs,' William said.

'Thank you so much,' Jade-Lotus said.

'I promise I won't steal him.' Snow-Flower winked again.

'Haha, very funny.' Little-Blossom nudged her sister-in-law.

'I trust William.' Jade-Lotus smiled. 'You're right that it's much easier if he stays with you in Shanghai tonight.'

'My driver will take him to the airport tomorrow morning,' Snow-Flower said.

'We must keep in touch as we find things out,' Jade-Lotus said.

'Please do come back whenever you can,' Grandma said to Snow-Flower. 'You three girls were born to be together.'

Jade-Lotus walked back from the train station after seeing William and Snow-Flower off. Once past the town centre where the tourists huddled, the streets were almost deserted. The townspeople, behind the faded wooden doors, were probably napping their traditional afternoon naps and dreaming their conforming dreams.

William travelling away for work had long been part of life, but in the townspeople's minds the shield of his man presence had left with him. As a leaf, could she complete her two heavy quests, even with Snow-Flower's and Little-Blossom's daggers and horses? Jade-Lotus kicked a small stone and listened to the hollow dings as it bounced on the narrow path framed by the tall whitewashed walls. The rolling tea-bush-smothered hills, necklace-like strands of gleaming rivers and canals, the forever rich smell of flora and home cooking, and the echo of hurried wooden clogs in the lane, made Blushing Lotus all so alluring and idyllic. But its stubborn character, darkened and scarred by ideologies, was soul-destroying. The journey ahead was certainly going to be bumpy. Mama's matter had only just begun, but it had already turned into a tangled skein. How could it be so complicated? But if no one could explain, truthfully, how Mama had died, and no one knew where her body was, it was indeed weird. Could the Three-Legged Ding really get to the bottom of it? And what if a choice had to be made between Mama and the baby?

She arrived home; the courtyard house felt eerily empty. She climbed the stairs to her bedroom – Mama's room – kicked off her shoes and threw herself onto the bed; all her limbs felt heavy. Dust particles floated in a sunbeam; songbirds chirped in the distance. Mama's mission might have stalled, but maybe it was time to go and find Little-Blossom to have a good natter about the baby. She sat up, put her shoes back on and headed out.

She strolled through the garden and along the ornate corridor. The lake beyond the fringe of willow branches was calm; young lotus leaves peeped up through the water. A pair of mandarin ducks glided past; painted eyebrows tweeted a crisp song. Spring was really springing, bringing new lives into the world; soon the bundle of happiness would arrive.

She opened the gate to the Shans's garden and followed the path. As she turned the corner, she saw Little-Blossom pacing, her hands hugging her belly.

'Hello there!' Jade-Lotus said.

Little-Blossom looked startled, but quickly wiped her face; the tip of her nose was red and tear-stains reflected the light. 'Ah ah, Cousin.'

'Are you all right?' Jade-Lotus said.

Little-Blossom squeezed a smile. 'I'm all fine, all fine.'

'Are you sure?'

'It's just my hormones.'

Jade-Lotus stared at her, 'You know, for a second, I thought there was something wrong with the baby.'

'No, no, nothing is wrong. Baby is growing well.' Little-Blossom patted her belly.

Jade-Lotus smiled. 'I'd say you're not showing much for four months.'

'She's hidden in layers of fat, just like Spring-Cherry was. At least it's warm in there, like a thick duvet.'

'That's nice.' Jade-Lotus coiled her arm around her cousin's, and walked side by side, heading towards the Shans's house. 'So, what are you doing here near our garden?'

'I didn't realise where I was, just far away from the house, I guess. I don't want to disturb my napping girls.'

'OK.' Jade-Lotus waited, but Little-Blossom didn't offer any more. 'Um, you look a bit miserable if you don't mind me saying. I worry you're going to stress the baby.'

'You're going to be a good mum; I can feel it.' Little-Blossom stroked Jade-Lotus's hand. 'She's a lucky girl, she really is. And don't you worry; I'll make sure she's all fine.' She straightened her back. 'I'm really sorry Cousin. I have an urgent work thing, and have to go.'

'OK.' Having lived in England for many years Jade-Lotus had learnt not to always dig out roots and chisel at the base. 'Anything I can do to help?'

Little-Blossom shook her head. 'No, but thank you.' She fanned her face. 'Hormones again. I promise you I won't stress the baby.'

Jade-Lotus nodded. The questions about the baby could wait; they would be spending many months together. 'I'll walk you home.'

'Actually, I need to go back to the academy,' Little-Blossom said.

'OK, I'll say goodbye here.' Jade-Lotus hugged her cousin. Their lives were entwined again, and forever, by the baby.

11

Knots of Worry

Little-Blossom hurried to her office and let out a big sigh.
Ah ah, that was terrible of me, wasn't it, to lie to my best cousin.
All is fine, but nothing is fine, is it? She leant on the back of
the door, her legs heavy, as if having run around the entire
lake. The newly restored room somehow looked vulgar
now; its elaborately carved and painted high ceiling and
polished flagstone floor were more befitting of the palace
it had once been than of an office. Aihh! She shifted her
weight and looked down, rubbing the floor with the ball of
her ballerina shoe. The crumpled letter in her pocket began to
bear fangs and brandish claws; she tried to press it down, but
it disobeyed. Taking a deep breath she pulled it out. With eyes
shut, she slowly smoothed it, crease by crease. 'It's there; it's
not. It's there; it's not... Please, please, make all the words on
the letter disappear.' However, when she gingerly opened her
eyes, the red characters of 'FINAL REMINDER' stood there
solidly, each stroke sharper than before, like a bloodstained
dagger. And the chunky figure for three months arrears stared

at her, almost laughing. *Ah, how could this happen? HOW? What are we going to do? What am I going to do?* 'Aaaaah...' *Oh Buddha! That doesn't sound like a good woman's voice, does it? More like a fat duck held by its neck on a chopping board quacking. Stop! Stop being so pathetic! Just work out what to do before River-Cloud comes back from Shanghai.*

Dong! Dong! She was jolted by the school bell in the ancient Shan Tower. *Already four? The teachers are coming to say their daily goodbyes.* She stuffed the letter in her pocket again, straightened her linen jacket and opened the door.

'Ah ah, Mrs Wang, happy birthday to your son! Nine now, isn't he? I bet you're going to have a feast tonight...'

'Mr Lin, is your mum's knee better? Say hello from me when you call her...'

'Congrats, Miss Yan! I can't believe it's been six years, can you?'

'Bye there! Have a lovely evening!'

The teachers really are the pearls in the palm of the school, aren't they? It's good that they get to go home and enjoy their family evenings, probably lit with orange lights and scented with orchids. But I must stay and face this horror. Little-Blossom locked the door as the last teacher left through the moongate, and marched towards the desk. In the soft slanted sunlight she paused, staring at the glistening scroll of River-Cloud's calligraphy hung on the wall behind the desk: 'STUDY BROADLY, ASK RELEVANTLY, THINK DEEPLY, DISTIN-GUISH TRUTHFULLY and ACT CONSCIENTIOUSLY'. The wise words of Confucius and the moto of the school. She chewed her lip at them before resuming her march and sat down in River-Cloud's throne-like chair. The high spirits of being a Ding again at brunch had entirely evaporated;

in fact, they had begun to disperse right after coming back to the office and opening the letter. It got worse when the school accountant confirmed that all the usable reserves had already been used. *But it can't be true, can it? Buddha, Buddha, please, please let there be an error!* She slowly reached forward and picked up the printed breakdowns. Narrowing her eyes, she scrutinised every line, every column, every sub-total and every total. When she eventually finished, she threw them down. *There are no errors, none at all!*

Her leg jiggled, she tried to hold it down; she loosened another button on her shirt, grabbed a notebook and fanned her face. The numbers weren't balanced; the outgoings were greater than income, and had been so for a while. *How are we going to pay our teachers' bonus following the exam results? How can we afford the much-needed new computers? And how are we going to expand the business as long planned? Most worryingly of all, there are three months' arrears on River-Cloud's large loan.* She pulled out the letter from her pocket again and scanned it to find: 'If we don't receive the stated sum in 30 days, as of today, we'll proceed to foreclose on the loan.' *Oh Buddha, great Buddha, we would lose the campus! Three hundred years of glorious history would vanish like the morning mist on the river! No Shan Academy in Blushing Lotus? It's almost as unthinkable as the sun rising in the west! It's one of the most prestigious private schools in the south of China.*

Founded by River-Cloud's ancestors, Shan Academy educated hundreds of literati and officials for Imperial China, and more recently many influential people for modern China. Yes, it closed a few times, due to wars, and most recently the Cultural Revolution, but it had always survived.

Could it now be lost while in our hands? She stared at her hands, beads of cold sweat breaking out on her forehead and her body pricked with heat. *Oh Buddha! Greatest Buddha!* She prostrated herself on the desk and sobbed, her shoulders shaking. 'It's all my fault, I let him down; it's all my fault, I pushed him to it; aah, I wasn't there when he needed me, aahaah…'

When she finally calmed down and raised her head, the sunlight had dimmed to a soft grey. She wiped her face, staring blankly. Things on the huge desk gradually came into focus. A computer screen, covered with a thin film of dust, had lost its fight for space with a sea of piled-up books and papers. A dark granite polished bar in the shape of a Toblerone, carved with 'Principal River-Cloud Shan' in golden characters, was drunkenly pushed aside. Instead of facing outwards to announce to the world who was in charge, the name was facing inwards. *Is he reminding himself he's still the head of the academy? The head of this unnecessarily large office? The head of this bespoke desk with dragons carved all over its legs?*

Ah ah, anger doesn't help, does it? She pulled the elastic band that chained mala beads on her wrist and let go. As the beads hit her skin, her face twitched; she repeated the action several times, her wrist turning red. Lowering her head, she mouthed a silent thanks to Buddha before raising her eyes. On the right corner of the desk prominently stood a set of the Four Treasures of the Study: a pile of silky rice paper, neatly unfolded; an ink stick, poking out from an elegant box; a deep, white porcelain dish, covered in half-dried ink; and a tall matching porcelain pot, full of different-sized brushes – one brush, with its hairs black and stuck together, stood out from the crowd of clean peers. Everything bore the academy's crest – a black lotus motif. *He still displays my gift to him on his fortieth birthday! His face had lit up when he opened the package; he brought it into the office and, like a boy with a new silk kite, showed it to everyone. It truly is an exquisite set, isn't it? The porcelain was made using the best kaolin clay, rice paper with the highest percentage of sandalwood bark and the most expensive wolf hair for the brushes. It was difficult to find a family workshop to produce them, and they cost a fortune, but for him, my true love, it was worth it.*

Little-Blossom sat softly back into the chair and stretched out her legs, the corners of her mouth tilted up. *Although Grandmother hadn't approved of him at first; ah ah, Buddha bless her. She just couldn't get on with the idea that you can find your perfect husband without a matchmaker: her matchmaker in fact. But it wasn't her fault, was it? People like us growing up in a mountain valley, all we saw every day was bald mountains wearing a moody sky cap; no woman, locally born and bred, would ever have set a foot out to go and see what was behind those mountains. Even as the wife of our clan leader Grandmother was illiterate, spending all her life spinning yarn, looking after families and chanting Buddhist and Confucian scripts. When Mother and Father were locked up in a labour camp to be re-educated, the twin brothers got to go hunting hares with Grandfather on the mountains, but Grandmother kept me with her to make sure I learned to be a good girl. After the Cultural Revolution, Mother and Father were released, and Mother visited her parents in Shanghai. On her return, she brought with her some text books and wanted to set up a school in the village for both boys and girls, the first in the villagers' living memory. But Grandmother just rotated the handle of the shiny wooden loom and mumbled, 'What use for girls to learn to read? Once grown, they'll just get married and bear*

140

sons. Confucianism is all we need. Come Little-Blossom, recite the Three-Character Classic Confucian tenets for me...' I would then obediently chant in my milk-voice as I passed the thread to Grandmother, 'Man on earth, kind at birth; the same nature; altered by nurture...' A year later Mother did manage to open the school, but had to compromise – to include Confucianism in the school curriculum. So chanting Confucius's lines filled our girls' school days; twin brothers and other boys could dream of being a doctor or scientist. Aihh, it was only with the help of Jade-Lotus and her grandma, I got to visit them in Blushing Lotus and met River-Cloud and he changed everything. At the train station, he, an educated, treasured son from a literati family, offered to carry my basket! During those long, lily-stained days, he taught me how to swim; I never dared tell Grandmother about that! At the Shan Academy's summer camp, such a privilege, Snow-Flower chose Jade-Lotus to be her second in command, and he chose me to be his! In the following summer holiday, he came back from university, and with so much passion told me all about it and said I would enjoy it too. At the end of that holiday, he gave me a pebble with a black lotus motif carved on and said it was the Shans's crest. As the train rolled off, I watched his waving arm turn into a line and then a dot; as the moist, jasmine-perfumed air was ousted by the mountain breeze, I knew that he was the one. He made me believe in myself, believe I could be equal with him, and walk hand in hand to the end of the earth, until the end of time...

The following years have been like spring breeze, all warm and full of vitality. As the first ever girl from our village to go to university in Shanghai, Grandfather lit one-thousand firecrackers and invited everyone for a feast, although Grandmother still insisted it was all done by my citing of wise words from Confucius. Ah ah, Buddha bless her. On the day I got my degree, River-Cloud asked me to marry him, embroidering flowers to the already rich brocade! But 1999 topped everything in my life! It started with River-Cloud and I tying the knot under snowy cherry blossom, and I formally became a Shan, such an old admirable name. That summer I got my master's degree in business management, after lots of hard part-time study! Cousin even called from the UK to congratulate me; so happy to hear that she was proud of me. In autumn, our apprenticeship was over and my parents-in-law gave the full ownership of Shan Academy to River-Cloud and me! What an honour! And in winter, on my thirtieth birthday, I was pregnant with our first child! So perfect wasn't it? When we discussed how to celebrate the new millennium at a family dinner, I boldly suggested that we should bring Confucianism back to the campus, in line with the trend of the time. It got a quick thumbs up from Grandpa Autumn-Rain; he said it fitted nicely with the Academy's history and its award-winning teaching and social ethics. River-Cloud was only too happy to oblige and had Confucius's wise words carved onto huge rocks placed around the campus to be our school's new motto.

As her eyes once again fell on the numbers, Little-Blossom's stretched lips slowly contracted. *Aihh, looking back, it's so true, isn't it? 'Extreme joy will turn to sorrow, like the sun climbing to noon and falling, and the full moon waning,' Confucius says. I'll never forget the first time I visited the Shan ancestral hall at the Spring Festival. In the hazy smoke of the burning incense, I listened to my father-in-law read out one by one the name of a man in each generation of the Shan family tree. There were twenty-two of them, and peeping at River-Cloud's serious face I realised what was expected from me even though he never said anything. 'The worst failure of filial piety as a wife is not producing a son,' Confucius says. I held onto my pregnant belly and prayed hard for it to be a boy. But it didn't help, did it? Instead of a seed to continue the Shan name, I had Summer-Lily, a leaf! How delighted my parents-in-law were seeing the baby for the first time, but their smiles froze on the news that it was a girl. The family matriarch Nine-Pound Old Lady didn't even bother to show up at the one-hundred-day baby event. So, I persuaded River-Cloud to try again, against the government's one-child policy. Determined to do it right this time, I avoided all my favourite chilli dishes, ate tons of pickled cabbage, drank gallons of bitter herbal tea, endured endless acupuncture and swallowed numerous precious 'boy pills'. I even consulted a feng shui master, re-arranged the position of our bed and ensured we made love on the right days by the lunar calendar, but, aihh, as fate had it, it was another girl. On the day I came back with my newborn Spring-Cherry, a leaf flag dangled lifelessly above the gate. My parents-in-law welcomed me home, but their cheer was a bit too loud. Grandma from next door and Snow-Flower came with lovely baby gifts, but then Nine-Pound Old Lady turned up with her friends, each dressed in sombre black, holding small baskets of dry leaves. They scattered leaves everywhere; Nine-Pound Old Lady pointed at the baby with her walking stick and laughed hollowly, 'I just knew someone from the barren hills couldn't be trusted to continue our precious family line.' She then gave River-Cloud a fierce glare before walking away.*

Aihh, things only went downhill after that, didn't they? Little-Blossom stared back at the Four Treasures of the Study. *It wasn't long after Spring-Cherry's first birthday, that TV documentary series about Chinese literati came on... River-Cloud watched every episode and said numerous times that he wanted to be one. Although I couldn't see how he, as a literati, so removed from real life, could run a renowned academy. I bit my tongue. I had another girl; I wasn't in a position to say anything, or crush his dream (or mid-life crisis) was I? Aihh! So, when his big birthday came, I presented him with the set, which would have been the envy of any literati, from Confucius to today. River-Cloud was happy, very happy; that's all that matters, isn't it? As his suits gradually changed to floaty silk robes and he became more aloof and philosophical I should have taken more control of the school, shouldn't I? But all I could see was the smoky Shan ancestral hall, and all I could think about was that there wasn't a boy's name at the bottom of the long family tree. One morning, I was readying for an important meeting about the new curriculum, where I needed to make River-Cloud see that literati philosophy did not need to be a core subject for our students, but I was unable to get out of our bedroom and just cried and cried. In the end, River-Cloud had to call a doctor. Eventually I was diagnosed with postnatal depression, and felt completely crushed. Mother had to step in and suggested that I should stay with them in the countryside for a few months, with the girls, to recuperate. River-Cloud was so kind and told me to stay as long as I needed and that he would take care of the academy. So off I went. He came to visit me often, to help me recover, but when I came back twelve months later River-Cloud gave me a big surprise – the old ratty courtyard houses, long used as storage, had been completely restored to their former Qing glory, and turned into offices. When I asked where he had found the spare cash, he told me not to worry – it was a small loan and the academy was doing extremely well; and if I chose to, I could stay at home to continue my recovery. So, I became a full-time mum. Only now, as River-Cloud is away at his conference in Shanghai, have I stepped in and opened that letter. After a quick check with the accountant, it turns out that the loan was in fact a large one, and River-Cloud has significantly increased the number of non-paying students from poor backgrounds whilst I was away.*

Worse still he's stopped chasing unpaid bills from students' parents. Aihh, he's a literati through and through, isn't he? He always felt that acting like a common businessman was beneath him and believed people would pay soon. How naïve can he be? Business is business; how can he not know that! Ah ah, stop being angry. She pinged her wrist with her mala beads again until she became calm. *Aihh, but one hand can't clap, can it? I share the blame, don't I? When we were handed the ownership of the academy, my parents-in-law said confidently that they could now relax because River-Cloud had me, a business brain. At first, using what I'd learnt we modernised our labour-intensive cost allocations, cash flow and bookkeeping, adopted innovative marketing and created a state-of-the-art website, so the Academy was doing great. But then I slipped onto the old narrow path of squeezing myself into the bull's horn of producing a baby boy! It sounds inconceivable, doesn't it? The last few years have been really hazy and, like a bookworm, I don't know whether I belong to the book world or the worm world. Instead of carrying my end of the pole and sharing the load fairly, I threw it all to River-Cloud and let my brain turn to mushy turnip. Even when I was recuperating in the countryside I wanted to try again. And here we are, pregnant again! 'Rotten wood can't be carved any more,' Confucius says. When Jade-Lotus called and asked to adopt my unborn baby girl, it was like she had beat me on the head with a stick! 'What? It's a GIRL, you know?' It's difficult to believe that I could quack like that! But I did, loud, clear, unplanned and unscripted! And the moment of silence that preceded her saying that they'd love to have a baby girl felt really long. Although she didn't say anything, I can imagine her huge disappointment in me. Aihh, the truth is crystal clear, isn't it, that I've become an ugly baby machine programmed with a single task – to produce an heir for the family, the one thing that all of us –*

Jade-Lotus, Snow-Flower and I – had despised growing up.

Little-Blossom pulled back her legs; her shoes made a sharp screech. She shifted her bottom in the chair; the leather squeaked. Fanning her face with her hand, she stood up. *Dong! Dong!…* the school bell chimed six times. She put the papers in her bag and left.

It was quiet on campus; the boarding students were in the dining hall eating dinner. She took the longer path along the lake; the evening breeze cooled her senses. The sun was setting, painting a wavy, golden ribbon on the water; the four-foot-tall granite rock, one of the five, stood proudly on the bank; its carved golden calligraphy – 'ACT CONSCIENTIOUSLY' – shimmered in the rosy sunlight. *Confucius is right on that, isn't he? I must act and do something. 'When fate throws a dagger at you, you can either die by its blade or catch it by its handle and throw it back,' Father used to say. Yes, I may not give the Shans the son that they secretly hoped for, but I can do something to save the academy and make them proud.* She nodded, sped up and headed home.

As Little-Blossom quietly entered, the house was dim and still. The low lamp above the dining table had been left on; insects circled around it, bravely tapping. In the middle of the table sat a dome-shaped quilted cover, under it a bowl of rice congee and some fried dumplings. Nanny must have left them for her. Beside the dome was an open exercise book. Ah ah, Summer-Lily's homework. The poor girl must have waited and waited for her mummy to come home and check it for her. Looking at the childish characters that filled the entire page, there wasn't a single error. Little-Blossom blinked her eyes hard. *If I had been back earlier, I could have told her how well she had done.* She sighed and reached to the sideboard drawer for the sticky stars. As she pressed a gold star on the back of the page, she could almost see the delight on Summer-Lily's little face on seeing it. She took off her jacket and peeped into the girls' room; they were both fast asleep, their faces peaceful and sweet. A wave of tender love splashed over her. *They're really little angels, aren't they? Sensible, smiley, giving their love unreservedly to everyone around them, rarely crying or making mischief. At their tender age, they have no knowledge of the dark side of people, know nothing about the age-old tradition that favours boys and the chilling facts of each family's secret preference.* She pressed her hand over her heart. *I'll always favour you, my little darlings, and give you my special love, care and protection. But now I must write a business plan.* She gently closed the bedroom door.

She took out the breakdowns and sat down to her dinner. As she ate, she scribbled in her notebook. When she had finished her food and plans, she stifled a yawn and felt a movement in her tummy. *Ah ah, my baby!* She caressed her belly; her eyes moistened. *There is a new life inside me; I must look after her. For Jade-Lotus and myself.*

A loud scream broke the serenity. Little-Blossom jumped up and rushed into her daughters' bedroom. Spring-Cherry was crying. She hurried over and picked her up. Summer-Lily moved across to cling on to her. Little-Blossom held both of them, gently rocking, and sung an old lullaby:

The moon's bright, wind's delight,
  Leaves caressing the window so light.
  Crickets happily singing,
  As if guzheng plucking.

147

My little baby, go to sleep,
Sleep, and may your dreams be sweet.
The moon's bright, the wind's delight,
Cradle's rocking gentle and slight.
My little baby, close your eyes,
Sleep, and in the morning rise.

12

Reeling Silk from a Cocoon

Jade-Lotus wandered in Grandma's garden. A day had passed, and all was quiet. William would be on a flight on his way to New York; Snow-Flower, Little-Blossom and Grandma were all back at work, with routines to follow and lives to weave. It was unreasonable to expect them to stop hoeing and hang up their sickles just for her.

What to do now? No immediate lead on Mama, and nattering about the baby with Little-Blossom was also out of reach for the moment. She kicked a small pebble; it clicked and clacked on the path. When it stopped, she kicked it again, with a force that sent it curving into the air. She watched it land near the outer path, the 'path to heaven' solely used for funerals, which led to the place where Mama was remembered; perhaps it was time to talk to her.

The outer path, invaded by rampant jasmine bushes and arching prickly brambles, was narrower; it was impossible to imagine its former glory. Grandma had said that a four-horse-driven hearse, followed by a phalanx of sixty-four trumpeters and hundreds of mourners dressed in white linen, made their way along it to the family graveyard when her grandfather died.

The record time, as a teenager, was nine minutes, running from the house; it was doubtful she'd be able to make that at nearly forty. Back then it was about rushing to clear frustrations, but today it would be better to take time and think what to say.

Perhaps the first thing to tell Mama was that her little girl was about to become a mother too, and then that the Three-Legged Ding had started to dig into the past, trying to unearth what had really happened in the autumn of 1969.

She arrived at the family graveyard at the foot of the hill. The area had been framed by moss-nibbled stumps back in the 1970s, but was now protected by the trees Grandma had planted in the eighties. The fragrant camphor trees at the back appeared sturdy, dense and lush, as if they had always been there, their menthol smell wafting in the breeze. Grandma had said that the aroma defended the ancestors' spirits. The ginkgo trees, with their fresh green fan-shaped leaves, looked like elegant dancers circling around Swan Lake. The graveyard – once a mass of dug-up graves, their headstones toppled by the Red Guards and made to lean drunkenly towards the east – looked formal and proper now, with new headstones standing like sentries. She headed to the corner, the place chosen to remember Mama, because it was next to a huge tree stump, and full of flowering dandelions. Grandma had taken a small slate slab from the cover of the well and placed it down as a headstone, although Mama's name had never been inscribed on it. The corner looked different now – curbstones circled a small area in which a small osmanthus tree held a leafy umbrella over a lonely white headstone with 'Peony-Grace Lu, 1946–' carved on it and stained in red. *Red?* Only the living use red. Was Grandma still holding a pocket of hope, or just refusing to accept Mama's death until her body was found? When had Grandma done this? She had never mentioned it.

She knelt down and stared at Mama's name. Light sieved through the leaves, dappling the shade, like her feelings towards Mama. The love for Mama was always there, like the sun and the moon, but sometimes it was nibbled by a sinister suspicion. Yes, High-Fly had many stupid insults, but one had taken root, resonating with one of the lowest notes in the repertoire of her own darkest thoughts. She could almost see him saying it right to her face, and smell his bad breath.

'Yeah! We've got into the best high school in the county!' Snow-Flower shouted.

'Let's go and celebrate! Grandma is waiting,' Jade-Lotus said.

Arm in arm, marching perfectly in step and giggling, they headed into town.

As they were crossing the town square, they heard a loud whistle. High-Fly and his gang sat by the ancient well, each holding a long sword, the silver blades glistening.

'Don't look,' Jade-Lotus said, 'whatever they're doing, I'm not interested.'

'I'm so glad he won't be in the same school as us any more.'

'Hello,' High-Fly shouted, 'a little bird told me you got in to No. 5 High School. I heard snakes lurk in the corners of the classrooms there, not nice.'

Jade-Lotus pretended not to hear him.

'Just like here then, where our snake tries to be funny and has crabby eyes,' Snow-Flower shouted back. She always knew how to retaliate.

His gang cleared their throats loudly, as if trying to restrain themselves from laughing.

Jade-Lotus wanted to giggle, but didn't. Never give him any attention.

High-Fly laughed coldly, stood up, stepped forward and turned his wrist to point his sword at them.

For a second, Jade-Lotus thought he was going to use it as a weapon, so she stopped and stared fiercely at him, as did Snow-Flower.

High-Fly waved his sword in a fluid showy way, and said, 'You know this is a Tai chi sword, a traditional art form.'

Jade-Lotus rolled her eyes; since when was he traditional or arty?

He came closer, and in an insidious tone said, 'And I'm sure you know our town's tradition too,' circling his eyeballs in their sockets, 'just ask yourself why your mama only brought you back here, and where did your little brother go?' He drew a question mark in the air with the tip of his sword and winked at her. 'I bet it was somewhere much nicer!'

Jade-Lotus felt her face burning. The urge to break his sword was overwhelming, but she just stood rigidly. Over the years there had been many insults, mainly political, from him, but this one really hurt. She curled her fingers into tight fists.

Snow-Flower tugged her sleeve, 'Let's go, don't listen to his rubbish!'

Since when did you give up so easily? Jade-Lotus sneered at him and left angrily.

The celebration at Grandma's teahouse, with eight other

students who were also going to the same high school, was a real buzz, but Jade-Lotus struggled to keep up with the excited conversation. Even Snow-Flower wasn't as bubbly as usual – she seemed to be somewhere else too.

When it finished, Jade-Lotus and Snow-Flower walked back home. Neither of them said much. Once Snow-Flower had turned off to her house, Jade-Lotus broke into a run for the Yang's graveyard. Kneeling in front of Mama's slab she cried out loud, wiping tears from her face. She held her jade pendant and asked, 'Was it true? Was it because I'm a girl?' But Mama didn't answer – she never had – so she grabbed a handful of damp earth and threw it onto the slab. A small rock bounced, as if to announce one of the greatest crimes, in deeply filial Blushing Lotus, had been committed. She collapsed to the ground, curled into a ball. Yes, High-Fly was nasty, but he might be right. There was no one to talk to about it: Grandma might get angry at such unfilial thoughts; Snow-Flower and River-Cloud might just laugh. The suspicion had been like tinder hiding in the dark, and now High-Fly had lit it, it was a raging fire. How could her parents do that?

The air began to smell of burning wood; it must be dinner time, and Grandma would be back from her teahouse. She crawled over to Mama's slab and wiped the earth off it with her sleeve.

A loud burst of birdsong brought Jade-Lotus back to Mama's grave. She felt that standing in this special corner should bring her a feeling of closeness to Mama, but somehow guilt, mixed with stubborn suspicion, had created a foggy barrier. High-Fly's malicious words had wreaked havoc, and it had been difficult to dislodge them. For years they had been eroding her soul like rust.

She let out a slow heavy breath. It would probably never be known why Mama had brought her back to Blushing Lotus; to accept it and move on was the only option. Caressing Mama's name she said sorry. Mama would probably look on her kindly and say it was alright. It was time to find out what had happened to Mama and where her body was. She got up, waved to Mama, and turned to head home. Grandma had said all Mama's things were in the room adjacent to their bedroom; it was time to look at them.

Jade-Lotus had never been inside the adjacent room before; growing up its door had always been locked and hidden behind a large wardrobe. Grandma said it was Mama's old den, so it should be a treasure trove with pretty dolls, colourful pens, origami creations, fragrant purses, precious jade bangles and embroidered silk dance shoes. But all that was there was a two-seat bamboo bench, topped with a bamboo-patterned pad and matching scatter cushions, and a short chest used as coffee table. *Where are Mama's things?*

Grandma often said that their house had many secret hiding places, so she examined the walls, but no section moved. There was nothing underneath the chair, and the chest appeared solid with no openings. *Hmm, where has Grandma hidden them?* She sat down on the chair wondering where to look next. Leaning back, with hands bridged behind her head, she stretched her legs and hooked her toes under the chest. Something hard seemed to push back. She sat up, groped under the chest and found a small button. *What is it?* She tried to slide it around, it didn't move; she pulled it, it didn't obey; she pushed it, and – *pa!* – the top of the chest popped open. *Gosh, open sesame!* The inside was lined with cream silk, and a shoebox nestled securely in the middle of the padding. She lifted the shoebox out, put it down next to her on the chair and opened it. Her heart thumped as she tipped out the contents.

The chair was covered in red. A little red book with Mao waving majestically in sunrays; a couple of red enamelled lapel badges, featuring Mao's self-satisfied smirk; a red metal pentagram, about the size of a beer bottle top, pinned to what looked like a red armband. *Hmm, Mama was a class enemy, how could she have these things?* Only a Red Guard would be honoured with this stuff. In fact, if Mama had been one her life would have been so much easier. Inside a folded A3 sheet, underneath a red Mao, with his God-like hand pointing to the east, embossed gold characters said: 'This is to certify that Comrade Peony-Grace Lu has correctly studied Mao's cultural policies.' A red stamp sealed the bottom right corner with the name of Mama's national newspaper. Another certificate of merit honoured Mama for having married for the great need of the revolution. Further down was an empty coupon book, three enamel school badges and a red poster with 'Sailing the seas depends on the helmsman' under Mao's fat, comic face. *Where are Mama's real things?* There didn't seem to be anything personal in this box.

Jade-Lotus had long realised she knew very little about Mama. Some personal items would help to know her as a person, not just her job as a news editor in Beijing or how red she had been before she became a class enemy. Something like her old school text books, a matchbox containing a beloved butterfly specimen, some colourful hair ribbons, a poster of an adored singer or a secret-soaked diary. But there was nothing. It was as if Mama was someone mass-produced from a mould. Robot No. 598 was just a copy of Robot No. 1. All their personalities the same, individuality non-existent; they did exactly what they were programmed to do – shouted the same slogans: 'Long Live Chairman Mao!' and sang the same song: '... the East is red, Mao is God...'

And there was nothing in the box to give a lead for the search. Out of disappointment, she thumped the bottom of the upturned box with her hand. Instead of a hollow sound there was a dull thud. She turned the box over, stared at the inside and slipped her fingernail around the edges. The bottom seemed to move slightly, so she carefully wiggled it – a false bottom! – and managed to lift it out. An envelope was taped inside containing three faded black and white photos.

Jade-Lotus picked up a photo and studied it, as if it was a precious white-jade elephant. It was of two smiling twin-like girls, in their late teens, rowing a boat. The one on the left looked a bit like Mama; Grandma only had one child, so who was the other one? Growing up, Grandma had told her very little about their family and she had never asked. Those relatives would only bring troubles. She picked up the next photo. It was of a young mother, joyously staring at the baby in her arms. *Is it Mama and me?* She turned the photo over, but as with the first there were no words on the back. The third was only half a photo, its jagged edge severing the left hand of a girl that looked like Mama's twin in the first picture, but slightly younger. Interestingly the background was half of the Tiananmen Tower. *Who is she? And who was in the other half?*

'Ah, you're here,' Grandma said at the door, 'I see you've found your Mama's stuff.' She smiled and entered.

'You hid it well,' Jade-Lotus said.

'You never know when the wind will change direction.'

'Is this *all* Mama's stuff?' Jade-Lotus piled everything back into the box and patted the chair.

'Yes,' Grandma sighed and sat down. 'Most of her possessions were smashed and burned. Those red things,' she nosed at the bloody pile, 'they didn't dare burn them.'

'Eh, was Mama a Red Guard?'

'Oh no, definitely not. She wrote an article about them and was given all that stuff.'

Jade-Lotus nodded, relieved. 'Do you know about these photos?' she passed them to Grandma.

'Ah, you are a good detective,' Grandma said. 'Not many photos of your mama survived.' She sighed again.

'Is this Mama?' Jade-Lotus pointed at the first photo, 'and are they twins?'

Grandma put on the reading glasses that had been dangling from her neck, 'Yes, this is your mama. Haha, no, they're not twins but cousins. Cousin Lemon-Moon, Little-Blossom's mother. They were very close, like sisters.'

'They look so similar.'

'Their fathers were twins.'

'Do you know where the photo was taken?'

'Somewhere in Beijing, I think. Lemon-Moon went to visit your mama one summer holiday. And this one,' Grandma moved on to the second photo, 'is you and Mama. It reminds me of when I had your mama.' She was captivated, and without lifting her eyes added, 'You do know your mama loved you very much, don't you?'

Jade-Lotus nodded. 'What about this torn one?'

'That's Lemon-Moon too, but I don't know why it was torn.

It was in your pocket when you arrived in 1969.'

Jade-Lotus widened her eyes. 'I need to visit auntie Lemon-Moon.'

'Talk to Little-Blossom. It's about time you met her mother,' Grandma said.

The next Sunday morning, Jade-Lotus and Little-Blossom sat down in a busy train carriage. Opposite them was a pregnant woman, her husband and a live cockerel in a small cage. 'Haha, matching,' the woman said pointing at Little-Blossom's belly. 'Can't wait for my fat boy to arrive, bet you can't either.' She giggled.

'Ah ah,' Little-Blossom said, 'actually, I'm having a girl.' She blushed slightly, holding her belly, showing off its soft curve.

Jade-Lotus turned to her cousin in awe.

'Oh!' the woman said. The humming of the other passengers' conversations filled the silence. Eventually she twisted her bottom, leaned forward like an old friend and whispered, 'I've done –' she raised three fingers '– abortions!' With puppy eyes, she turned to her husband, who nodded smirking; their cockerel tutted. She then reached across, grasped Little-Blossom's hand and said kindly, 'I can give you my doctor's details.'

'No, I'm fine,' Little-Blossom said, taking her hand back, and turned to Jade-Lotus, 'Look, the cherries are forming.'

Jade-Lotus gave her cousin's arm an approving squeeze. Outside, the passing trees were dotted with hundreds of tiny fruits, and would channel all the energy gathered by their leaves into growing and ripening them, nurturing the seeds within. Once ripe the fruit would be enjoyed by birds, which would then spread the precious seeds, but the leaves would simply fall and be blown away. The trees would be happy as their next generation was surely secured. Who cares about leaves? The beautiful Lin Daiyu had famously buried fallen flowers and leaves and held memorial services to honour their sacrifice. *I will always love, cherish and care for my leaf.*

The train stopped at a station, and the pregnant woman stood up to get off. 'You still have time,' she said to Little-Blossom softly.

'Gosh, three abortions,' Jade-Lotus whispered as the woman disappeared into the crowd.

Little-Blossom whispered back, 'I couldn't face going through even one.'

'Is that why you didn't do scans before your girls?'

Little-Blossom nodded, patted her belly and said, 'There's a beautiful life in here.'

Jade-Lotus shifted her bottom, crossed her legs and didn't know where to put her hands. The stories of adoptions failing and going to court because the mother changed her mind circled in her head.

'And it's yours.' Little-Blossom nudged her.

'Thank you.' Jade-Lotus felt her face burning.

'Ah, a kick!' Little-Blossom said, grabbed Jade-Lotus's hand and put it on her belly.

Jade-Lotus held her breath. At her cousin's 'Another one!' she felt a tiny, almost undetectable touch on her fingers. So gentle, it provoked the tenderest feeling; so fleeting, yet able to grab her heart. She sank into a bubble, warmly hushed and rose-fragrant, just her and her baby snuggled together…

The train whistled, and a village nestled in a valley emerged.

Jade-Lotus sat at a round table in her Auntie Lemon-Moon's

cottage. Opposite, on a bed that occupied half of the room, sat Little-Blossom's grandmother in the lotus position. She caressed the tartan cashmere blanket that Jade-Lotus had given her, and smiled a toothless smile. Little-Blossom and Lemon-Moon shuffled in and out of the room bringing tea, small walnut cookies, a plate of fresh elm leaves and some wrapped sweets. Outside in the garden, Little-Blossom's father was feeding the chickens and rabbits.

Lemon-Moon was a slender woman, with an oval-shaped, benevolent-looking face, and dark tanned skin, although deep wrinkles made her look older than sixty. Would Mama look like this if she had lived? Behind the spectacles her dark eyes appeared thoughtful, seemingly wanting to tell a story – a sad story perhaps. 'I hope your grandma is in good health,' she said, her voice low and calm, filled with warmth, 'I haven't seen her for a long, long time.' She waved her hand invitingly over the sweets.

'Yes, I'd say excellent for her age, still doing Tai chi every day,' Jade-Lotus said and accepted a cookie at Lemon-Moon's warm insistence. It was surprising they had never met before, but the days when everyone was locked to a town by their ration book and had no spare money weren't that long ago. 'Thank you for agreeing to help, Auntie.'

Lemon-Moon smiled; her motherly gaze felt comforting.

Little-Blossom poured tea and took a cup to her grandmother.

'Eh, what do you want to know about your mama?' Lemon-Moon said quietly, sitting up a little rigidly.

'I'm hoping, you can tell me about these photos.' Jade-Lotus handed over the picture of Mama and Lemon-Moon on the boat.

Lemon-Moon studied it; childish delight sparkled in her eyes. 'Ah ah, it was in Beihai Park, in –' she looked at the ceiling for a moment, her body seemingly relaxing '– in 1965. That summer holiday, I went to see Peony-Grace in Beijing University and we cycled to the city centre. We rowed that boat all afternoon, talking about our future after graduation. The happiest time...' Lemon-Moon trailed off and shook her head gently.

'What about this one?' Jade-Lotus passed the torn picture.

Lemon-Moon took it, but her hand shook and dropped it as if it was blazing hot. She turned, and from inside the small sideboard behind her took out a metal box, the size of a shoebox. She undid a button on the overlapping front of her home-spun quilted jacket, fumbled out a small key, opened the box and took out some photos. She spread them on the table, picked out a torn one and put it next to Jade-Lotus's photo.

Mama was in the other half!

'It was late 1968,' Lemon-Moon sipped her tea and began, 'I had to take leave from my labour camp and get back to Shanghai to see my mother; her arm had been broken by a Red Guard. Peony-Grace happened to be in Shanghai on business and came to see us. She was quite pregnant at the time, with your younger brother. When my mother fell asleep, Peony-Grace whispered to me that she couldn't spy on her husband any more, as she had grown to love him. She believed that something terrible would happen if she stopped reporting on him to Mao. I didn't know what to say, so I hugged her and cried, feeling scared for her, and she cried too.' Some tea spilled from the cup, but she didn't seem to notice.

'Mama spied on Baba for Mao?' Jade-Lotus said. 'Why did

she do that?'

'You don't know?' Lemon-Moon frowned. 'Eh, your parents had an arranged marriage, and the matchmaker was Mao himself. Your baba had just returned from overseas and was working for Mao as an economic advisor. Mao ordered your mama to forget her puppy love and marry for her country. After the wedding, Mao told your mama to keep an eye on him and report on him regularly.'

'Oh my Buddha!' Little-Blossom said.

Jade-Lotus was speechless, but eventually managed to ask, 'Did my grandma know any of this?'

Lemon-Moon shook her head. 'At that time, the Cultural Revolution was at its peak, everyone was living in fear; there was no way Peony-Grace would tell her mum anything about the spying.'

Jade-Lotus nodded and stared back at the photo.

'When we stopped crying, I took this photo from my purse, and tore it apart. I gave my half to Peony-Grace, and asked her to stay quiet until the baby was born. I held the half with her in it and she held the half with me in it, and we said together, "We'll meet again." It was our promise to stay alive for each other, to complete the picture. But – but Peony-Grace never came back…' Lemon-Moon turned away and wiped her face with her sleeve.

Silence fell; a fly hummed.

Jade-Lotus reached for her auntie's hand and caressed it.

Little-Blossom refilled teacups.

'Why this photo?' Jade-Lotus said.

Lemon-Moon re-composed herself. 'It was our favourite, taken on our first trip to Beijing,' she sighed. 'We were so excited, as sixteen-year-old girls invited to one of Mao's private dinner parties!'

'Really?' Jade-Lotus said.

Lemon-Moon nodded, 'Our grandfather took us. He was a good friend of Mao's in fact, a financier and supporter of communism. The dinner party wasn't too big, and we were introduced to Mao. He seemed friendly and easy to talk to. I was too shy to say much, but he was mesmerised by Peony-Grace.'

'Gosh!' Jade-Lotus said, 'Grandma never told me.'

Lemon-Moon pushed up her thick spectacles. 'I never told my children either. Because of this relationship, in spite of our wealth, our family fared better in the many purges. But things changed. Just after your brother was born, our grandfather wrote to Mao and criticised his Cultural Revolution, and soon our family's fortunes changed. Grandfather's villa in Shanghai was ransacked, all his Ming vases smashed, all his books and several unfinished manuscripts burned. At over eighty he even had to endure the 'taking a flight' torture. Then your mama stopped reporting on your baba.'

'"When a nest is overturned, no eggs will survive",' Jade-Lotus said through gritted teeth.

Lemon-Moon nodded, sighed and collected the photos together.

'Can I have a look at the rest?' Jade-Lotus said.

'OK,' Lemon-Moon said. 'I've never shown them to anyone before.'

The photos told the story of Auntie's life. She had been a university lecturer in Shanghai, but was sent to the poorest mountain village to be re-educated, where she fell in love with a kind young man, the son of the local clan leader. When Mao's power fell she was at last allowed to return to Shanghai, but she chose to stay with him in these mountains.

'Who was Mama's puppy love?' Jade-Lotus said.

Lemon-Moon stared into her teacup for a moment and said, 'Eh, I met him once. He didn't talk much, but there was a dreamy, scholarly air about him. Later, Peony-Grace showed me some of his letters. He wrote beautifully, and I joked that he matched his name well. Rich-Knowledgeable – ah yes, that was his name.'

'Who is he? Where is he today?' Jade-Lotus said.

'Blushing Lotus I assume. He had a brother, who I heard was the leader of the rebels during the Cultural Revolution, and later became town leader.'

'Mark Lee's brother?!' Jade-Lotus almost screamed. 'How could Mama fall for someone in that family?'

Lemon-Moon frowned, but smiled kindly. 'They were in the same class right up to high school. I heard he was very different from his brother. He seemed crazy about Peony-Grace, and she liked him too.'

'Grandma said he disappeared, and people thought he had died,' Jade-Lotus said.

'I never heard that,' Lemon-Moon said.

'Every lead seems to go back to Mark Lee's family,' Little-Blossom said.

Jade-Lotus nodded, 'But we can't talk to them. Have you found anything about Mad Girl?'

'The mother of one of our students came from the same village as Mad Girl's aunt, and she's going to talk to her,' Little-Blossom said.

'Didn't you say Nine-Pound Old Lady knows everyone?' Lemon-Moon said, touching her daughter's hand. 'Can she help?'

Little-Blossom shook her head, 'She doesn't like Jade-Lotus or Grandma.'

'We need to find Mad Girl,' Jade-Lotus said.

13

Wearing Out Iron Shoes

'So how did it go with Little-Blossom's mum?' William said, his enthusiasm rushed across the Pacific.

Jade-Lotus was quiet for a moment. Speaking by phone daily was not the same as having him in the room. 'It went really well,' she said, mirroring his enthusiasm. 'Guess what though? Mark Lee's brother and Mama were... um... good friends.'

'Really? But why would the wet nurse want to kill her husband's good friend?'

'Um... you know, *really* good friends.' She coughed.

'Really!'

'It makes sense, don't you think? Demonstrating her red heart for Mao could just have been rubbish; it could have been pure revenge.'

'Gosh. What next?'

'We know nothing about this brother, so our best bet is probably still Mad Girl. Little-Blossom may have a lead.' Just saying the word 'lead' somehow brought more positivity. 'So, how's progress on your side?'

'Well, I've read the reports. If they were accurate Mark Lee wouldn't need us!' He laughed. 'I'm running with some ideas and I've reached out to a few old pals; Nick in Hong Kong seems interested.'

'Oh, that sounds great!' She smiled; this was very William – if he wanted to do something his single-mindedness was relentless.

'I have to go now. I'm travelling to California tomorrow for a conference, and then on to Hawaii on Friday for the sales kick off. So I may not be able to call you every day.'

'No chance you can come here for Qingming then,' she murmured.

'Sorry, you broke up?'

'Nothing, darling.' It would be nice to sweep ancestors' tombs together, fulfilling a bit of filial piety, and it would make Grandma happy. *Grr, filial piety…* She shook her head. 'Have a safe trip! I'm going to be busy too. Just call me when you can. Love you.'

'Love you more than yours!'

Jade-Lotus put the phone down, and shut her eyes, as if wanting to bask in the warm sunrays of his love for a little longer. The longing for him intensified, plucking at every heart string, just like meeting him for the first time had all those years ago.

Jade-Lotus softly sang 'Say You, Say Me' on her way back to the office. The breeze on the campus was warm, scented with lilac wisteria. *What a nice song, the lyrics are so memorable. How did Snow-Flower manage to get the original cassette from the US?*

'… Xi… zh-u… ren?' A foreigner tried to speak Chinese just

167

ahead of her.

'We don't understand,' two young men answered in Chinese.

'The dean's office please?'

'We no English.'

Jade-Lotus looked up. A tall blond-haired man stood looking lost while the Chinese students he was trying to communicate with waved their arms.

She hurried over and the students shrugged and left. In front of her stood a rather handsome young man. His blue eyes sparkled.

'Do – do you speak Chinese? Sorry, silly me, I mean English?' he asked. He put his hands into his trouser pockets, but immediately took them out; he hid them behind his back before holding them together in front of him.

She smiled. 'Yes, I do. I speak both. Where do you want to go?'

'Oh great. I have a meeting with the dean in his office.'

'I can take you there. I work in the same building. We can take a shortcut over there.'

'Oh, is there a longer route? Sorry, I'm a bit early.'

She giggled. 'Of course, we can carry on here along the lake if you want to kill some time. The lake is pretty, full of fresh lotus.'

They walked side by side along the path.

'Your English is superb; did you say you work here?' William said.

'I'm an English lecturer.' She smiled again. 'What brought you to Beijing University?'

'Oh, I'm setting up a programme for my company to take on the best graduates.'

Silence fell between them.

168

'Oh, I – I'm William Hampshire by the way.' He stretched his hand towards her.

'I'm Jade-Lotus Yang.' As she shook his hand the tips of her fingers tingled. Something stirred inside, like a gentle wind teasing a calm lake.

'Beautiful lotus – sorry, I mean your name.' His face reddened.

She giggled again. 'In my hometown in the south there are a lot of lotus plants, their leaves as green as Jade. I'm named after them.'

He turned to look at her, but suddenly lost his balance. Without thinking she grabbed his hand and pulled him towards her. His chin brushed her hair and for a moment his hand firmly held hers and their eyes met. She felt her face burning, and gently took her hand back as William steadied himself. In awkward silence they resumed their walk.

'You saved my life! Thank you,' William said.

'You're welcome.'

'In my country we worship our saviours. Am I allowed to worship you?'

That was a cheesy chat up line, but it didn't matter. She nodded with a smile, feeling her face burning again, as hot as the sun in the sky.

Jade-Lotus touched her face, as if it was still burning. It had been great being a Yin and Yang, a complementary oneness, in every step of life, always working towards the same goals. Now William was making good progress; it was time to step things up. It was three weeks to Qingming; three weeks to find something to tell Mama.

Jade-Lotus hurried to find Little-Blossom, hoping for some news from Mad Girl's aunt. She knocked on the door of her cousin's house, but nobody answered. She hesitated for a moment, then headed off to the Shan Academy.

It was a bright morning. Fog-capped hills in the far distance were faintly visible, as if in an ink-wash painting; vibrant pink cherry-blossom trees added a finishing touch to the otherwise lush green vegetation and deep-blue lake, as if dotting the eye on a painted dragon. She sped up; the campus loomed ahead.

But the grey Russian-style two-story building, that had been quickly erected in the mid-sixties and used as a primary and middle school, had disappeared. In its place stretched a grass field, on which a game of football was being played at one end and rows of students practiced Tai chi at the other. She stopped and looked around. It should be a great feeling, shouldn't it? The horrible building was gone; nothing to render people into powerless potatoes, ready to be sliced, chopped and harshly stewed, like in the past. But a kind of disappointment brewed. After years of digesting, forgetting, and preparing to face that old hell, there was nothing to see. It was as if a severely beaten kung-fu fighter had jumped up to strike back, but was unable to find the opponent. She sighed and resumed her walk. Once down the little hill, she stopped again. Her eyes widened. The once dormant, but prominent Qing courtyard houses – the original academy – had woken up. Their swooping roofs glistened like jade; yellow roof-ridges crawled like dragons. They had used to be boarded up, left to deteriorate, and used to punish students like her: 'Go to stand in front of the feudal rot, and cleanse your dirty unrepentant black mind!' But the grey bricks of the courtyard walls, the silent houses behind the gate, the flowering dandelions in the crevices and the morning dew on spider webs had been somehow soothing and inspirational, much better than being duck-fed red communism in the stuffy classroom. In the distance, at the foot of the dark hills, the white Mongolian pagoda was still there, head held up high, seemingly content with its restored kingdom. An oath had been sworn with Snow-Flower and River-Cloud, 'I, solemnly promise, in front this sacred ancient pagoda, that I'll always be your friend.' Even though the pagoda's head had been missing at the time, a legacy of the Cultural Revolution.

She arrived at the moongate; the slate nameplate above the round arch announced Shan Academy. No longer a 'wild west' with lizards, snakes and other creatures hiding in the tall grass, the courtyard looked manicured and spacious with neat beds of blossoming camellias and magnolias. The surrounding two-story buildings were beautifully restored, humming with teachers and students. She crossed the courtyard and came to a Ming-vase-shaped doorway, an entrance to another courtyard building named Gardener's Place. The couplet, written vertically either side of the arch, was an old poem: 'A spring silkworm won't stop spinning silk until its death; a candle burns on till all its tears dry up.' Although a poem about love, it had long been used to describe the dedication of teachers. Indeed, she saluted all good teachers! Through the doorway the courtyard was more intimate; a cross-shaped slab path sectioned it into four areas of disciplined bonsais. A tall man in a long dark robe stood on the top step of the main building, the principal's office, staring at the adjacent building.

'Hi River-Cloud.' Jade-Lotus waved and hurried towards him.

'Oh, hello,' he answered, continuing his stare.

'What are you doing?' Jade-Lotus climbed the steps.

He didn't answer, and just pushed up his spectacles.

She followed his eyes and through the large lattice window saw Little-Blossom having an intense conversation with a man in a suit. 'Is she OK?'

'I hope so,' he said without turning.

'You hope so?' She raised her voice.

River-Cloud turned to Jade-Lotus. 'Oh, Little-Blossom is... is talking to our bank manager.' He reddened. 'Do you want her?'

She nodded.

'She should finish soon, very soon,' he murmured looking at his watch.

'I can wait.' As silence sprouted between them, Jade-Lotus looked up at the intricately carved fascia. Out of the corner of her eye, she saw River-Cloud still looking at his wife. 'Are you worrying she'll run away with the bank manager?'

River-Cloud laughed and pushed up his spectacles again. 'OK, let's wait inside.'

Jade-Lotus followed him into his office. 'Goodness, what a palace!'

'Haha, not that grand.' His quiff bounced and his lips curled into a smile. 'You like my restoration?' He brightened up.

'No, I don't like it.' Jade-Lotus paused to watch him frown. 'I love it!'

'Thank Buddha!' He rolled his eyes before gesturing towards the bay-window area where a throne-like cushioned bench was flanked by a pair of horseshoe chairs. As they sat down, he continued, 'I wanted to do justice to its history as the top place to educate the top students.' His neck grew taller in its mandarin collar, but fell back again as he sighed. For some reason he looked like he was stroking a floaty beard, but he didn't have one. 'So, how's life being back here again?'

'Great,' she said.

He said nothing, his eyes penetrating, although kindly, just like all those years ago in primary school.

'OK, OK. Everything is difficult, and I'm stuck, so I've come to see if Little-Blossom has found Mad Girl.'

He got up, piled his hands together behind his back and paced. '"The winding mountain road in Sichuan is *difficult*, maybe more so than scaling up to heaven",' he recited a Li Po poem, 'but we're in a small canal town.' He patted her shoulder as he walked past; his slim long-robed back looked as if it belonged to a different era and a different person, like in a film about the old literati. He stopped at the window and looked out again, before turning to the nearby drum-shaped stool. He sat down and plucked the strings of a guzheng that lay flat on a wooden frame in front of him. At once, a cascading waterfall bubbled down, hitting rocks along its way before joining the river...

Jade-Lotus went over quietly and watched him pluck away. His eyes were shut, his quiff bounced with each note. The fatter end of the chestnut-coloured guzheng reflected the dappled sunlight, its mother-of-pearl inlay of a blooming lotus coming alive, as if floating in the river he had just created. The formidable walls of the room crumbled, revealing fishermen returning in a rosy sunset, happily singing, their nets full of jumping fish...

When he pressed down on all the strings, and the last note gradually faded, she clapped. 'Bravo! Wow, you've mastered the guzheng. I remember Grandma tried to teach us both in secret.'

'Oh yes, hemp strings on a washing board; no wonder we both gave up so quickly.' He massaged the tip of his fingers. 'A few years ago, Grandpa Autumn-Rain gave me some lessons on a proper guzheng, and I've been hooked ever since. I play all the time, even in my dreams.' He laughed.

'You play really well! Bet Little-Blossom is impressed.'

'Hm.' He stared at his hands. 'Jade-Lotus, do you think a man is a real man if he just wants to play guzheng?'

'Of course, there are professionals.' Seeing him gently stroking a string, she added, 'Oh, is that what you want to do?'

He chewed his lip and eventually nodded.

The office door opened and Little-Blossom came in.

River-Cloud jumped up, rushed to fluff up the scatter cushions on the bench and gestured for his wife to sit down. 'So? Did he agree to extra time?'

Little-Blossom slumped onto the cushions and let out a big sigh. 'No, he was sharper than shark's tooth. One month, and that's all we have.' When she saw Jade-Lotus, she blushed.

Jade-Lotus came to sit next to her. 'Everything OK?'

'Ah ah, it's just a work thing.' Little-Blossom said quickly, brushing a piece of fluff from her lapel. 'Oh, I managed to talk to Mad Girl's aunt.'

'And?'

'Unfortunately, she doesn't want to help. I'm the bearer of bad news, sorry.'

'Did she say why?'

'She's not really against you. It's just after what happened to her niece, she hates everyone in Blushing Lotus, and you taking Mark Lee's boat didn't help.'

'Oh, so she thinks Mark Lee and I are jackals from the same hilltop?' Jade-Lotus said hotly. 'Can't people just stop assuming!' She breathed loudly. 'Our light from the hole in the wall has gone.'

Silence fell.

'Well, I remember someone who'd never stop until she reached the Yellow River,' River-Cloud said, looking across at Jade-Lotus. 'I'm sure you'll find Mad Girl one way or another.'

Little-Blossom nodded.

Jade-Lotus stared at them.   In the torchlight of their friendship, it would be OK to march into the dark night.

'What do we do now?' Little-Blossom asked gently.

'OK. I'll ask Grandma to ask her teahouse customers again. Besides that… do you think you could try Nine-Pound Old Lady?'

'Of course, no harm trying I guess.'

'Can I do anything to help?' River-Cloud said.

'I don't know what you could do, so not at the moment, thanks,' Jade-Lotus said.

A week went by. Finding Mad Girl was like trying to spot the legendary yellow crane.

Another week passed. It would have been easier to find an auspicious qilin-shaped bronze weight in a deep well. And Nine-Pound Old Lady had finally answered Little-Blossom, 'I wish I knew something, so I could enjoy flatly refusing that bad-fate girl even more.'

At the end of the third week, Snow-Flower confirmed that there was no official record of Mark Lee having had a brother.

Qingming came; it drizzled, just like on all other Qingmings.

175

'Do you think the weather god knows it's Qingming?' Jade-Lotus said on the way to the ancestral hall, carrying a heavy picnic basket.

'The sad ghosts must have nagged her,' Grandma said, carrying another full basket.

The feathery mist fluttered; their footsteps echoed beside the lake.

'Do you still remember the old ancestral hall, my little treasure?'

'Yeah. Not really a hall, is it? More like a ruin.'

'Ah, that was a long time ago. I can't remember the last time we visited it together.'

'I remember. I think it was the last time I came home for the Spring Festival, before I started working, so 1989.'

'So long ago.'

'Yes, a very long time ago.'

Once they passed the lake the drizzle stopped and the sun peeped out to paint a rainbow. Ahead, among the steaming tea bushes, white-walled courtyard houses nestled at the foot of the hills; the gatehouse, with a flying green-tiled roof, matched the one to their main house. Supported by the solid hills, softened by a half-moon-shaped pond to the front, and guarded by the family graveyard to one side, Grandma had always said the hall had excellent feng shui – the ancestors had chosen well.

They climbed the gentle slope to the gatehouse. As Grandma fumbled for the key to open the butterfly lock, Jade-Lotus sniffed; the camphor smell from the thick wooden doors was so strong it would definitely deter intruders, alive or dead. Once inside, the courtyard was surprisingly clean and spacious, neat white azaleas lining the walls. Right in

176

the centre at the back was the ancestral hall itself; with its flamboyant roof, varnished lattice doors and windows, it wouldn't have looked out of place in the Summer Palace in Beijing.

'You refurbished the whole place?' Jade-Lotus said.

'Yes. It's the least we can do.'

Jade-Lotus looked at Grandma, but didn't say anything. Grandma had always been filial, the only pillar holding up the family traditions. When meeting William's parents for the first time, William's mother, Georgina, proudly introduced the people in the big painted portraits lining the wall of the sweeping staircase in her house and animatedly told the glorious stories and colourful scandals of the Hampshire family. Georgina then said, 'You must have a lot of ancestors too.' She had just nodded without offering more.

'We'll cleanse our hands first,' Grandma said, heading to the well in the corner.

'Isn't there a ghost in the well?' Jade-Lotus hesitated. Grandma had said the reason that the whole place hadn't been burned down was because of the rumour of a resident ghost, of whom even the Red Guards had been scared.

'I've never met one.' Grandma dropped a small wooden barrel into the well. 'Even if there is, it's our family's ghost, it won't hurt us.'

Could it now be Mama's ghost? That would be a nicer ghost. But would it be disappointed that Jade-Lotus had made no real progress finding out what had happened? Jade-Lotus turned the handle and helped to draw the barrel up.

Once their hands were cleansed, they walked across the courtyard to the ancestral hall.

Jade-Lotus slowed down as they approached the big stone

threshold; on the other side, the Yang ancestors would all be there waiting, and probably scowling. Growing up, they had been a heavy black wok on her back; like a snail, making progress had been really hard. Grandma had never said much about the ancestors, thank goodness. The politics lesson every day in school had taught her to hate them.

The inside of the hall had the aura of an art gallery; painted portraits lined the walls. Right at the centre against the back wall was a long black altar table on which small tablets stood neatly and solemnly on tiered steps. Above them hung a long roll of Chinese painting in a silk frame, flanked by a pair of calligraphy scrolls that made an antithetical couplet. The painting looked familiar, yes: it was the one Grandma had always brought out and hung in the sitting room for a short time at each festival. It was Grandma's favourite ancestral portrait, by a famous Qing court painter. Although its background had yellowed and one corner peeled back a little, the proud rider, sat on a white horse, was vivid and handsome. 'What a hero my Manchu great great grandfather was!' Grandma would say.

Grandma opened the shutters; light flooded in. All the male ancestors in the portraits looked robust and prosperous; no wonder the communists had accused them of being exploiters. Surprisingly, there was also a lady in a black-and-white photo, wearing a long Qing embroidered robe, her unbound feet encased in platform shoes, and her head decorated with a magnificent headdress. A framed page hung below the photo, with brushed ink characters snuggling tightly together. Just as she leaned closer to read it, Grandma said, 'That was my grand nana, a fascinating royal lady; and thanks to her, all women in our family escaped bound feet.'

178

'Oh, I see,' Jade-Lotus said, thinking of Nine-Pound Old Lady's feet.

'All the ancestors I know of are here, and each has their life story on a page.'

'Is Mama here too?' Mama's name was still in red on her gravestone.

Grandma sighed. 'Over there, but her page is empty.' She stared across as if to say, it's all down to you now.

Mama's portrait was her graduation photo, the same one as in her bedroom. The blank page was conspicuously white.

Grandma took the offerings from the baskets and placed them carefully on the altar – a vase of fresh willow branches, a gilded lacquer bowl full of thumb-sized golden papier-mâché yuanbao, a jar of yellow wine, two glasses, a plate of green sticky-rice cake cubes, a platter of colourful fresh fruits, and small plates of sliced cured duck, deep fried whole carp, salted duck eggs and sautéed snails. There had never been anything like this much to offer before.

Jade-Lotus lit the candles and incense sticks; Grandma began to softly chant Buddhist scripts. In the fragrant smoke, the ancestors' faces appeared intermittently, their eyes staring sternly. Were they angry? Was it time to get to know them and show them some well-deserved respect? William's family history could be traced back over three hundred years and there were three books about it! Now there was a baby on the way, and when she grew up, she would probably want to know where the family had come from, and need the solid foundation of being a Yang rather than teetering on stilts like her mum. Grandma had curated every ancestor's story; it was time to fill Mama's blank page. Aihh, a whole month had passed, but progress to find the truth was like a donkey going round and round a millstone. It was as if there was an invisible net preventing it being uncovered, or an unseen hand putting up a big stop sign. Perhaps it would be easier to just lay down the dagger and beat the court drum to adjourn. But Grandma needed to know and her future daughter needed to know too.

'We'd better go and sweep the tombs before the drizzle comes back,' Grandma said after their final bow.

As they swept the already tidy and clean tombstone of Mama, and put more green willow shoots in the water pot, Jade-Lotus stared at the red characters of Peony-Grace Lu, and made a promise. 'I'll find out, Mama, I will.'

But how?

Sombre Qingming came to an end; the night stretched out long and shadowy. Under the crescent moon ghosts hurried back to the other world; brooding insects hummed, searching for blood. Jade-Lotus climbed into her mosquito-netted bed, and opened her copy of *Jane Eyre*. *Ah, where did I get to?* It had been a while. She turned the pages, managed to find the small leaf bookmark that was buried in the book and began to read Chapter 11, but the letters became ant-like and crawled away. Would Mad Girl come to wail on this damp Qingming night? Each reachable stone had been upturned and every plausible strand had led nowhere.

A strange sound drifted in; she stretched to listen, but it went away. She stared back at her book, but the sound came again: 'Aaaiiiyaaa…' She threw down her book and listened more intently. 'Aiiiiyaaa, you bastard… aaaiiiyaaa…' It was just like the moan on the night of Lantern Festival. She jumped off the bed and opened the window wide, risking being nibbled by mosquitos. 'Aiiiiyaaa, you bloody killer…

180

Heaven punishes you! Aaaiiiyaaa…' *Oh my gosh! It is Mad Girl!* She rushed out, but quickly rushed back to put on her shoes and grabbed a torch. Oh, women shouldn't go out alone after dark, particularly not on the night of Qingming and definitely not in pyjamas. Sod it! Jade-Lotus ran out of gate, following the wailing onto the main street. The streetlights were dim; the dark river hissed next to her. The wailing stopped; Jade-Lotus stopped too, catching her breath. *Where is she?* The night was quiet; the shutting of the nearby houses' windows was conspicuously loud. *Where did she go?* A breathless sob close by broke the darkness; Jade-Lotus turned around slowly. At the corner of a lane just off the main street, a ghostly shadow moved slightly on a whitewashed wall. Jade-Lotus quickly shone her torch at the shadow; a small-framed woman sitting on the floor put up her arm to hide her eyes.

'Hi there, are you…' Jade-Lotus stopped; it would be too rude to call her mad right to her face. 'Are you OK?' She moved the torch beam away.

The woman dropped her arm. She looked about thirty-five or -six, with a bony pale face and boyish short hair ruffled on top. Wiping away a tear with her hand she sneered, 'What do you care? Go away!'

'I need to talk to you.'

'I know who you are, and I'm not talking to you. You're running with the wolves!' She gritted her teeth, her face icy.

'What do you mean?'

'You took their boat to the Lantern Fair, I saw you! And they wined and dined you, I heard.' She spat onto the floor.

'Ah, it's not what it looks like,' Jade-Lotus sighed, 'I'm definitely not with them, quite the opposite…'

'You think I believe you?'

181

Jade-Lotus sat down next to her, standing the torch on the floor between them, beaming into the dark sky.

Mad Girl stared sternly at her but didn't move away.

'I assume you know that I'm back here to adopt my cousin's baby?'

'Yes, I heard.'

'Mark Lee needs my help, and won't approve the adoption unless I do something for him. He pretended to be welcoming by sending his boat and buying us lunch, but his real intention was to get my husband William to attract foreign investment for him.'

'Really? And you've agreed to it?'

Jade-Lotus nodded.

Mad Girl sneered again. 'You're still running with the wolves.' She looked away.

'Aihh, I don't blame you for saying that. You know Mark Lee better than me; we really have no choice but to play his game. The only consolation for us is that we are doing it for Blushing Lotus, not just him.'

Mad Girl was quiet, her breathing still heavy.

The night exuded spring dampness; insects circled above the torch.

'I know you were married to High-Fly, and what the Lees did to your baby girl. I can't imagine the pain and grief you've been through, I'm really sorry.'

Mad Girl turned to stare at her. 'Why are you sorry?'

'Because what they did was totally wrong and ghastly!'

'You're the first person to say that. Everyone pointed their finger at me, even my parents. How mad is that! And they called me Mad Girl! All I do is moan for my daughter to remind them about what they did to me.' She gritted her teeth

182

again.

'That's this stupid small town for you.' Jade-Lotus sighed and put her arm around Mad Girl, who didn't shirk; together they sat in silence. 'Sorry, I don't even know your name.'

'New-Dawn Chen.'

'New-Dawn, I need your help.'

'How can I possibly help you?' Her tone had softened somewhat.

'I'm trying to find out what happened to my mama back in 1969; I think Mark Lee is covering something up.'

New-Dawn sat up straight, her eyes shining. 'I'm listening.'

'You used to live with them, so I thought you might know something, like where Mark Lee's younger brother is.'

'High-Fly had no uncle on his father's side.' New-Dawn shook her head, 'I was constantly reminded that Mark Lee was the only son, High-Fly the only seed, and that's why we had to have a son. Humph!'

'Really!'

New-Dawn stared at Jade-Lotus for a moment. 'Is there anything else I can help you with? I hate that devil Mark Lee so much; I'd give anything to see him fall!'

'Not for the moment, but thank you. It's getting late, can I walk you home?'

'No thanks, I'm fine. Will you promise to tell me if you get anything on him?'

'Yes, of course. Good night, New-Dawn!'

14

Shanghai Shock

Once slumped into the seat, Jade-Lotus held her hand over her chest, the adrenalin of running onto the platform and squeezing through the shutting train door pumping around her body. Thank goodness! She had caught the last fast train in the morning rush hour to Shanghai. Mother Li's husky voice on the phone earlier whispered again, 'Please come, please, please come quickly and don't tell the Shans.' What had happened? Why hadn't Snow-Flower gone to sweep Wave Wang's family tombs yesterday – a tradition utterly unmissable for a daughter-in-law on Qingming – and instead locked herself in the bedroom, refusing food and water? What could really have happened to her friend with four Ps?

Raindrops' fat faces streamed into horizontal tears on the train window like a surrealist painting, intensified by the misty greyness that seemed to be trying to extend Qingming. What could have happened to Snow-Flower, really? Yes, she could be dramatic sometimes, but it was so unlike her to have not shown up at the Wang's family graveyard. After all,

Qingming was the one day that everyone submits themselves to the tradition of respecting their dead ancestors. And Snow-Flower had taken pride in always being the first of the Wang clan to turn up and light the incense. So, it would have to be something horrible that had happened to her. Hmm, but what horrible thing? On top of Pretty face, Professional job, Perfect husband and Powerful connections, Snow-Flower was also intelligent, loveable, polished and slick in all social situations; she was simply indestructible, incredibly strong and steadfast, refusing to be victimised by anything. And in the search for Mama, Snow-Flower was an important pillar, with her journalistic approach and ability to keep up everyone's morale. Jade-Lotus felt her face burning. That was selfish. Whatever had happened, Snow-Flower wouldn't have to face it alone. The train slowed down to approach the platform; the sweaty sign outside said 'Shanghai'.

As the lift doors opened, Mother Li appeared instantly from Snow-Flower's apartment and waved to Jade-Lotus to hurry. She looked older, her face tear-stained and the scar on her cheek raw. With her palms together in a praying position she sighed and said, 'Thank Buddha!'

   With no lights on, the hall was dark and gloomy; Jade-Lotus entered, quickly took off her jacket and changed into the slippers.

   'Ahya, she's still in her bedroom,' Mother Li mumbled, setting off at such a pace that Jade-Lotus had to run after her. 'My Buddha, she won't open the door.'

   Jade-Lotus knocked gently. 'Snow-Flower, it's me. Can I come in please?'

   They waited, but there was no response.

185

Jade-Lotus raised her hand again, but didn't knock. 'I found Mad Girl! Do you want to know what she said?'

Mother Li looked on anxiously.

Eventually the door opened, and Snow-Flower appeared: black silk pyjamas dangled from her sharp bones, her long hair now untidily cropped, her face extremely pale and her eyes bloodshot.

'Ohmygosh!' Jade-Lotus exclaimed.

'Oh Buddha, what happened to your hair?' Mother Li screamed.

'Chopped off,' Snow-Flower said weakly, shrugging. 'Why are you here, Jade-Lotus?' Seeing Mother Li standing help-lessly by, she added softly, 'Can you please cook us some hot soup-noodles? I'm hungry.'

With tears welling up Mother Li headed off, almost running again.

Jade-Lotus closed the door behind her, looked around the room and said, 'Oh!' The spotless bedroom, with two walls of mirrored wardrobes and a tennis-court-sized, cream-rugged changing area, that had been one of the tour highlights last time, seemed to have been bombed. A mountainous pile lay in the middle of the rug; three large suitcases stood to one side. 'Are you moving house?'

Snow-Flower didn't answer, and just continued her zigzag march.

Jade-Lotus followed. The teetering mountain was in fact made of lots of shoe boxes. It looked like someone had used them to build a tall wall on one side and a short one on the other, then an earthquake had struck, both walls collapsed, and some of the lovely shoes involuntarily jumped out. The mirrored wardrobe doors that were guarding the pile had giant characters on them, smeared in what looked like red lipstick: 'BASTARD!' on the left and 'SHAME!' on the right.

Snow-Flower finally stopped at the cream leather sofa by the bay window overlooking the misty river below. She sat down on one end and tilted her head to signal Jade-Lotus to sit down too. But the rest of sofa was covered with a half-empty tissue box, a laptop, a mobile phone and a photo album.

Jade-Lotus chose the adjacent chair instead.

Snow-Flower just sat there like a statue, staring out of the window. Her cropped hair stuck up here and there, her fringe looked like it had been chewed by a dog, her face was puffy and unwashed, and her eyes were those of a heavy drinker starved of sleep. *Hmm, this is so unlike her.*

Jade-Lotus got up, moved a few things from the sofa, sat down next to her and sniffed the air.

'I haven't been drinking!' Snow-Flower snapped.

'OK, then tell me what's going on.'

Snow-Flower looked in Jade-Lotus's direction, her eyes blank, before turning back to the window again.

Outside, a mist drifted amongst the indistinct old buildings of the Bund, floating towards the river.

Jade-Lotus twisted her bottom; the sofa squeaked. It was really heart-wrenching to see her friend like this, but it would be unkind to press her.

'What did Mad Girl say?' Snow-Flower eventually muttered.

My old friend is coming back. Jade-Lotus stretched a smile and said, 'You won't believe how I met her…' She told the story at great length and in minute detail, as if this might distract Snow-Flower from whatever she was going through.

'So, the bottom line is she knew nothing,' Snow-Flower said

sharply.

'Well, yes, you could say that. I don't feel New-Dawn is mad though. Calling her Mad Girl is more a reflection on the townspeople, don't you think?' *This might get her talking; Snow-Flower can never resist a social debate.*

Snow-Flower didn't answer, just bit her nail; the bright pink varnish was already chipped. As her face tightened and reddened, she started crying and sobbed out, 'Mad, they're all mad!'

Jade-Lotus hugged Snow-Flower, who heaved with sobs. Outside was grey, inside was grey too. She gently patted her back until the flood of tears became a quieter stream. 'What's happened?' she whispered.

Snow-Flower let out another big sob. 'I'm – I'm – I'm going to divorce that egg of a turtle, bastard of a bear! I – I want to kill him, cut his heart into pieces and feed it to dogs!' she blubbered, wiping tears and snot onto Jade-Lotus's jumper.

'What?' Jade-Lotus said. 'Di – divorce... your perfect husband?'

It was simply impossible! Their marriage had been perfect with a capital P, the precise definition of what a good marriage should be, and the model that every mother and daughter in Blushing Lotus had aspired to. While doing a master's degree, way past her 'shelf life', Grandma had even used it to nudge her. Their fairy-tale love story had been passed around and around Blushing Lotus like a legend.

'Hello hello hello!' A young man wearing a dark baseball cap rushed to Snow-Flower; the peak of his cap was so low that it covered his eyes. 'Welcome, welcome, newcomer! I'm Grand Liu, the student chairman of the department. What's your lovely name?' He laughed. 'Our department has a tradition, which is every pretty newcomer has to be interviewed by senior students.'

'Ignore him,' another young man with long hair pushed forward and said, 'he is abusing his fake power.' He smiled a sunny smile, throwing back his hair. 'Just relax, this is only the Meet and Weed. Hey, Chaiman Liu, you're ruining the reputation of the Journalism department.'

'But you two are ruining the reputation of Fudan University,' shouted another young man with wraparound sunglasses, who had just squeezed through the small gathering of young men on the playing field where Snow-Flower stood. 'I'd ignore both of them if I were you.' He grinned, showing his horse-like front teeth.

Snow-Flower just smiled and waved. 'Hello everyone! I'm Snow-Flower Shan. I'm really glad to meet you all. I have to say this Meet and Weed is a great event for us "newcomers" to meet you "old stayers". But it looks like I'm behind everyone else on clearing up my patch, are you all here to help?' Her dimples deepened.

'Of course, I'll help you!' each young man shouted, striving to be the first.

Snow-Flower bent down to work, pulling out knobs of weeds. After a couple of minutes, she screamed, 'Ouch!'

A disoriented bee flew up.

Her arm became red and swollen, and she cried.

The charming flock of senior students just watched, with their mouths dropped open.

A jogging student in a tracksuit stopped in front of them and asked, 'Do you need help?'

The young men quickly stepped aside and Snow-Flower

looked up. It was as if a Chinese Han Solo had dropped out of the sky.

He didn't wait for her answer, knelt down, examined her arm and commanded, 'Someone go and get me a bar of soap, quick!' He then poured some water from his drinking bottle onto her arm and sucked the swelling.

Snow-Flower blushed as the handsome student worked on her arm, while the flock watched on with wide eyes. Strangely, the pain was gone.

'My grandma taught me this,' he explained as one of the flock returned with the soap. He rubbed the bar onto her wound and said gently, 'You'll be OK in a couple of hours, but you need to stay still to stop the poison spreading. Perhaps someone should carry you inside?' He looked around, but none of the flock moved. He lifted Snow-Flower up and, carrying her in his arms, headed off towards her dormitory. 'I'm Wave Wang, by the way.'

Snow-Flower just wrapped her arms around his neck and rested her burning face onto his broad chest, hoping the walk would last forever...

That walk had certainly lasted. A year after their meeting, Wave Wang had graduated in law, top of his class, and because of his father was offered a position as a junior judge in Zhejiang province. But he turned it down and took a district government job in Shanghai so he could be with Snow-Flower until she finished her degree. After she graduated, and got a job as a newsreader at Shanghai TV, they got married and lived the city life to the full...

Snow-Flower finally stopped sobbing and sat up.

'Why?' Jade-Lotus cried out.

Snow-Flower didn't answer, and just twisted the end of her damp sleeve until it was tightly wound. It was as if she was trying to wring out her tears or bitterness; her knuckles were white. 'He cheated on me,' she muttered.

Jade-Lotus almost fell off the sofa. 'What? It can't be! It can't be…' How could their perfect bone-china marriage ever be chipped? 'How? I mean what happened?'

Snow-Flower remained silent, her finger nails digging into the back of her firmly clasped hands.

'Oh.' Jade-Lotus put her arm around Snow-Flower's shoulder, who leaned back onto her. 'Um, how did he…?' She swallowed hard.

'He and his assistant had – had…'

'An affair?'

'No!' Snow-Flower snapped, pushing away from Jade-Lotus. 'A one-night stand! Drunk and stupid!'

'OK. But, um… how did you find out?'

'He called and told me. Bastard! Fucking bastard! F…' Snow-Flower raised her voice; the air seemed to vibrate, like evening haze in the desert. She hammered down her fists on the sofa like it was a drum, 'Bastard, bastard! How could he do this to me!' She collapsed and buried her face in her hands.

Jade-Lotus held on to Snow-Flower; a thistle pricked her heart. 'I'm so, so sorry,' she whispered. There were no words that could make her feel better.

Snow-Flower grasped Jade-Lotus's hands forcefully, as if needing some extra strength. She slowly rose up and stared blankly out of the window again. 'It got worse,' she mumbled, a tear rolling down her cheek.

'Worse?'

'The girl is pregnant.'

'Oh!'

'It's a boy and he wants *us* to keep it!' With her eyes fixed somewhere far away, and her hands white, Snow-Flower looked like an ice statue. 'His parents were ecstatic; they always hated us for choosing a childless life. The assistant is young and doesn't want the child or Wave, so she offered him to us.'

'Oh I see!' Jade-Lotus found her own tone icy too.

'Speechless! I was totally speechless! I didn't even notice when he hung up. I just sat there, my mind totally blank, till my alarm clock went off. It was 4 a.m. on Qingming, and in an hour's time, my driver would come and pick me up, and drive me all the way to the family's graveyard in Zhejiang. I got angry. Furious.' She gestured to the mirrors. 'I'd done this. I couldn't face leaving. I told the driver to take the day off. Suddenly I was so tired and empty. On the day we mourn the dead, I felt my marriage was dead. Fucking dead!' She glared up at the ceiling and blinked hard.

It was dark and gloomy, the air damp and stifling. The aftershocks after an earthquake were turbulent. Jade-Lotus gently stroked Snow-Flower's back, tears forming in her own eyes.

'My head was all mushy, it was like I'd been hit with a stick; my legs turned to noodles. I collapsed onto the bed, covered my mouth with a pillow, screamed and cried. I've never cried that much in my whole life!' Snow-Flower wiped a tear with her sleeve. 'When I finally stopped, I felt so numb. Can you believe that I even thought about his wish for us to keep the baby? Can you believe that?' She stared hard with her big empty eyes before letting out a repressed sob. 'That way, his parents would be happy; we'd be together. I truly, truly love him, and I believe he truly loves me too.' Another tear rolled down and dropped onto her hand.

Jade-Lotus hugged her again. It wouldn't be a good idea to keep the baby, but she bit her tongue. There were so many ways to make a marriage happy; there was no right or wrong really.

After a little while Snow-Flower broke away and smiled weakly, as if to thank Jade-Lotus for not judging. 'I basked in this rosy delusion that I could be happy with it, but you know as well as I know, if it was a girl Wave would have aborted it and kept quiet. I went to visit him at the Spring Festival, for God's sake; he didn't say a word! Bastard! And his parents wouldn't be so involved and he wouldn't have wanted to risk breaking our marriage to keep it!' She balled her hands into fists, her chest heaving.

Jade-Lotus held Snow-Flower's fists, her throat a huge lump. Inside, it was as if an old dragon was clawing her heart.

'For so many years, I've worked hard to give a home and education to abandoned girls, to try to give them a voice, and to try to educate people that baby girls are just as good as baby boys. Wave always supported me. How could he do this to me, eh? And how could I ever consider keeping the baby…?' Snow-Flower choked. '… but I can't face separating from Wave, I can't,' she blubbered, her face red and taut.

Jade-Lotus passed Snow-Flower some tissues. Were there any right words for a situation like this?

Snow-Flower wiped her face, blew her nose loudly. 'I don't know what to do, I really don't know. I even tried using my shoe boxes to help me decide.' She turned to the mess in her dressing area. 'But one wall is much taller than the other.'

Jade-Lotus widened her eyes staring at the earth-quaked walls; what answer would the tall wall represent? It would be the right one, but perhaps the painful one too. Saddened, she gazed back at her friend.

'Don't look at me like that,' Snow-Flower said. 'I know it's the right decision, but, but…' She took a heavy breath and sighed.

'What are those suitcases for?'

'I got angry again, wanting to remove every trace of Wave. I took a pair of scissors out and cut off my long hair that he so loved; I got out every item of his clothes, the expensive dresses and jewellery he had bought me over the years too. I had a mad desire to burn it all in front of the Wang ancestors' tombs, but common sense came back. I'll set up a divorce dump on my charity website and sell everything in aid of my rescued girls.'

'Is it… um… a bit too soon? Maybe you two can take some time and work it out?'

Snow-Flower turned and stared at Jade-Lotus for a long minute, as if considering it, before shaking her head firmly. 'No. I can only see broken hearts. However much he apologises, it would never be enough. He shot two arrows into my heart. He's a pig! A wolf! A bastard!' She sobbed.

'But please, please take time to think about it?' Jade-Lotus helped to wipe Snow-Flower's face with a clean tissue.

Eventually Snow-Flower sat up. They sat in silence, staring down at the river outside the window. It had started as a fresh Himalayan spring, but had gathered rubbish on its long journey and looked repulsive. Now it was heading to the East Sea, to join the blue ocean and be purified. Right in front of them however, it was murky.

There was a loud knock at the door, and they heard Mother Li's muffled voice from the other side. 'Noodles are ready.'

'We'll be right there,' Snow-Flower shouted, and quickly wiped her face and combed her short hair with her fingers. As she put her dressing gown on, she added, 'Not a word to Mother Li, OK?'

'She seems to care a lot about you,' Jade-Lotus said.

'Exactly. Not a word.'

Mother Li turned and smiled as they entered the kitchen, the decorative beads on her hairpin sparkling in the kitchen light. She pointed at the table, where two bowls of steamy noodles beckoned, and said, 'Eat while they're still hot.'

'Thank you,' Jade-Lotus said to Mother Li, whose face blushed as she resumed her washing up.

'You made fresh noodles?' Snow-Flower said as they sat down at the table. 'They smell fantastic!'

Seeing Snow-Flower had colour returning to her face as she ate, Jade-Lotus leaned over and said, 'I should stay with you for the weekend.'

'Why?' Snow-Flower raised her head from her bowl. 'You want to feast on Mother Li's cooking?' She laughed dryly.

'I want to make sure you're OK.'

'What can you do? Sorry,' Snow-Flower squeezed out a quick smile. 'Look, I'm already two days behind at work. Tonight, I have to attend a gala, tomorrow an important charity do, and on Sunday I need to get back to work. See? I've no time for you – no offence.' She shrugged.

'But I'm worried,' Jade-Lotus said.

'Don't be. I'll be fine.' Snow-Flower gave a special stare, as if to remind Jade-Lotus not to continue to fuss. 'Now, tell me where we are with your mama.'

Jade-Lotus stared back at her and shook her head. 'Well, if you insist. We're stuck, completely. New-Dawn knew nothing, Grandma's customers had nothing. Little-Blossom even asked Nine-Pound Old Lady; again nothing. And you found no record of Mark Lee having a brother.'

A loud bang and crash made Jade-Lotus and Snow-Flower jump.

'Oh Buddha!' Mother Li shrilled. A large porcelain bowl was smashed to pieces on the tiled floor by the sink.

'Are you OK? Are you hurt?' Snow-Flower rushed over to Mother Li, whose face was completely white. Jade-Lotus followed, looking around to find a brush and pan.

'I'm sorry, so sorry. It slipped,' Mother Li murmured.

Jade-Lotus found a brush and pan. As she knelt down to collect the broken pieces, Mother Li bent down too. 'Please, let me.' She grabbed the brush and pan. 'Sorry!'

'It's OK,' Jade-Lotus said.

'Please go, don't let the noodles get cold,' Mother Li said, her voice trembling.

Snow-Flower stared at Mother Li, who seemed to want to be left alone, and said, 'OK then.' As they sat back down, she continued, 'So, where were we? Oh yes, stuck.' She studied her chopsticks for a while. 'We need to find a breakthrough. Let me think about it.'

'No, you have too much on your plate already. Little-Blossom and I will try to find a way.'

Snow-Flower shuffled her slippered feet and said, 'It'll be a good thing to distract me. You don't want me sinking back into my angry and sad state, do you?' She gave the sloth-eyed look.

'OK. But will you promise me that you'll take time to sort things out first?'

After she had finished sipping the last drop of soup, Snow-Flower nodded. 'You know, the Three-Legged Ding won't work if I'm missing?' She smiled weakly, her dimples blossoming. 'Have you finished? You'll have to leave soon; I don't want you to miss your train.'

'Really!' Jade-Lotus stared at her friend. This was so Snow-Flower, so stubborn and annoyingly strong. There was no way she would want help, not at the moment; to be honest, there wasn't much she could offer anyhow. She reached out and wrapped her little finger around Snow-Flower's. 'You promise?'

'Yes, I promise,' Snow-Flower said in a much softer tone, her eyes glittering.

Jade-Lotus was almost pushed out of door by Snow-Flower. As the train sped up, she looked out of the window. The drizzle had stopped; the sky was brighter, but still shrouded in grey. It had been a miserable day, inside and out. What had happened to Snow-Flower was a surprise, and no surprise really. It was really sad that in this land, beneath the ancient civilised, graceful and gentle culture, a girl's life was stamped from birth, like a slave's. The road for a leaf was indeed very long.

15

Ambushed From Ten Sides

Tall, whitewashed walls. A crumbling temple. A giant willow behind it waved and sighed, its leaves moulting. She pounds and pounds on the faded wooden door, the sound of babies crying growing louder...

Jade-Lotus was dazed, staring at the knotted ceiling of a mosquito net. *That dream again!* She pushed herself up. The light through the muslin curtains looked bright; the bedside clock said 11.30. *Gosh, the whole morning almost lost in sleep!* She rubbed her eyes. Yesterday in Shanghai, the emptiness and despair in her gut all the way home and the tossing and turning thinking about Snow-Flower all night resurfaced. Aihh! She flopped down like frost-bitten spinach. The curtains trembled in the gentle spring wind and the sun came out. They say tomorrow is another day; she just hoped Snow-Flower would be OK.

Hmm, that dream. How interesting, the first time it had come since being back. Perhaps it was really just a dream, nothing to do with Blushing Lotus; otherwise it might have occurred more often here. Or maybe the matter of Mama had been all-consuming. She took out her pendant and held it, feeling its warmth. Blazing down the highway to try to find out what happened to Mama hadn't got anywhere and now the brakes were firmly stuck on; also, the other two legs of the Ding had their plates full. She sighed, caressing the pendant.

There was a gentle knock on the bedroom door before it was pushed open and Grandma came in. 'Ahh, you're up. Morning!'

Jade-Lotus opened the mosquito net. 'Sorry, I overslept.'

'Don't worry, as long as you're OK.' Grandma tied up the net like a pair of curtains and sat down on the bed. 'Is Snow-Flower alright?'

'She just wanted to talk.' Jade-Lotus squeezed a small smile.

'Ah, you're her best friend. Now, do you want to get up so we can have lunch together?'

Jade-Lotus nodded. 'You still don't want me to help out in the teahouse?'

'No. I've got a good manager and staff. Just concentrate what you are here for, you know, the baby and Mama.'

'Grandma, um… you said that there's no crumbling temple under a willow near here, right?'

'Yes?' Grandma's eyebrows knitted together.

Jade-Lotus shrugged. 'It's just that dream is back.'

'Ah, but no. And for the hundredth time, no. Don't waste time on that silly dream,' Grandma said firmly, smoothing out the wrinkles of the silk duvet.

Jade-Lotus nodded; Grandma was right. A dream was just a dream, nothing more, nothing less.

'Come on, I've brought home some sautéed bamboo-shoots, your favourite tofu balls wrapped in lotus leaves and some of Mrs Song's fish soup.

'Lovely, I'll be right down.'

'Oh, William called. He'll call again at lunchtime; he has some good news.'

Jade-Lotus smiled. Good news was what was needed.

'What? You've lined up investors already, two of them?' Jade-Lotus screamed.

'Yes, yes,' William said, 'I've drafted the business plan and shared it with Nick and his friend in Hong Kong. They're super interested and they want to come and see for themselves. We'll have to impress them!'

'Oh my gosh, oh my gosh! It's all happening! And they're coming? How do we impress them? Let me think, let me think... well, Blushing Lotus, with all its traditions, is at its most impressive when there's a festival.'

'When's the next one?'

'Um... Duanwu, the Dragon Boat Festival, in two months' time, in June.'

'That sounds great – one us Westerners know about. I'll email you the plan to pass on to Mark Lee. Then you'll have to get everyone together to put on an amazing show.'

'OK, OK. Let me go and tell Little-Blossom, then we can start planning. Oh my gosh, I can't believe it! It's the best news, for now.'

'It is, isn't it? I'll say good night, it's nearly midnight here.'

'OK, darling. Sweet dreams!'

Buzzing with William's good news, Jade-Lotus hurried to find

Little-Blossom.

It was a tranquil afternoon; spring stretched idly in the garden. As she scurried through the gate to the Shans' garden, Jade-Lotus heard faint music, and soon enough, River-Cloud playing guzheng on a bench by the bamboo grove came into view. As she approached, the melody ended with a couple of rounds of soft strumming.

'Hi there, lovely music for a lovely day,' Jade-Lotus said.

'Hi,' River-Cloud replied lazily, pushing up his spectacles and staring through her.

'Um, are you all right?'

He nodded and stared back at his guzheng, his face sombre.

'OK, if you say so.' He was probably absorbed in his music. 'I need to see Little-Blossom.' She marched on.

'She's gone to the county town, for business,' River-Cloud shouted after her.

Jade-Lotus stopped in her tracks and turned around. 'On a Saturday?'

'Yes.' River-Cloud sighed loudly. 'She's gone to save my arse,' he mumbled.

'What?'

'Nothing.' River-Cloud looked up at the sun, squinting, his neck restrained by the high mandarin collar of his silk jacket.

'OK, when will she be back?'

'She's probably on her way now.' He plucked a guzheng string forcefully.

'Um, are you sure you're OK?'

'Yes, couldn't be better.'

'OK then, I'll come back later.' Jade-Lotus turned to walk back home.

A few steps later, the plucking turned into a brash strumming. Jade-Lotus stopped and listened. After a short pause, another heavy chord crashed into the air, then another and another; the pauses between each chord shortened, the notes came fast and wild. Hmm, the music sounded familiar... oh yes, it was a well-known classical piece about a historic battle over two thousand years ago. She turned and watched; River-Cloud played elegantly, his hands as light as a cat's paws, his eyes shut. The battlefield of Gaixia came alive: a moonless December night, bitter and quiet, patches of fog meandering; but the peace was suddenly broken by many tens of bugles, hundreds of drums and the hammering footsteps of thousands of soldiers. Silence fell again; King Xiang Yu of Chu had figured out that the Han soldiers, led by King Liu Bang, were surrounding them, and a vile ambush was about to happen. He paced, up and down, over and over again. His hundred thousand soldiers had been trapped in the town of Gaixia for a while, tired, hungry and scared, and the Han soldiers out there outnumbered his own troops by six to one. In years of endless fighting, he had never lost a battle; how had he got himself into this situation? He gritted his teeth and gave the order: fight to the bitter end. A bloody battle was soon in full swing, soldiers on both sides running, riding on horseback, shouting, beating their metal drums, attacking, chasing, throwing daggers and firing arrows. As his foot-soldiers battled, King Xiang Yu and his eight-hundred strong cavalry valiantly fought their way out, but soon they were lost, with no idea which direction to take. The winter night was freezing and the damp fog seeped through the steaming pores of both men and horses. Behind them, thousands of torches blazed and tens of thousands of Han soldiers fired endless arrows. Eventually King Xiang Yu found the path to the river and they ran for it. When they reached the river, however, the planned hundreds of waiting boats weren't there. There was just one small rowing boat. Everyone wanted the king to take the boat, but he just stood there, tears staining his dust-covered face. He stared at the twenty-six soldiers, all that was left of his cavalry, and the scene of his beloved concubine Yu-Ji killing herself right in front of him to avoid being captured played again in his mind. Beyond, the Han soldiers beat drums, sang Chu folksongs and shouted, 'Surrender, and you'll live!' But how would he be able to face his people at home? No! No! No! As the Han soldiers hemmed them in, King Xiang Yu stood tall in front of the fast-flowing river and shouted, 'Fight!' His troops fell one by one; having killed hundreds of enemies, King Xiang Yu finally slit his own throat with his dagger. All became quiet, deadly quiet, after River-Cloud strummed the final chord.

'Wow, "Ambushed from Ten Sides"! You played so well!' Jade-Lotus broke the silence.

River-Cloud glanced up at her, peeling off the picks taped to his fingers, and muttered, 'That's how I feel.'

Jade-Lotus frowned and came to sit down on the bench next to him. 'You're ambushed on ten sides? By whom?'

River-Cloud rubbed his finger nails and stared at them for what seemed ages, before squeezing out words through his teeth, 'I hate Qingming.'

Jade-Lotus stared at him waiting for an explanation, but his lips seemed to have zipped up, his eyes lacklustre.

'Well, I don't like Qingming either, but we have to remember the dead, don't we?' Jade-Lotus shrugged.

'I've no problem with the dead; it's the living and their stupid expectations that annoy me so much.'

'Who?'

River-Cloud didn't answer, breathing loudly.

'Am I one of them?'

'Haha, no.' River-Cloud shuffled his feet. 'Every year we do the ceremony, and I have to recite each ancestor's name, all twenty-two of them, all male. You see my problem?' He loosened the top button of his mandarin collar.

'What problem?'

'I've no male heir to be put on that stupid Shan genealogy! At the remembrance meal, "seven uncles and eight aunts" ganged up on me, as they do every year, asking me when I'm going to produce a son to carry on the family line. This afternoon, I went to see Nine-Pound Old Lady, and she ambushed me too!'

'Oh, I see.' Jade-Lotus could see the frozen face of the Shan's matriarch. 'I've never thought about men suffering from this stupid tradition.'

'Trust me, we men suffer too. Growing up I always felt the pressure of succeeding at this and that, and my ears seemed to grow a callus every time I heard, "I wish my son to become a dragon".' He sighed, a little melodramatically, and crossed his arms in front of his chest.

Jade-Lotus shook her head. It must be so uncomfortable to walk in his shoes; she stared at his big leather brogues.

'On top of not having a son, I'm also rubbish managing the academy,' he mumbled, staring at the floor. 'You'd laugh at me, because I made a mess of our finances, and Little-Blossom, pregnant, has had to go to the county town for a bridging loan!' He blushed. 'Everyone just automatically thinks I can manage the school, and carry on the glorious family business, just because I'm a son. No one wants to know what I want for my life.' His face was completely red now.

'What do you want?'

'I want, I want to live the life of the literati. There, I said it. And… and I want to play guzheng!'

'Well, you're really good at guzheng; what's stopping you?'

'The academy of course.'

'I'm sure Little-Blossom could manage the business, if you let her.'

River-Cloud pushed up his spectacles, thinking for a moment before lowering his head to examine his nails and said to his hand, 'The academy has always been managed by the son; and I can't let her shoulder such a heavy burden all by herself. Worse still, she might feel ashamed of me, a husband who isn't a real man.'

'Well, the tradition won't change itself, will it?' Jade-Lotus shrugged. 'And you might be surprised how strong and able your wife is.'

River-Cloud rubbed his hands without saying anything. He stared at the guzheng, seemingly in his own world as he nodded, shook his head and nodded again.

A soft clunk nearby made Jade-Lotus turn around, but there was nothing. 'I'd better get going. When Little-Blossom comes home, can you please tell her I popped by? I have some important things to tell her, and you, if you are interested.'

'OK,' River-Cloud said without raising his eyes.

Jade-Lotus got up and left. When she glanced back River-Cloud was still deep in thought.

16

Willows Shading, Flowers Brightening

Why hadn't Little-Blossom called? Had River-Cloud passed on the message? Had he stressed that it was important? Jade-Lotus jogged along the river, questions popping up like bamboo-shoots after rain. It would be better to discuss William's plan with Little-Blossom and drum up some ideas before passing it to High-Fly and Mark Lee; 'Food and fodder must be prepared long before manoeuvring troops and horses'. But a whole twenty-four hours had passed. Was Little-Blossom OK? Had she got her loan? And was the baby OK? What if she was trying to call now? Jade-Lotus turned and headed back home, almost sprinting. The phone was indeed ringing as she got in; she grabbed it.

'Ah ah, at last!' Little-Blossom exclaimed. 'Can you please come round, now? We've got really good news!'

'Good news? OK, OK, I'm coming.' Without changing, Jade-Lotus ran out and sprinted along the Yang–Shan corridor. What could their news be? She sat down on her cousin's sofa, breathing hard. 'So, what is it?'

'Look at this photo!' Little-Blossom glowed as she handed it over. 'We went to help Nine-Pound Old Lady clear out her loft this morning, and found a bundle of old photos. As we went through them with her, she told us this was her sister and brother-in-law.'

Jade-Lotus narrowed her eyes at the couple in the photo. 'Her sister and brother-in-law?'

'They're Mark Lee's parents!'

'Oh my gosh! But didn't Nine-Pound Old Lady say she knew nothing?'

'She still knows nothing. Her sister, Mark Lee's mother, died in the early seventies and Nine-Pound Old Lady lost touch with her brother-in-law after that.'

'OK. So how does this help us?'

'I know where he is,' River-Cloud said brightly, 'and I can take you to see him.'

'What?' Jade-Lotus screamed, wanting to throw a cushion at him. 'You knew where Mark Lee's father was and didn't say a word? He could lead us to his other son.'

'Well, I know the man in the photo, but I didn't know he was Mark Lee's father. Nine-Pound Old Lady said he was an accountant, but to me he's Mr Guan, Antiques Guan, selling antique musical instruments.'

Jade-Lotus grasped her pendant. 'But are you sure it's the same person?'

'Absolutely.' River-Cloud combed his quiff with his fingers, looking smug.

'He's very good with faces,' Little-Blossom said.

'Can we go to see him?' Jade-Lotus stared at River-Cloud. It would be nice to grow wings and fly there this instant.

'Right after lunch, if that's OK,' River-Cloud said.

'Yep, I'll go and get ready.'

'I'll see you at our dock at one.'

Jade-Lotus nodded and sprang up to leave, but turned back to Little-Blossom. 'Sorry, how are you and the baby?'

'You just go, don't worry! We're both good, over five months now, can you believe it?' Little-Blossom gently patted her belly.

Jade-Lotus caressed Cousin's belly and smiled. *Really not that long now, dear daughter!* 'How was your trip yesterday?'

'Not good. But don't worry, I'll find another way. You also have something to tell me, don't you? Perhaps when you come back.'

'Yes, yes, see you later.'

As River-Cloud drove the boat at full speed towards the county town, Jade-Lotus sat quietly, although inside it was as if a bunny was hopping. Was Mr Guan really Mark Lee's father? Say he was, would he know anything? Would he be willing to share what he knew? After all, blood is always thickest. It could be a step closer to finding out what had really happened to Mama; she grasped her pendant. 'After endless mountains and rivers that leave doubt whether there is a path out, suddenly one can see willows shading, flowers brightening and a lively village spreading out,' the old poem from Southern Song dynasty said.

They docked the boat and hurried towards a residential area. After passing through a labyrinth of slabbed paths, they stopped in front of a bleached wooden door; its handle was a rusty lion's head biting a large ring. River-Cloud lifted the ring and pounded.

'How did you know about this place?' Jade-Lotus whispered.

'A student's dad is a guzheng player and he introduced me to Antiques Guan a few years ago,' River-Cloud whispered back. 'I've been a regular ever since. You won't believe the stuff he has!'

A square peephole above the lion's heads squeaked open, a pair of small eyes peered out. After a loud clunk the door slowly opened.

'Afternoon, Principal Shan, long time no see,' an old man in a long, faded dark robe said warmly, gesturing for them to come in. He looked to be in his eighties, his body thin and slightly bent, his face plain and placid, but his wild white beard boldly reached down to his waist, and his matching white eyebrows, similarly reckless, sheltered his eyes.

'Yes, it's been a while. So, how are you, Mr Guan? How's business?' River-Cloud said, equally warmly, as the old man shut the door behind them. They were now standing in a small courtyard, above them a dense and fragrant wisteria netted the sky.

'All the better for seeing you,' Mr Guan said breathily, 'but you know, I'm ticking along, and my business is ticking along slowly too.' He breathed like a steam train struggling up a hill; when he breathed out, there was slight gurgling sound. 'So,' he turned to lead the way, 'you're looking for another guzheng? And who is this pretty young lady of yours?' He opened the door to his house; a musty, mouldy smell wafted out.

'Ah, this is Jade-Lotus, my old friend visiting from England. Eh, Mr Guan, no guzheng for today, but we need your help.'

'Principal Shan, you know me, I always try to be helpful, haha. Just ask away.'

'Eh, maybe we can talk somewhere more private?' River-Cloud lowered his voice to a whisper. 'It's about your sons.'

Mr Guan stopped in his tracks and turned around to stare at Jade-Lotus.

'Hello, Mr Guan,' she said and bowed.

'Who are you again?' Mr Guan stared sharply from behind the strands of his eyebrows.

'She's the granddaughter of Mrs Yang, who lives next door to me, my only neighbour, remember?' River-Cloud said, slowly and clearly.

'Lady Emerald Lu-Yang?' Mr Guan muttered, his face seeming to slowly drop.

Interesting, no one calls Grandma by her full name!

'Ah, you remembered, and so well,' River-Cloud said.

'What did you say it was about?' Mr Guan straightened his face.

'Eh, about your sons, the second son in fact.'

'What are you talking about? I don't have any children; I've told you.' Mr Guan turned to his front room. 'We can talk here, I've no other customers today.' His tone was cold.

Jade-Lotus followed River-Cloud into the room, which seemed to double as a shop, with every available surface covered in piles of old bric-a-brac. The musty smell was more pungent, as if the past was being fermented here. Mr Guan sat down in his armchair, and with a nod and a bounce of his beard gesticulated for them to sit opposite him on the bamboo bench.

River-Cloud sat down, unbuttoned his mandarin collar and cleared his throat. 'Eh, Mr Guan, we've known each other for, eh, many years, so I won't go around in circles, I'll just be frank.' He cleared his throat again. 'I think you are related to me.'

Mr Guan was motionless, playing dumb as if he was a wooden cock.

River-Cloud shifted his feet and leaned forward. 'Now I know why you have always been so interested to hear about my family. It's not fair, is it, that you know all about me, but I know almost nothing about you. And in fact you lied to me about your sons.'

Mr Guan said nothing, looking indifferent.

'Well, Nine-Pound Old Lady showed me a photo of you and your wife, her late sister. I have it here.' River-Cloud took out the photo.

Mr Guan didn't look up, but lowered his head. His breathing became heavy as he mindlessly stroked his beard, as if trying to think.

'You're my granduncle-in-law!' River-Cloud said, in the way of someone who had been searching all their life and finally found a loved one.

The old man eventually looked up, let out a loud sigh and reluctantly took the photo. With shaking hands he put on the half-moon glasses that had been dangling on his neck.

As he examined it, Jade-Lotus looked up at the wall, on which hung at least twenty guzhengs, arranged evenly and artfully like pictures in an exhibition. Hmm, was he really Mark Lee's father, the old accountant? Even if he was, would he own up to a secret that he had buried so deeply for so long?

After what seemed a very long time, Mr Guan's small shoulders buckled and he began to shake. River-Cloud reached out to hold his arm, but he brushed him off. When

211

he managed to stop shaking, he covered his face with his twig-like fingers and sobbed, tears seeping out onto his white beard. He nodded, at last.

Oh My Gosh! He is *Mark Lee's father!* Jade-Lotus stared hard at the old man.

'Granduncle.' River-Cloud gently patted Mr Guan's hand.

Mr Guan wiped his face with his sleeves. 'Have – have you told anyone else of my secret?' he croaked.

'No, Granduncle. No one, not even Nine-Pound Old Lady. I only worked this out this morning, but Jade-Lotus really needs your help.'

Mr Guan turned to Jade-Lotus. 'What do you want?'

Jade-Lotus crossed and uncrossed her legs. 'Mr Guan, I'm trying to find your second son; he might know what happened to my mama back in 1969.' She managed to say it softly, not wanting to spook the fragile man.

'Rich-Knowledgeable?' Mr Guan widened his eyes. 'Aihh, heaven punish me! I brought up two beasts!' He put his hands together in front of his flowing beard, as if praying, or perhaps asking for forgiveness. 'I heard the rumours. Do you think, he… he was involved in killing your mother too?' He trembled, breathing hard again.

Jade-Lotus gently patted his arm until he calmed down. 'I don't know, Mr Guan. People said it was his wife, but she disappeared and many said she had died. I thought your sons would know what happened, but I can't ask Mark Lee, so I want to try his brother.'

Mr Guan sighed. 'I… I have to say I don't know… I don't know where Rich-Knowledgeable is. Sorry.'

Jade-Lotus looked at him; was he telling the truth? It was difficult to trust a person when their eyes were covered by their eyebrows. 'Mr Guan, I'm not looking to get him in trouble; I just want to know what happened. It'll give me and Grandma closure. You know her, don't you?' She managed again to keep her tone mild.

'Jade-Lotus is an old friend, you can trust her,' River-Cloud said.

Mr Guan twirled the strands of his eyebrows away, lowered his head and stared at the beard folded in his lap, a tear still hanging on one eyelash. 'Aihhh! It's so difficult to look back.' After a bout of gurgled breath he continued, 'Although my sons kicked us out of Blushing Lotus, at first we still heard from old friends there. We knew Rich-Peaceful and Rich-Knowledgeable got promoted, and then both got married and started families. We… we hated not being part of their lives, but we comforted ourselves knowing that our sacrifice was for their future – they wouldn't be burdened by our black… black background. Aihh!' He took a long hard breath. 'But the rumour… the rumour about Rich-Knowledgeable's wife being involved in your mother's death broke us. We knew your mother and grandma, well… well in fact.' He looked up at Jade-Lotus. 'My wife was… was so disgusted she became ill, and a few months later, died.' Mr Guan was quiet for a moment, as if still mourning his wife. 'After that, I… I decided I wanted nothing to do with them, and cut all my ties to Blushing Lotus, so I wouldn't hear more about their beastly crimes. Absolutely beastly.' His face was taut, his eyes bulging.

Jade-Lotus relaxed her tightly held hands. They say you don't get to choose your parents, but you don't get to choose your children either. Mr Guan seemed genuine in his emotions, presumably he was telling the truth. It was interesting that he had changed his surname, staying far away from Mark Lee's mountains.

Mr Guan breathed heavily again. 'But… but a parent is always a parent. When I read the local papers, I… I automatically searched for their news. Over the years, I've seen plenty of Rich-Peaceful, ah, Mark Lee now – horrible name – but… but never anything about Rich-Knowledgeable. I have old photos with me, and all I can do is look at them. A few years ago, a close friend of mine told me he saw a travelling monk at a temple fair who… who looked just like Rich-Knowledgeable in my photos. When I got there, the monk had already left, and that… that was that. I really… really don't know where Rich-Knowledgeable is.' He let out a long sigh and looked at peace.

Jade-Lotus looked at River-Cloud, who shook his head. She thought for a moment and asked, 'Mr Guan, do you remember which year it was? And where the fair was held?'

'Ah, I do know that. I kept a newspaper cutting, let… let me find it.' Mr Guan stood up, shuffled to a table and took a tin box out of its bottom drawer. When he returned, he took out a small pile of papers and went through them. 'Ah, here it is.'

'Can I make a copy please?' Jade-Lotus said.

'Yes, yes, I've an old photocopier I use for business.' Mr Guan took Jade-Lotus to the machine. 'Ah, will… will you try to find him?' he asked.

'Yes.'

'Please… please let me know if you do?'

Jade-Lotus nodded. 'Can I also borrow a photo of Rich-Knowledgeable, please?'

'OK, but the only ones I have are old.' Mr Guan rummaged in the box, pulled out a photo and gave it to Jade-Lotus.

'Thank you, Granduncle,' River-Cloud said. 'If you need

214

anything – anything! – just remember, we're your family.'

'Aihh, it's good to have family.' Mr Guan looked teary again.

Jade-Lotus and River-Cloud walked out and the old man closed the heavy door, locking it from the inside.

'I don't know how much help he was,' River-Cloud said.

'I think he was a great help, a new vine we can follow. Thank you, really!' Jade-Lotus said.

'No need. Ah, I feel really sorry for him.'

'Me too. Do you think we should tell Mark Lee, so he could do his filial duty before his old man dies?'

'I doubt he cares, but we Shans will keep an eye on him.'

'Er, you know, it's difficult to accept that Mark Lee and Nine-Pound Old Lady are your distant relatives.' Jade-Lotus sighed.

'Very difficult! Now let's get back to Little-Blossom and you can tell us your news.'

Little-Blossom sat up from her sofa as Jade-Lotus and River-Cloud came in. 'Ah ah, a useful trip?'

'Yes, yes, very useful!' Jade-Lotus said. 'Mr Guan really is Mark Lee's father!'

Little-Blossom tutted as they weaved the story. 'That poor old man, our relative! At least he's nicer than Mark Lee. But how are we going to find a travelling monk?'

Jade-Lotus frowned. 'I thought we could just go to the temple and ask about the fair? They must have a record.'

Little-Blossom wrinkled her nose. 'It's not that simple, I'm afraid. There would be many travelling monks attending that fair, and the temple may not have any records.'

'She's right,' River-Cloud said. 'It depends. If he helped host or was a part of an important celebration, there could be some kind of record. But if he simply stopped over for prayers or an alms round, no one would pay attention. And it happened seven years ago.'

'OK,' Jade-Lotus said. 'I've got his photo; can't we just go and ask the temple or even temples?'

'But monks are so private, they won't give away anything about other monks, and they're usually reluctant to talk to women. As he is a travelling monk, he can be from anywhere and there are quite a few Buddhist temples in the region. Sorry, Cousin. We need more ideas, don't we? Where's the other leg of our Ding? I've been too busy to call Snow-Flower, have you heard from her?'

'Good idea, I'll call her tonight.' Jade-Lotus quickly picked up a lotus seed and threw it into her mouth. 'Haven't had these for years!' It was wrong to lie to a dear cousin, but it wasn't right to break a promise to a dear friend either. 'Now, I've got exciting news too; William finished the plan.'

'Ah ah, do tell.' Little-Blossom began nibbling a dried mulberry.

'William thinks the easiest and most effective approach is to use what Blushing Lotus is already good at, which is tourism.' Seeing them both lean forward, Jade-Lotus carried on with more zeal, 'But he's thinking big, to put our small town on the international map. And he's already got two friends from Hong Kong interested in the luxury tourist market.'

'Ah –' Little-Blossom frowned and stared at her red-varnished nails.

River-Cloud leaned back and crossed his arms. 'So, they'll come and build modern hotels, restaurants, roads, an airport and so on? Another Mark Lee concrete zone?'

Jade-Lotus raised her eyebrows; this was an unexpected

reaction. 'No, not really. William thinks we should bring back traditions, festivals, costumes, and music etcetera, and restore our traditional buildings to showcase the amazing history of Blushing Lotus. Western travellers love the old, not the new.'

'Really? You mean bring the glamour of the past back? Like what I did with the academy?' River-Cloud sat up, uncrossed his arms and pushed up his spectacles.

'Yeah, something like that. And we need a show to impress those investors.'

Little-Blossom and River-Cloud exchanged a happy glance. 'What show? What can we do to help?' they almost said together.

'I've been thinking, maybe we can make the upcoming Duanwu festival the best ever.' Jade-Lotus stared at them keenly, as if they were back to their teenage years again. Together they had been like crystallised ginger, sweet and packed with a zingy force.

'Really?' Little-Blossom exclaimed. 'Do you think Mark Lee will let us organise that?'

'We have to persuade him; I doubt he and his officials know how to impress Westerners. We'll make sure it goes really well, for the adoption's sake, you know?' Jade-Lotus said.

'I know all about organising Duanwu; we'll just need a good theme. Last year we did flowers, the year before food…' Little-Blossom tilted her head, bending her fingers one by one to count. 'What should we do this year?'

'Well, I asked Grandma and she'd love to bring back some of the traditions from her childhood. Apparently, they were more colourful and flamboyant than today's, much closer to the old Duanwu song.'

'The old Duanwu song? It would be very impressive if

we could do that, wouldn't it?' Little-Blossom turned to her husband.

River-Cloud nodded and began to hum the tune, his feet tapping the beat.

Little-Blossom joined him.

Jade-Lotus hummed too; she was back in the shade under white wisteria where Grandma had taught her to sing it. 'We could use the song as the theme, couldn't we?'

Little-Blossom and River-Cloud both stopped humming and looked at each other.

'What a brilliant idea!' Little-Blossom said.

'Bringing back even more traditions. That sounds like a good theme to me.' River-Cloud rubbed his hands together as if he was ready for action.

'If it's done well, the townspeople would absolutely love it! But will Mark Lee allow it? He has an iron fist on everything,' Little-Blossom said.

'Well, if he wants investment, he'll have to play ball,' Jade-Lotus said. 'But... I'm more worried about the townspeople...' she tailed off, twisting her bottom. People in Blushing Lotus loved nothing more than their traditions, and had strong views about how they should be celebrated. Selling them any new ideas would be like selling green tea to Hangzhou.

Little-Blossom patted her hand. 'Don't worry. We'll win them over.'

'I have just the book,' River-Cloud said, leaping up, and returning with a spring in his step. 'Look, there is a chapter here about the history of Duanwu Festival in our region, and some pictures.' He leafed through it to show them.

'We can steal some ideas from it,' Jade-Lotus said.

'Let me see, let me see.' Little-Blossom took the book. 'I

love this one!'

'How about that one?' River-Cloud squeezed to sit next to his wife and pointed.

'Just look at their headdresses!'

Jade-Lotus smiled; it was as if they were all back in the upstairs room of Grandma's tea house, only this time it was real-life challenges. Outside, the rosy sun was setting across the lake. 'I'd better get going. Can I borrow the book please? I'll run some ideas by Snow-Flower tonight.'

Little-Blossom and River-Cloud nodded.

'Are you checking up on me?' Snow-Flower said sharply on the phone.

'Maybe I am,' Jade-Lotus said. 'So, how are you?'

'Numb, it's only been three days.' Snow-Flower's tone softened. 'I've been keeping busy if you really want to know.'

'Have you, um…' Jade-Lotus bit her tongue; nagging wasn't attractive. 'Um… you know?'

'Don't, just don't…'

'OK. I guess you can take your time, but don't take too long. Do you want a distraction then?'

'That's better! Go on.'

'We found Mark Lee's father and went to see him this afternoon.'

'We? Who is we? And without me?' Snow-Flower raised her voice.

'Well, your brother took me to see Mr Guan. Can you believe that he even changed his surname?' Jade-Lotus rewove the story. Although she gasped a few times, Snow-Flower didn't interrupt. She seemed a better listener these days.

'But how are you going to find this monk?'

'Er, we don't really know. I was hoping you might?'

'Now you're talking!' Snow-Flower said, the bells of her voice ringing. 'And I may indeed be able to help. We ran a documentary series a year ago about the life of Buddhist travelling monks in the Yangtze region. I believe we have a list of them. So you can leave it to me for the moment – send me what you have.'

'Are you sure about that? You know, you need to take time to...' Jade-Lotus stopped herself.

'Didn't you say I need distractions?' Snow-Flower was sharp again.

'OK, OK. Now, I have more exciting news,' Jade-Lotus said. It would have been easier to have recorded the conversation with Little-Blossom and River-Cloud and rewound it to play again for Snow-Flower. As she repeated her initial idea for the festival, the picture of it became more and more vivid.

'Don't go to Mark Lee yet, all right?' Snow-Flower said, 'I'll come back next weekend, and we can hammer out a solid plan for the festival. "Know yourself and know your enemy!" Ahhhh, can't wait!'

'Haha, we might need all the wisdom from Sun Tzu to win a battle with that chameleon,' Jade-Lotus said. 'And home may be good for you, you know?'

'Something in the water?' Snow-Flower said, probably rolling her eyes.

17

Town Hall Meeting

Jade-Lotus sat in the front row of the town hall, holding her hands tightly together in her lap. The Shan family on her left all sat upright, while Grandma on her right stretched her neck towards the entrance. None of the townspeople had arrived. A stale damp smell permeated the hall; High-Fly had said it was due to infrequent use. In the early 1970s, the town-hall meetings were a weekly event everyone, even children, had to attend. It was often a trembling-with-fear event, as Grandma and other class enemies were hatefully denounced, and then violently beaten. At other times it was a boring-to-death drowsy experience listening to Mark Lee loudly reading parts from Mao's little red book and finishing with everyone shouting slogans. As a little girl, the only way to block it all out was to shut her eyes and imagine somewhere else, somewhere with flowers, books and pretty dresses. Nowadays, according to High-Fly, the focus was on making money and under Mark Lee's slogan 'TIME IS MONEY', town-hall meetings were an annual affair, always held in the darkest, coldest and least profitable month of January. Thus the call for such a meeting on May Day had caused a stir.

The amiable townspeople began to trickle in, their faces a well-fed healthy glow, and their worries – Grandma had heard plenty in her teahouse – had probably been suppressed at the bottoms of their full stomachs. High-Fly had cunningly chosen May Day afternoon, because the townspeople would have enjoyed a delicious family lunch and yellow rice wine celebrating the national holiday, and would be more relaxed, mellow and agreeable.

'Do you think he's nervous?' Snow-Flower whispered, tilting her head towards the rostrum, where High-Fly, the newly promoted deputy town leader, sat between two older officials and Mark Lee behind a long row of tables covered with red tablecloth. He wore a smart new suit – the Boss label still attached to one of his sleeves – and a white shirt fully buttoned up, but without a tie. His shiny hair was neatly combed back, but he looked unusually pale and his estranged eyes darted back and forth between the gradually filling up hall and the papers in front of him.

'He shouldn't be, after all the help we've given him the last three weeks,' Jade-Lotus whispered back.

'Ah ah, I just hope it's going to be as easy as he thinks,' Little-Blossom said.

The clock on the nearby tower chimed twice, the echoes lingering. High-Fly's face turned crimson, but he quickly cleared his throat, looked around the hall, tapped the microphone and said, 'Good afternoon, townspeople!' His voice was thin and shaky, but high pitched and full of enthusiasm; he grinned like a blossomed lotus. 'How are you today? Have you had a good lunch?'

But the townspeople just looked at each other, seemingly not accustomed to such a greeting, and no one in the packed hall responded.

Jade-Lotus clasped her hands tighter; surely he knew what he was doing.

'Ohhaha, no answers? Well, I know you,' High-Fly chirped with his familiar cheeky smile. 'Who had dumplings?' Still the audience was quiet. He raised his head high like a cock in the morning, 'Well, I had dumplings and I dare say they were the most delicious in our whole town; NONE of you can match our Lee's recipe!'

A commotion and some hissing began in the audience.

Snow-Flower and Little-Blossom turned towards Jade-Lotus, frowning, as if to ask if she knew he was going to do this.

Jade-Lotus shook her head. But he was a seasoned politician and should know how to handle the townspeople. She glanced around. Ladies fanned their silk fans with vigour; their husbands shifted their bottoms. Those who seemed unable to contain themselves put their hands up. On seeing them, others, who were obviously unconvinced, raised their hands too. Whatever the era, food was always one of the most important things in the townspeople's lives, and they had high standards.

'OK, tell me about your dumplings then,' High-Fly cajoled.

The two officials frowned, but Mark Lee was motionless, as if deaf, his darting eyes fixed on the papers in front of him.

The audience erupted, shouting out their recipes. To enhance their already tasty pork filling, some added crab's meat, others put in minced raw prawns or scrambled eggs, and all used their uniquely mixed spices and herbs. As the fondness and pride radiated around the hall, the townspeople relaxed. Whatever worries that they might have had simply vanished, just like the dumplings had from their plates earlier.

'OK, OK, you win!' High-Fly shouted, his eyes glinting with satisfaction. 'Wonderful townspeople, thank you for sharing your recipes with me. Now I'll share my exciting plan with you. I'm sure you'll love it as much as your dumplings.'

The audience quietened down; this time they looked happy and were wide awake, necks stretched high. It was all in contrast to their usual habit of dozing off, which had been cultivated by years of Mark Lee reading pages and pages of communist good news.

Jade-Lotus felt slightly relieved for High-Fly.

His plastic smile vanished as he started to read his speech, 'Since the economic reforms in the eighties our town has made huge strides, and our living standards have improved significantly, all down to the great, great leadership of Mark Lee.' He paused, both hands, palms open, pointing towards his father, as if making offerings to the mighty Buddha. He persisted with the silly gesture, waiting for his photo to be taken.

Jade-Lotus sighed. Although he looked less prosperous than his father, and lacked his foxy schemes and foresight, he was starting to sound just like him! Surely that blowing-the-trumpet style had long gone, but here it was! And William had to do Mark Lee's job for him. The only consolation was that the development would be good for Summer-Lily and Spring-Cherry's future.

High-Fly continued, 'Now the county wants us to do more. Of course, no one, I say *no one*, can match the colossal success already achieved by our town leader, so all we can do is add a small flower of decoration to our already perfect town.' He raised his eyes and looked around, perhaps hoping the audience would roar with agreement or applaud, but they remained silent, their faces blank.

The new deputy soldiered on. 'So, what can we do? Where can we find a flower? In fact the answer is right under our noses.' He tapped at the tip of his flat nose, and stared at the audience. But they just looked at each other again, probably wondering what trick he was playing. He ignored them and read on, 'Our party leader once said, "Study the past if you want to define the future." We've a long, long history, many traditions that we can exploit, so we are going to use these to attract foreign investment and more visitors.'

The audience hissed again, and someone nearby said, 'That's a Confucian saying; when did it become a party line?' And someone else shouted, 'This is nothing new!'

'I hear you,' High-Fly said, clearing his throat. 'But this is like nothing you've heard before. We've drawn up the Golden Dragon Investment Plan to promote Blushing Lotus internationally, to put it on the world map, and use that to develop our tourism and silk industry. We'll put the details on the notice board as we go along, but at its heart we'll designate the town centre as a tourist quarter and return it to its Ming glory. Inside, cars will be prohibited and everyone will travel by foot, boat, sedan chair or rickshaw. We'll encourage new tourist shops, hot-spring spas, fine restaurants, boutique teahouses, various museums and maybe a small opera house. And we'll have artisan workshops to show off our famous traditional crafts of fine silk making, guzheng making and stone carving…' He spoke faster and faster, full of zeal, his hands waving as he further detailed the plan, eventually finishing with, '… maybe even an annual film festival. We'll definitely put our small town firmly onto the world map!'

'Where's the money coming from?' someone shouted from the audience; humming from others suggested broad agreement.

'That's a good question,' High-Fly replied, his eyes becoming crescents, presumably feeling smug that someone had asked the question he was well-prepared for. 'We have some foreign investors lined up already, looking to start joint ventures, and I'm sure we'll attract more. Right now we're talking to someone who wants to refurbish old houses and turn them into a boutique hotel, and another who wants to expand our silk production for use in designer clothes.'

The shabby hall became a wok of boiling water; the simmering hubbub of surprise grew into a vigorously bubbling clamour. The usually reserved townspeople were like a crowd of noisy school children. Women frantically fanned again, men grabbed their straw hats to fan too, their faces flushed with excitement, as if they had just got the best bargain ever at the morning market.

High-Fly nodded like a nodding dog in the back of a car, and winked at Jade-Lotus, as if to say what did I tell you – it's easy!

'Did he just wink at us?' Snow-Flower whispered. 'Just get on with it, silly toad!'

High-Fly seemed to suddenly remember that he needed to close the net quickly, tapped his microphone three times, and shouted, 'Excellent, excellent, lovely townspeople!' Once everyone quietened down, he continued, 'Of course we want all of you to get involved, so you can come up with even more ideas to add to the plan. We'll have a Golden Dragon management committee, and those with the best ideas may be invited to join.' He paused for a second, admiring the look of surprise on people's faces, his lips stretching into a smile, and carried on silkily, 'Well, I'm glad you like the plan so far. Now, last but not least, is our immediate action – to showcase Blushing Lotus! We'll host the first dragon boat race for the five towns of the Upper Canal District. Our potential investors have already agreed to come, and it'll be televised by Shanghai TV and the BBC. This is our big break!'

His announcement went down like throwing frozen sweet rice balls into a lidded wok filled with hot oil at the Lantern Festival. At first all was quiet and eerie, and then people exploded like the rice balls against the lid. The noise level in the hall was unprecedented.

High-Fly looked mightily relieved at having delivered the whole speech smoothly. Smiling and nodding, he glanced at the officials and gazed at his father, perhaps hoping for a pat on his back. He drank some of the iced tea which was in front of him.

Jade-Lotus nodded to Snow-Flower and Little-Blossom, her tightly clasped hands relaxed. High-Fly just needed to finish the meeting by allowing some questions from the audience. When they had suggested it earlier he was surprised, but decided to do it, as his father had never let anyone else speak. He qualified it, however, by saying that he just wanted to give them a taste, with no intention of paying attention to what they said.

Mark Lee, his darting eyes now lethargic, didn't return his son's gaze. What was he thinking? Was he not pleased? Jade-Lotus shook her head.

'OK, quiet please,' shouted High-Fly. 'Any questions?' But

no one seemed to take any notice; the tumult in the hall continued. He pulled his ear trying to listen to what the townspeople were talking about, their faces all red. 'QUIET! QUIET!' he tapped the microphone harder.

What was going on? Jade-Lotus exchanged looks with her friends.

Gradually, the boiling crowd quietened to a simmer.

'Ahem,' someone coughed loudly at the back. Jade-Lotus turned and saw a man stand up. He looked to be in his mid-seventies, his face pockmarked and fringed by a neat grey goatee. 'Good afternoon, Deputy Town Leader,' he shouted, 'congratulations on your new job! Now,' he coughed again. 'We've never had a boat race at Duanwu before. So, how can we host it on such a scale and make a success of it?'

There was a sea of nodding in the audience.

Little-Blossom whispered, 'That's Pockmarked Chou, Nine-Pound Old Lady's good friend.'

Indeed he was sitting not far from Nine-Pound Old Lady in the same row.

Pockmarked Chou sat down and a Michelin-tyre man next to him stood up.

'That's Fat Sun,' Snow-Flower whispered. 'He owns the crab restaurant, the one Mark Lee bought you lunch in.'

Fat Sun shouted, 'Yes, yes, Deputy, a wonderful plan; your first fire in the new job is impressive! The boat race sounds great; we can make tons of money. I vote yes with both hands.' Fat Sun put both hands up in the surrender position, smiles piling up on his layered face, his eyes disappearing into two curvy lines. Immediately, the scene of Mr Pumblechook asking, 'May I? May I?' before he shook the hand of Pip in his new London house came to Jade-Lotus's mind. Fat Sun put down his hands and continued, 'The boat race *is* indeed a challenge; perhaps our deputy could show us some clever tricks?'

Fat Sun sat down, another wizened man next to him stood up. Jade-Lotus recognised him as Old Qian, one of Grandma's customers. He shouted, 'Even the cleverest housewife can't cook a meal without ingredients! The only stretch of water wide enough and long enough for this race is between the town centre and Shan Academy, but that's where our dowager moors her boat to be rented out as an ice-cream parlour, and the rent from that is her only income.' He sat down, his large square spectacles reflecting the turbulent ceiling fan.

Pockmarked Chou stood up again. 'Ahem! I heard that the whole plan was invented by a FOREIGNER!' he shrieked, his eyes bulging like a frog's. 'Am I right, Deputy?'

Gasps leaked from all around the hall and many women instantly held their fans up to cover their dropped-open mouths. Everyone glared at High-Fly as if he had grown horns and turned into a demon.

High-Fly was ashen; he opened his mouth, but no words came out and he stared accusingly at Jade-Lotus.

Jade-Lotus stared back at High-Fly and shook her head firmly, as did Snow-Flower and Little-Blossom.

Discontent grew like bamboo shoots after a summer rain, and loud remarks flew around. 'Foreigners have never been nice to us!' 'They shamed our ancestors; remember the Shanghai concessions?' 'Is taking a worthless baby girl abroad not enough?'

'Don't listen to that rubbish!' Snow-Flower said, and Little-Blossom and Grandma shook their heads angrily.

It was OK, this was nothing new really. Jade-Lotus nodded

to them.

River-Cloud stood up, turned to face everyone in the hall, and like the conductor of an orchestra gestured for them to be quiet. The audience fell silent at once. 'Good afternoon, everyone,' he shouted. 'Are we letting our eyes be obscured by a single leaf and not seeing Mount Tai?' His voice was clear and resonant, his tone mild but authoritative. 'This development plan is all about investing in our beloved traditions; we should thank this foreigner for understanding us so well. Haven't we struggled all these years trying to build a modern town only to realise that we can't? Our strength comes from our past and we shouldn't be ashamed of that. About this dragon boat race, I'm certain we can do it, do it well and do us proud. My academy takes part in a dragon boat race every year, so we can help people train and practise.' He stared at the audience until they nodded.

Jade-Lotus looked at him, it was as if a warm hand had caught her fallen heart and was caressing it.

River-Cloud sat down and his grandpa Autumn-Rain stood up. 'Principal Shan is right,' he shouted. 'We should indeed thank this foreigner, whom our family happens to be related to by marriage, I'm proud to say. I'm sure my sister won't mind helping out by not mooring her boat there until after the race. And of course, we can help with any rent shortfall.'

'Ha ha ha ha!' Nine-Pound Old Lady boomed from the back row. 'Have I asked YOU, my little brother, to speak out for me? Do YOU, decide where and when I moor my boat?' Despite her age, she sounded like thunder rumbling before a storm.

Jade-Lotus closed her eyes; the nemesis had risen again!

The stuffy room hushed; everyone seemed to hold their

breath.

'How dare you thank a foreign devil!' Nine-Pound Old Lady yelled. 'You seem determined to make my life difficult lately, don't you? First, bringing a shame on our family, conceding to the adoption of an unwanted baby by foreigners, and now speaking out for me! The old proverb says, "A drop of water in need should be returned with a bursting spring." But I don't need you to thank me for all of your life, I don't need you speaking out for me, and I certainly don't need your charity.' Her words were delivered slowly, each syllable clear and sharp like a shard of broken glass.

Jade-Lotus felt nauseous. *Just don't vomit! Definitely not at this moment.* She opened her eyes.

Autumn-Rain was speechless, his face the colour of raw liver as he sat down.

Grandma gritted her teeth.

Nine-Pound Old Lady snorted loudly, turned her stern gaze to High-Fly and shouted, 'And you! What a fool! If you want to fledge your new wings, you need to do your own homework, instead of repeating the words of a foreigner like a parrot. You're WEAK! You're USELESS! You expect us to respect you? You couldn't even stop your mad ex-wife wailing in our streets! You're allowing a foreigner to adopt a baby girl and now letting a foreigner tell us what to do. Shame on YOU! To be absolutely clear: my boat will moor at its usual place on the usual day!'

The quiet hall suddenly exploded into chattering. Pock-marked Chou and his friends all turned to their dowager, like a myriad of stars surrounding a bright moon, nodding in awe, their eyes shining with admiration.

Jade-Lotus turned back, her brain mushy, as if someone

231

had hit her on the head. She then looked at Snow-Flower and Little-Blossom, who both looked dumbfounded.

High-Fly's face, which had been crimson when the uproar started now turned white, in fact a shade paler and more ghostly than white. He stood up, and without a word stormed out of the door. His small and lonely back disappeared; the heavy wooden doors slammed shut behind him with a loud clunk.

One of the officials announced the closure of the meeting; Mark Lee left looking grey.

The townspeople just looked at each other and shrugged. Some appeared victorious, but some sighed. Once everyone was out of the shabby hall, all became calm again, the ripples dissipating on the nearby canal.

On the way back home, Grandma and the Shans looked sombre and were quiet.

Jade-Lotus walked quietly too, the humid heat prickling. 'Why was Nine-Pound Old Lady so mean?' she eventually said.

No one answered; all that could be heard was the echoes of their steps on the ancient cobbled street.

After a while Little-Blossom whispered, 'She brought Grandpa Autumn-Rain up single handed after their mother died. He's in debt to her.'

'We all paid a hefty price for our beloved traditions!' Grandma mumbled.

'Sorry for my sister's behaviour,' Autumn-Rain said.

'You don't need to apologise for her any more than I for my brother,' Grandma said.

'What do you mean, Grandma?' Jade-Lotus said.

Grandma didn't answer, just shook her head.

'I'm afraid we have to keep our promise,' Autumn-Rain said.

Jade-Lotus raised her eyebrows to Snow-Flower and Little-Blossom, but they shrugged and mouthed a 'Don't know'. Mm-mh, fog seemed swirling around the history of their two families.

River-Cloud, seemingly somewhere else, marvelled, 'Well done William, great idea to bring back guzheng making!'

It was late afternoon when they arrived home.

'I'd better go and practise guzheng,' River-Cloud said and headed off.

'I need to rest,' Grandma said, 'and mull over what has just happened.'

'Me too,' Autumn-Rain said and waved goodbye.

Jade-Lotus looked at the other two.

'The crab-apple flowers in our teachers' courtyard are blossoming; should we go and sit there?' Little-Blossom said.

'Why not?' Snow-Flower said lethargically.

Jade-Lotus nodded and they carried on walking. None of them spoke again; the silence stretched like pulled noodles. Their footsteps echoed on the slabs, clear and hollow as was their defeat.

When they arrived, Snow-Flower slumped onto the bamboo bench beneath the snowy umbrella of the crab-apple tree, and patted the space next to her. 'You can put your feet up now, Little-Blossom.'

Jade-Lotus helped lift Little-Blossom's feet onto the bench, and sat down next to Snow-Flower. They leaned on each other, catching their breath.

'So, what's next then?' Snow-Flower said, eventually.

Jade-Lotus shrugged, her brain still mushy.

The white crab-apple flowers were elegant, bordering on haughty, although their faint, sweet, cinnamon-like fragrance flirted dissolutely with the buzzing honeybees.

'Little-Blossom,' Snow-Flower said.

'Yes?'

'I've something to tell you.'

'I hope it's something good, not hail on top of heavy snow.'

'Um, it's about Wave.'

Jade-Lotus sat up and stared at Snow-Flower, who smiled a tight smile. Keeping a secret from loved ones was so hard; at last Snow-Flower would share hers with Little-Blossom.

Snow-Flower gave a bullet-point briefing about the affair and the baby. She seemed much calmer now, and took a long pause before whispering, 'I'm going to divorce him.'

Little-Blossom abruptly sat up and planted her feet heavily back down on the ground. She gazed at her sister-in-law, then hugged her. 'I'm so sorry. I don't know what to say! How could Wave do that to you? How could a perfect marriage be destroyed so easily?' She snivelled, her tears dribbling onto Snow-Flower's shoulder.

Snow-Flower held her, and didn't seem to mind the tears wetting her fuchsia silk shirt.

Jade-Lotus looked at them, her heart wrenching. Snow-Flower had said the D word back in Shanghai, but it hadn't really clicked. There was hope that things could be patched up between them; now to hear it for real was a heavy blow.

Eventually they untangled themselves. Little-Blossom leaned over to Jade-Lotus. 'You knew about this, right?'

Jade-Lotus nodded. 'Sorry, she really wanted to tell you herself.'

'It's OK, it's OK,' Little-Blossom mumbled, blushing and

smoothing the creases in her dress. 'I'm no better either. I've been trying hard to save the academy.'

'Save the academy?' Snow-Flower said.

Little-Blossom looked down, rubbed her hands slowly together and sighed. 'The school has been in arrears with a not-so-small bank loan for several months now, and the interest is snowballing.'

'How can that be?' Snow-Flower frowned.

'Because of all of this.' Little-Blossom opened her arms, pointing at the refurbished academy; her face twitched, as if she didn't know whether to smile or cry. 'Ah ah, it's my fault really that River-Cloud took out the loan...'

She spoke softly as she told the story, but never blamed her husband once, and instead was self-analysing and self-criticising. It was as if Little-Blossom had to go through the pupa stage of hard-on-self Confucianism before turning into a butterfly. Snow-Flower didn't interrupt her; perhaps she was resonating with Little-Blossom's dilemma: to stand up as a free, modern, educated and successful woman, or to buckle down under Confucian values and produce a son.

Silence fell again; a gentle breeze rolled in. The sweet scent turned almost resinous; a few petals fell like snow.

'Are we all doing something wrong?' Snow-Flower said eventually.

Jade-Lotus glanced at her and then turned to look into the distance, squinting. The setting sun was smearing the darkened bamboo and white azaleas with a shimmering coral glow. In the centre of the courtyard stood a huge bronze statue; its stout kimonoed body, long flowing beard, and hair, tied in a knot on top of his head, all glistened. He wasn't handsome but looked benevolent; his eyes were long and narrow, appearing thoughtful; and his knotty hands, one wrapping the other in front of his chest, seemingly held much persuasive power. He was the quintessence of ancient China, and for over two thousand years had shaped, and was still shaping, the lives of Chinese people. 'Do you think he's the problem?' she said, tilting her head to the statue.

'You mean Confucius?' Snow-Flower said, squinting too.

Little-Blossom leaned forward, opened her mouth, but closed it again.

Snow-Flower shifted her bottom, and raised a hand to ruffle her short spiky hair. She glared at Jade-Lotus, pouted, bit her lip and pouted again, her dimples playing hide and seek. 'So, you think we, modern, well-educated and successful women, have lost to him after all?' She narrowed her eyes.

Little-Blossom blew her short fringe, as if feeling hot. Probably she was digesting the indigestible.

Jade-Lotus picked a crab-apple petal off her jeans. 'I think his infamous saying: "There are three un-filial acts: the greatest of all is the failure to produce a son" is behind our misery, isn't it?' It felt like mentioning the C word – everyone knew about the ugly tumour, but no one wanted to talk about it. It was as if by refusing to talk about it, it would simply go away.

'My goodness!' Snow-Flower said. 'That old rotten line! I haven't heard it uttered for, like, ever. I thought modern women had long buried him.' She crossed her arms.

'Perhaps in a shallow grave?' Jade-Lotus sighed. 'It doesn't need to be uttered; people just follow it. This time back, I see it more clearly. Confucianism is an invisible cloth wrapping us all; like a chilly winter fog, it penetrates every cell of our souls. It's behind everything we do; our philosophy, virtues, ethics, and morality all bear its mark. It's so entangled with our culture; you can't separate it.' She took a deep breath.

The air seemed to vibrate; the rosy light reflecting from the statue diffused.

'It's true,' Little-Blossom said quietly. She shifted, rearranging her dress, her face the colour of the sunset. 'I grew up much more immersed in Confucian values than you two, and it feels natural for me to shrink behind it. To be honest River-Cloud never said it directly,' pointing at her belly, 'but I just felt I needed to… needed to have a son to continue the precious Shan's name, following the same old track Confucius laid out two thousand years ago.'

A screech drilled through the perfumed air as Snow-Flower dragged her leather soles across the stony slabs. Above them, crows cawed from their nests.

'I can't believe I've let the rotten little man win!' Snow-Flower said.

'I don't think it's you or me,' Jade-Lotus said, 'who is calling the shots. We grew up with Confucianism, our bones are engraved with it, just as our parents and their parents had been. Well, the communists tried to scrub it off – have to give them credit for that – but they failed. For two thousand years it has breathed down our necks, bored through our bodies and become our backbone. People accept every word of it, like God-given wisdom, and never challenge the awful values. With filial piety at its core, we women almost don't exist – our role is to serve in the male-controlled society. So, whatever we do, we lose.' Her chest was heaving. The heat – gathered over the years as a Confucian woman living in the West, observing the stark cultural differences – erupted.

Little-Blossom and Snow-Flower stared at her intensely.

'You see,' Jade-Lotus continued, 'in the West, people love Confucius, believing his wise philosophy to be an antidote to modern life. In my office colleagues came to me first, as I'm faster than Google on his lines. To be fair, many Confucian sayings are wise, philosophical, insightful, even saintly, like my motto: "Learning without thinking begets ignorance; thinking without learning is dangerous".'

'"Everything has beauty, but not everyone sees it" is my motto,' Snow-Flower cut in.

'"What you don't wish upon yourself, extend not to others" is mine,' Little-Blossom said.

'Exactly – we can all say a few without thinking. Even High-Fly quoted Confucius today. But the West doesn't know the dark side of Confucianism – its male chauvinism,' Jade-Lotus sighed again, 'like the "three obediences and four virtues"?'

'"Women and vile characters are equally difficult to deal with" is another one,' Snow-Flower said through gritted teeth.

'"A woman with no talent is the one who has merit"!' Little-Blossom quietly added.

'Unbelievable!' they shouted together.

'We need to prove how wrong he is!' Jade-Lotus said with determination.

'Absolutely! We can't let him win and ruin our lives.' Snow-Flower beat her thigh forcefully.

'Indeed!' Little-Blossom said. 'But it's slow progress, although "It doesn't matter how slow you go, as long as you don't stop".'

'You're quoting Confucius again!' Jade-Lotus and Snow-Flower shouted and laughed.

Little-Blossom laughed too. 'I'm his loyal victim.' She held her belly. 'And this won't let me forget.'

'Well, if you hadn't tried to do your filial duty, she wouldn't be here to adopt,' Snow-Flower pointed out.

'Absolutely true,' Jade-Lotus said. 'Ironic, isn't it, almost hypocritical!'

'Something good has to come out of it,' Little-Blossom said firmly.

Jade-Lotus nodded. 'For the sake of our baby girl I must go and find High-Fly, and get him back on track.'

'And I must save the school,' Little-Blossom said.

'I'll find the monk,' Snow-Flower said.

They smiled at each other.

The sun had set; the shimmer faded from the statue that loomed above them.

18

Grabbing the Blade

'What? High-Fly just quit?' William said on the phone. 'You have to find him! And we have to make him a hero.'

'A hero? Are you joking?' Jade-Lotus said.

'No. He lost face and we need to make him glow again. It's the only way we can get our baby. You'll have to work fast, there's only six weeks left.'

She sighed. 'OK, I'll try.'

'Sorry, darling, I've got another call now. I hate to rush you off, but I know you *can* do it! Love you lots!'

Jade-Lotus put the phone down. A wave of longing for him along with self-pity and disgust at bargaining with Mark Lee tangled together, twisting with pain; she lowered her head. *Stop! Just pull yourself together!* She breathed slowly in and out a few times and dialled High-Fly's office number. But he wasn't there, so she left a message with the assistant for him to call back.

By lunchtime the following day, High-Fly hadn't called; according to the same assistant he was still not in.

'Please, please, I really need to see him,' Jade-Lotus said.

'But he hasn't shown up. It's so unusual,' the assistant whispered and then resumed her formal tone, 'I'll pass on the message.'

On the third day, High-Fly was still a no-show. The assistant whispered again, 'Don't say I said this, but I'd go and check out the Mongolia Karaoke Bar if I were you. By the way, I love the development plan.'

No time to waste. Jade-Lotus hurried to the town centre, and eventually found the bar tucked away down a backstreet. She pulled open the heavy door, entered and found herself in darkness. After a few seconds her eyes adjusted. She looked around. A starry artificial sky illuminated a round room with a straight path through the middle as if bisecting a watermelon. The sofas on either side, that had a large flat screen hanging from the ceiling in front of them, were empty. At the end of the path sat a dimly lit curved bar counter, a curved wall behind covered in glinting bottles. There seemed to be no one around – well, it was mid-morning – but as she walked towards the bar, she heard a door squeak open.

'Jade-Lotus Yang!' said a lady.

'Yes?'

'Remember me?' The lady brightened up the lights. She was stick-like, wearing a white T-shirt and denim dungarees, topped with a mop of explosive permed hair.

'Is that you, Forever-Progress Wu?' There had been a slender girl sitting between her and High-Fly in the back row at primary school.

Forever-Progress smiled. 'Ah, you do remember me! So, what blows you to my bar? You want to sing?' She laughed

241

a low and throaty laugh. 'But I've guessed why you're here! Come with me; it's about time someone sorted him out.'

Jade-Lotus followed her along a curved dim passage. 'I'm not surprised that you have a karaoke bar, you always liked singing.'

'Well, my forever progress ended up in a bar.' She laughed again as they arrived at the entrance to a large tent. 'This is my Mongolian Yurt, our VIP guests can mingle here if they wish.' She seemed to have grown taller before striding again, along the torch-lit path that circled outside the tent. After passing seven doors, she stopped and whispered, 'This is his special room and he's been here ever since – you know – the town hall meeting.' She winked and left quietly.

Jade-Lotus knocked on the door, but there was no answer. The sliding cover on the small window was open, so she peeped in. High-Fly sat in a corner, lit only by images of flowers flickering across a huge TV screen, seemingly fixated by the lyrics that were popping up. She knocked much harder.

Eventually High-Fly opened the door, his shoulders droop-ing, his shirt wrinkled, his face grey and his cheekbones more chiselled than ever. 'You!' he snarled, anger burning in his bloodshot and spiritless eyes. 'Why are you here?'

'May I come in?'

'Why!' He didn't move.

'I want to check if you are OK.' Jade-Lotus looked into his eyes.

He studied her, still blocking the door, but in the end leaned aside to let her in. As he closed the door, he bellowed, 'What do you care? You'd love nothing more than seeing me humiliated in public!'

'High-Fly, I do care, and I care a lot. My husband has put

242

his heart and soul into writing this plan to satisfy you and your father; without investment, our adoption will be at risk; and this is the future of my hometown and my baby. What Nine-Pound Old Lady said to you was wrong and cruel, but running away and hiding isn't right either.'

He stared at her, seemingly dumbstruck, then walked past her and threw himself on the long sofa, the anger that he had worked up on seeing her vanishing. He slouched down, shrivelled like a deflated balloon trampled on the floor after a birthday party, and his eyes drifted back to the TV screen on which a singer sang silently, '...the past is like snow, infatuation hard to let go; trying to escape with wine, still seeing your eyes shine...'

Jade-Lotus knitted her eyebrows; High-Fly had never been like this before. She pursed her lips before sitting down next to him; on the screen the song had just started again.

'Do you want to put the sound back on?' she said.

He didn't say anything, but pressed the remote control.

Jade-Lotus listened to the entire song with High-Fly. He was quiet and motionless throughout, but bent forward, arms tightly wrapping across his tummy, when the final lyrics repeated: 'I'm loath to let you go, our love rooted long ago; I'm loath to simply part, you once ran wild with my heart.'

When the music faded, he reached for his remote control and switched the system off. They sat silently in the dark for a long time before he switched the ceiling light on. In the cold light, he looked more composed, although still sombre.

'Do you want to talk about it?' she said.

'What's there to talk about? All's long gone, she's long gone.' He looked down at his clasped hands.

'Who's she, can I ask?'

He turned to her, his hollow eyes taking time to focus, his lips quivering. He lowered his head and mumbled, 'Sometimes I wish I could be as brave and strong as you.' He paused with a dramatic sigh. 'There isn't a single day that I don't think of my first wife,' he said, shaking his head, 'I know it's not fair on my current wife, but I can't forget her and how happy she made me.'

'New-Dawn Chen?' Jade-Lotus managed not to call her Mad Girl.

'You know her?' He brightened up. 'She truly was the dawn of my life.'

Really? She nearly sneered, remembering Mad Girl's story, but it wasn't the time to challenge him. 'How did you meet?'

'At college,' he said, his lips stretching up. 'Unlike you, it took me three attempts to scrape through to an average college in Nanjing. Aihhh, but do you believe in fate?' He became lively, his small eyes sparkling.

Fate? But you're a communist! Jade-Lotus said nothing, and forbade herself to touch the mole above her lip. He wouldn't be interested in her answer anyway.

'"The old man lost his mare, but it all turned out for the best",' he continued quickly, now with a plastic smile. 'I was in the second semester of a teaching course, but hated it. I missed home, had no friends and the course was so dull. I organised some political events, but other boys just wanted to have fun with sports, pop music, and girls.' He rolled his eyes, his dark eyeballs almost disappeared. 'One day I gathered all my courage to ask a girl out – she wasn't even pretty, by the way – but she turned her nose up so high I bet you I could have hung my bag on it, and rushed off. I chased and caught up with her, but she said there was no way she'd go out with the secretary of the Communist Youth League!' He ground his teeth.

Jade-Lotus pictured it vividly, but managed not to giggle.

He bit a nail. 'I was so annoyed and took off for a walk. By the lake there was a crowd of students, all bending down and stretching their necks like stupid giraffes staring at the water. I pushed in and as I bent down by the lake trying to see what was going on, a girl suddenly rose out of the water right in front of me, holding a young duckling. She looked at me and then placed the duckling in my hands!' He cupped his hands together in front of him, his eyes burning brightly. He seemed so tender and loving, but how come? He had been a truly emotionless bully, his heart filled with nothing but communism.

Still, she stared into his hands too.

'I'd never held such soft little life in my hands before, so cuddly and so lively! But you know me, I always fucked up! So I just stood there, dumbstruck, and even worse, tears streamed down my face. Sooo embarrassing! The girl pulled herself out of the water, sat down next to me and smiled; the crowd applauded. I'd never had a pretty girl be so nice to me, but then I said the most stupid, *stupid* thing, "Are you going to cook it?"'

Jade-Lotus shook her head.

High-Fly ignored her. 'She giggled and said, "Silly you! I've just rescued it, it was trapped." She dredged more water out of her hair; I just stared at her, at the pale freckles on her cheeks, like I'd been bewitched. I followed her as she got up, walked a few steps, and released the duckling to join its family. Seeing her shivering I took off my jacket and put it on her shoulders. Without thinking I offered to make her a hot ginger tea and she said yes. That's how it started. Aihhh, the two years we spent together in the college were the happiest time in my life!' He sat back, sinking comfortably into the sofa, and beaming at the screen, but his mind was elsewhere, somewhere he wanted to stay.

Jade-Lotus wanted to sit back too. Underneath layers of oily fake veneer he had real passion, was able to fall in love and be enchanted by the magic of it. But how could such a loving couple end up aborting their baby and getting divorced? She turned to him and raised an eyebrow.

'Aihhh, after I graduated, things changed,' High-Fly eventually said, his tone becoming icy. 'My father wanted me to work for him in the government rather than do a thankless teaching job, but that wasn't all. Humph! He arranged a marriage for me, can you believe that! To a "past-sell-by-date" daughter of a high-ranking official in the county town! In his words, so he and I would have "a better political future"!' He mimicked his father's way of giving a speech. 'I argued with him, trust me, big time. In the end, I had to give in on the job, but not New-Dawn; my life would be nothing without her! And we were married once she had finished her studies, a big victory, yeah! For three years our life was like a long honeymoon and I never wanted it to end. Never!' He stretched his lips into a broad smile. 'But when we finally gave in to our parents' pressure and tried for a baby, it went wrong. Aihhh!' His infectious smile receded like a wave on a beach, his face littered with lines of sorrow. He stared down at his shoelaces, and seemed to have aged ten years. 'I guess you've heard the rest.'

The humming of the ceiling lamp became noticeable. Under the florescent light, he reverted back to his passive and solemn self. He then bent forward, put his head between his hands and curled up like a hedgehog – outside defensively spiky, but inside soft and vulnerable.

Jade-Lotus cleared her throat. 'But why did you help your father abort your baby girl?'

'You believe that rubbish?' He sat up abruptly, his eyebrows arching upwards.

'Well, I haven't been given any reason not to. I think the fact that New-Dawn divorced you says it all.'

He went red, clenching his hands into fists; however his aggression seemed more at himself. 'You see, you and I are very different! You're a fighter, but I can't face confrontation, especially not with someone I love, I just buckle and shrink. New-Dawn blindly accused me of helping my father kill our baby and demanded a divorce. I was so shocked that she could even think that I was capable of doing such a thing. I told her that it was my baby too, but she became deaf. So I stopped talking; it was hell for me to digest what'd happened. And she stopped talking too. In less than a year, we were divorced! What's the point of staying together if you can't trust each other?'

'So you think you're blameless? I can't believe you didn't fight your corner, and gave up on a loving marriage just like that! You were such…'

'A wimp? Maybe I was. The only crime I committed was telling my parents about us going to the temple to bless our unborn baby. I've never forgiven myself for being so naïve. Look,' he stretched out his right hand and wiggled his slightly bent forefinger and middle-finger. 'After I was locked in the temple, I was terrified in the dark and worried to death about my wife and baby. I shouted and kicked at the doors, but they didn't move. I tried to prise them open, but the doors sprang back, breaking these fingers. It was well over two hours later before they let me out and took me home; New-Dawn was already home, hysterical.' He sighed, straightening his deformed fingers.

Jade-Lotus sighed too; perhaps both sides of the sad story were true. 'Do you regret the divorce?'

'Every waking moment,' he said to his hands. 'I only really feel alive when I feel the pain of that regret. I let myself become my father's puppet; whenever he pulled a string, I obediently moved. Guess what? I married again, to the spinster of the official my father had originally chosen, and soon had a little boy which fulfilled my family duty. But honestly, I'm like a piece of drift wood, totally dead inside.' High-Fly leaned back and seemed at peace, having told the story that he had probably buried deep for all these years. 'I don't know why I'm telling you this.'

'Because you need... a friend?' Jade-Lotus said. *A friend? Really!*

'A friend, haha.' He squeezed a closed-mouth smile. 'Actually I'd like that.'

'Time heals; maybe after all these years...'

'Seven years eight months,' he interrupted.

'Well, it sounds like you still care. Maybe you and New-Dawn should talk, and settle the past, so you both can move on and start to live again. Perhaps she won't need to scream and wail in the street any more.'

'You think it would be that easy? I knew she was back, but I don't know if she's still around.' He played with his bent fingers for a few seconds before raising his eyes. 'It might sound weird to you, but her wailing is the only thing that reminds me that I once had love.'

'It is weird. But I'm surprised your brutal father didn't try to stop her.'

'Ah, like father like son. I knew how to blackmail him.' He winked. 'Believe it or not, he has a "pension pot", literally a pot containing the valuable stuff he confiscated from families during the Cultural Revolution. Bet there's something from your grandma in there. He should have handed everything back to the owners or the government in the eighties, but he kept it all in a secret room in our house.'

'Gosh! Is there any crime that Mark Lee isn't capable of?'

'Hahaha! Right now he's not happy with me; he doesn't believe I can lead the townspeople to make William's plan work.'

'Then we should help each other, and make it the best Duanwu ever. But we don't have much time. I've given it some thought: Little-Blossom and I can help organise things; you can handle the official stuff and use your connections to make things happen, can't you? Together we can pull it off. If the festival is a success, I'm sure everything else falls into place.'

High-Fly was seemingly lost in thought. 'New-Dawn always liked festivals. If we make it amazing do you think she'll come?'

'I'm sure she will.'

'OK. I'll do my best, and show her I have a backbone!'

Jade-Lotus nodded.

High-Fly reached for the remote control and pressed a button, the blinds opened. Outside was a prosperous day.

On the way back home, Jade-Lotus skipped. Had that really happened – sitting down with High-Fly, talking like a friend and even feeling his pain? Tell that to her younger self! But time had changed and there was a new focus; in just over three months' time the baby would arrive. *Must go and find Little-Blossom, and start organising the Duanwu Festival.*

Jade-Lotus jogged to Gardener's Place, where the doors of the principal's office were wide open and the courtyard was full of staff, each with a glass of yellow wine. *What's going on?*

Little-Blossom tapped her tumbler with a spoon and said, 'Hello!' beckoning to Jade-Lotus while looking around at everyone, 'We're gathered here to congratulate River-Cloud on his new post at the Shanghai Conservatory of Music, starting in September. He'll head a new programme called China's Ancient Music Treasures to write up a comprehensive guzheng handbook and lead a team of musicians to record a collection of classic pieces using traditional musical instruments.'

The Shanghai Conservatory of Music?

'To give River-Cloud time to prepare, I'll take over his role with immediate effect.' Little-Blossom stood upright in a silver linen trouser suit, her tummy protruding proudly. 'I hope for your steadfast wonderful support, and we'll continue the brilliant success of Shan Academy. Now let's toast to River-Cloud's exciting new adventure and wish him every success!' She raised her tumbler and drank what looked like lychee juice.

'Thank you, Little-Blossom.' River-Cloud raised his glass. 'This is a toast to my dear wife, to wish her great success managing the great academy!' The sunlight danced on his spectacles; as he downed his wine, his face blossomed.

Jade-Lotus smiled at him. He had finally got his wish and would absolutely thrive in his new role. It must have been a huge step for him to let his wife take the reins of the ancient Shan Academy, but he appeared comfortable with it. He already had the makings of a good literati.

'Now come and enjoy these delicacies from Shaoxing!' Little-Blossom said. The staff buzzed around the table in the middle of the courtyard and mingled.

Jade-Lotus moved over to Little-Blossom and said, 'Gosh, what a nice surprise!'

'Come, let's sit down in River-Cloud's... actually, my office now,' Little-Blossom giggled, 'and I'll tell you everything.'

As they sat down on the cushioned bench, Little-Blossom beamed. 'I used up my last life line and it worked.'

'OK?'

'Ah ah,' she sighed a happy sigh. 'In desperation to save the academy, I left my pride at home, and went to Shaoxing to meet with an old student, Tiger Liu. He owns a high-tech company and is now one of the richest men in China; so, he was my saviour!' Little-Blossom looked up as if to thank Buddha. 'Over a lunch, I frankly told him of our embarrassing situation and asked for a bridging loan. He asked me how much, then wrote down a number and two characters on a napkin, and passed it to me. Guess what he wrote?' She widened her eyes.

Jade-Lotus shook her head.

'He wrote a fat seven-figure number and the two characters for "gift". Can you believe that?' Little-Blossom shrieked. 'I said oh my Buddha I couldn't possibly accept such a generous gift, but he insisted and wouldn't take no for answer. In the end he accepted a tiny number of shares in the academy in return. It was as if the harsh north wind had suddenly changed to a warm southerly breeze; all my financial pressures melted away. How relieved I was! How relieved! Now I can pay off the bank straight away and use what's left on the many plans I've had in mind for years.' She closed her eyes, basking in the dappled sunlight streaming through the open window, probably dreaming about a rosy future.

Jade-Lotus smiled. It had been torture to watch Little-Blossom running around like an ant on a hot wok, and unable to help. Now she could relax. Little-Blossom had really been the Mount Dizhu towering in the middle of a torrent and managed to turn the tide, and more importantly she was back to her old confident self.

Little-Blossom opened her eyes. 'Sorry, I was drifting away, wasn't I? And there's more! Tiger and I then chatted like old times. He was an orphan, and the first free student River-Cloud had persuaded his father to take on. During his three years in our academy, he became part of our family. I told Tiger about River-Cloud's frustrations. By the way, I overheard him telling you in the garden that he would rather play guzheng than manage the academy. Then Tiger said he had an idea. A good friend of his is the head of new programmes at the Shanghai Conservatory of Music, and the institute was struggling to get financial backing for an ambitious programme: to revive Chinese traditional music and record it for future generations. He phoned his friend straight away and offered to back the programme on the condition that River-Cloud manages it. His friend was only too happy to oblige! Unbelievable, isn't it? So, one arrow, two golden eagles!' Little-Blossom giggled, her face glowing and her hands caressing her protruding tummy.

'Wow, that's so wonderful! Somehow, I just knew you would find a way to sort things out.' Jade-Lotus gave Little-

Blossom a gentle shoulder-nudge. 'But are you OK to manage the school while… you know?' she said breezily, tilting her head at her cousin's belly.

'Absolutely! I'll manage things much better without River-Cloud in the way! Don't tell him I said that.' Little-Blossom giggled again.

Jade-Lotus zipped her mouth with her fingers. Little-Blossom's giggles were infectious, as was her self-belief, and her courage to wear the trousers in an institution dominated by framed male faces for three hundred years. Headmistress Shan would suit her well and she would be brilliant. And it would be a proud story to tell future daughter one day.

'I want to tell you about a lovely thing that happened this morning. I was out for a break, and a mulberry catkin fell on my belly! Do you know what it means?' She pulled a tissue parcel out of her pocket and revealed the catkin.

Jade-Lotus studied it, and shook her head.

'It means my baby – actually, yours – is going to be lucky and wise when she grows up.'

'Really? I've never heard that saying before.'

'My grandmother said it every year. Mulberry trees only flower when they're sure that spring is definitely here to stay, and in our mountain village when we saw the catkins we knew the bamboo shoots would soon be ready and all the other crops would follow, and no one would be hungry any more.'

'A wise and lucky little girl. I'm happy with that.' Jade-Lotus nodded.

'I never thought she would change my life the way she has.' Little-Blossom sighed. 'If you hadn't wanted to adopt her, I don't know what I would've done. You even gave up your job to come and wait for her. It's like…' She was suddenly tearful. 'It's like you've shaken me hard and woken me up.'

Jade-Lotus hugged her. 'Thank you again for letting us adopt her! Waiting for her I get to spend time with you.' She paused for a second and screamed, 'And now we're going to organise the Duanwu Festival!'

'You found High-Fly?'

'Yes, and he's back on track.' Jade-Lotus winked at her and told her about the karaoke room.

'Well done you, well done! We've both done so well, I wonder how Snow-Flower is getting on with finding the monk.'

The phone on the desk rang and Little-Blossom answered. 'Do you have ears that can hear from a thousand kilometres away? I'll put you on speaker, Jade-Lotus is here too.'

'Hello,' Snow-Flower's bell-voice came through. 'I just knew you two were glued together. I tried both your home numbers, but no one answered! What's that background noise? Are you having a party? I'm jealous now.'

'Actually Little-Blossom is having an office party, and River-Cloud is taking up a post at the Shanghai Conservatory of Music!' Jade-Lotus blurted out.

'What? How come?' Snow-Flower shrieked.

'And thanks to Jade-Lotus, we're back on track with Duanwu,' Little-Blossom shrieked back.

It was like a school playground as Jade-Lotus and Little-Blossom fought to tell their stories. The years vanished, and the jellybean sandals were back on again.

'I have news too!' Snow-Flower screamed.

'You've found the monk?' Jade-Lotus straightened her face.

'Well, yes and no,' Snow-Flower said. 'We managed to track

him down, but he's out travelling and teaching, so we'll have to wait for him to come back. But his abbot is happy for us to talk to him.'

19

Duanwu Dragon Boat Festival

Jade-Lotus rushed upstairs, two steps at a time, and threw the window wide open. The returning fishermen sang the Duanwu song as if in a choir, joined by Tai chi practitioners on the riverbank, children playing in the square, men airing duvets high up on poles bridging the narrow lanes, and housewives laundering clothes by the river.

AYY HAYY HAYY...
  The fifth day of the lunar May,
  Duanwu Festival on its way.
  Ay hay hay, ay hay hay...
  Hanging wormwood on the wall,
  Zhong Kui, calamus deck the hall.
  Venomous creatures held at bay,
  Evil and disease can't find a way.
  Ay hay hay, ay hay hay...
  Delicious zongzi on the boil,
  Fragrance wraps like a coil.

Five-colour eggs well cooked,
Realgar wine jars hang on hooks.
Ay hay hay, ay hay hay...
On dragon boats, men raise oars,
Drums drive them, hot sweat pours.
Yummy zongzi thrown in sacrifice,
Hungry dragon truly in paradise.
Ay hay hay, ay hay hay...
Wish good fortune for all next year,
Favourable weather and harvest cheer.
Dragon's leftovers have fish served,
Great poet Qu Yuan is preserved.
Ay hay hay, ay hay hay...
On the shores, women smile heartily,
Fully made up and dressed for the party.
Pinning precious douniang in their hair,
Wearing woven Ai-Hu as a dare.
Ay hay hay, ay hay hay...
Children running around happy,
Painted faces looking like candy.
Pressing eggs, pulling grass blades,
dancing under mulberry shades.
Ay hay hay, ay hay hay...
The fifth day of the Lunar May,
Duanwu festival is today.

She hummed along, shrunk back to the three-year-old girl in a pinafore, leaning against Grandma's knee, learning the song for the first time. Grandma had taught her the traditional lyrics rather than what was blasting out of the loudspeakers at the time:

The fifth day of the lunar May,
Great Helmsman on his way.
Ay hay hay, ay hay hay...
Mao's posters on the wall,
Shining axe and sickle deck the hall.
Capitalists and reactionaries held at bay,
Monsters and demons can't find a way.
Ay hay hay, ay hay hay...

As the song ended, she leaned out of the tearoom window. The cobbled streets looked fresh. Chains of sea-green zongzi-shaped lanterns hung vertically, side by side, curtaining the white walls. Rainbow-coloured bunting, with pendants shaped as teapots, lotus flowers, butterflies and fish, was draped across the canals. Bundles of tied wormwood and calamus were suspended from front doors and the arches of the Three Bridges, to ward off evil and poisonous creatures. The aroma of pork zongzi being slowly boiled, painted eggs being simmered in tea, and green plums being stewed with sweet spices, drifted up and up, pushing the heady waft of jasmine to a back note. On the river, the morning mist had burnt off, revealing a newly erected giant scaly red dragon, its mouth wide open, ready to blow fire and smoke once the winning boat crossed the finish line. The town centre looked ready for Duanwu, probably as ready as the beautiful bride who had inspired the King of Yue to change the town's name to Blushing Lotus had been before their wedding two thousand years ago.

But...

She bit her bottom lip as she closed the net curtains. It had been five weeks since finding High-Fly in the karaoke room;

almost everything had come together – the town decorations, the festive activities for the big day, the intensive training for the hand-picked racing team, the band and choir, the VIP guest invitations, and confirmations from the TV stations. But Nine-Pound Old Lady still wouldn't let them use her water. Without that, there would be no boat race – the life and soul of Duanwu – and the first boat race for the five towns of the Upper Canal District would be a dragon made of mud or a dog made of straw. There was no going back either. High-Fly had sent the invites and the other four towns had enthusiastically accepted. In a week's time, William and Snow-Flower would be back, followed by the investors the next day, and then bang, the Duanwu Festival! Time was really running out, as well as the ideas to win over Nine-Pound Old Lady. Snow-Flower's strict talk ended with her being thrown out with a basin of water; Little-Blossom's gift of a jade comb was refused; River-Cloud and Autumn-Rain couldn't even get past her front door; Forever-Progress showed her pictures of a beautiful Samoyed puppy from Mongolia and offered to get her one – she hesitated, but in the end it was 'No, thanks!' This morning, the very reluctant High-Fly was going to visit her – assuming he didn't quit halfway – with an offer 'she couldn't refuse'. Well, hopefully that would work. Still it wouldn't hurt to have plan B ready, just in case.

She began to lay the table for breakfast, digging out the best china from the sideboard. Having lined up the teacups and saucers, bowls, chopsticks and their rests, she opened the lid of the oval bamboo bento box to check if everything was still warm. At last, she sat down at the eight immortals table, waiting for Grandma to come back from her Tai chi practice. A clunk from the lift door vibrated the air, and Grandma came in.

'Morning Grandma!' Jade-Lotus jumped up. 'You must be starving! Here, I've got your water and soap ready.' She pointed to a wash basin on top of the sideboard.

'Ah, my best teapot and Mrs Song's bento box! What's the special occasion?' Grandma washed her hands.

'Nothing special, just thought I should treat you once in a while.' Jade-Lotus smiled a sunflower smile.

Grandma sat down and threw her a suspicious glance.

Jade-Lotus stretched over and poured some hot soya milk from a thermos into Grandma's china bowl, carefully opened the lid of the bento and picked up a deep-fried fluffy bread-stick. 'Here you are. It's still nice and warm.'

'Thanks.' Grandma began to tear her breadstick into pieces, dropping each piece into her soya milk. 'Song's breadsticks are really the best in town.'

'Absolutely!' Jade-Lotus began to tear hers.

Grandma breathed in the steam from her soya milk and looked up. 'What do you want, my little treasure?'

'How do you know I want anything?' Jade-Lotus laughed.

'All of this. And you chewed your lip, and you're doing it again now.'

'Does anything escape your hawk-eyes?' Jade-Lotus laughed again. 'OK, Grandma, I'd really like to know the old secret between you and Nine-Pound Old Lady.'

Grandma dropped her eyes and tore her breadstick with more force.

'Grandpa Autumn-Rain said you two had to keep a promise. What promise?'

Grandma pushed the bread pieces down with her spoon, and watched them float up.

'I suspect whatever it is is why Nine-Pound Old Lady has been making trouble from the beginning.'

Grandma took a slow sip of soya milk. 'A promise is a promise,' she said without looking up.

Jade-Lotus arched her eyebrows and waited. *Well, I have to be more like Snow-Flower, the Jingwei bird who never gives up.*

Grandma avoided eye contact and concentrated on chewing a piece of bread.

'Only eight days left, Grandma! Nothing has worked to warm her icy heart; our time is running out. And you know what's at stake.'

The ceiling fan beat the air; spoons scraped the bottom of bowls.

Grandma took her time, sipped the last drop of milk and cleaned the grease from her fingers with a linen napkin before letting out a long sigh. 'It's been nearly seventy years.' She tucked a strand of loose hair slowly back into her chignon. 'But if I tell you, you'll have to promise not to tell anyone, not even Little-Blossom or Snow-Flower.' She looked serious.

Jade-Lotus frowned. 'OK, I promise.'

Grandma sat back in her horseshoe chair, looking solemn. 'As the tradition goes, our Yang ancestors would never intermarry with the Shans, because literatis and business people generally looked down on each other. Aihh! But times changed; our two families became great friends. Nine-Pound Old Lady's mother became ill, and before she died two marriages were arranged as she had wished.' She stared at the print of dancing cranes on her teacup. 'Nine-Pound Old Lady was engaged to my second eldest brother, and I to Autumn-Rain. At the time we were just children; I was only five.' Her stare was unwavering.

'A childhood arranged marriage! Really?'

'That autumn, my brother turned fourteen. With a mission-ary's help, he sailed off to France to study Western medicine. He had been really excited about it.' Grandma gazed into the distance. 'Before he left, the wedding day was set for after his graduation. Nine-Pound Old Lady was very happy. During the five-year wait for her fiancé, while helping to bring up her younger siblings, particularly Autumn-Rain, she blossomed, became really pretty and had perfect bound feet. Sometimes she tutted, looking at my free growing feet, and said my nana had robbed me of the chance to be waited on when I grew up.' Grandma shook her head. 'But she was kind to me, often called me little sis-in-law, and even allowed me to touch her wedding dress and the hand-made silk shoes for her three-inch golden lotuses.' Grandma squeezed a tiny smile. 'My brother graduated with a good degree and was due back for his wedding. But he didn't come, and instead sent a telegram to say that he rejected the arranged marriage and couldn't bear to marry someone with traditional bound feet.'

'Oh.' Jade-Lotus widened her eyes.

Grandma leaned forward, re-organised her bowl, spoon and teacup and saucer into a straight line. 'My nana and parents telegraphed my brother, and ordered him to come back at once, but he refused. In the end, our family had to tell the Shans and apologise. The news broke Nine-Pound Old Lady's heart; she was furious, and made her father cancel my engagement to her little brother too. To protect Nine-Pound Old Lady's reputation, her father begged my family not to tell anyone that she had been rejected, and also insisted my brother should never come back to Blushing Lotus. Our family accepted reluctantly and kept the promise. Soon my parents engaged me to one of the twin sons of a well-known lawyer in Shanghai. As fate had it, my brother died of typhoid in Europe soon after.' Grandma lowered her head.

'Oh my gosh, so… tragic! I'm so sorry about your brother.'

Grandma closed her eyes and said a quiet prayer. When she finished, she looked hollow, but nodded.

'Um, were you furious about the cancelation of your engagement?'

'Well, I was ten then, and being brought up to love Autumn-Rain and to be his bride one day. We read and played together often, and I loved playing with him; he was always so kind and gentle to me.'

'Do you, um, still love him?'

Grandma started to clear the table.

Jade-Lotus watched Grandma and sighed. 'I feel really sorry for Nine-Pound Old Lady now. I thought she'd been icy towards us because I'd been rude to her as a child, saying her feet were smelly.'

Grandma laughed. 'Oh no. Aihh, what she was proud of was also her downfall. Bound feet was a fashion started by men, and she was rejected by a man over hers!'

'Why didn't Nine-Pound Old Lady marry someone else?'

'Ah, there was another surprise. Months later, my brother's body was brought back, and Nine-Pound Old Lady attended his funeral. But instead of a white mourning dress, she came in her red wedding dress, and brought a priest and trumpet players. She held her wedding ceremony right there and then, and announced that she was his wife and would keep her chastity for him.'

'What? She wed a dead man and kept her chastity for a ghost? Was she mad? When was this? I thought that awful tradition died with the Qing Dynasty?'

'1937, just before the Japanese invaded the rest of China. I'll never forget that year; I lost my nana, parents, and two other brothers to the war. Only I survived.' Grandma was silent for a long while.

'So sorry.' Jade-Lotus caressed Grandma's hand. The family past was full of tragedies.

'Chastity lingered on in Blushing Lotus,' Grandma managed to continue.

'Nine-Pound Old Lady wasn't after a chastity arch, was she?' Jade-Lotus sneered. Like the twin sister of foot binding, widow chastity – young widows staying chaste and fulfilling filial piety to their husband's family – was another deformed Confucian ideal men had placed on women. For a thousand years, emperors had cultivated it as the top honour for a woman, awarding her a beautiful arch, placed in a conspicuous location, for people to respect and admire. 'Grandma, do you remember that arch on the way to your labour camp, the one you said got imperial approval?' Right outside of Blushing Lotus, there was a two-storey-tall granite arch, topped with three tiers of flying tiled roofs. The deep square beam had intricately carved flowers and birds on one side, and on the other the bold characters of 'Mrs Qiu' nestling between praise: 'As clear as ice' and 'As pure as jade'. On the large flat surfaces between the roofed tiers were neat characters, telling the movingly chaste story of Mrs Qiu; although eroded with time, it was still a moral beacon for women.

Grandma nodded. 'The most lavish one around here. She'd love to have had one like that from us Yangs!' Her tone was sarcastic. 'Aihh, I've thought about it for many years, and

I think it was her way of fighting back. Nine-Pound Old Lady was a prime beauty by the standards of the time. Being rejected by a man only because she had followed traditions set by men must have really hurt – and worse still, slashed her reputation as cheap as dirt. So she fought back the only way she could: by raising her status to become a most honourable Confucian woman.'

'But isn't it too high a price to pay?'

'Maybe. But she took control, regained her dignity, and lived by her principles and Confucian pride, which meant so much to her. Aihh, I wish she hadn't done it though; she wasted her whole life.' Grandma sighed. 'What time is it? I must get back to work; we have two groups coming at lunch time.' She stood up. 'I hope all this helps.'

'Tremendously! Thank you, Grandma!'

As she tidied up, Jade-Lotus couldn't help but think of Nine-Pound Old Lady. She had no way to defend her reputation other than to sacrifice herself. In the old dynasties she would have been honoured, no doubt, with a fine arch, her name, story, dignity and pride forever remembered. But now, in 2007, there was no way communist Mark Lee would allow such an arch. What could she do to win her over? Nothing would bring back what Nine-Pound Old Lady had lost. Hopefully High-Fly would bring good news.

As they waited, Jade-Lotus hummed the Duanwu Song, tapping her pen to the beat, and Little-Blossom and Forever-Progress soon joined in.

'Afternoon, ladies!' High-Fly burst through the door and slumped down.

'Did it work?' Jade-Lotus asked.

265

'"Money can make a devil turn millstones" – but not this devil!' High-Fly sneered.

'Perhaps you're so used to taking money rather than giving it out you were too tight?' Forever-Progress said.

'Oi, watch your mouth! I was so nice, offering her a handsome sum for the right to use her private waters, and a ten-year license for another ice-cream parlour right in the centre of the town, for free. But guess what? She just lifted up her three-inch golden lotuses and sat there inspecting them.'

Everyone giggled.

Jade-Lotus pictured him standing dumbstruck, staring at the old lady's bound feet. 'Thank you for trying. We're back to square one with her.' She shrugged.

'But can't Mark Lee just order her?' Forever-Progress said.

'No. Father is actually scared of her!' High-Fly said.

'She was the heaviest baby by birth,' Little-Blossom said.

'But surely she has a soft spot,' Jade-Lotus said.

'Really, that tough old boot?' Forever-Progress said, which made High-Fly laugh.

'We have to walk in her shoes to find what she'd really like,' Little-Blossom said.

Jade-Lotus stared at her, her eyes widening. 'You've just given me an idea.' She explained it.

'You must be joking!' High-Fly said.

'Do you think the salon girls would actually do it?' Forever-Progress said. 'My grandma's bound feet were always rotten in summer; the whole lane could smell them.'

'Well, that's the point, isn't it?' Jade-Lotus said.

'I think it could work,' Little-Blossom said, 'I know she misses doing girly things. Even her friends think she's as solid as a boulder, and they forget that underneath she's a

266

woman just like them.'

'I agree. "Utmost sincerity can pierce even gold and stone"!' Jade-Lotus said.

The following afternoon, Jade-Lotus knocked on Nine-Pound Old Lady's door. As she waited, she squeezed a tight smile at Little-Blossom, Forever-Progress, and a team of fresh-faced girls from the best beauty salon in town, who were carrying beauty kits and loungers. It was strange to knock on the door of a nemesis. Would it pan out? All chips were in for this final throw of the dice.

A wizened lady with a long chain of rosary beads on her chest opened the door. She grabbed her beads and screamed, 'Oh, you! Oh-my-Buddha, what in the world are you all here for?'

'Hello Mrs Qian,' Little-Blossom said warmly. Another lady, more stout, also came to the doorway, looking baffled. 'And Mrs Chou!'

Jade-Lotus took a deep breath and bowed. 'Good afternoon, aunties! We've heard that Nine-Pound Old Lady suffers a lot with her feet, so we took the liberty of arranging a proper wash and pedicure for her.' She gestured towards the girls. 'May we come in please? We'd also like to ask her about how best to wear a douniang headdress, my grandma said she was the town beauty when she was young and her douniang was always the best.'

The two old ladies frowned at each other. 'Wait here,' Mrs Qian said and went back inside. Mrs Chou looked serious guarding the door.

Mrs Qian reappeared and said to Jade-Lotus, 'You can come in. The rest will have to wait.'

'May I come too?' Little-Blossom said quickly.

'Don't worry,' Jade-Lotus whispered.

Jade-Lotus followed Mrs Qian into the lounge. An aroma of rose powder, similar to Grandma's bedroom's, mixed with herbal medicines, hit her. The walls were covered in lifelike bamboo-patterned silk panels, only the green had faded. A large chest was against one wall, draped with a cream silk cloth embroidered with flowers. Hanging on the wall were three long scrolls of watercolour painting: a pair of dancing white cranes, two golden carp and a pair of nesting orioles. Against the lattice window was a daybed with an intricately carved wooden-frame canopy, on which sat Nine-Pound Old Lady crossed legged, surrounded by an abundance of cushions, her pale lilac silk kimono shimmering in the sunlight filtering in behind her. With her eyes closed, her face placid, and her hands resting on her knees, she looked like a statue of Buddha. Was she expecting people to worship her?

Mrs Qian pointed at one of the two horseshoe chairs in front of the daybed, and gestured for Jade-Lotus to sit down. She then leaned over and stroked Nine-Pound Old Lady's arm, with the affection one would show a beloved pet, before sitting down on the other chair. She rubbed her hands together as if anticipating a dogfight.

Nine-Pound Old Lady opened her eyes, and said in her usual deep, calm, but unwelcoming voice, 'I can guess why you're here, Jade-Lotus, but I'm curious as to why you want these girls to wash my feet? To make me feel better? I'm just fine without it.'

'Well, they use a new pedicure technique that's all the rage in Shanghai and we thought you might like to try it.' Jade-Lotus tried to sound sincere, but her voice was a little shaky.

'Mrs Qian, do you think I need fancy toes?'

Mrs Qian let out a hysterical laugh, her shoulders shaking.

'Um, Grandaunt Shan, can we talk privately, please?' Jade-Lotus looked into her eyes.

Nine-Pound Old Lady raised an eyebrow. 'You want to wash my feet yourself?' Her tone was deliberate and Mrs Qian laughed even louder, rocking back and forth.

'Please, Grandaunt Shan! I persuaded Grandma to tell me your secret.'

Nine-Pound Old Lady put her hand up to stop Mrs Qian's laughter, and waved for her to go.

'Are you sure?' Mrs Qian stood up, and as she left the room glanced back several times before closing the door.

'What did she tell you?' Nine-Pound Old Lady pulled the lapels of her kimono together, as if feeling a draught.

'The truth between you and my granduncle,' Jade-Lotus said.

Nine-Pound Old Lady stared at her, emotionless.

'I'm very sorry for what he did. He thought he had bettered himself in the West and progressed beyond tradition, but he had no right to judge you and do what he did. It only showed he hadn't progressed at all. If I were in your shoes, I would be very very angry too.'

Nine-Pound Old Lady continued to stare, but her face relaxed a little.

'On behalf of Grandma, I want to apologise for my granduncle. It's a dark spot on our family history and we're very ashamed.' As her last word echoed, Jade-Lotus lowered her head. It really wasn't something to be proud of as a Yang.

Nine-Pound Old Lady didn't say a word, as if wanting to lengthen the time for Jade-Lotus to thoroughly chew her shame. She let go of her lapels, shifted her bottom, re-crossed her legs in the opposite way, and re-arranged the cushions.

Jade-Lotus raised her head and said, 'I can't take you back to that time and undo the harm; I can't imagine how hard it's been to live all by yourself, and I can't comprehend the huge loss you've been through. If there's anything I can do to make up for it, just tell me, and I'll do it. I know in old times, you would've had a fine arch erected for you...'

'You know about chastity arches?' Nine-Pound Old Lady cut in, her eyes shining.

Jade-Lotus nodded and sighed. 'I know it's not fair, but I don't think you'll ever get your arch, not under Mark Lee's nose. I'm sorry.'

Nine-Pound Old Lady was silent.

Jade-Lotus hesitated, but then slowly reached out, putting her hand onto Nine-Pound Old Lady's, expecting her to pull away. But she didn't, and closed her eyes, seemingly enjoying the touch. 'My granduncle didn't treasure your bound feet, but I do – not for historic reasons, but because they are a part of you, a strong and beautiful woman, like we all aspire to be, and I want to take care of them. May I hold one?'

Nine-Pound Old Lady looked at Jade-Lotus as if she was an alien, but then waved and invited her to sit on the bed. A tear ran down her cheek, which she quickly wiped away. As she stretched out her leg she nodded.

Jade-Lotus sat on the soft daybed and held one of Nine-Pound Old Lady's three-inch golden lotuses, wrapped in clean white cloth. There was a whiff of bad odour, but it didn't matter. Confucian women suffered so much! She shook her head as she gently massaged the top and the sole. 'Would you like to try this Shanghai pedicure? I haven't tried it, but they

270

tell me it's very nice,' she said softly.

'If I must.' Nine-Pound Old Lady smiled, looking beautiful.

Jade-Lotus returned to the front door and invited all the ladies in. There was a flurry of activity as the beauticians set out the loungers, towels, wash basins, bottles of aromatic oil and pots of cream.

Mrs. Qian and Mrs. Chou exchanged glances and said, almost together, 'Dowager, it's like a meaty pie has fallen free from the sky! Can we join in too?'

Nine-Pound Old Lady laughed throatily. 'So, you want me to share my pie? Typical!' However, her face glowed with pride, probably in the same way as it had when she was young and all her friends wanted to borrow her elegant handmade silk gowns.

'Of course Mrs. Qian and Mrs. Chou can join us,' Jade-Lotus said.

When all was set up, Jade-Lotus knelt down in front of Nine-Pound Old Lady, ready to unwrap the white cloth on her bound feet.

'What are you doing?' Nine-Pound Old Lady squeaked. 'You don't want to do that! It's very unsightly and smelly. Please just sit next to me, we can enjoy the pedicure together.'

Jade-Lotus smiled and obliged. Little-Blossom took the lounger on the other side of Nine-Pound Old Lady and gave a thumbs up.

When all the ladies had made themselves comfortable, the beauticians started to work. Amongst waves of soft oohs and aahs, Nine-Pound Old Lady started to giggle. 'Oh my ticklish feet...' Then she burst into laughter, echoed by Forever-Progress; soon, like a yawn in a room, everyone laughed.

'Oh, we haven't laughed like this for a long time.' Mrs Chou wiped her eyes.

'Indeed,' Nine-Pound Old Lady said, and covered her mouth, seemingly to stave off another wave of giggles.

'Grandaunt,' Little-Blossom said, 'can we please ask how you used to decorate your prize-winning douniangs?'

'Oh yes! I heard that women will be wearing douniang at Duanwu this year. I can't quite believe it,' Nine-Pound Old Lady said, sitting up, her cheeks glowing, 'it's been such a long time.' She settled back into her lounger again, and told everyone how to choose a good basic headdress; how to add feathers, precious stones and jewellery, shiny shells and even fresh flowers to it; and what angle to wear it at for best effect... In the gentle lavender-infused steam rising from the wash basins, as she listened to Nine-Pound Old Lady's happy, deep and almost magnetic voice, Jade-Lotus pictured her as a young beauty, smiling at Grandma as she took to the gilded Duanwu stage to be given a small jade cup for having the most magnificent douniang.

'So, are you up for the douniang competition, Grandaunt Shan?' Jade-Lotus said.

'Oh, definitely,' Nine-Pound Old Lady said. 'It's a shame that none of my precious old douniangs survived those bandit Red Guards! But I'm making one, and I'm going to win again, you know?' She giggled again.

'Of course you'll win!' Mrs Qian and Mrs Chou shouted together.

'Now, have you forgotten to ask me something else, Jade-Lotus? The reason you came here?' Nine-Pound Old Lady drawled.

Jade-Lotus suddenly felt hot. 'Ah yes, Grandaunt Shan. May we please use your water for the dragon boat race?'

'Yes, you may,' Nine-Pound Old Lady said, her voice ringing happily.

'Lovely! I can't wait for Duanwu! And we should have more of these girls' afternoons,' Little-Blossom said.

'Of course,' Jade-Lotus said, 'if Grandaunt Shan would like it.' She held Nine-Pound Old Lady's hand.

'I'd love it very much.' Nine-Pound Old Lady gave Jade-Lotus's fingers a firm and warm grip. 'And, please invite your grandma.'

'Deal!' Jade-Lotus said.

The Duanwu festival duly arrived. Townspeople were gathering in the centre under the bright mid-summer sun. It was as if the town clock had been rewound and Blushing Lotus had travelled back to its glorious past; or it was hosting a huge fancy-dress party where the dress code was historic and bourgeois. The shoulder-rubbing locals were turned out in clothes from the Ming and Qing dynasties; the eye-catching douniangs on the women's heads showed off their craft and ambition.

As William and Snow-Flower enthusiastically showed the investors around the pop-up festive stalls while they waited for the local officials and the mayor of Shanghai – Snow-Flower's friend – to arrive, Jade-Lotus quietly slipped away and headed to the main spectators' area. Snow-Flower had persuaded the abbot to call Mark Lee's brother Rich-Knowledgeable, now Master Deep-Water, back from his travels to lead the team of monks to bless the festival. To find him, and persuade him to join the private party in Grandma's teahouse after the celebrations would be the best chance to find out what had happened to Mama.

In front of the 'stage', a flat open space between the spectators and the river, Little-Blossom and her teachers and students, all dressed in Qing-style long robes, were directing people to be seated on the gentle grass slope. River-Cloud looked like an orchestral conductor, making sure all the performers for the opening ceremony were in position. Where were the monks? Oh yes, they were huddled in a corner, all wearing brown robes. But where was Master Deep-Water? He would be in a bright yellow robe and a red kasaya.

Jade-Lotus turned to take in the whole spectator area, that ran along the river and sloped up towards the town, and was packed with seated townspeople, but couldn't see him anywhere. She walked up the path to find her special helpers. Antiques Guan had come, keen to see his son; New-Dawn was here, wanting revenge; and Snow-Flower's housekeeper, Mother Li, had come as an extra pair of hands.

'Have you seen Master Deep-Water?' Jade-Lotus sat down next to New-Dawn.

'Yes,' Mother Li answered quickly and leaned over, her huge black hat with a peacock feather covering the sky and giant bug-eyed sunglasses covering much of her face. 'Only a second ago, he was there with the monks.'

'He won't be far away,' New-Dawn said. She was wearing a red baseball cap with a cute toy koala bear pinned to its side, and wraparound sunglasses.

Antiques Guan sighed. His long, now tamed beard and eyebrows suited his silver Qing robe, but his wide-rimmed straw hat looked a little out of place.

'Don't worry,' Mother Li said. 'We won't let him slip away.'

'OK. I need to get back to the investors.' Jade-Lotus stood up.

The clouds began to pile up in the sky, an auspicious sign for the townspeople, as by legend they brought the dragons. As she reached the path, Jade-Lotus was met by a big crowd that was following the BBC's reporter, David Kwan, who was talking to a camera. '… in mainland China, Duanwu is a much loved festival, ceremoniously celebrated each year on the fifth day of lunar May, which usually falls in mid-June in the western calendar. In my years of working in China I've seen it many times, in many different places. Although it varies, the main theme is the same – to commemorate the death of the patriotic poet and court official Qu Yuan, who drowned himself two thousand years ago when his country Chu fell into enemy hands. The legend says that people in boats raced to where he had drowned, beating drums and throwing hundreds of zongzi, which are bamboo-leaf-wrapped tetrahedral sticky-rice dumplings, into the water to feed the dragon and the fish, so that the body of the poet wouldn't be eaten. This year I'm in a small canal town called Blushing Lotus, fifty miles southwest of Shanghai, to see something new – a dragon-worship ceremony. The tradition dates back over two thousand years in this region, but it was banned by the communists in 1949 and then forgotten. Today, in Blushing Lotus, they've brought it back…'

Jade-Lotus tagged along at the back; an even bigger crowd following Ms Deng from Snow-Flower's Shanghai TV came up behind her. Ms Deng's voice was crisp and high-pitched, '… this year, we're following the new mayor of Shanghai in Blushing Lotus, a quintessential small town in the Yangtze region with a fabulously long history and its own colourful traditions. Our mayor is famous for his good taste in travel; join me, Bright-Moon Deng after the break to discover what attracted our mayor to this delightful canal town.'

David stepped up onto the grass slope. '… there are many customs unique to this town and one of the most spectacular is the wearing of elaborate headdresses called douniang. Like the extravagant hats at Royal Ascot on Ladies' Day, the women here compete to have the best douniang, and we can feast our eyes on this group of lovely ladies. This looks like a Monarch Butterfly, most vivid; and oh my, that one has a coiled serpent on it! Now look at this one!' The camera turned to Nine-Pound Old Lady's douniang. 'The lotus flower, pushed through fresh leaves, still has its dew; the green cicada attached to the bud looks so real, its golden wings spread open, almost transparent, its eyes so luminous…'

Nine-Pound Old Lady, who was sitting cross-legged on a rush-grass futon and chatting happily with her friends, turned to the camera and gave a big smile; her douniang trembled slightly. She wore a silver high-collared satin top, embroidered all over with pink peonies. Although her tiny feet were invisible, it wouldn't be difficult to imagine that they would be encased in matching little silk shoes.

Jade-Lotus gave her a little wave. Her douniang was indeed as magnificent as Grandma had predicted. The Lotus flower symbolised purity, and the cicada loyalty to principles. Nine-Pound Old Lady had certainly stayed pure and true to tradition, lived by her principles, and would probably die by her principles too. She might have been oblivious to the fact that times had changed and people had moved on; she might not have given much thought to whether traditions still have value when they become obstacles in a river of change. But, like Grandma, she was a lady of honour and dignity. She deserved to be happy and enjoy herself. It was the right decision not to wear Grandma's Phoenix douniang, a family heirloom from her royal great nana, full of rubies, pearls and gold strands, which had only survived because it had been hidden behind a hornet's nest near their ancestral hall. Although Grandma had wanted them to win the douniang competition, it would be much better if Nine-Pound Old Lady won. Jade-Lotus touched her own simple headdress, decorated with just a spray of red silk pomegranate flower, which matched the jacquard pattern of her muted rose-gold qipao dress. The pomegranate symbolised children and a happy family, and that was enough. Ah, it wouldn't be long now to hold that little bundle of joy.

Ms Deng squeaked, 'Our mayor has arrived! Dressed in a cream mandarin-collared silk robe and a white trilby straw hat, he looks so stylish, blending well with the locals in traditional costumes. He's now being introduced by our chief, Snow-Flower Shan, to the overseas investors. Let's get closer. We can also see a group of local politicians, all dressed handsomely, coming to welcome our mayor. I'm Bright-Moon Deng, join me again right after the break.'

Jade-Lotus pushed through the crowd and managed to quietly join William.

Mark Lee, with his sunniest smile, glided rapidly towards the mayor. With his hand stretched out, even though he was still a few steps away, he laughed and said loudly, 'Oh my, my great mayor, welcome, welcome to our humble small town!' On reaching the mayor he grasped his hand. 'Please forgive us for not coming sooner. I'm Mark Lee. Call me Mark, ah, a foreign name I know, but that's another story, hahahaha! Oh my, with your mandarin jacket, you look so handsome, hahahaha!' Like he had done with William when they first met, he shook the mayor's hand vigorously, and patted it with his other hand. His prosperous body shielded High-Fly and the leaders of the four neighbouring towns from the mayor's view, like a parasol hiding the sun.

'Nice to meet you, Mark Lee!' The mayor said, equally loud, like he was addressing a stadium. 'You've done wonders! How beautiful the whole town is, how beautiful! You must have all worked very hard. Don't worry about formalities; I'm here by private invitation.' He smoothly took his hand back.

'Hello, Mayor Chang,' High-Fly said, having stepped out of his father's shadow, but his voice was too quiet.

'My great mayor,' Mark Lee said quickly, elbowing his son back, 'you have excellent insight! Your kind praise makes me shy, hahahaha!' His eyes narrowed into crescents and he raised a fat little hand to shade his face, pretending to be a maiden from a Yue opera. 'But all the sleepless nights planning and making sure that things got done have paid off, really paid off!' He nodded dramatically, as if to try to add weight to his words.

'Hello, Mayor Chang,' High-Fly said again, a lot louder this time. 'Nice to meet you. The county leader can't be with us today, so private invitation or not, we'd like to ask you to be our most honoured official guest and open the ceremony. Would it be OK? Oh, I'm High-Fly Lee by the way.'

Mark Lee's eyes widened, his dark eyebrows knitting together, but quickly re-composed himself. 'Hahahaha, indeed, indeed!'

'Hello, High-Fly Lee,' the mayor said, shaking his out-stretched hand, 'I'm honoured to accept and I can't wait to see more of this fantastic festival.'

Mark Lee suddenly seemed to remember the other four

town leaders, and loudly introduced them to the mayor.

'Hello, may I introduce you all to our British investors from Hong Kong?' Snow-Flower said. With a happy ringing voice, she introduced everyone, while William translated for his friends. Hands were stretched in all directions to shake and be shaken; loud greetings and a veneer of laughter vibrated the air.

'We have VIP seats, please let's go and sit down,' High-Fly shouted and led the way.

At the bottom of the slope stood a long row of tables covered in red cloth, and a couple rows of red leather chairs, borrowed from Fat Sun's restaurant. The small town officials were hovering around the mayor like bees to honey, offering him the best seat in the front row. Mark Lee managed to grab the chair right next to him, poured him ice tea, passed him the local delicacies that were on the table, and fanned him vigorously. In the back row, Jade-Lotus exchanged a glance with William and Snow-Flower, and wanted to laugh, but restrained herself.

A gong boomed three times; everyone quietened down. After a burst of drum roll, with a high-pitched voice and stately wave of an arm, the mayor announced, 'The Duanwu Festival for the Upper Canal District is open – let the ceremony begin!'

Along the riverbank, a line of drummers, in front of a line of flagpoles on which white flags with embroidered golden dragons fluttered, began to hit heavy beats on their gigantic drums, their arms rising and falling in rhythm, to wake up the sleepy dragon. At first the drumming sounded like running soldiers' footsteps, and then it was as if a troop of apes were beating their chests before a fight, before it finally turned into deafening rumbles of thunder.

On the water, five boats, each with a majestic dragon's head on its bow and a scaly body painted in bright colours on the hull, glared at each other like tigers fighting for their prey. They eagerly awaited the start of the race, like arrows on bent bows.

The drumming crescendoed to a climax and suddenly stopped, as if someone had cut off the power.

The yellow-robed Master Deep-Water airily entered the stage, followed by a crocodile of brown-robed monks walking in pairs. As they raised their hands into the prayer position, they began to chant softly to soothe the temper of the newly awoken dragon.

Jade-Lotus stared at the Master, itching to get to him, as much as the ancient King Jing-Gong wanted to hurry to Yanzi. But it would have to wait until the ceremony was finished.

The monks went off, and the Tai chi practitioners came on. Dressed in white martial-arts uniforms with golden dragons embroidered on the back, identical to those on the flags above the drummers, they marched in a neat formation, each holding a sword by their side, its shiny blade pointing to the sky. Behind them was a giant dragon held aloft by agile puppeteers, its writhing serpent's body decorated with gold and green scales, its fierce-looking mouth open and a red globe resting on its tongue.

'Oh look – Grandma!' Jade-Lotus whispered to William, pointing at the leader of the Tai chi formation.

Grandma raised her sword and the whole formation started their Tai chi sword dance with the dragon. They moved in unison and led the dragon with slow and seductive move-ments of their swords, which sparkled in the sunlight; their uniforms floated like the white butterflies that were often seen at this time of year. The giant dragon was a little grumpy and jumpy at first, but became more co-operative, obediently following the swords and seemingly starting to enjoy itself. The watching crowds applauded, and someone shouted, 'What a beautiful dance! The dragon looks so happy; it'll reward us with a great harvest this year.'

As the subdued dragon was led away, Old Qian, Fat Sun and Pockmarked Chou, each dressed in a white kimono, gourds filled with realgar wine hanging from their shoulders and trays of zongzi in their hands, entered and lined up by the river. Chou lit the incense in the giant burner, they bowed together – once for the sky and once for the river – and then sprinkled wine and threw zongzi into the water as offerings to the dragon, to finish the dragon-worship ceremony.

As the incense smoke swirled into the air, a sweet-voiced girl sang the Duanwu Song, joined by a choir and accompanied by a band of guzheng players.

Jade-Lotus smiled at them and whispered to William, 'Look, Summer-Lily and River-Cloud.'

The song faded and High-Fly, in a heron-blue robe and a Qing skullcap, entered with a pair of cymbals in his hands. He raised them and shouted, 'One, two –' and brought them together as hard as he could in a loud crash, which set the dragon boats off down the river.

The boaters' paddles rose and fell to their drummer's beat, driving the boats forward faster and faster. For a few breath-holding moments they were equally matched, but quickly three of the boats surged ahead, goaded on by the shouts and cheers of the watching crowd. The gold and green one nudged its nose ahead, its crew paddled furiously, as if they were in a in a life and death fight; with just inches to spare they crossed the line first! The crowd yelled and roared; the giant wooden flame-red dragon blew fire and smoke into the air.

Blushing Lotus had just won the race! Jade-Lotus, William and Snow-Flower screamed; the mayor stood up, applauding loudly; Mark Lee punched the air with his fist. The towns-people behind cheered, chanted, whistled and clapped.

Jade-Lotus pressed her heart. *Calm down, calm down! Time to go and put an end to another story.* She exchanged a glance with William and Snow-Flower, and moved out of her chair quickly and quietly.

'Good luck!' Snow-Flower shouted after her.

Jade-Lotus almost bumped into High-Fly as she arrived at the stage.

'What are you doing here?' High-Fly said. 'Aren't you supposed to be with the investors?'

'I'm trying to find Master Deep-Water, have you seen him?'

'Why? Are you converting to Buddhism?' High-Fly laughed.

'I want to invite him to the party.'

'Ah, I've invited all the monks, and done your job for you!' He winked.

'Really?'

'It's customary to invite monks for a meal after a ceremony, don't you know? Besides Master Deep-Water was very nice to me at the rehearsals.'

'Are you sure he's coming?' Seeing him nod, she said, 'Thank you!' For once she was very grateful to him.

20

Tide Recedes, Rocks Appear

Grandma's teahouse was bustling. With abundant ice-cream supplied by Nine-Pound Old Lady's parlour, free-flowing vintage yellow wine that Autumn-Rain had brought from his renowned collection, and many festive nibbles, everyone was joyous.

The investors looked animated as William said, 'The teahouse is from the Ming dynasty, but Blushing Lotus goes way back before then, and there's even a legend about its pretty name...'

Jade-Lotus smiled; William was really playing his part. Although the mayor had left to rush back to Shanghai for an evening gala, his presence still lingered, like the grassy smell of the Creed cologne he was wearing. Snow-Flower struck while the iron was still hot, telling the investors just how close Blushing Lotus was to Shanghai. Little-Blossom jumped in to say that the level of English among her students was the highest in the country, and that they were all interns at the town's tourist attractions in the summer holidays. River-

Cloud added that their school also provided English lessons for adults in the evening for free. The investors were in great hands; it was time to find Master Deep-Water and the truth about Mama's death. Jade-Lotus looked around.

Mark Lee's face must be hurting, as he was still grinning, his hands tightly gripped on the trophy – a model bamboo boat, with a red dragon carved on its side, and golden characters that read '1st Upper Canal District Dragon Boat Race Champion'.

High-Fly seemed to have his mind somewhere else; with a drink in one hand, his lips gathered into an O, presumably whistling, he searched the room. Who was he looking for? New-Dawn perhaps. He had literally jumped when hearing that New-Dawn was coming to the party.

Nine-Pound Old Lady was sitting at a large table by a window, crowded in by her lady friends and other townswomen, who took turns to have a close look at her headdress and the small gold cup for this year's best douniang. Her whole face blossomed, her dentures gleaming in the sunlight.

Towards the back of the room, brown-robed monks sat around a table drinking tea, but the yellow-robed master was not with them. Jade-Lotus looked harder, and eventually found him standing not far from the other monks, but shrouded by Old Qian, Fat Sun and Pockmarked Chou, who were all laughing. Through organising the festival and working with these old gentlemen, they had become friends. So they probably wouldn't mind if she borrowed Master Deep-Water.

Another round of ice-cream, yellow wine and nibbles came by, and the Duanwu Song broke out again.

The fifth day of the lunar May,
* Duanwu Festival is on its way.*
* Ay hay hay, ay hay hay...*

More people joined in and sang loudly, their feet tapping to the beat.

Jade-Lotus headed towards the master, snaking through the crowd and eventually reached the master's little group, who were all singing and clapping. Hmm, how to approach him? As a woman, it was taboo to pull a monk away to talk privately.

'Greetings, Mr Chou. What a fantastic Duanwu and we won the boat race!' Jade-Lotus said.

'Afternoon, Ms Yang. Indeed, indeed, a proud feeling indeed.'

'Thank you all for your great help.' Jade-Lotus nodded to Mr Chou. 'Can you be ever so kind and introduce me to the master please?'

'Of course, of course.' Pockmarked Chou happily leaned over and shouted in the monk's ear.

Master Deep-Water nodded to her. In the photo, he resembled his brother Mark Lee, but in person, he was much slimmer and his facial features were kinder and more harmonious. With a clean-shaven head and a pair of thin-wired spectacles he perfectly fitted the stereotypical image of a monk, although there seemed to be a sense of mystery about him, which deepened as he didn't look her in the eye. Was it because of Buddhist rules?

Jade-Lotus put the palms of her hands together and bowed. Knowing it wouldn't be easy to talk privately, she had come prepared and presented him with a note.

285

Master Deep-Water returned her bow, took the note, stepped aside and read it slowly. He finished and remained emotionless. OK, maybe he hadn't heard clearly, but the note gave him all the information. Why did he have such a blank face? Had Buddhism given him supernatural control?

Jade-Lotus bowed again and pointed at the large decorative folding screen in the corner not far from them. The area in front of the screen looked quieter, but it was still in public sight.

He nodded, a little reluctantly, but followed her. Now away from the noisy crowd, he bowed again and said that Buddhism was all he could talk about.

But doesn't Buddha say you should help people? Jade-Lotus swallowed and bowed. It must have looked silly to everyone else as they just kept on bowing to each other. 'Master Deep-Water, we just want closure; Grandma is no longer young.'

Master Deep-Water bowed one more time, and began to massage the mala beads that hung in front of his chest as he closed his eyes and started to chant quietly.

'Please, Master. I heard you once loved my mama,' Jade-Lotus said.

Master Deep-Water lifted up one eyelid for a brief moment, but carried on chanting.

It was clear that he wanted to be done with her, but Jade-Lotus stood her ground. His chanting would have to end soon, wouldn't it? She felt a gentle tug on her arm and turned; it was Little-Blossom and Snow-Flower.

With her tummy protruding, Little-Blossom bowed to the master, her pink rose douniang wobbled slightly. 'Amitabha, Master Deep-Water. Please forgive me for interrupting. Buddha once said, "If you light a lamp for somebody, it will also brighten your path." Please, Master Deep-Water, please help if you can.'

Master Deep-Water stopped chanting, opened his eyes, and returned Little-Blossom's bow. 'Amitabha, Buddha also said, "Every morning we're born again; what we do today is what matters most." The past is gone, and I've let it go.'

Snow-Flower said, 'Didn't Buddha also say "Three things cannot be long hidden: the Sun, the Moon and the truth."? All we want is the truth.'

Master Deep-Water caressed his beads again and said, '"In the sky, there's no distinction of east and west; people create distinctions out of their own minds and then believe them to be true."'

This calabash isn't pouring. What else can be done?

'Ahem, Rich-Knowledgeable, do you remember me?' said a breathy voice from behind Jade-Lotus. It was Antiques Guan, arm in arm with New-Dawn and Mother Li. He was breathing hard, his chest heaving.

Master Deep-Water stopped caressing his beads, and for the first time looked up, his face animated. 'Father! Is that you? Is that really you?' He leapt forward, seemingly forgetting he was a monk, and held Antiques Guan by the shoulders, staring into his eyes. 'Oh my Buddha! It is you! But I was told you died, long ago! With Mother.' He put his palms together and bowed.

'Lies, all lies!' Antiques Guan said and coughed violently. When he eventually stopped, he beat his chest. 'Please tell Jade-Lotus what you know. I want to know too.'

Master Deep-Water froze like a sculpture.

Mother Li removed her black hat and sunglasses. 'Rich-Knowledgeable Li, do you recognise me?'

Master Deep-Water's eyes bulged. 'You're alive too! Am I in a dream?'

'You're *not* in a dream!' Mother Li said with gritted teeth. 'We're both very much alive it seems, and we can talk about that later. But if you're still the man I married, just tell Jade-Lotus the truth! I've suffered for it long enough!' Mother Li's face was the colour of aubergine, the scar on her cheek crawling like a caterpillar.

'What?' Jade-Lotus said. 'You were married to HIM?' She struggled to breathe, her face burning. 'So you're the wet nurse! YOU KILLED MY MAMA!' It was as if a bomb had dropped, with a deafening boom, it became eerily silent, and dust fluttered in the light from broken windows...

'Mother Li? Are you the...?' Snow-Flower screamed. '... And you...'

Jade-Lotus became deaf. When had the Duanwu song stopped? More people gathered around, but she couldn't see them clearly, they were just shadows. Murmurs of 'Wet nurse is alive!' faded into the background, like trains passing a backyard. A hand firmly gripped her arm, and she turned to see Grandma.

'You killed my daughter?' Grandma shook violently.

Jade-Lotus put her arm around Grandma, trying to stop her shaking; Little-Blossom held Grandma's other arm, while Autumn-Rain, River-Cloud and William came and stood solidly behind them.

Mother Li looked as dumb as a wooden hen, her face pale and ugly, her eyes two triangles, the scar visibly thumping.

'Mother Li, did you kill my mama?' Jade-Lotus said, each word as hard as rock to spit out, her hand rolling into a tight fist, her knuckles cracking.

The wooden hen came alive; Mother Li shook her head like a rattle-drum. 'No, no, no, no, NO! It's not true. NOT TRUE!' Her eyes were full of anger, almost teary, as she went up to Master Deep-Water, and beat him with both her hands. 'Your brother is a heartless, liverless, lungless egg of a turtle! You must speak now and tell the truth!'

Master Deep-Water winced, his face pink, but his palms firmly pressed together. The tearoom became still, the heat unbearable, throaty thunder brewing in the distance. He bowed down deeply, not to anyone in particular, and murmured 'Amitabha' before slowly rising up.

'If I could turn the clock back, I would.' His tone was desolate but calm; his fingers tightly held onto his beads and his eyes focused on a small piece of floor in front of him. '"One slip brings eternal regret."' He heaved a sigh, but quickly recomposed himself. '1969 was the year that changed my life forever. My brother got a call from Beijing to say that the traitors New-Star Ye and his wife Peony-Grace Lu were on the run with their children, most likely back to Blushing Lotus, and they ordered us to quietly catch them all alive. We took two loyal Young Worker Rebels and headed to the railway station, but couldn't find them. So, we split up to search. The YWRs spotted two women, one matching Peony-Grace's description, in a small motor boat going quickly down the river. My brother ordered them to take the fastest boat and chase them. He and I jumped into another motor boat and followed. The two rebels soon caught up with the women and we watched as one of the hotheads tried to grab Peony-Grace. For a second he had her, but she struggled; he lost his grip and she fell, hitting her head on the bow of her boat before sinking into the water. The other woman jumped into the river to rescue her; by the time we arrived the three of them had managed to pull her into a boat. Peony-Grace lay in the bottom, with a deep cut on her forehead, seemingly not breathing. I jumped onto the boat and tried to revive her, but… but she didn't respond; her face lost its colour, and – and I realised she was dead.' Master Deep-Water broke down sobbing, his face knotted together in a pained expression, the opposite of the removed, emotionless monk he had been earlier. Eventually he stopped and bowed. 'I am truly sorry, Mrs Emerald Lu-Yang, Jade-Lotus.'

Jade-Lotus felt cold, despite the stifling heat. Grandma's fingernails sank deep into her arm, but it didn't matter. The people around her blurred again; Mama's body was lying in the boat, strands of long dark hair spreading around her white face, ugly blue overalls clinging to her body. She wanted to touch her, but she couldn't raise her arm; she wanted to shout 'Wake up, Mama!', but she had no voice… Someone sobbed, someone stroked her arm, and someone was talking, the faint words eventually becoming clear: 'Is that it?' Yes, was that it? As if snapped to her senses by a magician's fingers, Jade-Lotus found herself back in the room, her mind crystal clear. 'So if you didn't kill my mama, why couldn't you just come and tell us that it was an accident?' She stared hard at Master Deep-Water, wanting to see into him. 'We've spent our life looking for Mama, and we've never had one day of complete peace or happiness, because we didn't know what had happened. How – how can you be so, so cruel?'

A murmur of agreement spread around the people nearby.

Master Deep-Water lowered his head. He should feel shame.

Mother Li reddened, staring at the floor, as if trying to find a crack to escape. Eventually she looked up, and gazed at Antiques Guan and New-Dawn.

Jade-Lotus followed Mother Li's eyes and found High-Fly stood right behind New-Dawn, his face full of schadenfreude. *What is he doing here? He has no place here listening in and laughing at our misery!*

'There's something else,' Mother Li murmured, poking Master Deep-Water. 'You tell!'

The monk sighed. '"One step wrong, all seems wrong",' he began, 'To our horror, the woman helping Peony-Grace was my wife!' Glancing at Mother Li, he continued. 'We asked her where Peony-Grace's husband and children were, but she said she hadn't seen them. My brother realised the seriousness of the situation and ordered us all back to our shared courtyard house and hid the body. We had failed the central government and my wife had helped the traitor. "The hens have flown the coop; all eggs are broken." We were in serious trouble! If we gave up the two young rebels, they'd be killed, but before that they'd be tortured and made to tell everything. My wife would have been publicly executed, and all the Li family would have been in danger too. My brother paced around, while my wife squatted in the corner, clasping our toddler son, crying and laughing.' He shook his head slightly.

'My brother finally had an idea,' he continued. 'The whole thing had to be coffined up. My wife had to go and never come back, and we needed to unitedly say that she had taken the matter into her own hands: wanting to show her red passion for the Great Helmsman, she pushed the mother and children into the fast-flowing river and drowned them, and then ran away. All four men made a blood oath to keep the secret. My wife absolutely rejected it at first, but eventually gave in, and wanted to take our son with her. My brother jumped in and said no way! My son was the only boy in our Li family – my brother's wife had given him three daughters and couldn't bear any more – and I sided with him. My wife wouldn't have it, and ran out with our boy, but my brother caught up with her. He tugged our screaming boy from her; she stumbled and fell, her face hit a stone step, blood everywhere. My brother's wife was a nurse, and quickly came to help. Once my wife's face was stitched and bandaged, we put her on the next train to Shanghai, where we had a distant relative.'

'Oh my God!' Snow-Flower screamed.

Mama had died; all you could think about was protecting yourself! Her stomach churned, as Jade-Lotus stared at the monk. *What did you do with Mama's body?*

It was as if Master Deep-Water had read her mind, when he continued, 'When we got back to the house, the winter sun had set. My son had gone to sleep, tears stained his little face. I felt so empty; it dawned on me that I'd never see my wife again. "The longer the night, the more dreams!" my brother said, so we carried Peony-Grace's body up into the mountains and buried her...'

'Where did you bury her?' Grandma cut in.

Master Pure-Water frowned and scratched his reddened cheek. 'I'm really sorry you weren't told. She's buried not far from the Forever-Light Temple. I tended her grave whenever possible.' He looked down for a moment. 'Sins! Terrible sins!' he mumbled. 'That night I couldn't sleep. Everywhere I looked, I saw Peony-Grace. I knew her well. We'd been in the same class for ten years; she was pretty, kind and clever, and helped everyone with their studies, and everyone adored her. Now she was dead, I blamed myself. I could've begged my brother to let her off, I could've seen the danger of the boat chase, and I should've anticipated what those two young hotheads would do.' His face reddened more, as if about to ignite.

Jade-Lotus wanted to roll her eyes, but didn't.

'That night, my brother's wife looked after my son,' he carried on. 'I heard him screaming across the courtyard. He must have been hungry. How could I bring him up on my own? I'm a man; I'd never changed his nappy, and I had no milk. The whole country was disabled, nothing in the shops to buy. My brother had rightly pointed out he was the only seed in our family. When dawn came, my brother and his wife ordered me to divorce my wife; otherwise, everyone would be in jeopardy. Then they wanted to formally adopt my son, so he'd have a much better future, away from the dark shadow of his "murderous" mother. I was shocked, but didn't have a better idea, so I nodded. My brother added that I should move away too, so they could bring my son up as their own, without complications. I thought about it; with me hanging around, the crime my wife "committed" would never go away; my son deserved better. So, I nodded again. I had nowhere to go, but my brother had a solution for everything. Right after breakfast, we went to get the divorce papers done and then I moved into the abandoned Forever-Light Temple, to concentrate on studying Mao's books. My brother promised me he would tell Peony-Grace's mother about the grave when it was safe.' He raised his eyes; they looked calm and peaceful. He may have told the truth.

'How did you become a monk?' Antiques Guan said.

'Peony-Grace's death shook me awake. I lost interest in the Cultural Revolution. Instead of reading Mao's books, I read the Buddhist scripts that I found in a hidden compartment in the temple attic, and found solace. With my brother's protection, no one came to bother me in the temple, so attending Peony-Grace's grave, studying Buddhism and foraging for food in the mountains became my life. When the Cultural Revolution ended, the monasteries reopened, and knowing my son was safe with my brother I left for the county town, shaved my head and became a monk. At the festivals, I often volunteered to be a travelling monk, so that I could come back and tend to Peony-Grace's grave. I hoped she would forgive me. I hope you can forgive me.' Master Deep-Water bowed deeply down towards Grandma and Jade-Lotus.

A tear rolled down her face; Jade-Lotus wiped it off quickly. How needless Mama's death had been; how unnecessary their suffering for all these years had been! When the whole country was tossed into a burning wok, fanned by searing political fanatics, and seasoned with rotten Confucian traditions, the resulting dish could only be an ugly mass, bile-bitter, ink-charred and totally disgusting! At Grandma's insistent grip, she returned the monk's bow. Should she forgive him? Could she? And would she? She felt a stroke on her back; she turned to see Snow-Flower and Little-Blossom. Yes, the Three-Legged Ding had solved the mystery; Grandma would be able to close her eyes when her time came, and Mama's ghost wouldn't need to float in the wilderness any more. For that she gave them a teary smile.

'Oh, you poor, poor thing!' New-Dawn broke the silence, turning around to High-Fly.

'Hello, New-Dawn!' High-Fly said, his face glowing. 'Why am I a poor thing?'

'Didn't you hear?' New-Dawn's eyes widened.

'Yes, yes, it's a very sad story; I'm sorry, Jade-Lotus.' High-Fly shrugged.

'Good Buddha!' New-Dawn said. 'Are you thick? *You* were the toddler! Master Deep-Water is your birth father and Mother Li, your birth mother.' She tutted.

'What?' High-Fly said. 'What are you talking about?'

Oh-my-Gosh! I'm as slow as High-Fly! Jade-Lotus slowly looked around, Snow-Flower, Little-Blossom, William, and even Grandma were all nodding. She stared back at High-Fly, her eyeballs wanting to jump out. He was the boy, the seed! Leaves from three generations have suffered for this one small insignificant seed! She couldn't breathe, and refused to touch her mole.

'You've been talking about me all this time?' High-Fly shouted, pushing past Antiques Guan and New-Dawn to face his parents. 'Is it true?' His tone was bitter, his voice thin and high.

Mother Li tugged the monk's sleeve. 'Yes, yes, I'm your birth mother.' She stretched out a hand, but pulled it slowly back.

Master Deep-Water, with mala beads in hand, bowed to his son. The tearoom suddenly darkened and mid-summer thunder rumbled outside, but his yellow robe and red Kasaya stood out as if under a spotlight.

'But I already have parents?' High-Fly grumbled, looking around the room, searching for someone. Mark Lee, presumably, but he was nowhere to be seen. His chest heaved as he stared back at his real parents. 'You'd never have told me if it wasn't for Jade-Lotus, right?' his voice high and shaky.

'I had no choice,' Mother Li said timidly.

'Everyone has a choice!' High-Fly bellowed. 'You should be

ashamed! I can possibly – I only say possibly – understand why you couldn't come to find me during the Cultural Revolution, but that finished a long time ago. You abandoned me! And you!' He glared at the monk. 'You were nice to me at the rehearsal, and I really liked you. But you were just trying to make up for your dirty, dirty guilt!'

'I'm truly sorry for what we – what I – did to you,' Master Deep-Water said.

'You expect me to forgive you?' High-Fly said hotly. 'It's not going to be that easy!' He breathed loudly through his nose.

'"Water has no feet, but it can run; time has no wings, but it can fly." I'm not asking for your forgiveness. I simply want to apologise,' Master Deep-Water said.

Mother Li sighed and said, a little louder than before, 'I'm very sorry too. I love you more than anything.'

'What's that supposed to mean?' High-Fly's eyes narrowed into two slits. 'Do you think an apology can wipe out forty years of guilt? Is that how you show love?' He turned, and marched towards the door, people quickly parting for him.

'High-Fly, how can you not see it?' New-Dawn shouted after him. 'You're the only seed, and your real parents could never have given you what you've had with Mark Lee, given what had happened. The stupid tradition had to be honoured, what choice did they have? And High-Fly,' her voice trembled, 'what choice did we have when our baby girl was brutally terminated?'

High-Fly stopped, presumably digesting her words.

Good on you, New-Dawn! People around her shifted their weight from one foot to the other, avoiding eye contact. It was as if she was holding up a searing bright light shining on the hidden ugly scars that each family in the small town possessed.

High-Fly resumed his marching. As he opened the heavy wooden door, the dark sky was lit by a blinding flash of lightning, turning his small frame into a dark silhouette and illuminating the smashed remains of the boat-race trophy, which Mark Lee had earlier held so tightly, on the stony floor beside the door.

The silent tearoom shook to a deafening crack of thunder. Another flash of light filled the doorframe, the door swayed in the stormy wind, making a ghastly rasping noise. And with more rumbles of thunder came the first heavy drops of rain. A second later the heavens opened and rain fell like sheets of arrows fired by armies of archers in the clouds. On the river, water danced in circles and bubbles burst to the surface; from the cobbled road, steam rose like many ghosts. In just a few minutes the lively small town was turned into an ink painting, with no clear line between the land and the sky, everything a muddy grey…

'Thanks dragon, the rain has finally arrived,' Nine-Pound Old Lady said.

'Oh dear, we've lost Mark Lee and High-Fly,' William murmured.

21

The Old Willow Temple

'Do you think Mark Lee will still allow the adoption, given what happened earlier in the teahouse?' Jade-Lotus said, applying moisturising cream to her hands.

'I don't know,' William said, 'but it wasn't your fault.' He put his arm around her shoulder. 'I think he should honour it; the deal was based on getting him the foreign investment.'

'So, they're going to invest?' She sat up.

'I think so. They want to meet Mark Lee again to discuss the terms, which is a good sign. Ideally before I leave with them, which is the day after tomorrow?'

'OK, I'll call High-Fly first thing in the morning.'

'The festival was really great, darling. I enjoyed it very much. Well done!' William kissed her. 'Let's get some sleep, we have work to do tomorrow.'

Jade-Lotus kissed him goodnight and in no time William was off, light snoring vibrating the damp air.

She settled herself under the sheet. Outside was ink dark; the raindrops pattered on the banana leaves, *pa-da*, *pa-da*… It was as if the satisfied dragon had decided to return the favour by turning on the rain tap, but had forgotten to turn it off. The stormy, blustery showers had changed into persistent, warm, fine drizzle – the month-long Plum Rain had arrived.

The revelation of what had happened to Mama had been like poking a hornets' nest. Judging by the smashed pieces of the boat-race trophy, Mark Lee must have been very angry. Would his sting be as venomous as a hornet's when it came to the adoption? She bit her lip hard. The extraordinary lengths he had gone to protecting the truth about High-Fly were insane!

Hmm, High-Fly. He had been friendly, even helpful recently, but he had mercilessly walked out on his real parents. Would he be spiteful? But the true villain here was really this decaying seed-over-leaf tradition; even his calculated, communist father Mark Lee had been unable to escape and fallen prey to it. High-Fly wasn't stupid; surely he would work that out overnight. With that gleam of hope, she held on to her pendant and closed her eyes.

'We'll answer any questions you have,' High-Fly said in the ornate upstairs room in Fat Sun's restaurant, 'and once the golden egg is laid, hahahaha, our county leader will join us for lunch.' He grinned at the investors, and broadened it to his father and William.

Clearly it had been a mistake to offer interpretation at this meeting, Jade-Lotus thought, as Mark Lee and High-Fly turned to William every time they needed translation. And as they all talked, they laughed, joked and teased, as if they had been best friends for life. As Mark Lee laughed hysterically again, she looked outside. The lead sky, the muddy river, the pregnant canals and the exquisite stone bridges were a fusion of shades of grey. If only the relationship between the Yangs and Lees could be as harmonious. But the timber had been turned into a boat. Suddenly all the men stood up and vigorously shook each other's hands. The rice seemed almost cooked. Time for lunch perhaps? Jade-Lotus made an excuse to leave; Mark Lee and High-Fly looked much relieved.

Jade-Lotus was upbeat walking home. The investment looked certain; next would be the arrival of the baby. Stopping on a small stone bridge, she looked down at the river. 'Not hammer-strokes, but the dance of water, sings pebbles into perfection,' Tagore had written in one of his poems. Perhaps that should be the approach to get the adoption through.

William and the investors had left for Hong Kong, but the Plum Rain stayed on and on. In the subtropical heat, green plums turned mellow yellow and red bayberries sweetened up. Rivers and canals swelled as if harbouring a grudge against the banks; magpie-robins sang, 'Yu jia jia…'. Green creepers and giant crab spiders webbed the town, and sticky mist and hot steam pervaded it like ghosts. The air was filled with the smell of camphor and mould, lichens mosaicked the white-washed walls, and moss made stones soft and weepy…

'Gosh, I can't believe it, the torturous Plum Rain month has almost gone. It was quite easy this year, wasn't it?' Jade-Lotus said.

'Ah, it's because you've been spending it with us,' Grandma said, looking up from the baby blanket she was knitting.

'And us!' Spring-Cherry and Summer-Lily shouted from the corner of the room, stopping a second from fighting with the kitten for a yarn ball.

Little-Blossom smiled. 'It's been one of the best summer holidays.'

'For me too,' Jade-Lotus said. 'Thank you for all the baby tips.'

'It won't be too long now, my little treasure,' Grandma said.

'Ah Grandma, when the baby arrives, will you still call me that name?' Jade-Lotus said.

'You'll always be my little treasure, dear.'

The phone rang, breaking the cosy harmony.

'Hello?' Jade-Lotus answered.

'Hey, stranger! Survived the Plum Rain?' Snow-Flower said.

'It's been ages, are you OK? Can't seem to get hold of you nowadays,' Jade-Lotus said.

'I've been suuuper busy!'

'We've survived, haven't we? Little-Blossom and Grandma are here, you're on speaker now.'

'Hi everyone! You cousins must be getting bored with each other! Time for some excitement, don't you think?' Snow-Flower said.

'Do we need excitement?' Little-Blossom said.

'Actually, I have a favour to ask you, Jade-Lotus,' Snow-Flower said.

'Anything.'

'Remember my documentary programme, *Unwanted*?'

'Yes, about unwanted baby girls, wasn't it? The one that your boss banned, for being too negative, or something like that?'

'You do remember!' Snow-Flower squealed. 'My boss is letting me revive it with a new angle, and I need your help.'

'How can I help?' Jade-Lotus frowned at Little-Blossom.

'I'd like to use your adoption story, um... if you, and Little-Blossom, of course, are OK with that,' Snow-Flower said.

'You're not setting me up as one of your awful examples of abandoning a baby girl, are you?' Little-Blossom said.

'Oh no, definitely not. Nothing negative, no one's being humiliated,' Snow-Flower said, almost in her work tone. 'In fact, the programme's called *Wanted* now, highlighting people like Jade-Lotus.'

'What? Me?'

'Yes, you!' Snow-Flower said. 'You coming from abroad to adopt a baby girl is very powerful. So, on top of your story, I'd like you to open the programme.'

'Oh, I've never done anything like that before.'

'It's dead simple, you just need to knock on a door.'

'Um...'

'Snow-Flower, dear, is that all?' Grandma said.

'Yes, yes, Grandma, I promise that's all.'

Little-Blossom whispered, 'Her work is really important to her, we should help.'

'OK, Snow-Flower. If it's important to you, it's important to us all; we're the Three-Legged Ding,' Jade-Lotus said.

'Aaaah! Brilliant!' Snow-Flower said, 'Thank you! Thank you both! Now, I've booked next Thursday for the shoot, forecasted to be dry and sunny. Is that OK for you guys?'

'It's still the school holidays, so no problem at all,' Little-Blossom said.

'Definitely no problem for me,' Jade-Lotus said.

'Yah!' Snow-Flower shouted.

'My little treasure, you don't need me there, do you?' Grandma said.

Before Jade-Lotus answered, Snow-Flower said quickly,

'Grandma, it'll be a nice day out in the mountains, escaping this muggy heat, and with good food and drink all on my company. My mother and Mother Li are already coming, so you should definitely come.'

'OK, my dear.'

The humid heat had begun to lose its sticky grip, and with clear blue sky and a gentle breeze, the end of July felt much more comfortable. Once everyone was on board, the film crew's boat gathered speed heading towards the mountains. Grandma, Mother Li and White-Azalea chatted like old friends. Snow-Flower directed her crew shooting the scenery.

'Where are we going, Snow-Flower?' White-Azalea shouted.

'An old temple,' Snow-Flower shouted back. 'Look! We're almost there!' She pointed.

'The West Hill?' The three older ladies shouted almost together.

Against the bright sunlight, the West Hill loomed like a giant bear, its thick dark fur of vegetation appearing almost cuddly. The boat rounded the bend. 'Ta-da! The Old Willow Temple,' Snow-Flower shouted and opened her arms, as if opening a show.

Nestled in the middle of the hill, the temple seemed half swallowed by dense surrounding trees, although its roof poked out obstinately. Unlike other temples in the region, there appeared to be no yellow or white walls protecting it. The footpath leading up to the temple from the small quay wound like a pale snake, crawling in conspiratorial grass.

Once the boat docked, everyone climbed up the steps to the stone terrace, embroidered with dandelions, and shaded by a huge willow tree.

'Oh Buddha!' White-Azalea said. 'Do we really have to go up there?'

Snow-Flower rolled her eyes.

Grandma pulled Jade-Lotus's sleeve and said quietly, 'An old temple is full of ghosts and creatures that would love to find a new motherly host; maybe we should just stay here and let them film?'

Mother Li nodded keenly.

Jade-Lotus shook her head and said quietly, 'We can't break our promise, can we? Besides I'm a Yang, not a Yin for the underworld!'

'OK, everyone, let's go!' Snow-Flower shouted. 'Gentlemen, please lead the way.'

Two men from the crew went ahead, each with a long stick tied with a bell to scare off the snakes. As dings echoed, they began the gentle climb: White-Azalea arm in arm with Grandma, Snow-Flower with Mother Li, and Jade-Lotus with Little-Blossom.

When they reached the temple, Snow-Flower and her crew set to work, while the rest sat on a large slab nearby, watching.

The cameramen started to film and everyone kept quiet.

The Old Willow Temple was unpretentious. From where she sat, Jade-Lotus could now see the moss-covered boundary walls, dotted with white patches. The walls had collapsed in many places, revealing colonies of bamboo bushes, which gently rustled against each other in the wind. A gap led the eye to an inner gateway across the courtyard, and through its opening, a two-story building could be seen in the distance. Its lower roof was mostly obscured by lush willow branches; a scaly trunk grew out of its upper roof, like a mermaid rising out of water. The crew gathered in front of the outer gateway that had a flying roof, a tall threshold and a pair of sun-bleached wooden doors.

'The Old Willow Temple has been here, hidden in the mountains, for centuries,' Snow-Flower said to camera. 'According to the sparse records we found, it wasn't always a tranquil place for Buddhist nuns to live and worship. For many years it was an unofficial orphanage for unwanted girls. Sad, reluctant mothers, would have turned up here with their baby girls, and left quietly in tears, without even knocking on the doors. The babies would have lain on this cold stone threshold waiting for the kind nuns to take them in and eventually find them a new home. Today, in the twenty-first century, a brave young lady knocks loud and clear at these heavy wooden doors, shut for so long. And the doors aren't the only thing she is knocking at. Cut!' Snow-Flower sliced the air with her hand. 'Now we'll film Jade-Lotus.'

Jade-Lotus ran up the steps and stood in front of the doors for a second, grasped the corroded ring and knocked heavily. The dull sound reverberated.

'Good! Stay there,' Snow-Flower shouted. 'Do a second take from the side, close up.'

'Hold on, I need to change the battery,' one of the cameramen shouted. 'I only changed it this morning!'

Jade-Lotus stood there, waiting. On either side of the gateway, jasmine bushes were rampant, their fragrance heady. Some kind of stone figure was hidden among the bushes; upon lifting a dense branch, a lichen-mottled lion's head appeared. Of course, most temples would have stone lions guarding them. She turned around, but the cameraman still wasn't ready. Behind him was a perfect view of the river, on which a boat passed by sedately. She frowned, and then widened her eyes, like a drowsy student hit on the head by the teacher's bamboo ruler. 'OH MY GOSH! It's here!' she exclaimed. 'Grandma! Grandma! It's NOT a dream, it's here! It's here! I WAS HERE!' In slow motion, she stared hard at the stone threshold, and, feeling faint, slumped down on it. It all came back to her – autumn 1969.

… the boat ran, then they ran and ran… it felt hot and bumpy on Mama's back… and finally Mama stopped.

'We're going to play hide and seek. Come and sit here, close your eyes and, and recite one of Li Po's poems,' Mama said, a bit out of breath.

'Which poem?'

'"Thoughts on a Quiet Night". Twice! Don't peep! If you can't find me, knock on these doors. Can you do that?' Mama hugged her tightly and kissed her.

'Yes Mama.'

'Close your eyes now.'

'OK Mama.'

Moonlight shines on my bed,
Looking like frost on the steppe;
To gaze at the moon, I raise my head,
I bow down, missing my homestead!
......
Moonlight shines on my bed,
Looking like frost on the steppe;
To gaze at the moon, I raise my head,
I bow down, missing my homestead!

She opened her eyes. 'Coming, Mama.'

The tall white wall wears green bamboo hair, the willow tree above it doesn't seem to like it, and is shaking its head. 'Where are you, Mama? Where are you?' *The doors are really big and shut, and the stone lions look a bit scary. But I'm a brave girl.* She knocked on a door. *Why doesn't Mama come?* She knocked harder. *There are babies crying inside, just like Didi does sometimes.* Aaachoo! *What's that smell?* 'Mama, where are you?' *On the river, there's a small boat disappearing. Isn't that our boat?* 'Mama! Ma-ma! Ma-ma...'

Jade-Lotus sat there, numb and deaf to the many voices surrounding her. When had all the ladies come and sat next to her, their faces full of concern? She stared at Grandma, White-Azalea and Mother Li one by one and said, 'You all knew, didn't you?'

'Yes,' Mother Li said quietly, her scar twitching. 'I picked you and your mama up from the station, and when I told Peony-Grace that she and her children were wanted by the local rebels, she told me to bring you both here...'

'I collected you from the nuns after I got the note from Mother Li,' White-Azalea said, lowering her head.

'Why didn't you tell me?' Jade-Lotus stared at Grandma.

Grandma rubbed her hands and sighed. 'I was worried about what you'd think of your mama, if you knew.' Tears welled in her eyes.

'Why did Mama leave me here? Was – was it because I'm a girl?'

Grandma quickly shook her head, as did White-Azalea and Mother Li.

'I've thought about it for all these years, and I truly believe in

307

that desperate moment your mama thought it was the safest place for you, and that growing up without the baggage of your family background would be better for you,' Grandma said.

White-Azalea nodded. 'I agree. I knew Peony-Grace well.' Staring at her tightly held hands she added, 'Only a mother can make a decision like that. It seems a contradiction to give a baby away, but a mother knows what's best.'

'That's why I had to give High-Fly away, and stay away,' Mother Li said.

White-Azalea raised her gaze and stared at Snow-Flower. 'And why I sent you to your aunty in Shanghai; she had more chance of finding milk for you.'

Snow-Flower opened her mouth, but closed it again without a word.

'So moving…' Little-Blossom said.

Jade-Lotus's shoulder suddenly felt heavy with the weight of Little-Blossom. She turned and saw her cousin's hand dangling limply. 'Little-Blossom? Little-Blossom? Oh my gosh, OH MY GOSH, she's fainted!' Jade-Lotus screamed. A chill shot up from her soles. *What's happening?* She shook her. 'Wake up, WAKE UP!'

'Lay her on the floor,' Grandma shouted.

In a flurry of movement, Jade-Lotus and Snow-Flower laid Little-Blossom down on the stone terrace.

Grandma frantically loosened Little-Blossom's blouse, Mother Li fanned her face, and White-Azalea pressed a thumb on her 'human centre' acupuncture point.

What to do? What to do? 'Yes, yes, we need to put her into the recovery position!' As if a switch had been flipped, Jade-Lotus remembered the first-aid training from work.

'I'm calling an ambulance,' Snow-Flower said.

'Little-Blossom! Little-Blossom!' Jade-Lotus called again. But she didn't respond, her face pale.

'Oh my Buddha, Oh my Buddha…' the older ladies muttered incoherently.

Fear smothered her like a sudden fog; Jade-Lotus couldn't see anything, so she closed her eyes. *What to do? WHAT TO DO NOW?* Taking a deep breath, she forced her eyes open. A bottle of mineral water stood on the floor not too far away, so she jumped up, dizzy with adrenaline, stumbled over and grabbed it. She emptied the whole bottle over Little-Blossom's head.

Little-Blossom gave a start and opened her eyes with a soft moan.

'Thank Buddha!' the three older ladies cried out.

'Are you OK, are you OK?' Jade-Lotus wiped the water off Little-Blossom's face with her sleeve, and held her hand tightly.

Little-Blossom nodded. 'Sorry, am I causing trouble?'

Jade-Lotus wanted to say yes as a joke, but just stroked her hand. 'No, you're not.' Her eyes were suddenly misty.

'Thank God you're awake!' Snow-Flower said. 'We must get back on the boat quickly; the ambulance is going to meet us at the county town main quay.'

'No need,' Little-Blossom said weakly. 'I'll be all right, probably just dehydration.'

'It's better to get you and the baby checked over,' Jade-Lotus said.

'We need to go now. My guys will carry you down to the boat, OK?' Snow-Flower said.

'Oh Buddha,' Little-Blossom muttered, blushing, but nodded.

In a frantic rush everyone got back on the boat, which headed towards the county town at full speed. Jade-Lotus wrapped an arm around Little-Blossom, letting her head rest on her shoulder, while Snow-Flower talked on the phone outside. The three older ladies huddled together praying.

Please, please, let their prayers come true. Jade-Lotus had never wanted more to believe in the power of praying.

'I'm sorry to hear that your mama left you at the temple,' Little-Blossom whispered.

'Ssh, ssh, you just rest.' Jade-Lotus patted her hand.

Trying to work out what the recurring dream meant had been a permanent itch, but not so itchy that it needed a cure. Now it had been accidentally scratched, deep beneath the surface in fact; a little blood seeped out. Why had Mama chosen that temple, an orphanage for abandoned girls? Was it really as Grandma had said? But now there were more important things to face. The boat's engine hummed restlessly; it felt slow even at full speed. The acute shock of seeing Little-Blossom fainting had evaporated, but wild wonderings filled the void. Was it just dehydration as Little-Blossom had said? Was it something more serious? Something wrong with the baby or its mother? Or both?

'My friends will help once we get to the hospital,' Snow-Flower said as she came back. 'It won't be long now.' She patted Little-Blossom's hand.

In the emergency department of the county hospital, long zigzag queues fanned out from each of the six registration windows; anxious people stood on their toes, stretching their necks to see when it might be their turn. But thanks to Snow-

Flower, they were met by a nurse, whizzed to a private suite, and promptly seen by Mr Liang. 'We'll just do a routine check,' he said gently to Little-Blossom, and added a comforting smile.

Jade-Lotus waved to her cousin as she was wheeled away. Even though Snow-Flower had said Mr Liang was the best obstetrician in the whole county, she couldn't take her eyes off that door, her heart pulled in all directions.

'River-Cloud's on his way,' Snow-Flower said as everyone sat down in the suite.

Jade-Lotus smiled a tight smile; Snow-Flower was able to keep a cool head.

No one spoke. Feet fidgeted; crossed and uncrossed legs rustled.

'She'll be all right, won't she?' Grandma said eventually.

'Yes, she will,' Snow-Flower said loudly. Although her tone was firm, her voice wasn't ringing in its usual way.

Jade-Lotus nodded, her fingernails digging into the backs of her hands.

The floor tiles had a repeat pattern, a small character for the sun after every ten plain tiles; the sun beamed on one of the characters, and the dust motes danced in the sunlight.

Snow-Flower's phone suddenly rang and she shot up. 'River-Cloud!' she cried out, 'Turn left at the entrance, we're in the VIP section.'

River-Cloud rushed in, his forehead covered with shiny beads of sweat. 'Any news?' He was catching his breath.

It was as if Mr Liang had heard him; the door opened and he marched in. 'I need to talk to the family,' he said.

'I'm her husband,' River-Cloud said and went up to shake the doctor's hand. 'Is she OK? Is baby OK?' The back of his silk shirt was a world map of sweat patches.

Jade-Lotus sprang up, as did everyone else; they circled around the doctor.

'Your wife's blood pressure is a little higher than we'd like,' Mr Liang said calmly, glancing around. 'She's thirty-eight weeks. We need to induce labour, to keep mother and baby safe.' He explained the pros and cons, and then asked River-Cloud to sign for the bill.

The pros were like water dripping into a sponge but the cons – bruised head for the baby, higher risk of blood clots for the mother – were amplified. 'Will they both definitely be OK?' Jade-Lotus had to ask.

'They *should* be OK, if there are no complications.' Mr Liang stared at her for a second and squeezed out a smile before heading back.

A strong urge flitted across her mind, to chase after him and make him promise that all would be OK, but all Jade-Lotus could do was watch the swinging door slow down and shut. Beyond it would be a white sterilised world where two leaves would fight for their place; on this side of the door, slumping down and curling into a tight ball like a pangolin was not an option. *Rhino horns possess telepathic powers; please, rhinos in every corner of the land, please let Little-Blossom and baby know that they are not alone.* She closed her eyes and repeated it to all the gods she could think of.

'Little-Blossom should be fine,' White-Azalea said, sounding like she was trying to convince herself. 'She had high-blood pressure when she had Spring-Cherry, but they were both fine then.' She began to pray.

'Do you want to call William?' Snow-Flower whispered.

Jade-Lotus shook her head; there was no point in worrying

him too.

'We'll have to just sit and wait,' Snow-Flower said, a little too loudly. 'Little-Blossom is in the best possible hands and is experienced at childbirth.' She laughed a dry laugh.

Jade-Lotus smiled. 'I'm sure it'll all be over soon; both mother and daughter will be absolutely fine.' Having said it out aloud, the prickly burrs on her back peeled off. After all, a child's birth brings happiness and joy; Little-Blossom had already brought two beautiful girls into the world, safe and sound. Perhaps this baby just wanted to meet her new mum earlier than planned, and that was all. Yes, yes, that was right, she just wanted to come early, and it was time to get completely ready and welcome her. 'I guess I'll stop dithering and decide her name now,' she said more energetically.

'What names are you thinking of? I think we all need a say, don't we?' Snow-Flower said loudly, looking around.

River-Cloud, who had been fanning himself vigorously, and taking his spectacles off and putting them back on several times, joined the debate: should it be an English name or a Chinese one, would there be middle names and what would the surname be? An hour passed. What language should she speak when she grew older? Should she learn to write Chinese characters? Another hour slipped away. How frequently should a baby be fed? How to get her to sleep more? What nappy should one use? Two more hours went by. The hospital staff had quietly brought in a couple of rounds of chrysanthemum teas and small cakes.

The door opened and Mr Liang marched in again, still in his 'theatre blues'.

Everyone jumped to their feet.

'Both mother and baby are safe and well. Mr Shan, congratulations, you have a healthy baby son,' he announced.

'A baby son?' River-Cloud cried out, staring at Mr Liang like a bull at a red cape.

'A baby boy?' everyone repeated; it was as if a whisper was passing around the circular wall of the Temple of Heaven.

'Are you sure?' Jade-Lotus stared hard at Mr Liang.

'Yes, of course, I can tell,' Mr Liang said, a frown furrowing, but then he nodded, seemingly knowingly. 'We need to keep Mrs Shan a little longer, to make sure her blood pressure is all good, but you can all go to the observatory to see the baby. He's in number twelve cot.'

River-Cloud seemed to have come out of his shock, and shaking Mr Liang's hand vigorously said, 'Thank you, thank you!' His eyes misted behind his spectacles.

'Oh!' White-Azalea said. Her raised eyebrows dropped comfortably back down, and her eyes brightened like dying ashes fanned by a welcome breeze. The corners of her mouth stretched up and a broad smile blossomed on her face like a morning glory seeing the sun. 'I just knew my daughter-in-law isn't a soft egg. See, it's a boy! It's a BOY! We Shans finally have a seed!' She seemed to have forgotten her usual elegant manners and almost shouted the last sentence, looking intensely proud, beaming at River-Cloud. 'We'll keep the baby now, won't we?'

River-Cloud stared at his mother, his mouth opened, but no words came out.

'Mother!' Snow-Flower shouted.

Jade-Lotus froze, everything becoming a blur, then there was a clunk, as if someone had shut the door right in front of her. The numbness churned into a sharp pain twisting in her stomach.

'How come it's a boy now? Didn't Little-Blossom have a scan?' Grandma muttered.

Jade-Lotus looked at her, unable to put words together.

'Oh Grandma,' Snow-Flower said, 'Little-Blossom did one illegal scan at an early stage of her pregnancy, which isn't always reliable.' She sighed.

'Shall we all go and look at our baby boy?' White-Azalea shrilled. 'Come on, River-Cloud!' She waved impatiently.

Jade-Lotus couldn't lift her legs; they were as heavy as sandalwood logs.

Snow-Flower tutted at her mother and came to wrap an arm around Jade-Lotus's shoulders. In silence, they followed and were the last to arrive at the big window of the baby observatory.

River-Cloud pushed to the front; with both hands pressed on the glass above his head in a surrender position, he shouted, 'There it is, cot number twelve!' He took off his spectacles to wipe his eyes.

'Oh, he looks just like you did when you were born,' White-Azalea cooed, elbowing River-Cloud. 'Ah, what a sweet little face. Look, look! He's twitching his nose, how cute!' She bowed. 'Thank you Buddha, thank you so much Buddha!' She glued herself to the glass, as if to make sure that her new grandson would not disappear like a bursting bubble.

As Snow-Flower stretched to get a closer look, Jade-Lotus glimpsed the baby through the gap between River-Cloud and his mother, her heart pounding. The long and precipitous journey was over: the baby was right there! The most joyous feeling in the whole world! What did his face look like? How much hair did he have? How bright were his eyes? What would it feel like to touch his little hand? What did he smell like? The urge to get closer was like a rubber duck in the bath, impossible to hold down. But… but… She bit her lip hard and clenched her hands into balls. The baby had turned out to be a boy, a desperately wanted and most precious seed that the Shans had been trying for years to harvest. Perhaps it was better not to look too closely at the baby, because the Shans would now want to keep him. Hadn't White-Azalea just said it loud and clear? Hadn't River-Cloud just cried? By not looking at him, he wouldn't burn his little face into a forever memory, and it wouldn't hurt so much to leave, empty handed, for England. The Shans in the front cheered aloud, applauding; they should, shouldn't they? The generations' dream had finally come true, their family tree would have a nice addition – River-Cloud would be able to relax in their ancestral hall on festivals – and their glorious name would now continue. Everyone else was an outsider, an observer, a spectator.

A father standing next to River-Cloud, laughed, wiped his face with his sleeve and said loudly, 'Mine's a boy! A BOY! His grandparents will be over the moon! What's yours?'

'A BOY too!' River-Cloud replied, just as loudly.

Jade-Lotus squeezed her eyes shut for a second, swallowed down her tears, turned and quietly left.

Around the corner after a long corridor, there was a seating area. Jade-Lotus sat down and looked out of the floor-to-ceiling window; the sky was clear and blue, just like the one back home in England. A feeling of exhaustion swamped over her; it would be nice to just go home, curl up in the big bed and sleep for days on end. On waking up, maybe everything would have, in fact, been a dream. The velvety pink roses on

316

the back terrace would look divine, their fragrance wafting; the rolling hills in the distance would be dotted with white sheep. In the far corner of the garden, the huge oak tree, onto which a handmade treehouse had long been planned, would remain solitary; it might remember the summer that had been full of leaves and dreams. The space where a children's slide could be erected would be planted with azaleas, and when they flowered they would perhaps stir memories of the best times spent with Grandma, Little-Blossom and Snow-Flower in Blushing Lotus.

The wall clock sounded four dull dings; it was nearly an hour since the doctor had announced the boy. Would Little-Blossom be back in the suite? Would she be awake? Was she sore? Was she all OK? Maybe it was time to head back to see her.

Jade-Lotus slowly got up. Turning left would lead her back to the private suite; she thought for a second and turned right. The white corridor seemed a mile long. Many people sat along each side, but they quickly faded, together with their hubbub. Gurgle, gurgle, her tummy rumbled. How long ago was breakfast? The adrenaline rush from realising the meaning of the dream, Little-Blossom fainting and the baby turning into a boy had turned into hunger pangs, chewing inside. Let it chew! Let it hurt! It was far better than the twisted pain growing inside! She carried on walking; Jane Eyre carried on walking on the moorland after leaving Thornfield, hungry and despairing. One must find her own saviour, candlelight of hope and peace of mind.

What would Little-Blossom be feeling now? Immensely proud, of course. She would have a seed lamp brightly lit and hung high above her front door for weeks, and fireworks would bloom in the sky above their house every day for a month. Endless visitors – Nine-Pound Old Lady would definitely be among them – would wear out their doorstep, bringing with them the sunniest smiles and loudest wishes for the baby and the family... Jade-Lotus shook her head. But then she nodded, slowly. Perhaps it was time to put herself aside and try someone else's shoes. Yes, it was time to feel Little-Blossom's happiness and celebrate the occasion with her. Their five months together, watching her belly grow, feeling the baby's kicks, had been priceless. As a vital leg of the Three-Legged Ding, Cousin had helped solve the Mama mystery. Her affection, sisterly love and friendship had filled a hidden void. Now it was time to do the right thing. She turned back towards the VIP section.

'Ah, you're here!' Snow-Flower said, 'Little-Blossom wants to see you.'

They walked in silence.

As they entered the private suite, Grandma jumped up. 'You're back! Are you OK? Are you OK?' her voice was slightly hoarse.

Jade-Lotus nodded. 'Are you OK?'

Grandma wiped her eyes. 'I don't know what's going to happen now.'

'Come, Grandma, let's sit down,' Snow-Flower said. 'The cousins will have to sort this out themselves.'

Jade-Lotus took a deep breath, knocked on the bedroom door and pushed it open. White-Azalea and River-Cloud sat on either side of Little-Blossom, and all of them seemed completely besotted with the baby, who was wrapped in a cream blanket, resting comfortably on his mother's bosom. It was a perfect happy family portrait.

Little-Blossom raised her eyes. 'You took your time!'

River-Cloud stood up quickly. 'We'd better go and help Mother Li bring back our late lunch.' He lowered his head as he passed. 'Come on, Mum.'

White-Azalea finally peeled her eyes off the baby. 'OK, I'm coming.' She avoided eye contact.

After the door closed, Jade-Lotus rushed to hug Little-Blossom and the baby, burying her face on her shoulder.

'Ah ah, gently please. You're here at last!' Little-Blossom said, her voice choked with emotion.

Jade-Lotus breathed deeply, taking in the baby's smell before letting them go. 'How are you feeling? Are you in any pain?' She sat down.

'We're all good, aren't we?' Little-Blossom said, looking lovingly at the baby. 'I'm pumped with painkillers and so exhausted. Ah, look at him! He's so so sleepy.' She then put her nose softly onto his little head. 'You're amazing, aren't you, aren't you? Do you want to hold him?' She turned to Jade-Lotus.

'Look, Cousin, I've been thinking, and I completely understand if you and River-Cloud want to keep him. I'll tell William tonight, and I'll go home next week. I'm really happy, super happy, for you, and I'm sure William will be too,' Jade-Lotus said sincerely. It was better this way.

Little-Blossom gently put the baby down on the bed next to her and took time to tuck the blanket in around him. 'So, you think I'm going to keep him?' she said. As her eyes narrowed, she blasted, 'Honestly? Honestly! I'm insulted! You should know better, after we've spent so much time together!' She tried to keep her voice down, but it was still much higher than usual; her delicate face was bright red.

'Oh, please don't be angry with me, you have to watch your blood pressure.'

'Don't you worry about that!' Little-Blossom snorted. 'You really think I'm going to keep him?'

Jade-Lotus nodded. 'It was going to be a girl.' She looked down.

'Now it's a boy you belittle me and assume the worst of me! How dare you? You did Snow-Flower's documentary to make a point, to educate people like me. I know you didn't do it to humiliate me personally, but you are now! You disappoint me, truly!'

Jade-Lotus stared at her; Little-Blossom had never been so angry before. The harsh words were like thrashing whips, but there was a lot of truth in them. She twisted her bottom; the cushion beneath seemed full of needles. 'I've seen how happy the Shans are, and heard White-Azalea say they would keep the baby now...'

'So you thought I'd be the same?' Little-Blossom cut in. 'But I'm not like her! I'm not! Ask me if I'm happy and proud to have a baby boy, I'll say a hundred yeses. But I would have been equally proud if it had been a girl. I've changed, been changed by you in fact, and your belief that boys and girls are of equal value. You've taught me well and now you think I'll fail the exam?' She shook her head, tears welled in her eyes and she looked away.

'But the Shans haven't changed.' Jade-Lotus found her mouth dry.

'That's not your problem, you can leave them to me! Now, do you want to hold your baby?'

'I do, I do,' Jade-Lotus said. The sweet little baby had slept through the heated argument that had sealed his fate. She put a finger gently in the palm of his hand and he curled his tiny fingers around it; tears streamed down her cheeks. She licked her tears; underneath the salty bitterness it was sweet. She hugged her cousin again. 'Thank you, thank you for giving life to my son.'

'He'll always be my son too, wherever he is. He'll always be in my heart.'

The door opened slowly and River-Cloud came in, with bags full of take-away boxes. As he laid them down, he said, 'Little-Blossom, I hope you haven't broken Jade-Lotus's heart. I've thought long and hard about it, and I don't think we should keep the baby.'

Little-Blossom raised her eyebrows at Jade-Lotus, before turning to her husband. 'Why not?'

'Lots of reasons, really. But most of all, how could we explain to our girls that we've kept the baby because it's a boy?'

'You're so right, my perfect husband! I'd better obey.' Little-Blossom turned and smiled to Jade-Lotus.

'What's happening?' White-Azalea came in with everyone else.

River-Cloud announced, 'We're still giving our baby to Jade-Lotus.'

'What? He's OUR son!' White-Azalea dropped her food bags onto the floor with a thud.

'Oh, Mum,' Little-Blossom said, 'didn't you say a mother knows best?' She stared at her warmly. 'It's for our son's benefit. Growing up in England will give him a much better life, don't you think?'

White-Azalea took time to process her thoughts. 'Oh, I see, I see! OK, for our seed's benefit, OK!'

'OK,' River-Cloud said. 'Now, for our benefit can we eat this very late lunch please?'

The baby opened his dark eyes and cried loudly, as if agreeing with his father.

Little-Blossom smiled and said, 'Can you all please go and eat in the other room? Our baby is hungry too.'

Once everyone had left, Little-Blossom took out a pump, extracted some milk from her breast, and handed the bottle to Jade-Lotus. 'Rather you than me.' She giggled. 'And you'll need to feed him every two hours, twenty-four hours a day. Welcome to being a mum!'

Jade-Lotus gently picked up the baby and sniffed his sweet scent. With wet eyes, she leaned him onto her chest and put the teat into his mouth; he sucked eagerly.

Little-Blossom looked on, wiping her own tears away.

Jade-Lotus looked at her son, his little fingers grabbing at the air, as if trying to grasp the many twists of his fate. She looked up at her cousin, a beautiful leaf, who had just given up the most-treasured seed, and smiled wholeheartedly.

Outside, the lush leaves of a parasol tree danced with budding seeds in a gentle wind; cicadas sang happily.

On the evening of the Zhongyuan Ghost Festival, the air was filled with the smell of burning paper-money and incense, and the cobbled road to the town centre was lined with thousands of lit candles. Jade-Lotus, with baby in a sling, William and Grandma joined the townspeople heading for the river.

It was hard to believe a month had skidded past, even with endless feedings, sleepless nights and many 'fountain sprays' changing nappies. Jade-Lotus had had to pinch herself every morning, on seeing her baby and William next to her. All the worries about Mark Lee blocking the adoption had proven unfounded, as not long after the Duanwu festival, he had 'jumped' to an early retirement, and with the county leader's good grace, High-Fly had taken over. Apparently, he had vowed to be a modern leader, and his first fire as town leader was to speed through the adoption papers. But when he said, 'Just remember this when I call for a favour one day,' it seemed that while the broth had changed, it was the same old medicine. There had even been rumours that he was going to run away with New-Dawn, but Nine-Pound Old Lady said she had gone to Shanghai, alone. Little-Blossom had started the autumn semester, so it was time to fly home – as a whole family!

By the riverbank in the town centre, silhouettes of people drifted in and out, befitting the festival. The full moon, with thousands of twinkling stars, lit the path for the travelling ghosts. Mama's coffin had been unearthed that dawn to Master Deep-Water's chanting, and reburied in the Yang's graveyard in the rising sunlight. Mama had come home at last.

In their hands, they held homemade paper lamps – Grandma's in the shape of a lotus flower, and hers a leaf. After William lit the candle in the centre of each lamp, Grandma gently placed hers in the river and bowed, happily telling the Yang ancestors that the family tree had a new branch and Mama's page in the ancestral hall was no longer empty. Jade-Lotus kissed her lamp, and placed it on the river too. Her handwritten words were illuminated by the candle: 'for Mama, endless love from Jade-Lotus, William and Adam Peace Shan Yang Hampshire.' Their lamps soon joined hundreds of others, lighting the path from earth to heaven.

Adam cooed, and grabbed her jade pendant. She held his little hand together with the pendant against her heart. Fate was not so bad after all.

Acknowledgements

The Great Wall of China was not built in a day by one person and neither was this novel. I would like to thank all the people who helped it come to fruition.

I am extremely grateful to my copy editor, Martha, for her meticulous work. With plenty of nits to pick and creases to smooth out she remained calm and humorous; she is the kind of editor that all writers dream of.

I am immensely appreciative of Kari Brownlie for her stunning book cover design. She conveyed the symbolism in this book more creatively than I could ever have imagined.

My deepest gratitude goes to Jacqui Lofthouse for being an amazing writing coach, for believing in my story and being generous with her time and support. She taught me dramatisation, among many other wonderful techniques.

I could not have taken this journey without my dear husband, who has been fantastically enthusiastic since the seed of this story was planted. He is my first editor – always able to guess the words and sayings I am trying to get across from Chinese culture. He was the sounding board for all my ideas, my emotional support, and almost as important as I was in getting this book finished. Thank you so much, darling.

From the bottom of my heart, I would like to thank my dear old friend, Tiffany Kemp, for always being there, giving me almost professional-level criticism and direction, and for being optimistic about my story and me.

The same deep appreciation goes to another friend, Joanna Swainson, for helping me edit this novel, twice in fact. Her sound industry knowledge and wise insight helped to make it so much better. I will never forget our shared love of Mongolian yurts.

And I am super grateful to my neighbour, Fiona, for being a brave test reader and giving honest feedback.

I am deeply indebted to Mama and Baba for bringing me up with love and for reciting idioms, proverbs and classic poems to me when civilisation was replaced by political turmoil and books were taken away.

Wholehearted thanks to Margaret, Robin, Barry, Kathy, Laura, Trevor and Ann for your love and unwavering interest over the years. And to Rosalie and Peter, my affectionate English 'parents', for motivating me by forever asking for the first signed copy. You will always be my young ducks! And to Ken and Marty, my kind American 'parents'. I will never forget our time together building a house for homeless people in California.

Sincere thanks to all the strong Chinese women I am lucky to know well.

Special thanks to Jill, Brian and Amy, Ali and Mark, Isabelle and Clive, Elaine and Simon, Sue, Dario and Amanda, Mei, Peter and Justin, Hui, Isobel, Simon, Jannie, Elsie and Sue for seeing me through the time it took me to write this novel with kind encouragement. And to Toby for keeping our secret.

Many thanks to James and Barry for seeing what I can do, not what I cannot. To Jan for all the warm chats about books. To another James for the many coffee sessions discussing writing. To Peter for opening a door to an IT career where I found my strength and confidence, and for all those stimulating debates about the differences between men and women.

Finally, I would like to thank Jo Connell OBE DL, Dame Hilary Cropper and Dame Steve Shirley. Your shining example of how women could become successful in the male-dominated world of IT had a huge impact on me and inspired me to write this story.

About the Author

Hana Yin grew up in China and graduated with a first class BA degree from one of the top universities in Beijing. After marrying an Englishman and moving to the UK, she worked in the IT industry.

While in China she had poems and short stories published in the People's Daily, Chinese Reader's Digest and Chinese Literature (English edition). *A Leaf in a Small Town* is her first English novel.

Printed in Great Britain
by Amazon

28308820R00189